Th
the situation

If the attack on them by the North Korean army was random, it meant some other, faceless enemy had known about his arrival. Perhaps the whole job was a setup to begin with. It was possible that Yang wasn't a prisoner. Maybe Yang didn't even exist.

Then there was the issue of the attack on Haeju. Another organization could have possibly expected an American response. He was already convinced the whole attack was a hoax, had been sure of it almost from the beginning. Nevertheless, Brognola and the cyberteam at Stony Man believed there was credibility to the issues. He had no choice but to proceed with the mission on the information he had.

But if trouble broke out, Mack Bolan would be ready.

DON PENDLETON's
MACK BOLAN®
Deception

A GOLD EAGLE BOOK FROM
WORLDWIDE®

TORONTO • NEW YORK • LONDON
AMSTERDAM • PARIS • SYDNEY • HAMBURG
STOCKHOLM • ATHENS • TOKYO • MILAN
MADRID • WARSAW • BUDAPEST • AUCKLAND

First edition March 2001

ISBN 0-373-61477-2

Special thanks and acknowledgment to
Jon Guenther for his contribution to this work.

DECEPTION

Printed in U.S.A.

Of the four wars in my lifetime, none
came about because the U.S. was too strong.

> —President Ronald Reagan
> June 29, 1980

None of the men and women of our
armed forces *wants* to fight a war. They
do it only as a last resort. Therefore, I will
carry on with my war and fight for them.

> —Mack Bolan

To all those who love this series
and have faithfully accompanied Mack Bolan
on his many adventures—Live Large

PROLOGUE

Yellow Sea, North Korean Coast

Droplets of sweat fell from Cho Shinmun's face.

The forward berth of the stolen South Korean submarine was hot and cramped, and Cho could see the tension in the faces of his men. They were hardened veterans of countless missions such as this one, and their strengths lay in their fighting abilities. Nevertheless, patience was just one trait of a good warrior, and it was the rule for Cho's crew rather than the exception. They would wait with him until the moment to strike was at hand.

Cho couldn't quell his reservations on this particular mission. The thought of murdering his own countrymen wasn't easy to endure, but he had a job to do. His orders were clear. Several good soldiers would probably die this night, a small sacrifice when he considered the greater good of his nation.

The actions of their enemies had driven Cho's superiors to implement these drastic measures. Despite repeated warnings, the South Koreans had elected to conduct their annual training exercise with the Americans. These acts were nothing more than blatant attempts to provoke the Democratic People's Republic of Korea to respond in kind. If America wasn't threatening to withdraw support for the construction of the nuclear power plants in Kumho, then the Japanese were manipulating the South to suggest military intervention.

In any case, Cho's controller was quite clear when he'd said, "We cannot tolerate the interference of foreign governments in our national sovereignty, nor will we allow them to dictate DPRK policy." Therefore, there was a distinct need for this mission and Cho would obey his orders despite any personal hesitancy.

The sound of the engines that powered their stolen submarine reverberated throughout the ship. Cho clenched his teeth against the grinding and groaning that had assaulted his ears for the past hour. He gripped the American-made rifle closer to his chest and whispered a prayer of wisdom to Buddha. The sounds ceased abruptly, and Cho took a moment to study the taut faces of his squad. Eleven good men awaited his instructions. They were the most loyal and dedicated soldiers in the Korean People's Army. They held neither rank nor title, but simply answered by number. Their operations were more secret than were those of any elite fighting force in the world. Even the Black Army didn't conduct such sensitive missions.

As he felt the submarine begin to rise, Cho quickly ordered his men to do a weapons check. They instantly obeyed, and his heart raced with the clack of the bolts as they slammed fresh rounds into battery. In a few minutes, Cho and his men would change the course of history. One day they would be hailed as heroes.

A buzz sounded from a communications link above Cho's head. He listened to the instructions, snapped an acknowledgment, then disconnected the transmission.

"Let's move," Cho told his men quietly.

The squad rose wordlessly and rushed toward the main hold. Cho positioned himself between his men, with three in front and the remaining members to the rear. Two of the forward guard would take point, and the third would act as a relay. The rear attachment would spread out behind him. They would all await his order to begin the mission. They had rehearsed the scenario a hundred times, and each man knew his assignment to the last detail.

Within minutes, the group left the sub and began the three-quarter-mile swim to shore. The water was so cold it chilled Cho to the bone. He had dismissed the idea of wet suits. Such needless equipment would only slow them, and they couldn't afford any unnecessary delays—timing was of paramount importance. Each man was an excellent swimmer and in top physical condition. They would all make it without a problem.

Eight minutes elapsed before the group was ashore and in position. The naval yard at Haeju wasn't a large installation, but Cho knew this was to his advantage. It made the mission less complicated. Their purpose here was to make it *appear* they had failed their objective; deep penetration of the complex wouldn't be necessary.

Cho gestured toward the fence that lined the eastern perimeter of the naval base. The pointmen rushed toward the ten-foot-high chain-link barricade topped with several rows of barbed wire. Each retrieved a pair of small bolt cutters from his butt pack and began to cut an entry through the fence. The hole would serve as an egress as well—*if* anyone made it out alive.

As the pair worked feverishly to cut through the heavy links, the relay maintained position in front of Cho and provided cover. They crouched in the darkness as the remaining team members spread into a half circle behind them. The leader checked his watch, then scanned the perimeter for the roving patrol. If everything went as planned, the patrol would "discover" them as they made their entry.

As if on cue, Cho spotted the sentries' shadowy forms thirty meters from their position. He signaled his men to begin the assault. The two at the fence completed their task and slipped inside the perimeter. They knelt and swept the area with the muzzles of their weapons as the remaining members converged on Cho. One by one, the team scuttled through the hole in the fence.

The sentries were now within range. One of them called a warning as the other started to bring his rifle off his shoulder.

Cho barked an order. The forward trio brought their weapons to bear and opened fire. The M-16 rifles spit 5.56 mm slugs at the pair of sentries. One of the men died under the hail of ball ammunition while the other dived for cover. The unfortunate sentry spun away and landed prone in the soft mud near the concrete walkway that bordered the fence. The second sentry propped himself on his elbows and returned fire.

Cho's men fanned out in a valiant effort to avoid the sentry's rounds. He recognized the distinct bark of the report from the sentry's weapon as he pressed his own body to the ground. The guard carried the standard rifle of the Korean People's Army forces. It was a Chinese Type 68, an import design based on the AK-47 Kalashnikov rifles. One of his men couldn't escape the onslaught of 7.62 mm Soviet rounds, which stitched a circular pattern in the soldier's chest.

Cho aimed his own weapon and triggered a burst. Despite his many hours of practice, he still felt uncomfortable with the M-16 rifle. It was large and awkward, and he would have preferred his own weapon right at that moment. Cho's aim was perfect, however, and the rounds blew the sentry's head apart. Slugs from the Japanese Type 89 weapons held by a few of Cho's men tore through the man's torso at the same moment.

Alarms and sirens began to sound throughout the base.

Cho rose and the remaining nine men with him followed suit. He'd lost two good soldiers in the encounter, thus far, and their mission wasn't even half accomplished. He could hardly stifle his regret at their deaths. He quickly checked his two fallen troops for anything that would link them to their North Korean heritage while assuring they carried their forged South Korean identification, then ordered his squad to continue with the operation.

Four men rushed across an open field in the direction of the dock facilities. The remainder sprinted with Cho and his new pointman toward the darkened administration buildings in the distance. One man from each team carried a satchel filled with high-explosive charges. The buildings of the Haeju naval yard were large, constructed from steel and brick. It didn't matter if there weren't enough demolitions to topple their targets. Again, the intent would be to create the appearance of havoc and destruction. It was imperative to Cho's mission that he *attempt* to destroy sections of the naval yard.

As Cho and his team raced nearer to the headquarters building, a squad of fresh soldiers bounced across the rugged field in a wheeled personnel carrier. They approached the team on an intercept course, and they would easily reach them before Cho's men could finish the job. Cho directed his pointman and another trooper to stand and fight while he and the man with the demolitions continued toward the building. Muzzle-flashes winked in the night as the pair quickly obeyed. They dropped to their knees and began to return fire with their Type 89 rifles.

One of Cho's men had a grenade launcher attached to

his rifle. He sighted on to the approaching vehicle and fired an HE grenade. The grenade landed aft of the vehicle. The resulting concussion lifted the personnel carrier off the ground and nearly flipped it end over end. Somehow, the driver managed to maintain control.

The squad leader continued to the building. He covered his demolitions expert as the man planted the charges and set the fuse timer. Cho saw one of his men chopped to shreds by the incessant fire of the naval yard's security response troops. He raised the M-16 to his shoulder and drew a bead on the personnel carrier as it slewed to a halt. He stroked the trigger with repeated motions. The head of one of the North Korean soldiers snapped back, and he toppled to the dirt. A second man quickly met the same fate as his remaining comrades bailed from the carrier. Cho saw his other man rise and try to retreat, but several troops shot him in the back as he ran.

Cho felt the anger rise into his throat in the form of bile—his own people fought with cowardice. Revenge burned in his gut as he again depressed the trigger on the M-16. Cho could see his subordinate rise and fire his own weapon. With quick precision, they dropped every remaining member from the carrier. The driver attempted to flee, but a heavy barrage from Cho's rifle and his demo man's Daewoo K-2 ended that escape.

"The explosives are set, sir," the demolitions expert said.

Cho nodded with satisfaction. "Then we must proceed to the rendezvous point."

The two men set off in the direction of the fence line. They would have to wait near the water, since the remaining members of Cho's team would need a few extra minutes. The distance to the dock area was considerable, and that didn't even take into account any resistance they might meet along the way. Cho looked at his watch. He wouldn't wait one second longer than planned—he couldn't. He'd already lost four men in the operation. That was twice the number estimated in the planning stages.

The two men reached the fence and passed through it at their original entry point. They proceeded to the shore and sought cover behind a heavy outcropping. The tide was rising, and he could only hope the extraction crew hadn't met with some unforeseen change of plans. If the boats didn't arrive soon, Cho would have to break up his team and find alternative means of transportation away from Haeju. The entire mission had to look like a botched insertion of the American and South Korean forces training in Seoul. Anything less was unacceptable.

Cho's eyes roved over the brightly lit expanse of Haeju. It was a great city, not like Pyongyang or some of the others in his country. It had its own, distinct appeal. Like many urban settlements in North Korea, there were the signs of poverty and decay, remnants of the Korean War and the decimation left in the wake of the capitalist nations.

Almost fifty years later, North Korean standards were still well below those of many countries. His people could barely afford to feed and defend themselves much less develop new technologies and more efficient methods of energy production. A good part of the North Korean economy still lay in the coffers of the elite and political families. The controller of Cho's squad was considerably wealthy and had financed them to date. This mission had been costly, and Cho expected a full recompense for recruiting and training replacements. His superior could afford it. He would have to afford it if he wanted Cho to continue conducting these kinds of charades.

Over the sounds of the sea and the distant explosions

within the naval yard, Cho detected the hum of the approaching extraction boats. Two motorized rafts appeared in the haze, and the North Korean soldier checked his watch. Less than a minute remained. Cho ordered his man to risk a look from their rocky haven. The soldier peered around a low point in the rocks. He quickly withdrew, and his dark eyes studied Cho with excitement.

"They are coming, sir," he reported. "All of them."

"Good. I am pleased with your performance. You will be commended, Net."

Cho could see his number-four man beam with pride. Commendations didn't come easy in the Korean People's Army. They meant honor and prestige—they were a source of pride when a soldier in the KPA advanced in stature and value. His family would be proud of him, and it would bring honor to both them and himself. Since the men of his squad couldn't hold rank, commendations were the only subsequent rewards for a job well done. Cho believed in rewarding loyalty and ability. His men had fought hard and well for him this night. They had brought distinct credit to him and reflected the fine traditions of the DPRK.

The remaining men joined Cho and Net as the boats reached the shore. He quickly identified his second in command.

Cho spoke quickly as the rest of the men headed for the boats. "Tul, I am glad to see you well. Did everything go as planned?"

"Yes, sir," Tul replied.

"And you left the items as instructed?"

"There will be no doubts when they are discovered, sir."

Cho nodded and the two men moved to the boat. He climbed into one and ordered Tul to command the other. The boats would follow the western shore until they reached the bay near the city of Onchon. From there, they would rest for a few days and let the incident pass before risking transport back to Pyongyang.

As the special-warfare personnel guided the boats away from Haeju and pointed them toward Onchon, Cho couldn't resist a smile. With their mission accomplished, his country could rally world support. The Americans and their allies would look foolish, and it would illuminate their warmongering ways. Powerful nations would rally beside the brave DPRK, and his country could again rise up to fight those who had oppressed them for so many decades.

Cho eagerly anticipated the beginning of the second phase of their mission.

CHAPTER ONE

Stony Man Farm, Virginia

Hal Brognola looked tired as he entered the War Room.

He'd spent the past six hours at the White House in conference with the President and the national-security adviser. The situation wasn't good; forty-eight hours had elapsed since the events surrounding what they were calling "the incident at Haeju." Negotiations between North and South Korea were now at a standstill, and it seemed obvious that the North Koreans were ready to cash in their chips and leave the table.

Mack Bolan could see an expression of relief spread across Brognola's solemn features when his old friend saw him. Bolan sat at the table with Barbara Price, and his icy blue eyes studied the man with concern. It didn't look as if the big Fed had slept since the attack on the Haeju naval installation.

The Executioner had to admit that he was as concerned as Brognola. Since the Korean War, political tensions continued between the neighboring countries. Neither country had ever signed a peace treaty following the war, simply ending the conflict by armistice. At the end of 1996, the United States tried to help moderate an official treaty to end the Korean War, but new tensions interfered with those proceedings when the North Koreans launched scathing accusations against Japan and its involvement in the conflict.

There was undoubtedly a capitalist influence in the South, while the Stalinist North wavered between a socialist and Communist system. Although they called themselves the Democratic People's Republic of Korea, Bolan knew there was very little to indicate a democratic foundation. The Communist and Red Chinese influence permeated their society. The conditions of starvation and poverty—present in so many Asian countries—created a susceptible platform for such political machinations. Target countries like these were easy pickings for the ideals of "equality and prosperity for each and every citizen."

Now it appeared those ideals had unveiled a new threat. It was one Mack Bolan was anxious to tackle, because he knew the alternatives could be devastating for the American people. The Executioner hadn't asked for this war, but he was willing to fight it his way and on his terms. Unfortunately, he knew he couldn't set the terms on this mission. He'd come only as a courtesy to the man who now stood before him.

Brognola shook hands quickly with Bolan before he seated himself at the head of the table. He gruffly called for the attention of Aaron Kurtzman, who busied himself in a corner printing mounds of data on what Bolan assumed had a direct relationship to the mission. The man known affectionately as "the Bear" rolled his wheelchair to the table, tossed a stack of data in front of Brognola, then returned to the computer.

"You can start if you want, Hal," Kurtzman announced. "I've still got some data to gather on this deal."

"Fine," Brognola said. He looked at Bolan. "There's

quite a bit of information here, maybe some of it worthless for you, Striker. I hope you'll indulge me."

"The more intelligence the better, Hal," Bolan replied easily.

"Of course," Brognola said with an appreciative nod. "As you know, the North Koreans allegedly thwarted a sabotage attempt on their naval base in Haeju. They claim to have evidence that the perpetrators were a special detachment of South Korean soldiers."

"What kind of evidence?" Bolan asked.

Brognola thumbed through the stack of organized papers until he found the technical data gleaned by Kurtzman's inside sources. He shoved the stack to Bolan, who picked it up and immediately gave the information a cursory read. The weapons that belonged to those enemy troops killed by Haeju security forces included American-made M-16 A-1 rifles and Daewoo K-2s. Explosive charges were set at several key places inside the base. One of the explosive stockpiles failed. Investigators recovered a U.S. satchel filled with C-4 plastique and detonation cord fuses. The report detailed other minor findings, but the evidence was all circumstantial to Bolan's way of thinking.

The Executioner let out a sigh. "This doesn't mean a thing. Any of these items are readily available on the arms market."

"You know that and we know that," Price interjected, "but try telling it to the North Koreans."

"Those are American-made weapons found at the scene," Brognola stated gravely. "That has the President very concerned."

"Daewoo Precision Industry developed K-2s for the South Korean army," Bolan said. "They started making M-16s under license and finally began production of their own rifles after they'd gained some experience."

"And what about the explosives with U.S. military lot numbers?" Brognola pressed.

"Easy pickings for the right price."

"The most compelling evidence was the discovery of a South Korean submarine signature. It was detected off the coast by the installation sonar crew just prior to the incursion."

Bolan looked hard at Brognola and asked, "What's the President's take on all of this?"

There was something in Brognola's manner that caused Bolan to realize he didn't want to broach *that* particular subject. This struck a nerve in the soldier. Was it possible the President actually believed North Korea's story? Anybody could see this was an elaborate hoax, maybe cooked up by the North Koreans themselves. Then again, it was possible an outside agency was responsible. Perhaps the DPRK government was a victim, as well as the Americans and South Koreans. The entire world knew the North was paranoid of its southern neighbor and the alliance formed between the South and the U.S. That made them a target for half a dozen terrorist organizations, not to mention possibly former KGB subversives or even a renegade group of dissidents.

That only left one question in Bolan's mind. If neither of the Korean governments had implemented this crazy scheme, then who else would stand to gain from increased tensions between the two countries? The Chinese didn't have any obvious stake in it, and the Russians had enough problems of their own without adding fuel to the fire. The remaining countries in Southeast Asia seemed unlikely candidates, as well.

Maybe it was an internal faction of the U.S. or South Korean militaries. It wasn't unheard of, particularly given the recent apprehension of North Korea over the joint military training exercise under way in Seoul. Bolan could already see the many directions this mission might take him.

"The President was handed an initiative by someone within the North Korean government," Brognola finally replied. "But I'll let Barbara get into that shortly."

"What about these South Korean troops who were killed?" Bolan asked.

Brognola shrugged. "The North Koreans refuse to release further information until they've concluded their investigation. They feel this was bound to happen in light of the training exercise."

"I knew that would come into it sooner or later," Bolan remarked.

"Frankly, the President has no reason to believe the North Koreans are lying about this incident. CIA connections inside the country confirm there *was* a skirmish at Haeju, and they're telling us with a certainty that this was no drill."

"Okay, I'll buy that. But what were they hoping to accomplish?"

"We don't know and neither do the North Koreans," Brognola said wearily. He paused, and then added, "I think it might help if you knew some history."

"Shoot."

"Back in June of 1999, the two Koreas began negotiations for the reunification of families and famine relief for the North. The talks were strained because their navies exchanged gunfire in the Yellow Sea just days before, and a North Korean submarine was sunk."

Bolan nodded. "I remember that."

"Okay. Eventually, the North Koreans dropped it and peace talks continued. Our last President took the initiative to assist the North Koreans with the famine relief, provided they would continue negotiations. But there was a greater concern, because a year before the North had launched a two-stage ballistic missile known as the Taepodong I. The missile flew over Japan and splashed into the Pacific. The same month the President went to visit North Korea they threatened to launch the Taepodong II, a missile with more than twice the range of the first. That made it capable of striking Alaska or westernmost islands in Hawaii.''

Bolan set the information he'd skimmed on the table and crossed his arms. "Is it possible the North Koreans just staged this ruse to justify reinstatement of their nuclear-weapons development program?"

"We considered that," Brognola replied, "but we don't have enough evidence to prove it. Not yet anyway."

"But you're working on something," Bolan stated, cocking an eyebrow.

"Perceptive as always, Striker."

The big Fed turned to Price. "Barbara, you can take it from here."

Price nodded and Bolan turned his attention to her.

The honey-blond mission controller was a looker by any standards and an invaluable member to the Stony Man operations. She could put efficiency experts to shame with little more than a few hours at her disposal, and she was knowledgeable in the intelligence game. She had contacts in places most people didn't know existed, much less hear about. Her savvy had repeatedly surpassed the expectations of everyone at the Farm, and her devotion to the Stony Man cause was unquestionable.

Throughout his relationship with her, Bolan learned Price was as dangerous as she was beautiful. She could tug on parts of him he thought had disappeared long ago, and she ventured into areas of his psyche that none other dared. Their relationship consisted of stolen intimacy forged by the basic need for human contact—both of necessity and convenience. That was it. There was nothing more or less to it, and neither of them had ever tried to make it otherwise.

"We did consider the nuclear-arms development as one probability," Price stated, "so Aaron and I went digging on the off chance the President was incorrect in his assumptions."

Price reached out and Kurtzman handed her a thin sheet of papers on cue.

"There's no question," she continued, "that deep divisions run between ourselves and South Korean officials on how to handle the North. Public and congressional opinion seems to be that the DPRK is run by little more than a group of manipulative thugs. The ruling party to be precise."

"Sometimes our politicians have trouble backing their words with some muscle," Brognola added grimly.

"That's where I come in?" Bolan asked.

"Not exactly," Price replied.

"What do you mean?"

"In the course of our investigation, we discovered that the buildup of nuclear arms *is* taking place. Reports from both the CIA and NSA confirm this." Price handed Bolan some data sheets. "With the exception of some minor countries, North Korea has one of the lowest wheat-production rates in the world. About two thousand metric tons annually, according to the Food and Agriculture Organization."

Bolan shrugged and furrowed his eyebrows. "What does that have to do with increased nuclear weapons?"

"Quite a bit when you consider the fact that these people are nearly starving. South Korea, Japan and the U.S. poured billions of dollars into North Korea, all in the name of famine relief. Much of that money was allocated for two light-water nuclear power plants presently nearing completion in Kumho.''

''The North Koreans agreed,'' Brognola interjected, ''to dismantle their nuclear-weapons program and use the two plants for energy production.''

''Instead, they secretly developed newer and more powerful weapons on their own,'' Bolan surmised.

''Exactly,'' Price replied, ''although it was hardly a secret. A complication arose when our agents in Pyongyang were approached by a high-ranking North Korean politician named Yang Tae-jung. Yang's attaché to the Korean Ministry of Foreign Affairs and extremely valuable to their government. He claims that there is a secret construction project nearing completion for a new missile with devastating abilities. Our last communication from him hinted at the fact the attack in Haeju was bogus.''

''This guy sounds bogus himself,'' Bolan replied flatly. His eyes narrowed as he scrutinized the photo of Yang that Price handed him.

''We thought so, too,'' she said, ''until he disappeared. Aaron managed to track him to a prison just outside of Pyongyang. The North Koreans have him under tight security, and the CIA contact inside the city who acted as liaison for this business says the place is virtually impenetrable.''

Bolan shifted his gaze to Brognola. ''Do you believe this Yang?''

''I'm not sure. I warned the President that we know very little about him.'' Brognola shrugged helplessly. ''Nonetheless, he's convinced that if there is some truth to the story then we need to mount a rescue mission. He personally requested you for the job, Striker.''

Brognola's last statement sounded hollow in the Executioner's ears. The President considered him a necessary evil. While he never burdened Bolan with a problem—out of respect for his rocky alliance with the Oval Office—he didn't call on him lightly. In that respect, Bolan could only assume there was considerable validity to the concerns of the President and his advisers.

He returned his gaze to the photo, then lifted his chin and fixed Price with a concerned look. "What do we know about the prison?"

"Bear can give you more on that, but there's something else you should know. One of the things Yang mentioned was the Taepodong III. He believed that factions within his government might launch the missile if someone didn't stop them. We found it odd that he made no mention of the government as a whole. That led us to conclude not everyone within the ruling party is on board with continued enmity between North Korea and the U.S. In light of recent tensions over the training exercise in Seoul, this could have disastrous consequences for the world at large."

Something stunk to high heaven about this, but Bolan knew her assessment was correct. If there was any truth to Yang's claims, they wouldn't be able to prove it until they got him safely out of North Korea. Moreover, Bolan knew his country's position on North Korea and nuclear arms. If some unknown faction could pull off an elaborate hoax like the incident at Haeju, it was certainly clever enough to make good on the threat to launch the new missile.

It was a perfect plan. Blame for the launch would fall on officials within the North Korean government. This would absolve any particular entity within the circles of power and support anonymity for their case. However, if Yang was rescued and started naming names, it could have converse consequences. That ruled out the idea of a terrorist organization, since terrorists were usually unconcerned with anonymity.

A long silence elapsed before Bolan spoke. "Let's assume I can get inside and pull this guy out. What kind of resistance am I up against? And how do I identify the enemy?"

"I'll admit that the whole thing is sketchy," Price acknowledged, "but we have little else to go on. Without Yang, relations will continue to be strained between the respective governments involved in this situation."

"Our paramount concern is twofold," Brognola concluded. "We want to get Yang out of his country without question. But in three days, a meeting is scheduled in Hungnam between a score of important diplomats."

"It's actually a multinational negotiations conference," Price added. "Hungnam is located on the eastern coast of North Korea. Ironically, it's not that far from Kumho."

"Where they're building the power plants." Bolan nodded with satisfaction. "They want to use Yang as a bargaining chip should things go sour at the conference."

Price nodded. "Probably."

Bolan turned to Kurtzman. "What do we have on this prison, Bear?"

Kurtzman spun in his wheelchair and smiled triumphantly at his friend. "They call it Ingchok, but don't ask me for the English translation. I'll send a diagram and layout for you, as well as a probable location where they're holding Yang. But make no mistake. The place is as tight as a drum."

"Electronic security?"

Kurtzman nodded. "Not to mention ten-foot fencing, an internal alarm system and infrared sensors." Kurtzman retrieved satellite photographs and other material. "The NSA's Comsat and AWACS network provided the better part of the information we have. Gadgets is compiling a list of hardware you'll need as we speak.''

"What about human resistance?''

"With their electronic surveillance, CIA estimates the assigned personnel is limited,'' Kurtzman told him succinctly. "Mostly Black Army detachment.''

"North Korean special forces,'' Bolan muttered, sifting through the photos and AWACS computer-graphics images. "This won't be easy.''

"We figured the best way to get you inside,'' Price said, "was the discreet way that left you the most options. Jack is on his way from a mission with Phoenix Force. He'll air drop you at night just off the western coast near the village of Onchon. From there you'll be met by a CIA contact named Wanfeld, who will provide you with transportation to Pyongyang. He'll also provide any additional weaponry or gear you may need.''

Bolan nodded slowly. "I want to recon this prison before I make entry. That's the only guarantee against errors or other nasty surprises.''

"Agreed,'' Brognola said. "But if things get hot, don't risk yourself, Striker.''

The Executioner studied Brognola with a knowing gaze. The mission was risky at best—as were most of Bolan's assignments—but the soldier understood what Brognola was trying to say.

Despite the fact Stony Man no longer had official ties with Mack Bolan, he was still a valuable asset. His ideals and dedication were the foundations of their project. Although the supersecret organization had boundaries that Bolan didn't, it operated on his principles. The morale, integrity and lives of its members hung in the balance. Phoenix Force, Able Team and the entire support staff all hung in there and gave their best because the man known as the Executioner chose to do the same. Bolan would go the extra mile, and he didn't do things because of some false sense of invulnerability but out of the necessity of duty.

Bolan knew his life would end one day. Nevertheless, the lives of the many people he defended would continue, and his cause was one that made it safe for people to sleep soundly at night. Many wouldn't recognize the face or the name, but they understood the reasons and the singular goal that drove the man called Mack Bolan. And that was enough for him.

"Okay, I'll get ready to leave," Bolan said. He checked his watch. "What time is Jack scheduled to arrive?"

"Four hours," Brognola replied. "If you want to grab something to eat or some rest, your room is just the way you left it. I'll wake you when he gets here."

Bolan stretched and threw Price a knowing look. "I could use a couple hours of sleep."

If either of the two men sitting in the room noticed Bolan's furtive glance, they didn't mention it. Everyone understood the situation and it never came up for discussion. Barbara Price caught the Executioner's look and smiled.

BOLAN'S ROOM SMELLED of sweat, sex and unrestrained physical passion. It wasn't passion defined in the most literal sense, but rather the combined nature of animal need and human urgency. He always made love to Barbara Price gently and with perfect attention to her own desires. There were moments Bolan could see the loneliness in her eyes. Yeah, she was incisive but also withdrew from close contacts.

Bolan usually felt accustomed to her introspective tendencies. He had a few of his own and he considered them while he quickly showered. Needles of hot spray splashed

onto his scarred chest. He traced a few scars as he thought
of his own vulnerability. They were just small reminders
of one too many close calls. Eventually, he knew, his luck
would run out. Then what?

Dammit, you're not getting any younger, he thought.

No, he wouldn't last forever in the jungles ruled by the
creature called man. Every day it seemed the human mind
of those who preyed on the innocent grew more capable
of conjuring worse atrocities than before. Sooner or later,
the weight of those horrors would crush the Executioner.
He could only hope that someone would stand up to re-
place him. But not today.

As he toweled himself dry and dressed in the pale
orange half light that swirled into the room through wind-
blown curtains, Bolan saw Price watching him from where
she lay under the sheets. He mechanically donned his
blacksuit and pretended not to notice the expectant look in
her eyes. She wanted to ask him something, and he
couldn't ignore her forever.

He slid into a shoulder holster that housed his Beretta
93-R and combed his damp hair. The muscles in his chest,
stomach and arms bulged against the skintight combat suit.
He was still in top physical condition, his body hardened
over the years by demanding conditions. Few could match
his stamina or reflexes in a close-quarters engagement.

"You seem preoccupied," Price said softly.

Bolan walked to a bureau and began to check the contents of his jump bag. He yanked a Desert Eagle Mark
XIX .50 AE from the bag to check the action; the slide
moved smoothly. He thumbed the catch and it fell forward
against the stop with a thunderous clank as it chambered
a round. The warrior set the safety and replaced the
weapon.

While it wasn't his normal side arm, Bolan had procured

the .50 AE from the Stony Man armory especially for this mission. He would have to make his jump into the water—toting a lot of extra firepower was impractical. Like the .44 Magnum, this weapon boasted additional features such as machined rather than precision-cast parts. The dovetail rib on the barrel allowed for scope mounting that didn't required additional hardware. The larger caliber and longer barrel meant a higher degree of accuracy with increased knock-down power.

Price didn't appear convinced. "Would you please look at me?"

Bolan whirled on his heel and studied her. He had to stifle an urge to bark at her. He had things to do—this was neither the time nor the place for lengthy discussions. Well, that wasn't her fault. She had insight on the soldier and there was little he could do about it. He wouldn't mistreat her for it now. She provided comfort and balance in a very uncomfortable and unbalanced world.

"Sorry," Bolan whispered. "I've got a lot on my mind."

"About this mission?"

"About a lot of things."

"Do you want to talk about it?"

Bolan shook his head as he continued perusing the bag. "That would only distract me more."

"Okay, but if I had to venture a guess I'd say you look...tired."

Bolan stopped and thought seriously about what she had just said. As profound as it seemed, she'd echoed his very thought. He was tired. Bolan knew Price didn't mean tired in the physical sense and it bothered him even more that she was so accurate in her assessment.

"I know it's a damn dirty war you fight," Price continued, "but you've never let down those you fight for. I admire you for that. I guess I never told you but I really admire you.''

Now Bolan turned and looked at her with a surprised expression. ''I never wanted anyone to admire me.''

''I know that,'' she said with a chuckle. ''You just want people to understand. I understand. Everyone here understands. But we all lean on your strength. When you hurt, we hurt. When you get angry at all the horror and injustice in the world, we get angry. The people here look to you for guidance, Mack. You're the example. The person we all wish to emulate.''

''It sounds as if you think I'm ready to give up,'' Bolan ventured.

''I don't think anything of the sort,'' Price replied softly. ''I think that the moment you *do* feel like you want to give up, that's when it will become fatal for you. That's when you might make a mistake.'' She paused a moment and looked at the light of the sunset diminishing around the window. ''I don't want to see that. I sure as hell don't want to think about it.''

''I'll be fine,'' Bolan said, touched by her honesty.

''Watch yourself, big guy,'' Price finally managed to say with a mischievous smile.

''Always.''

CHAPTER TWO

Pyongyang, DPRK Party Headquarters

Pak In-sung was pleased.

The attack on Haeju by Cho Shinmun and his elite squad had gone as planned. A perfect plan that was perfectly executed. Although the loss of four good men angered Cho, Pak refused to concern himself with it. Such things were trivialities when balanced by the good of the people of North Korea. Sacrifices were sometimes necessary—a few had to die for the many. Cho knew the risks and had elected to take them.

Their people had recently suffered many injustices. South Korea was undoubtedly conspiring with the Americans to discredit the North's sovereignty. The premier wouldn't continue to tolerate such intrusions into the affairs of the Democratic People's Republic of Korea. He'd rallied the cry for assistance and increased the number of workers to complete the construction in Kumho.

Pak believed in their cause, although he didn't care to admit it amounted to more than simple allegiance and loyalty to his nation. His primary concern was to ensure the uninterrupted flow of substantial cash that lined the party coffers. Pak's backer was a man of prestige and honor in his own country and one of the wealthiest men in the world. A nation as impoverished as the DPRK couldn't afford to look the other way when it came to financial stability.

Pak knew what it meant to be poor. His life began at the end of the Korean War with the submission of the capitalist invaders. Pak's father had served proudly as a unit commander with the Twenty-ninth Regimental Guard near Panmunjon. The end of the war signaled an end to his father's career—and his life. As Pak's father returned to his barracks one evening, a squad of South Korean deserters crossed the now infamous Thirty-eighth Parallel and killed more than one hundred men from the regimental guard.

As a suckling whose mother could barely provide to feed him and his four siblings, Pak learned hunger and poverty. Yet he also learned how to survive. By the age of ten, he was working as a servant for their village leader. Pak survived and he educated himself on the vast array of literature and information available to him in the company of the elite family. By fourteen Pak could read and write well in advance of his age.

The village leader saw promise in this strapping youth, and he began to help Pak seek out valuable scholarships. The DPRK university in Pyongyang—a Communist institution dedicated to training party leaders—finally accepted Pak In-sung. He never returned to his former life. He left his family, village and the only life he'd known. He studied continuously and avoided the Western influence in which his friends regularly indulged. To throw away the chances handed him on such perverse and worthless frivolities seemed childish and hedonistic to Pak.

As he grew into a man, Pak learned as much as he could. When his formal education was completed, he bounced from job to job but never established a career. He met his wife in the late seventies, and she pressed him to enter the political arena. Her beauty and connections landed him in the heart of a changing society and a people hungry for strong leadership. For more than twenty years, Pak rose through the ranks and vied for position.

He entered an orchard ripe for picking. Many members and their assistants in a thriving political machine had aged beyond their abilities. Pak was young and strong—a likely candidate for extreme wealth and prosperity. His long bonds of friendship and his no-nonsense approach in his business dealings brought him unshakable contacts throughout the world.

Now Pak intended to seek his revenge. He would right the wrongs and reap the profits while he was at it. He had neither the desire nor the aspiration to commit to a position as premier, although the offer had come on more than one occasion.

"An arrangement can be made," one strong supporter and influential party member had told him. "This is a title and position for which you were born."

Nevertheless, that wasn't Pak's way. He had complete control over the situation. He saw no point in compounding his troubles by serving as a figurehead for an ungrateful country. The changes he wanted were best implemented away from center stage—there was less danger of discovery and far fewer consequences. It was a most effective way of ruling people.

Although he dared not whisper it among even the closest of his most faithful supporters, Pak already figured he was the true power in North Korea. To elevate himself officially to such a position would only have served to publicly announce it to the rest of the world. He didn't even need to make them aware of who pulled the strings; this was egomaniacal and disrespectful. Those who had benefited most from Pak's shrewd dealings already knew who ran the country.

Cho Shinmun sat brooding before Pak in silence. Pak could see it in the man's eyes. Cho was anxious to execute the next step of the plan, but Pak had learned patience. He ran his hand through his thinning hair, the silvery strands distinguished against his unusually dark complexion.

"I understand your restlessness," Pak said, his voice a cool, clipped tenor.

"Do you?" Cho asked.

"Yes."

"I am simply eager to serve," Cho replied.

Pak smiled at this change of tack. He wasn't sure if he detected sincerity or distaste in his subordinate's tone, but he elected to not dignify it in either case.

"I remember a fond saying of one of my most beloved professors at the university. He said, 'Time is everything, and everything takes time.' Is that not profound?"

"I find it to be trite," Cho muttered, then quickly added, "although I mean you no disrespect."

Pak raised a manicured finger. When he spoke, his tone implied eloquence mixed with warning. "You and your men have served with honor. Do not waste this now on impertinence."

Cho looked at Pak, who kept his face impassive. Pak didn't fear the hardened killer seated across from him. He could make Cho disappear with a word. Not that he felt the necessity for such action would arise. Pak was a powerful and influential voice in the very highest halls of politics. He was also well-connected with the security agency. Cho knew this and he would never dare rebel against Pak.

Pak studied his office for a moment and let the silence weigh on his guest. A mixture of antiques and modern-day trinkets provided the general decor. Pak had a passion for the dark, burnished woods of the furniture and floor. Large ruby-colored curtains and tapestries hung from the walls, secured with ornate stitching and gold tassels. Rare Persian rugs covered select portions of the polished floor. Above Pak's desk hung the flag of his country.

"I must beg your forgiveness," Cho said with a bow. "I spoke out of turn. It is not for me to question your wisdom. I am ashamed of how insulting I have been."

"Think nothing of it," Pak replied with a wave of his delicate hand. "The matter is concluded."

"Thank you," Cho said politely.

"I do not suppose you have received any update from your contacts within the city?"

"No, but they have all agreed the Americans will likely respond with subterfuge." Cho snorted derisively. "The capitalists act with faultless predictability."

"Well-spoken," Pak replied with a complimentary smile. "You have learned much since I first knew you."

Pak didn't mean the comment to sound condescending. He'd employed Cho when the man was a young upstart and fresh to the Korean People's Army. Cho had struck a senior officer when that man insulted his heritage and questioned his family honor. To discipline soldiers was one thing, but to insult any North Korean's family was quite another matter indeed. The officer tried to charge Cho with insubordination and assault on a superior. Both were capital offenses deemed acts of treason and punishable by death. Such behavior was not tolerated in the KPA.

Cho appealed to his party leader, and Pak served in the position during that time. When Pak questioned Cho, he found him obedient, respectful and anxious for action. Pak dismissed the grievance and arranged for a "transfer." Subsequently, the officer lodging the complaint disappeared, and the KPA listed him as a deserter. The officer never resurfaced and most of the records related to the incident vanished as mysteriously as he had. Neither Pak nor Cho ever mentioned the matter between them; any such discussion was considered taboo.

For the next ten years, under Pak's watchful eye and careful training, Cho grew to be a competent and very effective soldier. He was an expert in every known form of Korean martial arts. He excelled in weapons and was highly educated in all concepts of modern, historical and guerrilla warfare. He obeyed orders without question, and he treated both his superiors and subordinates with paramount respect.

Cho was the model soldier in every sense and a formidable tool that Pak could use at will.

"I would think," Pak continued thoughtfully, "that we can count on their Central Intelligence Agency to send someone. A specialist, perhaps?"

Cho shook his head. "This is what we cannot predict. It would be favorable for this kind of response, but we can know nothing with certainty at this moment. However, I do have it on the strictest confidence that someone *will* come."

Pak nodded his understanding. "Yet there is no clarity on when or how, correct?"

"I would consider that to be accurate."

Pak rose from his chair and turned to look out the expansive window behind his desk. It afforded a misty September view of gray clouds along the Taedong River. Pak looked at the street below, which bustled with pedestrians, students and party officials. Their breaths crystallized in the cool air, and the gray fog cast a ghostly haze over the activity of the city.

"We must prepare for any eventuality." Pak whirled and fixed his subordinate with a serious expression. "Our people have suffered the disgraces of poverty and starvation for entirely too long. I act with the authority of the premier, and he does not question my methods. I am deemed a man of results, and I fully intend to see this through.''

Cho nodded sharply. "I understand."

"Excellent." Pak returned to his chair. "Now, I know of your concerns at the loss of personnel. Nonetheless, if the Americans respond as you have indicated, and I have every confidence your assessment of the situation is correct, it should not be troublesome to deal with it.''

"They will send three men at the most," Cho stated.

"I do not think we can afford to recruit and train replacements at this time."

Cho shifted stiffly in his chair but kept his silence.

"Furthermore," Pak continued, "it would be foolish for the Americans or South Koreans to respond to our assault on Haeju publicly or with any force."

"You are correct on that count, as well," Cho replied. "Resistance will be negligible."

"Then I trust you will deal with the situation should it arise?"

"It will be my pleasure," Cho said coldly.

AFTER CHO LEFT his office, Pak waited patiently for the telephone call he knew would come.

He busied himself with mundane tasks and attended private meetings among other high-ranking officials inside the party. His informants on the investigation surrounding the Haeju naval installation confirmed the citizens of his country were angered by the situation. His carefully produced propaganda had only served to strengthen the North Korean position on the training exercise in Seoul. No one appeared the wiser, and that pleased Pak immensely.

It was late as he made preparations to leave his office and go home to his estate on the outskirts of the city. His contact had obviously become occupied with more important matters and missed the opportunity to contact Pak. It was of no importance. The man would contact him when the time presented itself.

Suddenly, the phone rang on his desk, jangling twice for attention and then ceasing. A minute of silence elapsed and then it rang again. This time, Pak picked it up. "Yes?"

"You are working late," the heavily accented voice greeted him.

"Of course."

"I hope I have not kept you waiting," the man replied.

The tone was almost snide, but the caller could afford to be. There was no room for niceties. Pak had tremendous authority in his own government, but this man answered to no authority but his own. Pak knew the complications of his position, and he always conducted his business with a degree of politeness and honor. As usual, his aura of respect was lost on his backer. He tried to let it pass, but he couldn't help feeling the irritability that crept through him.

"I was just preparing to depart." Pak sat at his desk and nervously toyed with a pen lying there. "Have you heard of our success?"

"Yes. It will do a considerable amount of damage to the enemy's reputation."

"Then I am pleased, as well. I have ordered preparations for the second phase of my plan."

"This is what I have called to discuss," the man replied. "I want you to delay for a couple of days."

"I do not understand."

"I have decided to visit Pyongyang."

A chill crept down Pak's spine, and something cold and

hard knotted his stomach. This wasn't a piece of news he'd anticipated. They had always insisted on complete subtlety in their dealings with each other, but now the man was actually suggesting a personal visit to Pak's homeland. Pak considered this an insult in some respects, and he wasn't about to let the matter slide unchallenged.

"Do you think that's wise?" Pak queried softly. "It could become...complicated. Such an action seems rash in light of—"

"I am aware of the risks," the caller snapped icily. "I do not need you to remind me. Nonetheless, I have responsibilities of my own. Have you forgotten the tremendous fortune I've invested in these schemes of yours?"

"Of course not," Pak said quickly. "I mean no disrespect. But my people are certain that the Americans will send an agent to investigate the issue from the inside. This could pose a serious threat to you. To both of us."

"One man?" The caller snorted. "Hardly. I will have my own staff with me anyway. You can expect me tomorrow evening."

"I understand."

"I will send handwritten instructions by courier after I arrive safely in Pyongyang. Be prepared for my arrival."

"Yes, of course," Pak agreed. "I will take every step to assure sec—"

He cut himself off when he heard the unmistakable sound of a broken connection. He stood there for a moment and listened to the dead silence on the other end of the line before carefully replacing the receiver.

Pak was uncertain of how much longer he could suffer this rude and impudent treatment. He was unaccustomed to such hostilities. The man's entire demeanor spoke of a haughty sense of self-importance. Who was he to impugn Pak's competency and authority in these matters?

Pak finally had to admit that this was the man who had provided the material wealth that allowed him to conduct these operations outside the knowledge of the party. He knew he would have to endure whatever treatment the man saw fit to impart. For the time being, he would have to keep silent and let his arrogant, pompous benefactor inflate his position. Soon, they would accomplish their mission.

And then this man would simply disappear.

CHO SHINMUN STUDIED the woman with interest as she swayed her hips and undulated in every direction.

The Yang Tang club catered to American tourists with its Korean remakes of Western music and its gaudy interior, but a good number of Cho's own people frequented the place, as well. Some of them were surprisingly well-known, faces of men Cho had seen around party headquarters. The dim lights and smoky atmosphere made it difficult to tell, but Cho was even certain he recognized a close aide to Pak In-sung. It didn't surprise him, since the club was only a few blocks from party headquarters.

Cho sat at a long, gleaming bar that ran the length of one wall. The soft hues of red, blue and yellow lights glinted neatly off the reflective material of the bar top. From his position near the back of the club, Cho had a perfect view of the entire place. He couldn't afford to miss the man he was waiting for.

Hours had passed, and Cho was only nursing his third mineral water with lime. Alcohol wasn't particularly popular in his country. Intoxicants were forbidden from many religious standpoints. Buddhism and Chundo Kyo were the two primary forms of accepted religion in North Korea. There was a Christian population, but its influence was scattered and undoubtedly weak among the Asian cultures. Cho was less than perseverant in his Buddhist practices, but he didn't drink alcohol so no one gave him a second glance.

Except for the woman dancing on stage. While she tried to pretend to be preoccupied with her routine, Cho could see she kept watching him from the corner of her eye. At some moments, she would look directly at him and smile a gleaming row of white teeth. Her lithe and supple body seemed to bask in the glow of the lights, calling to him, taunting him to indulge in his own carnal desires. The woman tossed her silky black hair out of her almond-shaped eyes, and snapped her head back in a mock display of passion. She twisted from her position on her stomach to her back and arched her graceful figure before sliding back to the lit floor of the stage. She rolled onto her side and drew her fingers across her tongue, and Cho could feel the pleasurable sensation of lust settle in his groin.

Cho tried to focus on the task ahead of him. He needed more information on the American operation that was surely already under way. To think the Americans or South Koreans would do nothing was improbable. In no uncertain terms, Pak had made it clear that he neither wanted nor expected to hear about this little affair. Cho could use whatever methods he saw fit to deal with the problem.

In some ways, that didn't make a bit of sense to him. Pak knew what they would attempt to do as well as Cho did. If their ruse worked, the enemy would concentrate their efforts on rescuing Yang Tae-jung from Ingchok. Nothing less than a heavily armed tank division could overrun the impregnable defenses there. Any lone man who attempted such a feat would have to be insane, and he could forget escaping Ingchok alive—even if he could get inside. It would result in disastrous consequences, and Cho would be ready.

The man Cho waited to see strode through the door. He

was tall and good-looking by American standards, with thin brown hair and a dark complexion. The newcomer watched the stage and nearly tripped over several chairs as he wound his way to the bar. He ordered a drink and then continued to watch the show. As he counted out five hundred *chon* and set the money on the bar, he looked in Cho's direction and noticed the man staring at him. At first there seemed to be no sign of recognition. Slowly, the man's expression changed from one of indifference to surprise. He nodded to the bartender and snatched his drink from the bar before walking over to Cho and taking a seat next to him.

Whatever Sam Wanfeld ordered smelled strong and foul. The American had CIA written all over him, which was probably the only explanation of why he was still alive, in light of recent events. The Americans weren't popular with the North Koreans at present, and the little peace that coexisted between the two nations was quickly deteriorating. To see Wanfeld alive at all was nothing short of a miracle as far as Cho was concerned.

Wanfeld offered his hand, and Cho shook it without enthusiasm.

"Been a while since I've seen you around, Chang," Wanfeld said with a Texas drawl, fighting to make his voice heard above the blaring rock music.

"My name is Cho," the soldier replied tightly.

"Yeah, whatever," Wanfeld said. He took a large swallow from his glass and wiped his mouth with the sleeve of his jacket before looking at Cho. "What can I do you for?"

"I need to know if your people have planned an assault on Ingchok."

Wanfeld cocked his head and smiled. "Whoa there, Chong. That's a tall order, and I—"

"I told you that my name was—"

Wanfeld slapped Cho on the back and smiled. "I know, I know. I'm just giving you a hard time is all. Damn, hoss, you gotta learn to relax some."

"I would like an answer."

The music ended abruptly to the tumultuous applause of a handful of customers. The woman flashed Cho another smile, bowed slightly and tossed her head knowingly in the direction of the dressing rooms. Cho pretended to take scant notice of the woman and kept the majority of his attention on Wanfeld.

The CIA agent shook his head and downed the last of his drink. "She was a hot one. Hey, bartender, line me up!" he bellowed.

"Lower your voice," Cho commanded.

Once the attendant had rushed away with Wanfeld's glass, the American lit a cigarette and focused his dark brown eyes on Cho.

"Listen, hoss, I don't know what my people are up to anymore. They don't talk to me much these days, you know? It's all politics now. Not like when I was first in the Company. The word is getting around that Pak has stirred up a lot of shit. I—"

Cho unsheathed his knife and jabbed it into Wanfeld's ribs. The CIA agent looked down, and there was no mistaking the fear that filled his face. The man had allowed Cho an opening, and the combat expert planned to make of the most of Wanfeld's undivided attention.

"You know something, American?" Cho whispered, the threat implicit in his voice. "You talk too much. Get up and walk toward the dressing rooms."

"Look, I d-don't under—"

"Shut up and do it." Cho pressed the point of the knife harder into Wanfeld's side.

Cho looked into the man's eyes but kept his face impassive. He was going to teach Wanfeld the error of his ways. No one mentioned Pak In-sung in public, particularly not around Cho and especially not *to* him. His orders were clear. Nobody could make the connection between them and increasing unrest in the DPRK. It had to remain confidential, and no sacrifice was too great. Cho knew that even he and his men were expendable.

Wanfeld rose and walked calmly toward the rear of the club with Cho on his heels. The North Korean was ready for any deception that Wanfeld might attempt. Such a maneuver would have been stupid, even suicidal. Cho was younger, stronger and in better condition—he was also highly specialized and trained for such encounters.

Wanfeld didn't stand a chance against him.

They reached the rear of the club and Cho pushed Wanfeld through the dressing-room door. The woman who had just come offstage greeted the two men with wide eyes. Cho walked past her and noticed she had nothing covering her ripe breasts at the same moment as Wanfeld turned his head to gawk at her.

"Eyes front," Cho ordered him.

The two men continued through the dressing room to a door that led onto a narrow alley behind the club. Once they were outside with the door closed, Cho stepped in and drove his foot into the back of Wanfeld's knee. The CIA agent's leg buckled, and he dropped to his knees on the rocky ground. Water splashed up from murky puddles that reflected the moonlight. The skies had cleared, leaving Pyongyang bitter cold and deathly quiet.

Cho reached up and grabbed the man's hair. He yanked back and drew the sharp blade across the soft portion of Wanfeld's throat. Blood spurted from the carotid arteries and Cho snapped the severed neck before watching Wanfeld's body fall facedown into the alley. The American twitched in the shock of his brutal and sudden death as blood ran and darkened the already murky puddles.

Wanfeld finally lay still.

Cho spit on the man's body. "This will be a lesson to anyone who interferes with Pak In-sung."

He wiped his knife on Wanfeld's shirt and replaced it before whirling and heading to the door. Perhaps the dancer was still interested in him. He could allow himself a reprieve this night. He didn't have to return to Onchon and get his men until the following morning. In the next few days, he would probably face his mysterious new enemy. He couldn't help but wonder whom the Americans would send. Surely they would select someone that matched Cho's own abilities.

He was ready for a worthy challenge.

CHAPTER THREE

Yellow Sea

Icy, damp winds blasted Mack Bolan's face as he slid aside the door to the MAC RC-35 Learjet.

The reconnaissance plane flew low across the Yellow Sea about ten miles off the coast of Onchon. The whine from the twin Garrett turbofan engines roared in the Executioner's ears, competing with the howling gusts that buffeted the sleek craft. One particular jolt nearly tossed Bolan from the plane, and he stepped away from the edge of the exit with a quick shake of his head.

"Sorry, Sarge," Grimaldi's voice broke through over the earphones Bolan wore. "It's getting pretty rough. You've got the green light whenever you're ready."

"Check that, Jack," Bolan growled. "I'm already hooked up. Try to keep her steady."

"No problem."

The soldier wasn't exaggerating his status. His static line was firmly secured to the shuffle track mounted above his head. It dangled from the ceiling and was connected to the parachute for automatic release no more than five seconds after Bolan jumped. He wouldn't normally have used a static line, preferring a high-altitude free fall, but with the onset of the nasty weather he didn't have a choice.

The soldier wore an insulated wet suit over his skintight uniform, and a black wool cap covered his head. Attached to the front of his belt was a watertight pack that contained his trusted weaponry, protected by the case Bolan had brought with him from the Farm. The pack would accompany his descent and be the first item to touch the water. Bladders in outside compartments would provide buoyancy. The weight of the Desert Eagle, Beretta, ammunition and other special items wouldn't drag the Executioner to an untimely death at the bottom of a watery grave.

Timing would be everything in this jump. Bolan had both the elements and darkness against him. There were simpler methods to enter North Korea, but there were also contacts inside the American intelligence network he preferred to avoid. He was skeptical about working with someone from the CIA inside the country, but the penetration of Ingchok prison was a tall order and he wasn't about to throw away any help.

Bolan trusted few people with his life, but Jack Grimaldi was one of them. The ace pilot could handle the controls of anything that sported wings with the deft control of an expert. There were perhaps a dozen pilots in the world with Grimaldi's kind of talent, and he had pulled the Executioner out of more than a few hot spots since they first forged an alliance.

Bolan spoke into the headset microphone again.

"I'm out of here, Jack. Be careful getting back to Seoul."

"You, too, Sarge. Stay hard."

Bolan removed the headset, stood in the door and took a deep breath.

In the next moment, he pushed away from the plane, tucked his chin to his chest and pulled his arms and legs tightly together. The distance to the sea below ranged at somewhere in the area of a thousand feet. The chute deployed correctly, and the soldier dropped toward the darkness at thirty-three feet per second. As he released his pack to fall freely below his feet, he estimated touchdown in less than forty seconds.

Bolan relaxed his body and took hold of the risers, steering the chute into as straight a descent as he could manage. The winds buffeted him and the cold mists from the thick, dense fog licked at his muscles. The Executioner suppressed a shiver and fought the sudden cold despite the warmth of his clothing. He pushed any discomfort from his mind and concentrated on the task ahead.

White, choppy waves signaled his proximity, and Bolan yanked hard on the risers. As his boots touched the water, he sucked in a deep breath and slapped the quick-release tabs that disengaged the chute harness. He allowed his weight to pull him well below the area where the chute would come to rest. With the restless nature of the Yellow Sea, he knew there was an increased risk—he could get caught under his chute and drown.

Bolan swam fifty feet from his landing site before he allowed his pack to pull him to the surface. He floated in the cold water a moment to analyze his bearings before swimming toward the shore of Onchon. The village lights twinkled in the darkness, burning like miniature beacons of welcome.

The soldier swam toward his objective, propelling himself through the rough seas with long, even movements of his arms and legs. He kept pace with the rhythmic movements of his body by using a skip-breathing method. With every three strokes, he took a deep breath and held it, breathed deeper and then let it out fully. It was a technique commonly utilized by Navy SEALs. Powerful muscles forced Bolan through the water, aided by the waves that steadily surged toward the shore.

Within minutes he reached the shoreline. He pulled his pack from the water, hauled it onto one shoulder and climbed through an opening in a cluster of large rocks. Bolan quickly examined his darkened surroundings to ensure he wasn't observed. Then he dropped his pack on the ground, peeled off his wet suit and quickly pulled his military webbing from the pack. He donned the webbing, securing his Beretta 93-R in a shoulder rig and a Desert Eagle .50 AE in a hip holster. A combat knife rode secure in a sheath attached to one of the harness suspenders and a pair of flash-bang grenades dangled from the other. The soldier wasn't planning for trouble so soon but he couldn't shake the gnawing sensation that burned in his gut. Something about the entire mission had bothered him from the start and his sixth sense began to tingle.

Bolan checked his watch; he was ahead of schedule. It would be several hours before his contact arrived, and he began a reconnaissance to locate the rendezvous site where he would meet the man. The soldier's information on his contact was vague. Some guy with the Company by the name of Sam Wanfeld, supposedly a native of Texas. Wanfeld was a veteran observer of the political machinations of the DPRK ruling party. Barbara Price knew the man personally, and she'd assured the Executioner that Wanfeld had all of the information he needed on Ingchok.

He glanced at the luminescent dial of his compass. By his best estimate, the rendezvous site couldn't be more than five hundred yards from his position. He shouldered his pack and set off for the site.

For some reason Bolan smelled a trap. It seemed as if the American government had come by the details surrounding the incident at Haeju too easily. Moreover, it didn't make sense for the North Koreans to release only part of the information surrounding the investigation. The confiscation of the weapons and explosives was completely bogus—Bolan was sure of that much. Professional units didn't make such sloppy mistakes, regardless of whether they were American, South Korean or otherwise.

The Executioner reached a cleft in a line of jagged boulders and scrambled to where it overlooked the rendezvous point. He withdrew a pair of NVD goggles from his pack and studied the area. There was no movement. The waves rolled into the shore, and the temperature continued to drop steadily. Bolan lowered the goggles and looked at the sky. If it got any colder, it might snow. He retreated from his perch and quickly devised a makeshift shelter by propping a tarp from his pack over a pair of boulders. It wasn't much, but used in conjunction with a thermal blanket it would protect him from both the weather and observers.

If fate smiled on him, he would meet with Wanfeld, reach the Ingchok prison and escape with Yang before the North Koreans were wise to his plans.

If not, he would have to play the hand fate dealt him.

BOLAN WAS SUDDENLY alert to the steady rumble of engines in his ears.

He checked his watch and confirmed it was a good hour before the rendezvous. Moreover, his contact was supposed to be alone. The soldier heard multiple vehicles, which sounded like trucks. He snatched his field glasses, crept from his shelter and positioned himself at a point on the ridge above the rendezvous site. Bolan studied the area through the binoculars.

An old Jeep utility vehicle bounced and careered recklessly along a graded road of crushed rock, leaving a trail of flying gravel and mud. The Jeep quickly neared the point where the road ended and the beach began. A lone swarthy man drove, visibly fighting the wheel to keep his monstrous vehicle on the road. Bolan could make out only a few details. The driver wore a camouflage cap on his head, and a cigarette dangled from his mouth.

Bolan followed the road to the rear of the Jeep and spotted the source of the heavy equipment engines he'd heard. Two trucks painted in olive drab with DPRK markings followed the Jeep at a distance. The Executioner couldn't translate the foreign characters stenciled across the sides of the trucks, but there was no mistaking the armed men that rode in the rear of them. They were regular troops from the Korean People's Army and heavily armed. Bolan made a quick estimate and arrived at a number of about twenty. Each man carried what appeared to be a Chinese-made rifle. Lightweight machine guns with which Bolan was unfamiliar were mounted on the roofs of the cabs.

It was a patrol of some kind. The man in the Jeep didn't seem aware of its presence. He probably couldn't hear them over the noises from his own vehicle.

The soldier returned to his shelter and quickly stuffed it into his pack. He checked the actions of his .50 AE and Beretta and then began to trace the perimeter. He needed a better point from which to observe all of the new arrivals and determine what he was up against. There was a good chance someone had tipped off North Korean officials. Or someone inside the CIA had betrayed him. In either case, avoidance of this new threat was preferable to open conflict. The soldier had to scout the area and make sure he met with Wanfeld before the guy trapped them both on the beach. He'd wait for his contact at some place outside the perimeter.

Bolan skirted the edge of his makeshift cover and descended the ridge farther inland. Every few seconds, he paused to listen and assess the distance of the army troops. He reached the base of the quarrylike area and dropped prone in a patch of tall, dry weeds at the sound of an approaching vehicle. He peered over the edge of the brush.

The Jeep roared toward him, and something told the Executioner that this was his ride. The man seemed unaware that there was trouble. Surprise registered on his face when Bolan rose and stepped toward the Jeep. The guy jammed on the brakes and swerved to avoid him. The Jeep ground to a halt, churning up sand and loose rock.

The driver leaped up onto his seat and poked his head through the top of the frame. "What the hell do you think you're—?"

His voice dropped off when he noticed the Desert Eagle glinting wickedly in the light of dawn. Bolan had the business end trained on the guy's chest. "Wanfeld?"

"No," the man replied, his eyes never leaving the Executioner's weapon. "Wanfeld's dead. You're Belasko?"

"That depends," Bolan snapped. "Who are you?"

"Well, I—"

Bolan shook his head as the steady thrumming of the approaching trucks resounded in his ears. "Never mind," he growled, rushing to the Jeep and jumping into the passenger seat. "Time's up."

"What are you—?"

"Drive!" Bolan ordered, waving the hand cannon at the man. "Or we'll both be here a very long time."

Whether out of respect for Bolan's authoritative presence or simply fear of death by .50-caliber ventilation, the man did as instructed. He dropped into his seat and put the Jeep into a hard turn, headed directly into the arms of an enemy obviously eager for blood. The Executioner brusquely ordered the man in a direction that would take them off-road.

The guy studied Bolan with widened eyes. "Are you nuts? This clunker wouldn't stand a chance over that terrain."

Bolan gestured in the direction of the trucks with exasperation. "It stands a better chance than we do against a couple dozen troops."

As if in reply, the steady rattle of a machine gun barked through the crisp air. Heavy slugs chewed up the earth immediately in front of the Jeep as the driver veered from the gravel road and began to negotiate the rough terrain. The trucks laid in a pursuit course, seemingly more equipped to handle the rocks and crags in the uneven ground.

"They're following us," the man said after risking a glance behind him.

Bolan stood in his seat, faced the rear and swung the barrel of the Desert Eagle into acquisition on the nearest enemy vehicle. He squeezed the trigger successively and maneuvered the barrel in a corkscrew pattern while accounting for the changes in the terrain. A stream of 300-grain rounds hammered the windshield and punched through it. Several of them drilled through the chest of the machine gunner who stood atop the jouncing truck. The man toppled backward off his mount and landed among his surprised comrades. One of the KPA soldiers immediately took the unfortunate man's place.

Bolan couldn't take every one of them down like that. It was time to switch tactics.

"Slow down," he said firmly as he dropped the empty magazine, loaded a new one and then holstered the Desert Eagle.

"Why?"

"Slow down!"

The driver complied, and Bolan yanked one of the M-26 high-explosive grenades from his webbing. He struggled to hold on to a roll bar on the Jeep and yanked the pin with his teeth. The truck slowly gained on them. Bolan used a boulder to the left as a start point to time the truck's average speed. He counted four seconds—an estimate of the time from when he released the grenade spoon until the explosion—gauged the distance and then let fly.

The Executioner could hear machine-gun rounds whistle past his head and punch holes into the rear of the Jeep as the M-26 arced gracefully through the air. The grenade struck the ground and bounced once before slamming against the bumper. The throw was perfect. The truck engine erupted into flames as the grenade exploded, its intense heat melting the tires and boiling the diesel fuel. The nose of the truck dipped as the back lurched and tossed out half its occupants. The North Korean soldiers were slammed to the rocky earth amid a cloud of dust.

Bolan drew his Desert Eagle .50 AE and opened fire on the group before the gunners could scramble for cover. He wanted to create more of a panic than to eliminate numbers, keep them off balance and disorganized. The second truck rushed to provide cover for the first, and the Executioner took the moment to drop a magazine and slam in a fresh one.

They were steadily increasing their distance from the chaotic scene of carnage. A secondary explosion rocked the early-morning stillness, and flames engulfed a few of the troops who hadn't been able to extricate themselves from what was now nothing more than a hulk of smoking metal.

Bolan continued to watch the scene for a few more

minutes before he was satisfied their pursuers had abandoned the chase. He turned and slid into his seat.

"We're approaching one of the eastern roads out of Onchon," his driver said. He jerked his thumb to the back seat. "I remember seeing it on that map there."

"Good," Bolan replied. "The farther we can get away from here, the better off I'll feel."

When they had gone over a rise in the terrain and journeyed downward to a paved road, the man brought the vehicle to a halt. He half twisted in his seat and wiped sweat from his brow with one hand while offering the other to Bolan.

"You know, for what it's worth, thanks for saving my ass."

"Forget it," Bolan said easily, accepting the handshake. "My name *is* Belasko. Mike."

"Caleb Arkwright," he replied.

"You with the Company?"

"No. NSA, foreign intelligence section."

Bolan nodded. "You said Wanfeld was dead. What happened?"

"It's a long story," Arkwright said, glancing nervously behind him, "and this probably isn't the best place for it."

"Then let's find the best place for it."

Arkwright grinned as he put the Jeep in gear and popped the clutch. "Your wish is my command."

As they drove toward the village, Arkwright began to brief Bolan on the situation in Pyongyang. It seemed that the NSA had known about Wanfeld's dealings with the local citizens for some time. That was a particularly surprising bit of news for the Executioner, since he'd come highly recommended by Price.

Part of the blame for Wanfeld's "straying" could be directly placed on the CIA itself. In a way that incensed

Bolan. It wasn't the first time he'd seen what too much field time in a foreign sector could do to the men and women employed by the Company. Many of them were poor and fed up with the political quagmire that seemed to be the foundation of many CIA operations. Sometimes it made Bolan wonder if that secret branch of the government wasn't more of a hindrance than a help.

Nonetheless, like the NSA, it was an information storehouse, and this intelligence dictated American foreign policy. Some relations between the United States and certain countries were based solely on information provided by the CIA. This wasn't necessarily the best way to improve foreign relations since members of the Congress—as well as the executive staff—couldn't be one hundred percent certain the information was reliable. Many agents worked for themselves and many more were motivated by one central factor: money. And lots of it.

Bolan didn't have any proof that that was the reason for Wanfeld's ultimate demise, but it surely raised some serious questions about the information Stony Man had given him. Perhaps it was this element that had bothered him from the beginning.

"It's really too bad," Arkwright explained, "because the Company kind of treated this guy like a mushroom, you know?"

"I know," Bolan replied quietly.

"We had it early on that everything with Wanfeld wasn't on the up and up," Arkwright continued. "The guy was into everything. There wasn't enough evidence to really prove wrongdoing, but he *did* know quite a few of the locals intimately."

"What do you mean?"

"He knew people, man," Arkwright said, acting as if he almost couldn't believe it himself.

"What kind of people?"

"The influential kind, that's what kind." He shook his head. "I'm telling you, Belasko, this guy was heavily connected among the higher echelon. He went to quite a few parties where he was the only white face present. Everyone else at these functions was like…well, as Korean as it gets."

"Any thoughts as to why that might be?"

Arkwright shrugged. "A few of them hypothesized he was on the take, but nobody really gave a shit until my superiors began to wonder if there was more to it." He glanced at the soldier. "I guess they saw a chance for some good intel and they jumped on it."

"I'm guessing that's where you came into the picture."

"Right on." He paused before adding, "I was assigned to full-time surveillance on Wanfeld. I thought it was kind of stupid myself. It would have made more sense to put someone Korean on him. That's the only type he associated himself with. He didn't hang out with Americans. Ever. I never could figure that out about the guy."

Bolan looked ahead through the mud- and dust-caked windshield and took a moment to ponder Arkwright's statement. A CIA foreign desk agent rubbing elbows with the higher society inside the DPRK did seem a bit odd. Particularly if it was with some intent to help heighten the suspicions of the North Koreans against their southern neighbors. Furthermore, Bolan couldn't think of anyone better to head a misinformation campaign against Americans than an American in bed with a foreign power. A modern-day spy located in a foreign country who was virtually untouchable by that very assignment. The only question that remained was why Wanfeld would assist to hatch such a nefarious plot against his own country. Had he been motivated by money or something else?

"How did Wanfeld die?" he asked Arkwright.

"Got his throat slit behind a favorite hangout. And then I got my ass chewed out for it."

"You were tailing him at the time?"

"Yeah." Arkwright ran his hand across his face as he yawned before continuing. "He had a thing for Asian chicks. Any kind, you know? Anyway, he always went to this place after he left his office. I'd wait ten minutes, maybe half an hour or so before going in myself. I could usually keep an eye on him without being noticed because he was always half-sloshed by that time."

"What happened?"

"I went inside and he wasn't there. I asked the bartender if he'd seen him, and he pointed to a door in the rear. I found him outside with his throat cut from ear to ear. Somebody did him in good, man. Damn near decapitated the poor bastard."

"He must have met with someone inside, then."

Arkwright nodded. "That's what I figure. But it was closing time for the work crowd so the streets were pretty full. I didn't really pay attention to anybody entering or leaving the place. I had never seen the point."

"I can see that," Bolan replied sympathetically. "But maybe somebody was counting on this."

"How so?"

"It's possible somebody met him inside because they *knew* you were on him," the Executioner said. "If he was in over his head with these high-society associates or party members, then there's a good chance they saw him as a liability and eliminated the leak."

"Yeah, I'd never thought of that." Arkwright swore softly and pinned Bolan with his gray eyes. "You think he might have conspired with members inside the DPRK government against his own people?"

"It wouldn't surprise me."

They were in the middle of Onchon village when the engine began to sputter and miss. Arkwright fought to keep control of the Jeep as it surged forward and then chugged to a halt. He started to steer it over to the side, depressing the clutch and trying to start it again while they were still in motion. The engine turned over but immediately died each time after it rumbled to life.

"Dammit!" Arkwright exclaimed. "The damn thing's dead. And the gas gauge reads empty."

"Our little party back there probably got the gas tank."

"It's lucky we weren't blown to kingdom come," Arkwright snapped as the Jeep rolled to a halt on the side of a village street.

"The day is young," Bolan muttered.

"There's a guy I know a few blocks from here. He should be able to provide us with some transportation."

Bolan nodded and secured his weaponry inside the pack with the exception of the Beretta. He retrieved a windbreaker from the pack and quickly slid into it to conceal the pistol. There was no point in attracting the attention of the bystanders.

As they climbed from the Jeep, Arkwright studied his vehicle skeptically. "I hate to leave the thing here, but I guess it's not salvageable now."

Bolan shook his head. "It won't be here by the close of the day."

"Yeah," Arkwright said forlornly. "I know."

The NSA agent led Bolan down the village street. Despite its size, Onchon showed very few signs of prosperity. A handful of morning commuters bustled about their business and most of them gave scant notice to the two Americans. Evidently, Americans weren't an unusual sight to the villagers. A few of them spared the Executioner a second look, obviously taken aback by his strange attire. Bolan made a note to change out of his blacksuit as soon as they had reached their destination.

They rounded a corner where a narrow single-lane street intersected the main road through Onchon. The glint of light on metal from a window of a house at an angle and to the left winked in the soldier's peripheral vision. Bolan's eyes flicked in that direction, but he kept his head completely still.

"We're being watched."

"What?" Arkwright asked with alarm.

"Keep walking," Bolan ordered him. "Don't give it away."

Arkwright was apparently practiced in not letting on that there was anything wrong.

They continued along the narrow lane, passing several homes that were more like rickety shacks. Bolan noticed that the siding consisted of little more than cheap materials tacked to deteriorating wood frames. Onchon was hardly a model of industrial prosperity, and it wasn't the Executioner's first visit to North Korea. The sights of poverty and decay didn't surprise him.

As they reached a point directly across from where the observer had concealed himself, Bolan eased his hand inside his jacket. "You armed?"

"No," Arkwright said with a curt shake of his head. "I'm not much for guns."

"How far to this guy's place?"

"It's that brick building at the end of the street."

"As soon as I tell you, you make a break for it. And don't look back. Understand?"

Arkwright nodded.

"Go!"

Arkwright took off like a gazelle, and the Executioner

suddenly bolted to his left and rushed toward the window. As he drew near to the house, he could see the sudden look of panic on the Asian face, which was now clearly outlined behind the metal frame covered with steel mesh.

Bolan reached the house and snatched his Beretta from shoulder leather. He set the selector to 3-round bursts and thumbed the safety catch. The man disappeared from the window as the soldier snap-aimed and squeezed the trigger. The subsonic cartridges chugged from the muzzle with a report that amounted to little more than a loud cough. Three 9 mm Parabellum rounds punched through the window and nearly blew it from its frame. Bolan hit the front door and placed his foot to the lock with his weight behind it. The wood splintered as the door was ripped from its hinges. A muzzle-flash from an automatic rifle alerted Bolan he was under fire.

The Executioner dived to the floor as a fusillade of rounds buzzed overhead.

CHAPTER FOUR

Bolan rolled over and pressed himself to the floor.

He immediately spotted his attacker, who stood near a door frame clutching a Chinese Type 68. He tracked on the Executioner, swinging the muzzle for a new target acquisition. Bolan squeezed the trigger of the Beretta to keep his opponent off balance, then rolled to his right for a better position. A score of 7.62 mm rounds tore furrows in the floor where Bolan had lain, and wooden splinters showered him.

The soldier lined his sights at center mass and loosed another 3-round burst. One of the slugs shattered the stock of the Type 68 and drove it into the man's stomach. The second and third rounds drilled through the gunner's thigh, splintering bones and ripping flesh. The man dropped to the floor and writhed in pain, the echo of his screams dying with the report of the weapons fire.

The Executioner rose and moved quickly to his opponent's side. He kicked the rifle out of reach, then grabbed a handful of the man's shirt. The muzzle of the Beretta was still hot as Bolan pressed it against the Korean's temple. He studied the man for some reaction, but there didn't appear to be any fear in the dark eyes that stared back at his own—only resolute hatred.

"Do you speak English?" Bolan asked.

The man remained silent.

He pressed the Beretta harder against the Korean's skull and tightened his grip on the shirt. "I asked you a question. Answer it."

"Yes," the man whispered tightly, the tone in his voice betraying his pain.

"Why were you watching us?"

"Those were my orders."

"Whose orders?"

"My superior's," the man replied. "I was ordered by my commander to watch for any American activity."

"You're with the Korean People's Army?"

The man swallowed hard, and Bolan immediately knew that whatever the guy answered was going to be a lie. He didn't have the time for a thorough interrogation, and he didn't believe in torture. It was unlikely he'd obtain much in the way of information from the man. Whoever he was with, it was probable he was trained to resist questioning.

"Why did those soldiers attack us on the coast?"

"I know nothing of this," the man spit. "I do not work for them."

"Who do you work for, then?" Bolan asked through clenched teeth.

The man fell silent again, and it was evident he wasn't going to answer any more questions.

Bolan slammed the butt of the Beretta across the back of the man's ear and knocked him unconscious. His body went limp. The Executioner tore off a piece of the Korean's shirt and wrapped the leg wounds, then quickly searched the house. There was no evidence of habitation other than some empty containers of dried rice and fish. The place was deserted.

As Bolan left the house and went to find Arkwright, he considered the situation. If the attack on them by the KPA was random—and he could hardly believe in coincidence—it meant some other, faceless enemy had known about his arrival. It was either a leak that Wanfeld had made to his DPRK associates, or the whole job was a setup to begin with. It was entirely possible that Yang wasn't a prisoner at Ingchok. Maybe Yang didn't even exist. Perhaps officials within the American government had been duped.

The soldier couldn't accept the theory that Arkwright had set up the whole fiasco, although the guy still hadn't explained how he knew about Wanfeld's meet with Bolan. If Arkwright was working with the KPA, or some other foreign service, then he'd slip up sooner or later. The Executioner would eventually catch him in the act, and he'd deal with him. For the moment, however, he was going to have to trust Arkwright.

Then there was the issue of the attack on Haeju. Another organization could have possibly expected an American response. He was already convinced the whole attack was a hoax, had been sure of it from almost the beginning. Nevertheless, Brognola and the team at Stony Man believed there was some credibility to the issues. He had no choice but to proceed with the mission on the information he had. But if trouble started, Mack Bolan would be ready.

IT TOOK JUST under an hour to reach Pyongyang. Founded in 1122 B.C. and one of the oldest cities in Korea—with its southwestern edge only thirty miles from the Yellow Sea—Pyongyang was divided into old and new sections. Some areas of the city sported wide streets with modern office buildings, while others could barely support habitation. It was a city rich in culture and history, with reconstruction of pavilions and temples dating back to the seventh century.

Despite the magic and beauty of the Okryoo Hall and the Grand Theater, Bolan was reminded that Pyongyang was headquarters to North Korea's Communist Party. This explained the fact why the majority of workers were employed by the government and worked in government-owned factories, warehouses and offices. It also explained the educational foundations of the city. In addition to the DPRK university was the Kim Il Sung University and a number of academies for medical, social, agricultural and forestry sciences.

A large industrial complex sat on the southern bank of the Taedong River. Bolan watched as smoke poured into the area from the industrial section, the result of manufacturing in rubber, chemicals and ceramics. Pyongyang even boasted a major food-processing center for their agricultural products like wheat, millet, rice, cabbage, corn and apples.

Despite the progress, many of those in the city and the country on the whole continued to starve. Pyongyang had suffered tremendous damage over many centuries during repeated conflicts when it fell to the Manchus, the Japanese and several other cultures bent on complete domination of its people. During the Korean War, there was widespread destruction, and the rebuilding of Pyongyang was the result of mostly Soviet and Chinese support. Despite all of these obstacles, its people had survived and grown to an urban population in excess of two million.

"Where are we headed?" Bolan asked.

"To my apartment," Arkwright replied. "It'll give you a place to hole up until we can decide what to do next."

"I already know what I need to do," the soldier countered, "and I think you do, as well."

"Actually, I don't have a clue."

This was the moment Bolan had waited for, and now he wasn't sure if he wanted to even put Arkwright to the test. It was possible the NSA man really didn't know what had brought the Executioner to North Korea. But if he'd been tailing Wanfeld for the past few weeks or so, the soldier couldn't see how Arkwright wouldn't know. Nevertheless, if he didn't let him in on his plans to rescue Yang from Ingchok, then he could hardly ask for Arkwright's help. Bolan figured he could probably proceed without outside assistance, but part of the plan had called for support from Wanfeld. His death had thrown a real monkey wrench into the works.

Bolan was in a difficult spot, and he knew that it now fell on instinct. He had to trust his intuition. Arkwright was a good guy—the soldier was sure of this much. Maybe he didn't possess the skills of a soldier and experienced combatant, but that didn't make him any less valuable. This deep inside enemy territory, the Executioner needed all the support he could get. If not Arkwright, then nobody. Bolan decided to take that chance.

"You ever heard of a guy by the name of Yang Tae-jung?" he asked.

"No, I don't think so. Why?"

"He's with the North Korean Ministry of Foreign Affairs."

"Wait a minute," Arkwright said, snapping his fingers. "I do remember now. Yang? Yeah, sure. That was one of the dudes we identified with Wanfeld one night at a major party shindig."

Bolan nodded. "Supposedly, that's how my people made connection with him to begin with."

"I've only seen the guy once," Arkwright said. "I wasn't impressed."

"What do you mean?"

"He wasn't one of those that stood out in a crowd." Arkwright looked at Bolan. "You know what I mean? Not like some of the other guys whose faces we've finally managed to pin with names."

"Well, somebody considers him a threat. Enough to toss

him in one of the best prisons in this country." Bolan studied Arkwright as he added, "That's why I'm here."

The NSA agent looked at Bolan in disbelief. "You're talking about Ingchok, aren't you?"

Bolan nodded.

"Oh, cripes," Arkwright said, forcing himself to avoid the Executioner's cold blue gaze. "That's not good, Belasko. That's not a good idea at all."

"Maybe not, but that's the deal," the soldier replied. "Wanfeld was supposed to help me get the additional stuff I need."

"What the hell do you want to go into Ingchok for, man? Are you nuts? Have you completely flipped your lid?"

"Look, I don't have a lot of time to explain this," the Executioner shot back. "I have to get to Ingchok, make a quick recon, then commit to the project or scrap it altogether, which is unlikely."

"You say Wanfeld was supposed to help you, huh?"

"Yeah."

"Well…shit." Arkwright fell silent, obviously contemplating his options.

Bolan could understand the man's reluctance. Arkwright hadn't counted on this much trouble when he'd made Wanfeld's rendezvous at Onchon, which led the soldier back to the other tidbit that bothered him. Arkwright hadn't explained how he knew about the rendezvous. He had just shown up out of nowhere with a bunch of KPA troops on his tail. Arkwright hadn't betrayed anything in his manner to suggest he was in bed with the enemy, but the absence of an explanation puzzled Bolan. He had to admit he was wary of his new ally. He decided not to broach the subject. To hold his cards and see what transpired was the better tactic here.

They arrived at a small three-story building a few blocks

off the highway. It wasn't the best neighborhood in Pyong-yang, but the other buildings along the block looked sound and the place was quiet. The echo of dogs barking in the distance was the only noise to break the solitude. Ark-wright backed his car into an alley adjoining the apartment building and parked it strategically. He killed the engine and flashed Bolan a wicked smile.

"Just in case we need to leave in a hurry."

"You learn quick," Bolan answered.

The two men exited the car and proceeded up an exterior stairwell to the second floor. Arkwright led Bolan to a rear-facing apartment. The place was perfectly tidy, with sparse furnishings that testified to the simple tastes of their owner. A small, waist-high refrigerator unit and electric stove oc-cupied the better part of the kitchen, which separated the bedroom and living room. The bathroom was as meager as the remainder of the house, with a simple sink, shower and one of the old-fashioned toilets where the tank sat above the bowl and water was released by a pull chain.

"Nice place," Bolan offered.

"Not really," Arkwright replied, "but thanks for saying so."

"It's small."

"Yeah, but it's home," Arkwright replied with a nod. "I eat most meals out, whenever I get the chance." He walked toward the kitchen and began to rifle through a cabinet until he found a small glass jar with an orange top. "I've got some instant coffee from the States. You inter-ested?"

Bolan nodded and Arkwright put on a kettle of water to boil while the Executioner seated himself on a battered tan love seat. The threadbare material was well past its prime. A long coffee table sat in front of him. Bolan pulled a map and some of the satellite photographs of Ingchok from his bag.

Arkwright entered the living room and sat in an old overstuffed chair at the head of the table. Bolan handed him several of the photographs.

"These are pictures someone in the NSA provided for my people. They show the complete layout of Ingchok and the surrounding area."

Arkwright took the pictures and studied them intently as the soldier unrolled a large mechanical drawing of the prison facility itself. He signaled for Arkwright's attention and pointed to a long narrow road that ran from the outskirts of the city directly into the facility.

"From what I've gathered, this is the only access into the prison," Bolan continued. "It's been my experience that you should make an exit the same way you made entry. It cuts down on the variables and prevents having to neutralize more opposition on the way out."

"Sort of the proverbial trail of bread crumbs?" Arkwright asked.

Bolan shrugged. "That's one way to look at it."

Arkwright studied the photographs again and then directed his eyes back to the drawings. "Something's wrong here," he announced.

"What's that?"

He shoved the satellite pictures under Bolan's nose and pointed to a light, curving line along the back of the prison area. "See this here? That's a service road that leads north from the village of Sungho-Dong. It ends on the southern outskirts of the prison perimeter. It's not marked on your blueprints, but I know the damn thing's there because I've been on it before."

"What kind of condition is the road in?"

Arkwright snorted. "Like most of the roads outside the urban centers. Pyongyang invests so much money in their political infrastructure, they can barely maintain city roads much less offer aid to outside areas."

"In other words it's impassable."

"I wouldn't say that," Arkwright replied. "Let's just say I wouldn't take a fancy sports car up there for a leisurely Sunday drive."

"Then what would you suggest?"

"We could probably get much closer off that road, but we'd have to secure something a bit tougher in the way of transportation. Yeah, definitely tougher and definitely four-wheel drive."

"That sounds like your department."

"Thanks."

"Wanfeld was also supposed to help me out with some weapons," Bolan continued. "Any ideas?"

The kettle began to whistle for attention.

"Saved by the bell," Arkwright cracked.

He excused himself and went into the kitchen. Bolan watched carefully as the NSA agent spooned a couple of heaping mounds of instant coffee into two cups and poured the water. He still couldn't bring himself to trust the man completely, and it bothered him a little. The idea that Arkwright might try to slip poison or something into the Executioner's drink seemed arcane, even corny, but he couldn't take any chances.

Arkwright returned with their drinks and grinned. "It's instant, but it's one hundred percent American."

"Thanks." Bolan took a few tentative sips of the strong brew, then placed the cup on the floor near his boot. He didn't want to risk fouling up the diagrams of the prison.

"My sister sends me a care package once a month. You know, the usual like coffee, cookies and so on." Arkwright took a couple samplings of his own, then sat back in his chair with a gratified sigh. "I have a Korean pal who's pretty high up in the customs chain, so I can say with certainty that a little bit of kindness *can* go a long way here."

"And some money, too," Bolan quipped. "Now, what about the weapons?"

"I don't know, Belasko," he said skeptically. "That's a tall order. I certainly couldn't justify it through the agency. Hell, my own people don't even know you're in the country. They'd string me up if they knew I was helping you at all."

Bolan saw an opening. "How *did* you know I was coming?"

Arkwright's expression changed to one like a trapped animal. He stared at Bolan across the top of his cup, as if he were trying to evade the Executioner's icy stare. The silence in the apartment was like a heavy weight, and the soldier could sense a mounting tension. His sixth sense began to tingle, the alarms resounding in his head like fire klaxons.

Arkwright finally lowered his cup and frowned. "You don't trust me, do you?"

"Trust is something you earn."

"Yeah," Arkwright shot back, his eyes narrowing and his face turning red. "It is. But after all of that crap back in Onchon, you still think I'm playing for the other team."

Bolan disliked this game. He wasn't trying to insult the NSA agent, but there were still a few things unexplained. How could he blame the guy for hating his guts? He'd saved the Executioner from an ambush—one that he'd appeared to be unaware of himself—and opened his home for sanctuary at considerable risk. He'd even provided assistance when he'd had neither reason nor duty to do so. These were just the kind of espionage games that solicited enmity between potential allies. Nonetheless, Bolan had a job to do. If there were to be any trust at all, he couldn't mince words.

"You haven't answered my question."

"Look, if it's that important I'll tell you. I had Wanfeld's place tapped...that's part of my job, you know. I got wind from a phone call he received from somebody. That's how I knew about the where and when of it. I didn't find out the why until you showed up and told me.''

"Who else did you tell?"

"Nobody. Like I said, *my* people don't even know you're here. Hell, I doubt the Company knows you're here. You see, I was ordered to take a few days off after he got his throat cut." Arkwright shook his head. "Not that anybody was all that choked up about it, okay? The guy was dirty, and I hated soiling my hands on his kind. But I couldn't just let you sit in the cold. Do you see? You're still an American, and Americans stick together."

Whether it was the hurt expression on Arkwright's face, the even tone in his voice or a mixture of the two, Bolan knew he was hearing the truth. He nodded with satisfaction and cleared his throat.

"I didn't like that any more than you did," the soldier said, "but I've learned to be careful in my business."

"Forget it. Water under the bridge," Arkwright replied with a dismissive wave. He tapped the diagrams and added, "Let's concentrate on this now."

"Right. So you can't get weapons through traditional means. What options are left?"

"Well, there's no shortage of firepower in this town," he said matter-of-factly. "You got a list?"

Bolan nodded, whipping a piece of paper from his windbreaker and handing it to Arkwright. The agent studied it for a minute and finally whistled his disbelief. "You planning on starting another war here?"

"If necessary."

"There's a guy I know on the south side of the city," Arkwright finally said. "Not too far from here, actually. I think he can swing this."

"Then let's wrap it up and go see him."

CHO SHINMUN STOOD beside Tul as two of his men deposited Net's unconscious form onto a stretcher and carried it out of the house. He would get the finest medical attention possible. They had left Net to watch their shelter while they went to investigate reports of fire traded between an army patrol and two unidentified Americans. Cho was thoroughly convinced these were the same men who had ambushed Net.

It seemed perfectly clear that the enemy had successfully landed their opposition inside his country. A radar system had detected the penetration of DPRK airspace by a small jet, which then turned south. It was possible the jet had simply veered off course in one of the many storms that rode inland from the Yellow Sea at this time of year. Cho had a hard time believing that. There was something more to it, and he had the deep suspicion that the American intelligence network was behind the two men seen on the shore, then later in the morning in Onchon itself.

Cho couldn't believe his fortune, having unwittingly stumbled onto the Americans without even knowing he would. There was little doubt in his theories surrounding this new turn of events. Buddha had smiled upon Cho and his crew. It wouldn't be difficult to follow the Americans to their final destination. They would probably go to Pyongyang, right into the heart of enemy territory. The Americans weren't foolhardy; they were just predictably stupid.

Cho might never have known about their arrival had it not been for their chance encounter with the Korean People's Army. Two men in an old American-made vehicle. That implied someone on the inside was working with them; probably someone from one of their intelligence groups. Maybe the information had come to them from an operative inside the DPRK. That meant it was possible Wanfeld had lied about his ignorance to their plans. It didn't matter. Wanfeld had been an idiot, and his death was no loss to their cause.

The fact there was only two also meant that the Americans had sent just one man to do their dirty work. Good. The man was probably an expert, although Cho doubted he was worthy of the faith the Americans had in him. Nonetheless, this man had penetrated North Korea in hazardous conditions and against tremendous odds. Obviously, Cho was dealing with someone highly specialized in such operations. Perhaps he had found an equal, his long-awaited worthy adversary. He would visit revenge upon this man.

"We must make them pay, Shinmun," Tul said quietly, echoing Cho's thoughts.

Cho put a hand on his subordinate's shoulder. "Oh, we will most certainly see to that. But first we must find these two men. That is our priority. I am certain I know where they will go. Once we find them, we will take action."

Tul looked at Cho. "You know that I will follow you into hell itself. You are both an honorable superior and friend."

"I know," Cho replied with a nod. "Where is Colonel Shinri?"

"He is outside and demanding to see you."

"Send him in and then see to the care of Net," Cho ordered.

"As you wish." Tul quickly bowed and left.

Shinri entered the house a moment later. He was tall for a Korean, with hair as dark as Cho's despite his age. Cho didn't know Shinri personally, but he knew of the military man's reputation as a soldier and leader. Their failure to apprehend the two Americans could not occupy Shinri's thoughts lightly. Cho wouldn't mention this. It wasn't honorable to do so, and he understood the disgrace Shinri still faced with his superiors. He'd lost nearly half his unit.

Cho bowed. "Colonel Shinri, I am honored by your presence. Your reputation precedes you, sir."

Shinri studied Cho a moment before returning the respectful gesture.

Cho would have to use caution with this man. Technically, neither Cho nor his unit existed outside the realm of Pak In-sung's control and influence, and they bore no official ties to the Korean People's Army. Shinri would certainly seek to restore his honor and in that respect he might not elect to cooperate with Cho's plan. It was preferable for him to keep the details to himself and visit retribution on the Americans at his leisure.

"I regret that I cannot atone for my error, sir," Cho continued. "I have no authority here. However, it would seem that the invasion of our shores by a foreign power is *my* failure. I take full responsibility."

Shinri's face immediately brightened at this suggestion. "Proceed."

"My men are a special detachment. They were assigned to Onchon for disciplinary actions following their inability to repel the recent sabotage attempts on the Haeju base."

"I see," Shinri said, clasping his hands behind his back and rocking on his heels.

Cho kept his face impassive and stood at attention as Shinri circled him. He finally stopped after several repetitions and looked Cho in the eye. Cho dropped his eyes in respect, leaving Shinri with the impression he wasn't worthy to look directly at him. Inside, Cho was laughing. It appeared that Shinri was snared by the ruse.

"Continue with your report."

"The man injured here was left behind when we embarked early this morning for night training. It appears that his injures were self-inflicted."

"Are you saying he shot himself?" Shinri scoffed, canting his head.

"I believe so, sir," Cho said, adding quickly, "although it was an accident."

"And how is it that you are to blame for the American presence?"

"We were on the shore when they arrived and we failed to detect them. Again, we have miserably cast dishonor upon ourselves. Therefore, I would request permission to return to our superiors in Pyongyang and report this failure. I will ensure that your unit is vindicated of any wrongdoing."

Shinri appeared to consider the request, and his face went through a series of contortions. Cho began to wonder if he would even approve. It was rare for a subordinate to accept the consequences of such a bumbling failure, but Cho was certain Shinri wouldn't let that stop him. He had his own head to protect, and Cho's solution provided the perfect excuse.

"And how do you intend to explain that two Americans took out nearly a dozen of the best soldiers in our regiment?"

"They set booby traps obviously," Cho said quietly. "Have I assumed incorrectly? I was under the impress—"

Shinri lifted his hand for silence. "Oh, no, you are absolutely correct. They would not have been able to do this if you and your men had seen them to begin with."

Cho fought to repress a grin.

"Your request is approved. You will proceed immediately to Pyongyang and report everything just exactly as you have to me. Is that clear?"

"Yes, sir."

"I will also send a sealed report with you on all of the intelligence I managed to gather. Everything that I observed, of course. Deliver it into the hands of the regiment commander."

"Yes, sir."

"You are dismissed."

Cho left the house, grinning.

Shinri would probably hang within a week and his men would be transferred to different units. The whole incident would be forgotten, and any reference to Cho or his unit would disappear. In time, even Shinri's men would move on in their careers and dismiss the incident outside of On-chon. The plan had worked perfectly. Now, it was time to find the enemy and deal with them.

Permanently.

CHAPTER FIVE

As night fell, Mack Bolan studied Ingchok through his NVD binoculars.

The Executioner had concealed himself amid heavy brush that grew from a ridge. His position allowed a perfect line of sight onto the prison facility spread below him. There was no question in the soldier's mind that he had his work cut out for him. Getting into Ingchok wouldn't be easy. Getting out would probably prove even more difficult.

Arkwright waited patiently in the Ford Bronco he'd acquired from a friend. The vehicle was parked on the access road about one hundred yards to Bolan's rear. The NSA man had also managed to get everything on the list with the exception of a few explosive charges. While weapons seemed easy to obtain in the DPRK, demolitions were quite another matter. That was okay with Bolan, however, because Arkwright had already proved himself to be more valuable than originally anticipated.

The soldier scanned the fenced perimeter and noted the location of several large transformers that Gadgets Schwarz had guessed supplied power to the intruder system. Their locations were clearly marked on the blueprints Stony Man provided the Executioner. Using explosives to neutralize them was out of the question, since it would alert the entire security force. He would have to take out the infrared sensors by neutralizing the manual override.

Bolan quickly noted the location and direction of the main road, which wound its way through some low hills and terminated at the front gate. He counted a half-dozen sentries on the gate with one man inside the guard shack. Several additional men walked the fence in a staggered rotation. They wore camouflage fatigues, military webbing and toted heavy-caliber assault rifles. Many of the weapons were Kalashnikovs and Type 68 rifles, but he noticed several of the sentries carried Russian-made VAL Silent Snipers.

While full examination by intelligence and weapons experts hadn't yet been possible, Bolan could recall a recent information sheet Kissinger had circulated among the Stony Man teams. Created in about 1993, the VAL fired 9 mm subsonic cartridges. The cyclic rate of fire was unknown, but the weapon was said to have a 20-round clip and chambered a special tip that could penetrate body armor at ranges of four hundred meters or better. The fact some of the men below carried this weapon was proof positive that Bolan would face Black Army troops.

The prison itself was another matter. It was two stories, excluding the subfloor cells where Kurtzman and Arkwright had both agreed was the likely place for them to house Yang. From the information Stony Man had gleaned, the building was constructed of thick concrete with interior walls reinforced by steel mesh and iron rebar. The place was a veritable fortress, and it would have been an impossible job for an ordinary man.

The Executioner was anything but ordinary.

Bolan scrambled from his hiding place and loped back to the Bronco. Arkwright sat behind the wheel, obviously fighting to stay awake. He couldn't blame the NSA agent, who was unaccustomed to hours and sometimes days without sleep. Bolan, on the other hand, lived his life around such bizarre schedules. A soldier ate and slept when he could. The four hours of shut-eye Bolan had managed to get early that morning could keep him going until he could snatch a few more.

"How does it look?" Arkwright asked quietly, although there didn't really seem to be any reason to whisper.

"Like this could be the last mission I ever take," Bolan muttered as he pulled his harness from the back of the Bronco and slid into it.

"Don't hold back," Arkwright said with a grin. "Tell me how you really feel."

Two grenades remained on the webbing; one white phosphorous and the other high explosive. The combat knife was on the opposite suspender, and the canvas belt supported several ammo pouches, as well as a hip holster containing the Desert Eagle. The Beretta was still in position in a shoulder holster under his left arm.

Bolan retrieved the pack and a Daewoo K-2 from the floor of the vehicle and slammed a clip home. He set the selector switch to safety and slung the weapon across his back, then double-checked the magazine loads for his two side arms. He jumped up and down several times to ensure that there were no loose items that might make noise. With that task completed, he quickly and expertly applied black combat cosmetics to his face and hands.

Bolan finally looked at Arkwright. "Give me one hour and no more. If I'm not back by then, you can bet I won't be coming back."

"Who should I call if—?"

"Nobody," the soldier cut in sharply. "Officially, I'm here on my own."

"I wish there was something else I could do," Arkwright murmured. "I feel so useless."

"You've done enough."

The two men fell silent, and there was something distant in Arkwright's eyes. His somber expression made Bolan realize the guy had formed a bond with him.

There were people who wanted to emulate Bolan, but it just wasn't possible. He was who he was because destiny had ordained it for him. Fate had given him special skills and talents as a soldier, and the circumstances of his violent life—fueled only by his desire for right—had haphazardly propelled him through one dangerous situation after another. But nobody could ask the Executioner to take responsibility for that.

Arkwright smiled and offered his hand. "If things go wrong out there, Belasko, it's been a real pleasure."

Bolan nodded and returned the gesture. "Same here."

"Good luck, man."

IT TOOK BOLAN nearly fifteen minutes to reach the base of the ridge paralleling the access road that ran down to the perimeter of Ingchok. He crawled the last fifty yards to the fence and quickly scanned the semidarkness. Bright two-way spotlights encircled the main building and illuminated the area in every direction, their beams overlapping.

The fence was in a rectangular shape that resembled the facility itself. Tall metal towers rose from its four corners, each connected to the next by metal-grate catwalks. Bolan couldn't see any soldiers walking along them, but he couldn't take such a possibility for granted.

He had positioned himself at a point directly under the southeast tower. Gadgets Schwarz was convinced from the wiring diagrams that a manual override for the alarm system was located there. Moreover, intelligence suggested the infrared sensors occasionally had to be turned off to allow the change of sentries or the use of dogs. If Bolan were to get inside undetected, he would have to first disable the motion detectors.

He used a pair of hand cutters and quickly stripped enough fencing away from the tower to access the perimeter without making the damage obvious. He waited several moments in the shadows and watched for the enemy, but the area around the base of the tower was still. Bolan checked his watch and estimated he had four minutes to disable the override before the next sentry passed that point.

Bolan entered the tower and climbed the enclosed, circular ladder well as silently as a cat stalked its prey. He reached the top and poked his head through the opening in the floor. A guard stood with his back to him, facing in the direction of the front gate, apparently interested in something there. Rising from the shadows, the soldier wrapped his forearm around the guard's throat, pulled backward and twisted his arm in the opposite direction, snapping the man's neck. He lowered the body soundlessly to the floor.

The links would most likely be mounted directly to the power source. Bolan quickly located his objective, a small switch box attached to the side of the wall. He used a miniature solder tip to melt away the wire link that secured the front cover, then pulled it away and studied the inner workings.

"The Koreans wire stuff a lot differently than we do," Schwarz had said. "The only wire that has a color is the ground, and it's usually white. Every other wire is black or striped, so you'll have to work on that premise."

Bolan found the wire that left the override switch itself and exited toward a hole drilled into the wall of the tower. That was the power source. Luckily, the override was part of a series circuit on the hot side of the power source. A direct disconnect would activate an alarm, and a technician would probably be sent immediately to investigate the problem. He gingerly reached for the wire next to the one he'd identified as the power source, unsheathed his combat knife and used the wire strippers to bare the exit terminal. He did the same for the entry side and connected an insulated wire with clips on either end to the exposed wires. A brief spark immediately followed by a popping sound cinched the job.

Now the sensors were disabled, but those inside the prison would have no idea anything was wrong. From where they sat, it would appear as if the sensors still worked and power was intact.

Bolan half climbed and half slid down the ladder well. When he reached the bottom of the tower, he crouched against the inside wall and waited. The sentry moved past the tower almost on schedule, and Bolan tensed when the man stopped just outside the tower entrance. The soldier fisted his knife, ready to alter his plans if necessary. A few moments later, the acrid smell of cigarette smoke invaded his nostrils and the sentry moved away.

The Executioner waited a full minute, then left the guard tower. The second sentry would pass that point in two minutes. He crossed through the disabled infrared field and continued toward the prison building. In the darkness, it took him several minutes to find what he was looking for, a large boxlike structure that seemed to have grown from the ground. It was actually a housing for one of several large fans that recycled fresh air into the underground ventilation system.

Bolan again used his torch and burned through the bolts that secured the housing to its concrete base. When he'd accomplished that task, he pushed the massive housing aside enough to create sufficient space to pass. He dropped into the dark shaft. The landing on the base of the shaft jarred his teeth even though he'd anticipated the impact.

He slid the housing back into place and then worked his way farther into the shaft.

Once he reached the ventilator fan, Bolan risked using his miniature flashlight. He stepped between two of the three massive blades, struggling to wedge through the confined space with his gear and pack. It was time to lose some of the weight. Bolan shed the pack, retrieving only the small black box from it that Schwarz had sent with him. The kit contained several other little devices that the Stony Man electronics whiz felt might come in handy for the Executioner's mission. The rest of the pack contained clothes and some rations. He would have little use for it now.

Bolan continued along the shaft on his hands and knees, his large frame brushing the sides of the cold, narrow space. Only a dusty film covered the otherwise gleaming, oily appearance of the shaft. He nearly choked on the musty, dank air that pressed upon him. Actually, it wasn't as bad as some of the places he'd found himself in, and these conditions were mild compared to those of past missions.

Yeah, it could have been worse. Much worse.

PAK IN-SUNG RECEIVED the instructions by courier just as promised.

At the indicated time, he deposited some paperwork into his briefcase and left his office. His meeting with the new arrivals would probably last until the early hours of the morning, which made him nervous. Primarily because the instructions had specified he come alone, without escort or personal security.

Pak understood the need for secrecy, but that didn't mean he trusted it. He would have preferred to have Cho accompany him to his meeting, but he knew that other, more pressing matters demanded the soldier's attention.

His news of the skirmish between the two unidentified Americans and Colonel Shinri's troops was disturbing. Moreover, Cho was convinced the intruders had come to Pyongyang with the singular purpose of rescuing Yang Tae-jung from Ingchok.

Pak wasn't comfortable with the idea of allowing Cho to employ his methods so close to the home front, but he didn't see much choice. Too much was invested at this point; he couldn't reverse direction now and run from his responsibilities like some aging coward. Such a tactic was neither practical nor honorable. He'd implemented too much of his plan to just drop it.

The feeble attempts by their enemies to take Yang from the country were hardly a problem. Cho would find the capitalist invaders and eliminate them. Pak was certain of that much, and for the moment he could find solace in it.

Pak ordered his driver to take him to the meeting place on the outskirts of the city. He had originally found the purpose of this meeting senseless but now looked forward to it. The man who had provided so much financial backing to ensure the future security of the DPRK had always shrouded himself in mystery and anonymity. They had never met personally, but their relationship was based solely on trust and respect. At least from Pak's perspective.

While he didn't think this man respected him, Pak couldn't dismiss both the shrewdness and efficiency of his partner. He commanded respect, just as Pak did, and he got results. The power plants in Kumho were nearing completion, as were the preparations for Seoul. Soon Pak's country would rise to its proper status in the political and military world and would command the respect of allies and enemies alike.

The lights of the city faded behind him. The drive to the meeting place took nearly a half hour. The chauffeur parked the car at the curb in front of a newer two-story building made of brick. Ornate windows were set in the house and covered by artistic wrought-iron bars twisted into unique decorative patterns. The man had obviously rented the structure for his stay in the DPRK, and from Pak's point of view no expense had been spared.

Pak was impressed but simultaneously couldn't curb his feelings of resentment. Certainly, there was nothing wrong with wealth—Pak was quite wealthy himself. After all, fortune meant power and power meant that he would want for nothing. But Pak also knew what it meant to be poor, and he found it hard to accept the attempts of this man to flaunt his money. A foreigner had entered Pak's country and lavished on himself every kind of luxury while others within the DPRK wanted for basic necessities like food, clothing and shelter.

Pak exited the vehicle and instructed his driver to proceed to his home with a message for his wife. "Inform her I will be detained for some time, perhaps many hours."

The chauffeur nodded his understanding and immediately drove away.

Four Japanese men wearing suits seemed to materialize from the shadows. The apparent leader frisked Pak, then instructed him to open his briefcase. At first Pak considered refusing the request but then submitted to an inspection. He had nothing to hide from his benefactor, and he didn't wish to sully his reputation for honorable business practices.

After the man briefly inspected the briefcase, Pak was escorted up the flagstone steps and into the modern flat. Expensive rugs covered the floors, and the interior was decorated with stylish furnishings made of polished woods and brass. Paintings, some of them priceless by Pak's estimation, hung on the walls. Distinctly familiar music resounded through the house from hidden speakers, and there was a strong odor of incense that clung to air like the smog that floated over the city.

The men ushered Pak into a comfortable sitting room, then departed as quietly and quickly as they had appeared outside.

He sat patiently, but as the minutes began to elapse he started to feel the first pangs of impatience. Who was this mysterious and impertinent man that rudely kept him waiting? Pak had to admit that he would only tolerate this treatment for a short time before responding in kind. He'd always been a tolerant man, but he had a large stake in this operation, as well. It was presumptuous of his benefactor to think that Pak's only responsibilities lay in the service of others. The very idea was ridiculous.

A short, thin man with jet-black hair stepped into the sitting room. He had a petite nose that jutted from a round face, and his lips seemed as lifelessly pale as those of a corpse. The man's stature and features betrayed his Japanese lineage, and the teal-and-red kimono he wore enhanced those effects.

He smiled a death's-head smile, one that sent an uncomfortable sensation down Pak's spine. While his presence seemed to emanate an aura of intelligence and authority, there was something cold and calculating behind those dark eyes. He studied Pak with little more than mild interest, and when he spoke his tone reeked of its usual disdain.

"Thank you for coming," he said in flawless Korean.

Pak only nodded, wondering if he should even speak.

"You came alone?"

"As you requested," Pak replied. "I—"

The man raised his hand for silence as he seated himself in a chair across from where Pak sat.

The party leader considered such behavior to be insolent, but he didn't dare voice his irritation. Pak had thought that this meeting might change the man's attitude, but he quickly realized this wouldn't be the case. Again, he'd been manipulated into the position of an underling rather than one of an equal.

"I have heard some disturbing news since my arrival," the man said. "It concerns me greatly."

"I'm afraid I do not understand."

"I think that you do." He paused for effect before adding, "The Americans seem to have taken an interest in this plan you have conceived. A very dangerous interest."

Pak nodded. "It is true that they have sent someone to investigate. However, I have the problem under control."

"Do you?" the man asked with another cold smile. "I think you should reconsider your position. Even now my informants tell me that an operation is under way right here in your own city."

"As I have said," Pak answered, narrowing his eyes, "the situation is not one with which you should concern yourself. I have my own team in place to neutralize this threat."

"I would remind you that this is not the time to have to deal with something of this nature." The man's tone implied a threat.

"The Americans are hardly of consequence," Pak interjected. "As you recall, I tried to tell you that there would be a slight danger. It is not as if we hadn't anticipated this kind of response from our enemies."

"Is it possible that they know more than you had foreseen?"

Pak again had to ignore the man's condescending tone. "Before yesterday my people had quite an invaluable source of information positioned among the ranks of their Central Intelligence Agency. Now that man is dead. This will most likely require me to solicit other avenues of information."

"And what of Yang Tae-jung?" the man asked. "If he is retrieved, this could have terrible consequences for us."

"Then it is the Americans who are in for a surprise," Pak countered. "This morning, I had Yang transferred to a prison on our northern border with China."

"Good," the man replied slowly with a nod. For the first time, he appeared impressed. "Very good. Now, let us discuss our plans for Seoul."

BOLAN DROPPED from the ceiling grate, landing just behind the guard and snatching a fistful of his fatigue collar. He pulled back and wrapped his hand around the man's throat. A quick squeeze of ironlike fingers crushed the guard's windpipe, then he eased the body to the ground.

The soldier crouched in the shadows of the dimly lit corridor and took a moment to assess his surroundings. He was definitely in the subfloor, probably on the south wing of the cell block. At least the schematics provided by Stony Man had proved fairly accurate. According to his estimate, there were eight individual units within the basement cell block. Ingchok was a political prison, and it was unlikely the place was full. Hardened criminals weren't imprisoned within the facility, so it wouldn't take long to locate Yang. *If* he was here.

The Executioner cleared the Beretta from its holster and catwalked down the corridor, sidestepping to keep his back pressed to the wall. He continued a silent, rhythmic pace until he reached the end of the hallway, where he crouched again and took a moment to recall the facility diagrams. The left branch terminated in a stairwell that led to the upper floors, and the right would take him to the cell block.

As the Executioner entered the intersection, he swept the muzzle of the Beretta in both directions. No one appeared to challenge him. He moved toward the cell block and began to run the numbers in his head. He figured ten

minutes remained before someone discovered his handi-
work with the guard.

There wasn't much time left.

Bolan reached the end of the hallway and peered around
the corner. This corridor was similar to the one where he'd
made his entry, except that four cell doors lined each wall
in staggered formation. The doors appeared to be made of
vertical steel bars that were reinforced in three spots by
horizontal plates. A heavy mesh covered the bars on the
inside, and small boxes were attached near handles on each
door—that meant electronic access. He seriously doubted
there was anything in Schwarz's bag of tricks. Besides,
there wouldn't be time. When he found Yang, he'd have
to melt the damn thing with his torch.

The soldier slipped around the corner and crossed the
hallway until he reached the wall. He moved quietly, his
ears ringing in the deadened silence. Somewhere in the
distance he could detect a faint hum. Probably generators
or an isolated power station. Ingchok operated indepen-
dently of any outside utility sources. It used wells for water, and large conductors powered all of the systems. It
also had computer systems and communication terminals
linked directly to satellites, and solar collectors on the roof
provided reserve energy. The North Koreans had obviously
thought through the construction well before they built the
facility.

Bolan used his flashlight to carefully inspect each cell.
He checked the entire block quickly and efficiently, only
to wind up at the other end with the same frustrating results. The place was empty. The Executioner was considering his options when the sound of movement at the far
end of the cell block from where he'd begun the search
reached his ears. He sought cover behind the nearby wall
and crouched, keeping the Beretta high and ready. The

sound of boots slapping the floor behind him echoed through the hallway.

Bolan whirled to see the shadowy figures of a half-dozen soldiers moving down the corridor toward him from a second stairwell that mirrored the location of the first on that side of the cell block. More footfalls resounded from the other end of the same hallway where it intersected with another corridor, and from the sounds of it that brought the count to twelve or more. Bolan ducked back into the cell block. Yang was either on another floor or he wasn't there at all, and the soldier was betting on the latter.

He tried each cell door even as he was certain he wouldn't find any of them open. A quick check revealed his worst assumption, and as the enemy soldiers appeared around the corner at the far end of the cell block hallway, Bolan spun to face them. There was no question that he'd been deceived, and there was now little hope he would escape Ingchok alive.

CHAPTER SIX

Bolan holstered his Beretta and unslung the Daewoo K-2 in one fluid motion.

He knelt as his new arrivals lurched forward and bunched themselves in the narrow corridor. The Executioner took quick advantage of the tactical blunder, flipping the selector switch to full-auto and squeezing the trigger.

The first two guards fell immediately under a salvo of 5.56 mm NATO rounds. The muzzle of the K-2 spit bright orange flames as Bolan swept it in a zigzag pattern. The weapon was stouter than its American counterpart and felt a little awkward in his hands, but it packed the same punch. The NATO slugs rocketed into their targets and ripped open chests and bellies. As a third guard met the same fate, the remaining troops realized their mistake and beat a hasty retreat to the cover of the walls at the end of the corridor.

One of the retreating guards reached the corner when Bolan shot him in the spine. The impact carried the man forward and slammed him into the wall. He slid to the floor at an awkward angle, but Bolan was already on his feet and retreating up the corridor.

Two more guards rounded the corner and nearly ran into the Executioner. He was too close to bring the K-2 into play, so he swung the butt of his rifle under his opponent's arm and caught the point of it on the man's chin. The guard's jaw broke with an audible crack, and the blow knocked him senseless.

Bolan immediately followed up with a sweeping attack and slammed the side of the K-2's stock against the second attacker's face before the man had time to react. As the guard landed against the wall, Bolan brought the muzzle back into play and shot him at point-blank range. The short burst punched gruesome holes through the man's skull and blew out the back of his head. A mess of shattered bone and blood left a gory mark on the wall behind him.

Angry rounds whizzed past the Executioner as the guards down the hallway returned fire from positions of cover. Bolan raced into the hallway and sprinted toward the stairs. Getting out the way he'd come in was out of the equation. He'd be an easy target inside the narrow ductwork of the ventilator shafts. The only way out of the prison hellhole was a straight shot through the opposition. There was only one problem with that—they would be expecting it.

As Bolan reached the stairwell, he risked a glance behind him. A fresh team of soldiers had pursued him and was now sighting in on his position. He cut loose with a fresh burst of gunfire before ascending the stairs two at a time. The climb was long and tedious; his heart and lungs worked furiously to supply his body with desperately needed blood.

Gunfire resounded in the stairwell, causing his ears to ring. Above him, coming down the stairs, Bolan detected the shouts of new arrivals. A tactical retreat was out of the question. He gripped his weapon tighter in anticipation as he continued to climb the stairs. The only way to handle the threat ahead was swiftly and efficiently. They would never know what hit them.

Bolan reached a landing one flight below the first floor and waited in the shadows. Four soldiers appeared a moment later, and the Executioner triggered his weapon. The first two in line took the brunt of the autofire, and Bolan's controlled bursts slammed them into their comrades. The other pair tripped over the entangled mass of torn flesh and toppled down the remaining steps to the landing. Bolan finished the job with single shots to the backs of their heads.

He started to step over the bodies and continue up the stairs when an idea hit him. He quickly retrieved a VAL Silent Sniper from one of the guards, as well as a code card, then dragged the bodies into a disorganized pile. The guards from the basement were obviously taking their time, probably proceeding in leapfrog fashion up the stairwell. They had learned their lesson about charging madly at their enemy, and this mess would give Bolan a little extra time.

As he heard them approach, the Executioner yanked the HE grenade from his suspender and pulled the pin. He set the bomb under the shoulder of the body atop the pile he'd made. It was an old trick but it would probably work. They would have to move the body in order to advance, and they wouldn't be expecting such a tactic. In the confines of the stairway, the results would be devastating.

Bolan continued up the stairs and passed through a door to the first floor. The poorly lit corridor stretched out in either direction, the walls painted the same dismal gray as those in the basement. He quickly judged his direction, then took the left side, heading in the direction of the exit.

He wondered if the entire facility was on alert. He had heard no warning alarms, and the floor seemed deserted of any personnel. Perhaps they had been reassigned to capture the Executioner on the lower level. Bolan decided not to spend time looking for Yang. Something in his gut told him that his prize wouldn't be found anywhere in the prison. And even if he'd been moved to another area of the facility, Bolan stood almost no chance of rescuing him now.

It was time to split.

ONLY FORTY MINUTES elapsed before Caleb Arkwright realized something had gone terribly wrong.

He was observing the guards through the NVD goggles Belasko left behind when he noted an increased amount of activity occurring near the southeast tower. A minute later, the sentries left the perimeter and were charging toward the main building. The guards at the front gate now spread out and began to circle the perimeter in their stead, and one man exited the shack at the front gate and began to bark at the seasoned troops.

Arkwright didn't hear any alarms but he knew it didn't matter. Somehow Belasko had been discovered. His instructions were to wait one hour and then take off, but Arkwright knew he could never bring himself to abandon the man. There was something about Belasko that he admired. Maybe it was the guy's personality and maybe something else. Arkwright knew one thing for sure. If the roles were reversed, Belasko wouldn't turn chickenshit and run. The NSA agent wasn't about to run out on his newfound friend. He had to do something.

But what?

Another view at the guards gave him the idea. He would have to create some sort of diversion. He had no weapons or explosives, so there was little more he could do from where he was. But down there he could do quite a bit to elicit their attention. He knew what he had to do.

Arkwright ran to the Bronco, started the engine and steered it down the road.

THE EXECUTIONER HAD nearly crossed the finish line when fresh resistance appeared—eight heavily armed troops guarded the exit to the prison building. Aside from them, the only other obstacle apparent to him was a large steel door behind them that opened by coded access. He could only assume that door led to the outside. Otherwise they wouldn't have so many men guarding it.

Bolan sought cover and weighed his options. A direct assault was tantamount to suicide. He could probably take out the majority of them before they responded, but one might get off a clean shot and that would end his hope for escape.

He looked down and noticed one of the overhead lights reflect off his remaining grenade. The incendiary didn't carry a very powerful charge, but it burned long, hot and bright with oxygen as its fuel. There was plenty of that around. It was his last resort, and he would have to make the most of it. It would do the trick nicely if he could get them close enough together. With a little help from the VAL.

Bolan slung his Daewoo and traded it for the Silent Sniper. He adjusted the selector from auto to single shot and leaned around the corner. The only nearby cover was a heavy desk, and the rest of the area was open. The reaction of the guards was certainly predictable.

The Executioner sighted in on his first target. He took a deep breath, let out about half of it, then stroked the trigger. The weapon stood up to its name. Bolan hardly felt the recoil as the first soldier went down clutching his side. The VAL let out a popping sound that was even quieter than the Beretta.

A distant explosion echoed down the corridor. The crew chasing him had apparently found his grenade. Bolan processed this information in a split second as he swung the fixed sights onto another target and fired. The second soldier was lifted from his feet as the 9 mm subsonic slug tore his throat apart and splattered a nearby trooper with blood and bits of wet flesh.

Several of the soldiers dived for cover behind the desk, but a couple looked in every direction and tried to pinpoint their attacker's location. Bolan switched to full-auto and continued his assault. He dropped two more of his targets with the expert control that had earned him his name as a sniper in the jungles of Vietnam. Before the last man hit the ground, Bolan rushed the position, the incendiary grenade leaving his hand.

One soldier peered over the top of the desk and saw Bolan on a direct course toward the exit door. He called to his comrades and brought his weapon to bear on the black specter that rushed him, but Bolan dived to the ground as the grenade bounced once off the enemy soldier's rifle and exploded. Bolan covered his head with his arms and pressed himself as flat as he could. Milliseconds elapsed before he felt the intense heat of the flame pass through the air over him, nearly searing his skin.

When he raised his head, three fiery forms lay on the floor and a fourth soldier was a running, screaming mass of flesh awash in bright flames. The metal top of the desk had melted under the intense heat. Bolan rose to his feet and used the VAL to pump a quick trio of mercy rounds into the human torch. The guard's screams died away as his body collapsed.

As Bolan turned his attention to the door, a fresh cluster of enemy troops appeared around the far corner. They immediately spread out and took up firing positions. The Executioner whirled and inserted his access card into the lock. The LED on the door changed from red to green, and it began to roll aside obediently. The first things to appear beyond the doorway were the exterior lights of the prison yard.

Followed immediately by four more guards rushing toward him.

ARKWRIGHT HAD THE GAS pedal to the floor of the Bronco by the time he'd completed his descent of the bumpy access road. He aimed the vehicle in the direction of the fence and ducked behind the dash as a pair of sentries began to fire at him. The metallic plinking sound of the slugs hitting the exterior panels reverberated in his ears, and the NSA agent suddenly remembered that he didn't own the vehicle. Ted was going to kill him when he saw the damage to his Bronco.

The fence tore away easily enough, but a portion of the metal caught on the bumper and dragged behind the big vehicle. Arkwright made a suicide run for the front doors. He had no idea what to do when he got there, but he could figure that out then. Maybe if he ran one of the guards down he could acquire a weapon.

That still didn't solve the problem of finding Belasko.

A moment later, Arkwright knew he wouldn't have to worry about it. The big guy appeared at the main door and looked no worse for the wear. Except for the soldiers from the perimeter who were charging toward him. Arkwright swung the nose of the Bronco into an intercept course as Belasko made a beeline toward it.

The unwary sentries were caught completely off guard by the sudden appearance of Arkwright's vehicle bearing down on them. Only two of the four managed to dive out of the way in time. Arkwright struck the other pair head-on, leaning on his brakes and executing a hard spin as they flew off in opposite directions.

One of the guards who had escaped that fate discovered his luck had run out when the section of fence Arkwright dragged with him dislodged from the careening Bronco and struck him in the head. A razor-sharp strand of concertina wire ripped through the guard's neck, and the force cleanly decapitated the man. His headless body dropped to the ground a moment later.

Bolan leaped into the Bronco as Arkwright slowed long enough to allow him inside. He stomped the accelerator and made for his hole in the fence.

The Executioner looked at him from the corner of his eye. "Going out the same way you came in?"

"Absolutely," Arkwright snapped. "It cuts down on the variables and limits opposition."

Bolan's eyes flicked in the direction of the front gate where an identical pair of utility vehicles had just arrived. Arkwright followed the soldier's stare and noticed the guards within the compound stop and gesture in their direction. Arkwright turned his attention back to the path ahead.

"I think the fun's just beginning," Bolan said over the roar of the Bronco's engine.

"Great."

CHO SHINMUN ARRIVED with his squad at the front gates of Ingchok in time to witness serious activity on the prison grounds. He leaped from his position in the front seat of the lead Hyundai Galloper and stared at the chaos with fury in his eyes. His heart beat against his chest, and it took only a moment to locate the senior officer, who was yelling at his men and pointing to an American vehicle tearing from the compound.

"What is this?" Cho demanded from the man. "Report!"

The officer whirled and his eyes widened. "Wh-who are you?" he stammered.

"Never mind who I am! What's going on?"

"There was some sort of breach in security and an explosion." He gestured to the American vehicle again, which had now reached the perimeter fence. "They are escaping!"

"No, they are not," Cho stated, climbing into the dark gray Galloper, where Tul sat behind the wheel. He waved in the direction of the Bronco. "The Americans are here, just as I had hoped. We must stop them."

"Yes, sir," Tul replied.

Cho's second-in-command yanked the gearshift into Drive and spun the utility vehicle into a parallel course with the fence. Another pair rode in the back seat, and three more men followed in a second Galloper. The gleaming vehicles tore mud, grass and gravel from the ground while their drivers maneuvered along the rough terrain. The heavy engines groaned in protest as they increased speed.

The Bronco was older, bulkier and slower than the new 4×4 vehicles under Cho's command. Cho knew there was no question they could catch the Americans before they escaped from the area. Everything depended upon it. If they had managed to steal Yang from the prison, Pak's plans would come to ruin. Cho had allowed them to slip past him once—he wouldn't let it happen again.

It would end here and now.

"THEY'RE FOLLOWING US," Arkwright told Bolan.

"No surprise there."

The soldier glanced at Arkwright and noticed the man's face was twisted in concentration. The guy had guts even if he didn't know how to follow instructions, and the Executioner had to admit he was grateful that Arkwright had disobeyed orders. It left no doubt in his mind that the man was as trustworthy as they came. Once again he'd done something for Bolan when he had no duty to do so. Yeah, he had to admire the guy.

"I don't suppose we could step it up?" he asked.

Arkwright shot him an angry glance. "What, do you think I've got a Cummins turbocharged diesel under this thing or something?"

"Just do the best you can." Bolan looked back toward their pursuers and noticed they were rapidly gaining.

"What about those guys?" Arkwright said as he coaxed the Bronco up the hill.

"Just worry about the road," Bolan ordered, "and I'll worry about them."

The Executioner reached over to the dash, lowered the rear window and climbed over the front seat. He quickly checked the magazine on the VAL, tapped it against his thigh, then returned it to the well. He palmed it home and yanked the charging handle as he turned the selector to single shot.

Now was the moment of truth. Bolan would get the opportunity to test the weapon in probably the worst conditions he could ask for. Cowboy Kissinger would be very interested to hear about his experience with this new weapon, although Bolan wouldn't have chosen to test it in such an uncontrolled environment.

"Keep it as smooth as you can," Bolan called to Arkwright.

"Oh, you're funny," the NSA agent replied as he hit a huge rut in the road.

Bolan's head banged against the top of the roof, and the blow nearly knocked him senseless. He ignored the sharp pains running through the top of his skull and centered the rifle on the lead vehicle. This particular weapon was equipped with a scope, although it didn't have night-vision capabilities. It would be an unquestionable challenge for the Executioner, firing at a moving target in the dark and at a range in excess of one hundred yards. He knew it was unrealistic to expect to disable the vehicles. Maybe a lucky shot would take one of the tires. The purpose was to keep them off balance and slow them. Bolan assumed that Arkwright knew the topography of the area well enough that he could shake their pursuers.

He pressed his chin to the weapon, keeping his eye about half an inch from the scope. He didn't want to blacken it with the sudden twists and bumps he knew lay ahead of them. The lights from Ingchok glinted against the mirrorlike finishes of the utility vehicles pursuing them. Bolan waited for a momentary lull as the Bronco crested the hill.

He took his first shot, keeping his cheek locked against the VAL's cold stock. Sparks flew from the hood a moment later. Bolan corrected for the deficiency and fired again. The vehicle swerved erratically for a moment, then continued on course, climbing the hill and continuing to gain ground. The one following it had nearly rear-ended its lead, so in a way the crude plan had been slightly effective.

Bolan's target disappeared from sight as Arkwright steered the Bronco onto the winding access road.

"How far to that village?" the Executioner asked.

Arkwright's eyes flicked to look at Bolan in his rearview mirror. "What village? You mean Sungho-Dong?"

"Yeah."

The NSA agent shrugged. "About ten minutes, give or take. Why?"

"Because these guys won't give up easily." He turned momentarily to watch the rear, waiting to see the lights of their pursuers as the Bronco rounded the first curve in the road. "Is there another road off this one we could take?"

"Not really," Arkwright said. "We've got mountain ranges to the left and a steep drop to the right. You saw it in daylight, remember?"

"Unfortunately."

Bolan also remembered the fact that the access road was

treacherously winding and narrow. In the dark they would have to watch their speed. The big Bronco was a work-horse, but it had neither the speed nor maneuverability of the other vehicles.

Arkwright slammed on the brakes and nearly tossed his passenger into the front seat. Bolan was about to ask what the hell his problem was when he saw the backside of a deer disappearing into the foliage on the other side of the road.

"That's great," Arkwright complained, wiping his brow as he brought the Bronco under control. "If those fanatics don't kill us, the wildlife will."

"There's one difference," Bolan growled.

"What's that?"

"Deer don't have guns."

"Touché."

They drove down the hillside, and Arkwright carefully negotiated each switchback like an expert. The Executioner was impressed with the man's control. The intelligence agent didn't have a tremendous amount of field experience, but he was fairly calm under fire. If they made it out alive, he would have to remember how well Arkwright had performed in these conditions and pass it along to Brognola. The big Fed might be able to use a good man.

Eight minutes elapsed and the first lights of Sungho-Dong began to appear off to the left. Suddenly, Bolan caught the sweep of headlights come around a bend directly ahead of them. A small Korean-made sedan was on a direct collision course for their vehicle, and Bolan knew they had nowhere to go.

"Watch it!" he warned.

Arkwright swerved from the oncoming vehicle and aimed the nose of the Bronco toward the inside. The vehicle plowed through trees and brush as the NSA man pumped the brakes for all he was worth. Twigs and large branches snapped off, and the Bronco finally ground to a halt nearly fifty feet from the roadway. The sudden jolt tossed Arkwright forward, and he struck his chin on the steering wheel. Blood splattered the dash and began to flow down the front of his shirt.

Bolan's knee slammed against the back seat with considerable force, and a pain shot up to the soldier's thigh. After the vehicle halted, he quickly checked himself over. Everything seemed to be working with nothing broken.

"You all right, Arkwright?" he asked.

Somehow, the NSA agent had managed to maintain consciousness. He wiped the blood from his split chin with the sleeve of his shirt. "Yeah, fine," he replied weakly. "Thanks for caring."

"Kill the lights and let's get out of here."

Bolan left the Bronco, abandoning the VAL on the seat and whipping out his Beretta. He swept the edge of the tree line with the muzzle as Arkwright shut off the lights. The NSA agent tried to open his door, but the impact had crunched the metal and jammed the mechanism. The NSA man exited on the passenger side. Bolan unslung the Daewoo and passed it to him.

"You know how to use this?"

"I suppose," Arkwright said, accepting the weapon reluctantly. "Do I have to?"

Bolan nodded and brought his finger to his lips.

A shadowy figure illuminated in the taillights of the sedan stood at the edge of the woods. The long, flowing hair and shapely figure couldn't have belonged to a man. The hips, the accentuated curve of the shoulders, the protruding chest—even the legs that peeked out from the white satin dress she wore under what appeared to be a black leather jacket. The woman stepped closer to the wood line and whispered loudly, her voice almost melodic.

"Belasko," she called hoarsely. After a momentary silence, she called his name again.

At first Bolan couldn't believe what he was hearing. A beautiful woman stood at the edge of the woods, like some forest elf, and called him with an insistent and almost parental tone. He didn't recognize the voice, but there was something about the woman that he instantly mistrusted.

"Who wants to know?" Bolan challenged the woman.

"My name is Kawashita Arisa. We have mutual friends. I've been searching all over Pyongyang for you."

"Why?" Bolan pressed.

The woman's head turned away from them briefly, then she returned her attention to the woods. "There is no time to explain now. You must come with me. I will take you to a safe location and then I will answer your questions. You must trust me."

"Like hell," Arkwright piped in.

"Explain now," Bolan demanded.

The roar of approaching engines reached his ears before Arisa could reply. He needed to make a decision. There was no question in the Executioner's mind that he and Arkwright stood a better chance against an unarmed woman than they did against a score of enemy troops bent on their immediate erasure from existence. The men in the utility vehicles certainly didn't want to chat.

"What do you think?" Bolan asked Arkwright.

"You're calling the shots here, chief," he answered. "I'll trust your decisions before my own."

Bolan nodded and motioned for Arkwright to follow. They rushed to the woman, who was now moving toward her car. She jumped behind the wheel as Bolan climbed into the front passenger seat and Arkwright reached for the rear.

The utility vehicles suddenly appeared around the corner and ground to a halt. A group of well-armed Koreans burst

from them and quickly moved for cover. They were togged
in black, tight-fitting fatigues that weren't too dissimilar
from the Executioner's own combat suit. Machine pistols
were clutched in their grip, and they moved with the well-
ordered drill of professional combatants.

The driver in the lead vehicle was the first, closest and
best target. Bolan swung his Beretta out the side window
and triggered a 3-round burst. The 9 mm rounds chewed
flesh from the driver's shoulder and sternum, and pitched
him onto the road.

The other soldiers fanned out and began to fire on the
tiny sedan. The Executioner heard a groan behind him and
turned in time to see Arkwright slump against his open
door. The fingers reflexively squeezed the trigger of the
K-2 and sent a flurry of rounds in the opposition's general
direction. Bolan bailed from the sedan and pushed Arkwright into the back seat, following behind the man and
slamming the door shut behind them.

"Go!" he ordered Arisa.

The woman put the sedan into a sharp U-turn and sped
from the area. Several bursts from the machine pistols
shattered the rear window and showered Bolan and Arkwright with glass before Arisa managed to round the corner.

"Aw, sh-shit," Arkwright sputtered, holding his side.
He tried to sit up, but his strength was waning quickly.

Bolan studied the NSA man with concern, his cool blue
eyes probing for wounds. He tried to plug a few of the
holes with his hands, but he could already see the life
fading from Arkwright's eyes. Bolan coaxed him to hold
on, then ordered Arisa to find the nearest hospital.

"I am not sure where it is," she said.

A moment of silence elapsed before Bolan said, "It
doesn't matter."

"What?"

"He's dead."

CHAPTER SEVEN

Kawashita Arisa drove her sedan through the village of Sungho-Dong with the efficiency of an expert. She negotiated the twists and turns of the narrow streets like a native, and it was quite apparent to the Executioner that this wasn't her first visit to North Korea. For a moment, he studied the woman in her rearview mirror as she spared an occasional, furtive glance at him. Mostly, those dark and sensuous eyes set above high cheekbones probed the streets ahead. Every angle of her face was flawless from an aesthetic standpoint. Arisa's full red lips were pursed in concentration. She had a light complexion that seemed luminescent in the glow of the moonlight. Her hair was full and thick and cascaded past her shoulders.

The woman had a definite aura about her—she exuded confidence with a touch of calm assurance. It was immediately evident to Mack Bolan that he was dealing with an extraordinary individual. There was something behind the beautiful visage that related intelligence and wisdom beyond her years.

Whether he could trust her was another matter, and one the soldier intended to establish quickly. He lifted the Beretta over the seat to make sure that Arisa was aware of its presence. She looked at the gaping muzzle of his pistol for a moment with surprise, then studied the Executioner in the rearview mirror for a second time. Something cold and hard replaced her expression, and Bolan contemplated the look. She continued to stare at him until she saw something in his grim eyes that seemed to frighten her. Bolan watched as a visible shudder ran through her.

"You are just as your friends described you," she said quietly.

"We need to get out of this car," Bolan replied, completely ignoring her observation. "They'll be looking for it."

"I can take us to Pyongyang. We have a house where we have set up a base of operations."

"Who is 'we'?" the soldier countered.

"I will be happy to explain it when—"

"No, you'll explain it now." He gestured to a small alleyway ahead. "Pull in there."

Arisa appeared at first if she were going to argue with him, then steered the car smoothly into the alley and stopped. She shut off the lights and turned in her seat. The anger in her eyes was evident now, but Bolan was unaffected. Things were moving entirely too fast for him, and he needed some answers before making a decision on how to proceed.

"It seems like too many people are involved in this operation."

"More than you know," Arisa shot back in a challenging tone. "That is why I was sent to find you."

"Why?"

"To keep you from breaking into Ingchok."

"What's your interest in this?" Bolan asked.

Arisa let out a sigh and shook her head. "You were misled into thinking that Yang Tae-jung was there. He was transferred by the party early this morning to Namso, a prison on the North Korean–Chinese border."

"Who ordered the transfer?"

"That is part of what I do not know," Arisa replied quickly, "but I intend to find out."

"How did you know about my mission?"

"As I have said already, we have mutual friends. My orders were to find you. To prevent this from happening." She looked at the still form of Caleb Arkwright lying on the back seat. She let out another shudder, and tears welled up in her eyes. "I was too late."

Bolan was surprised by Arisa's reaction. None of this made sense to him, and she wasn't really giving him any of the answers he sought. Nothing in his mission had gone as planned so far. At least his suspicions were now confirmed about Yang and the operation to break into Ingchok. So someone in the North Korean government was pulling strings and creating a crisis. That also left no doubt the attack on Haeju had been bogus, as well.

"So someone set us up to think that Yang was a political prisoner?" Bolan asked her.

"Oh, he is definitely a prisoner," Arisa explained, "but of his own accord. Information about his whereabouts was purposely leaked to a man in your Central Intelligence Agency."

Bolan nodded in understanding. "Wanfeld."

"Yes." She pointed to Arkwright. "This man was innocent of any wrongdoing. He became involved when Cho Shinmun killed Wanfeld. He knew nothing of the party's plans to deceive your government into believing that a crisis was brewing in North Korea."

"So a member of the North Korean ruling party killed Wanfeld?"

"No. Cho Shinmun is a terrorist and guerrilla-warfare expert, among other things. Those were his men who attacked us on the road. Cho intended to intercept you when you arrived in the country, but we think Wanfeld wouldn't discuss it."

"This is starting to make sense," Bolan replied. "Arkwright said that Wanfeld was rubbing elbows with some pretty big hitters inside the political hierarchy, including Yang."

"We have not identified the North Korean behind this operation," Arisa continued with a nod, "but we know for a certainty that someone from my country is involved."

"Then that brings us to who you are and what you're doing here."

"I think that I have answered enough questions for now," she stated. "The longer we remain here, the better our chances of another encounter with Cho Shinmun. We must return to Pyongyang. I promise I will explain, but let us leave this place now."

"Fine, but I'll drive." He stepped from the vehicle and walked around to the driver's door.

Arisa inclined her head toward him and slid into the passenger seat. Bolan took the wheel and started the engine. He backed out of the alley, then followed Arisa's directions to the highway that would take them back to the city. They rode in silence. Arisa respectfully left Bolan to his thoughts.

So someone with the party was calling the shots here. Someone high in the echelon wanted to blame the training exercise on the South Koreans and Americans, so they rigged an attack on Haeju. Then they let it slip about Yang and coerced the man into making Wanfeld think he had information vital to the security of the United States and its allies.

Naturally, America and South Korea wanted to avoid armed conflict, since they were in the middle of negotiations with the DPRK, so Bolan was sent to spring Yang. Someone faked the entire thing and figured when the American arrived they could simply eliminate him and publicly claim the Americans were using subversive tactics to determine their weaknesses. This would make the training exercise seem more like a mobilization for invasion in the eyes of the rest of the world.

North Korea could then justify launching the Taepodong III in preparation for an attack. Other countries would rush to their aid, particularly the Chinese and Russians. They could rally support for arms, food and supplies. Their allies would rush to the call, and the whole situation could blow up in their faces. It would mean war for America and South Korea, another Korean conflict that would give the Chinese and Russians the excuse they needed.

It would also make those in power extremely wealthy. There would be a substantial increase in funding for completion of the power plants in Kumho. Nuclear energy would change the tide, and put the Democratic People's Republic of Korea on the map as a nation rising to power and defending herself against her enemies. War could bring poverty and destruction, but it almost always brought jobs, food and outside political and military aid at the outset.

The North Korean people would see this and sing the praises of the ruling party. Anarchy would reign in North Korea, and an armed conflict of horrible proportions might ensue. The DPRK had already proved it would launch nuclear weapons with little or no provocation. The concept of a nuclear war had long been a threat, but the imminence of it now struck the Executioner like a hammer. They had implemented their little plan of deception without considering the consequences of their actions. Now it was time to alter that plan.

As they entered the outskirts of Pyongyang, Bolan knew he would have to contact Stony Man. The negotiations began tomorrow morning in Hungnam. That didn't leave much time. Certainly, the party would try to salvage the events of the past twenty-four hours and turn the tide of support in their favor. Bolan needed to know more about the meet. He needed intelligence and he needed it fast before he could determine his next course of action.

"There's a multinational conference scheduled to begin in Hungnam tomorrow," Bolan said quietly. "What do you know about that?"

"Members from America, Japan, the two Koreas and other concerned countries are drafting an agreement for more aid to the DPRK. Most of the parties involved believe that North Korea will use this as a platform to attack the United States and its allies."

"So this is all part of the ruse," Bolan announced.

"Yes."

The Executioner fixed her with a contemplative look. "How did you get involved in this?"

"I cannot disclose that information," Arisa replied. "I can only say that I work for the Japanese government. My people are concerned because whoever is behind this scheme has the support of a very influential and wealthy businessman. My mission was to observe his actions and report any subversive activities to my superiors."

"Who are you after?"

"Have you ever heard of a man named Sumio Hakajima?"

"No."

"This surprises me since he is one of the richest men in Japan. His company is a business conglomerate operating throughout Asia. Hakajima-*san* has contacts in every nation on earth. He operates under a blanket of political and financial support. He was a major supporter of the nuclear plants being constructed in Kumho."

"And you think he's pulling the strings of someone within the ruling party?" Bolan concluded.

Arisa nodded emphatically. "We are certain of it." She glanced at Bolan with a concerned expression. "My government is concerned that he will betray us. While Japan may not maintain its own military, Hakajima's money is made from the export of defense products. Primarily weapons and explosives, but he also dabbles in electronic and computer hardware used solely for the purpose of military applications.''

''Does he export to the United States?''

''Absolutely. His company invented one of the satellite missile-defense programs currently being tested by your government.''

''The North Koreans claimed that U.S. and South Korean munitions and demolitions were used in the attack on Haeju,'' Bolan concluded. ''I'd bet a plug nickel they were supplied by Hakajima.''

''That would be a correct assumption.''

Everything fell into place for Bolan in that moment. He could hardly believe it. Japanese and North Koreans, bitter enemies for centuries, now involved in a conspiracy to discredit America and its allies? It was almost too much to fathom—it was also too tidy. The only thing Bolan couldn't understand was motive. What would have prompted such an unholy alliance between these factions? What did Hakajima stand to gain from supporting the DPRK's ruling party leaders?

With every solution, Bolan found a whole new set of questions. The plot thickened by the minute, with one mystery piling upon another. There would be many layers to peel before he could get to the heart of the issue. All of the players involved had something to gain. It wouldn't be easy to see these motives until he had a clearer overall picture.

One thing was absolute. There were factions manipulating the situations and individuals like string puppets. Bolan knew he would find the answers he sought at the core of these complicated facades. He was certain he knew where to find them but he would have to go to Hungnam.

And he sensed the enemy would follow.

SUMIO HAKAJIMA WATCHED from a window as his men escorted Pak down the flagstone steps and into a waiting sedan.

When the vehicle had departed, Hakajima adjusted the folds in his evening kimono and sat contemplatively in his chair. He took a moment to study the Oriental decor and ponder their conversation of the past few hours. He was anxious to receive word on the American agent who had arrived in North Korea the previous day.

In many respects, Hakajima had to admire the Americans for their tenacious audacity. It was political suicide to risk discovery and public humiliation so close to the beginning of the peace talks in Hungnam. His capitalist enemies were courageous, if not a bit foolhardy, to think that there was a true crisis brewing in North Korea. The Koreans always had some sort of crisis in the works. Why were the Americans treating this any differently? It hardly mattered now. As long as he could benefit from them, he wouldn't concern himself with their foolishness.

Fame and fortune were commodities into which Hakajima had been born. His father had worked long and hard to support their family name, and he had done so honorably. As an only child, Sumio Hakajima bore considerable attention and was spoiled by his father. He'd been brought up in lavish surroundings and wanted for nothing. Although many other families descended from noble houses wouldn't have dared speak of it, Hakajima had become corrupted by his lifestyle. In Japan he was nothing less than royalty, and the community abroad had dubbed him "the King of Tokyo."

Hakajima didn't subscribe to these beliefs, although he

did nothing to dissuade such banter. He couldn't deny that he relished his legendary status. To be a legend was to be respected, and to be respected was to be feared. He ruled his own Rising Sun empire with an iron hand. Discipline and honor were the traits of his family and his businesses. A person thought twice before crossing his house, and if someone did, it was usually his or her last mistake.

The Japanese considered himself a businessman first and foremost, and like all businessmen he thrived with one goal in mind. Profit. His father had reared him with a strong hand and taught him discipline. Hakajima attended the best schools in the world, and he owned export corporations in nearly every country. It angered him that his own country didn't have the right to defend itself. The Americans were so narrow-minded in such matters. Their lack of vision would be their undoing. They put faith in a tattered, archaic document: their beloved Constitution. Meanwhile, their country rotted from within, filled with poverty and strife.

He had no political aspirations, despite what Pak In-sung might have thought. Pak was a politician in every sense of the word. He manipulated situations and used people until they were spent. Hakajima preferred a more subtle approach. A true success didn't manipulate. To be successful, one had to work and slave and earn the respect of one's peers. Then when the stage was set, underlings knew themselves to be subordinate and would simply fall in line. They would readily serve their leader to the death. This was the honorable way—the Japanese way. The Hakajima way.

And it was totally effective.

Gaiesh Koto silently entered the room and bowed long and deep. Hakajima let him wait a moment before acknowledging his chief enforcer's presence. Koto was a short, stocky man with wavy hair and long, slender hands.

Hands that were as deadly as razor-sharp knives. He moved with the grace of a cat and the strength of a lion. His stature wasn't to be underestimated, for he was one of the finest martial artists in the world. His expertise was matched only by the calm manner in which he undertook any task.

In all of the years Sumio Hakajima had known Koto, he'd never heard the man raise his voice or lose his temper. The man conducted himself with the utmost degree of self-control at all times, and this pleased the Japanese tycoon. Koto believed in the way of the shogun and the samurai. He would defend Hakajima to the death, and he obeyed orders without question. He was as dangerous and efficient as they came, and Hakajima found him to be an astute confidant.

"You have something to report?" Hakajima queried.

"Yes. The Americans escaped Pak's men."

Hakajima fixed his protector with an inscrutable gaze and narrowed his eyes. "This is not the news I had hoped you would bring."

Koto bowed again. "I am sorry."

"How did it happen?"

"The Japanese agents that followed us here. They interfered and helped the Americans to escape."

"We shall not continue to tolerate this liability."

"Pak's men are excellent, my master," Koto protested softly. "I am impressed with their skills. Pak has assured us that—"

"Pak is a fool, Koto," Hakajima cut in, raising his hand for silence. "And like all fools, we cannot allow him to compromise our position."

"I understand. What do you wish me to do?"

"I am certain that Pak will offer some feeble excuse tomorrow. I must attend the conference in Hungnam. I have neither the time nor the inclination to entertain his whims.''

''I would concur.''

''I think it is time that we eliminate the meddlesome lot, including Pak's men. They pose a considerable risk.''

''Begging your forgiveness for my presumption,'' Koto replied with another bow, ''but do you think it is wise to fight among our allies?''

Hakajima now rose from his seat and whirled to face Koto. The enforcer continued his gesture of obeisance as Hakajima strolled to him and put his arms on his shoulders.

The Japanese tycoon didn't take offense at Koto's suggestions. He never let personal feelings get in the way of better judgment. They had known each other too long for such pettiness. Koto was as devoted to his master as a son to his father. With no offspring of his own, Hakajima looked upon Koto as one of his own children. He had nurtured him in the enforcer's younger days. Koto was his devoted servant; he was also his protégé.

''Our cause must remain our only goal. I cannot undo what has been done. The Koreans have brought this upon themselves, and they would attempt to sink us with them. I cannot allow this, Koto. You know that.''

''Yes, my master. But I do not wish to leave your side. My place is with you.''

''I do not think this will be necessary. Send your best students. I have complete confidence that they will do what Pak's men could not.''

''And what of Cho Shinmun and his men?''

''They do not pose a threat. Not at this present time. They are only a secondary annoyance, and we may deal with them at our leisure. For the moment, we must concentrate our efforts on the greatest danger.''

''Understood. It will be done tonight.''

Hakajima nodded once, then turned from Koto. He

walked to a nearby table and began to indulge in a water pipe. The harsh smell of opium burned in the air as Hakajima inhaled deeply. He didn't offer any to Koto, since such a gesture would have been deemed an insult. His protector and constant ally was pure in body and spirit, and did nothing that would alter his state of mind. He ate only the finest and purest delicacies, allowed no spices in his food but only minerals and natural herbs.

Koto trained two hours in the early morning and another two in the evenings. Hakajima loved to watch him somersault through the air, lunging and parrying with lightning-fast kicks or hand techniques. He would study Koto with interest as the martial artist felled four or five attackers at a time, or placed them in effortless holds until they surrendered with the pain he inflicted.

Koto hadn't moved from his spot, and Hakajima realized that there was still something on the man's mind.

"What is it?" Hakajima asked.

"There is the matter of one of the agents from our country. She followed us, but I have not wished to trouble you with this information. Nonetheless, Kawashita Arisa is helping the Americans."

Hakajima felt the blood rush to his head, and he knew it wasn't the effects of the opium. His could sense his face had flushed and his heart began to beat faster. His ears started to ring, and he fought back the urge to scream and vomit at the same time.

"I have asked you," Hakajima said quietly, "not to mention that name in my presence. Ever."

"I am sorry, master," Koto replied. "Please forgive my transgression."

Hakajima smiled and forced himself to remain calm. "You are forgiven. And you have your instructions. Eliminate all of them."

"Yes, master. It shall be done before the next dawn."

With that Koto turned and departed, leaving Hakajima to sit in stony silence.

CHO SHINMUN HAD assessed the damage done to Ingchok by the American subversives.

He rode in silence as Yadul drove the Galloper up the Pyong Ni Highway and proceeded north. They followed the sedan at a safe distance, having picked up the tail by waiting on the highway. It was the only logical way out of Sungho-Dong and it now appeared that Cho's vigilance had paid big dividends.

The lights of the city burned as bright and hot as the anger within Cho. A pang of remorse stabbed his gut as he thought of his longtime friend and faithful first officer. Tul had died gloriously, but Cho could hardly find a reason to celebrate. He turned an angry glance to the city's skyline and sullenly mulled over the situation. They had failed a second time.

Pak hadn't been pleased with this news when Cho called him on the satellite phone inside their vehicle, and Cho couldn't say he blamed his superior. He'd never failed this miserably on an operation before. Up ahead of them, the American and his passenger were probably laughing at him.

They had brought down part of the enemy, but Cho remembered the hardness of his opposition. The man who they had cut down on the road into Sungho-Dong was sloppy and unprofessional. But the other one—the one wearing all black and with the eyes of a demon—he was as experienced as they came. The man had shot Tul with true marksmanship, considering the firestorm laid down by the rest of Cho's men. Yet he had also risked himself to save his conspirator despite the fact the man's life was already lost.

To Cho, this showed a devotion and spirit that could

only be appreciated by a fellow soldier. No, the American commando was not new to combat. He was an experienced professional and extremely dangerous. Their next encounter would be their last. Cho would be ready for the man this time. Failure wasn't an option.

The appearance of the woman further troubled Cho, primarily because he recognized her. He didn't know her name, but he knew she was Japanese and worked for her government's intelligence service. Cho realized he couldn't take this at face value. It seemed strange that the Americans would solicit the assistance of the Japanese warmongers in their plans. While there was obvious animosity between his people and the Japanese, he couldn't see their stake in this game of cat and mouse.

Pak had been unable to offer him any insight.

Despite Cho's reported failure, Pak chose not to administer any kind of punishment. Perhaps it had been because Cho was tailing their quarry, and he'd begged for a chance to correct his mistake. Pak could be merciful when he chose to be, and Cho had appealed to this. He would promise anything, do anything, to restore the honor and respect of his men. Yes, Cho would follow his targets and drive them to their knees when the time was right. He would make them wallow in the dirt of his beloved country, and eat the dung of its animals.

And then he would finish him for all of the world to see.

CHAPTER EIGHT

A burly Mongolian-looking man attired in a black suit cast a dubious look at the Executioner as he exited Kawashita Arisa's sedan. A second car, this one silver in color, was parked facing out of the driveway.

Although the man visibly relaxed at a hushed word of caution from Arisa, Bolan kept his hand close to the Beretta just in case. The broad, flat, yellowish face stared at him, dark eyes sizing up the warrior. Bolan marked the man as a lookout, probably posted outside the single-story house to alert its occupants if any trouble arose. Not that the guy would need any help. His body was as thick as the trunk of an oak tree, and muscles strained at the seams of the suit, threatening to tear it from his body.

The house the lookout guarded sat back in a cul-de-sac, isolated from the other units along the street it faced. It was nestled among the working-class residents on the north side of the city. The soldier studied the structure, his hard blue eyes scanning it for any weaknesses. It wouldn't be easy to approach the place undetected, and Bolan found he could relax some on that note. Nevertheless, he would proceed with caution as always.

Arisa gestured for him to accompany her up a few steps to the entrance. As Bolan stepped up, the giant shuffled aside without hesitation. His movements were surprisingly graceful, and Bolan was acutely aware that the man could move with speed and agility despite his enormous size. His eyes, still filled with skepticism, watched the Executioner, but the soldier ignored the glare. There was no point in taking it personal—the guy was doing his job.

"That is Sajn," Arisa offered when they reached the front door.

Bolan looked behind him to spare another glance at the human behemoth.

"He is also a faithful associate. Do not let him trouble you."

"No trouble," the soldier replied.

The two went inside the house and were immediately greeted by a pair of inquisitive expressions belonging to well-dressed Japanese males. They were obviously relieved to see Arisa had returned unharmed, but they appeared to give the Executioner scant notice. Bolan could see that the woman was unquestionably in charge of their operation. If the soldier was okay with her, then it seemed he was okay with the rest of the group. Although he still had his doubts about Sajn.

Arisa introduced the larger of the two men as Eichi and his partner as Yutaka. They bowed respectfully to Bolan, and he returned the gesture, but they never took their eyes off him. Their movements were precise, without wasted motion, and the soldier quickly concluded he was dealing with professional combatants. Undoubtedly, they were trained in the martial arts, and Bolan figured they were also employed by the Japanese government.

Bolan took the time to observe his surroundings. The house was clean and appeared well maintained. Most of the furniture and art in the foyer where they stood, as well as the adjoining rooms that were visible, appeared Japanese in origin. A large table occupied one room immediately off the foyer, and Bolan noticed a large map spread across it. Several areas on the map were marked in grease pencil, but he couldn't see enough details to clearly identify what area was represented. Aside from that part of the house, the remainder seemed posh without displaying a sense of gaudiness.

After nearly a full minute of conversation, Arisa looked at Bolan and smiled.

"I have vouched for you and explained the situation. It will take some time, but I think they will come to trust you."

"Fine," Bolan told her, "but I don't plan to stay long enough to earn it."

Arisa's expression went cold. "I see."

Bolan couldn't understand her haughty demeanor. They were in the middle of a predicament, and time was the one luxury he didn't have. The Executioner certainly wasn't going out of his way to be rude, but he needed to contact Stony Man and bring them up to date on where the situation stood. He was also going to need the support of Jack Grimaldi, and it would take the ace pilot some time to reach him.

"Is there a phone I can use?"

She gestured to a closed door at the end of the hall. "Through that door are my quarters. We shall remain here so that you may have privacy. Eichi and Yutaka will take care of Arkwright-*san*'s body."

Bolan nodded in way of thanks, then proceeded immediately to the end of the hall. He pushed through the door and closed it behind him, leaving it partially ajar. The room was sleek and elegant with a bed covered by satin sheets and a small bureau with a mirror and stool. There was a bathroom toward the back corner, and the smell of jasmine hung strongly in the air.

Bolan found the phone on a nightstand. He sat on the bed and dialed the special, encoded number to Stony Man. A series of clicks and whirs sounded in his ear as the phone line went through several cutouts before keying the satellite telecommunications center at the Farm eight thousand miles away. Even if the receiver was tapped on Bolan's end, the encoder would scramble the signals and prevent anyone on the outside from eavesdropping. It was a technical marvel invented by Kurtzman and his crack team of cybernetic specialists, and considered to be nearly foolproof.

There was a single ring before Aaron Kurtzman's voice resounded crisply in Bolan's ear.

"It's me," the soldier greeted the Farm's resident computer whiz.

"Hey, buddy," Kurtzman boomed. "What's happening there?"

"Well, I can tell you the eagle has landed but it's hardly been smooth sailing along the way."

"We heard. I trust you're still in one piece?"

"For the moment. Is the head Fed in?"

"Right here. Hold a sec."

There was a pause before Harold Brognola came on the line.

"Are you okay?"

"Yeah, I'm fine. But things have definitely gone sour on this end of the world."

"What happened?"

Bolan began to explain the recent events, detailing his landing at Onchon, the death of Wanfeld and the encounters in and near Ingchok. He also filled Brognola in as to his unexpected rendezvous with Kawashita Arisa and her overall involvement with the mission. Brognola listened in complete silence, never interrupting the Executioner as he gave the complete rundown. When Bolan had finished his report, Brognola sighed deeply.

"I'm sorry about Arkwright. I will personally see to the arrangements for the return of his body to the States."

"He said something about a sister. You might want to contact her."

"Sounds like he was more of a victim than a willing party."

"He assumed the risks," Bolan replied.

"I understand. As far as Arisa is concerned, Barbara sent her to find you. They've worked together on numerous occasions, and the information about the Japanese involvement came after you were deployed. We had no idea something like this would occur."

"I know. What's done is done."

"Agreed. What did you have in mind for your next move? Extraction?"

"Not yet," Bolan said sharply. "Unless you have other ideas."

"The ball's in your court, Striker. It's your call all the way now. The original mission has been scrapped. I can't believe we allowed ourselves to jump into this without soliciting all of the facts."

"Nobody could have seen it coming," the soldier said quietly. "The way I look at it, I have two problems to deal with."

"I'm listening."

"The Japanese government seems convinced that this Hakajima isn't operating alone. He's working with someone high up in the party. They haven't identified this other player, but they know he's got a team of soldiers operating under his direct orders."

"Do you think we're talking about a military coup of some kind?"

"No," Bolan interjected, "this is definitely under the table. I don't think whoever's working with Hakajima has the blessings of the North Korean government. According to Arisa, this team is led by a man named Cho Shinmun.

They're hard-core professionals, be they a mercenary unit or otherwise."

"How do you propose to deal with them?"

"It's better if I let them come to me."

Brognola hesitated to reply to this information, and the soldier could tell that the big Fed wasn't exactly keen on the idea. Bolan could have offered more of an explanation, but he didn't want to give too many details.

"What's the other problem?" Brognola finally queried.

"I think the meeting in Hungnam is the key to this whole deal," Bolan replied. "I also think that if I'm right, all of the major players will scramble to stop me. Arisa agreed with that much."

"Okay, I can buy that. But the peace conference is scheduled to begin tomorrow. I assume you'll need Jack?"

"Yeah. I need him in Pyongyang any way he can get here, and damn quick. I also need you to send him everything you can on Cho and Hakajima."

"Okay, that won't be a problem. He's holed up at the air base on Guam. That storm apparently forced him to divert. I'm sure he can be there in a few hours. It's pulling the strings to get him into North Korea that will take time."

"I have every confidence in you, Hal," Bolan said, smiling into the phone. "You'll make it happen."

"Sure. Anything else you need from us?"

"A list of the attendees and the details of the meet itself, an agenda, anything you think might help. Maybe I can figure out who our mystery player is."

"Done." There was a momentary pause. "Hey, Striker?"

"Yeah."

"Be careful over there."

"Check. Out here."

Bolan broke the connection and sat in silence. He

mulled over the conversation with Brognola and knew his friends at the Farm were concerned. Brognola had echoed the thoughts and sentiments of all the Stony Man crew in that statement.

Now there was a whole new set of circumstances boiling in this caldron of deception. It was like an unruly game of chess where only the law of the jungle ruled. It seemed like a millennium had passed since one of Phoenix Force's earliest missions against the crime syndicate known as MERGE. Yakov Katzenelenbogen had mentioned the mission to Bolan in a moment of passing, referring to it as one with no rules, no referee.

But if Bolan had learned anything, it was that the rules didn't apply in his War Everlasting against the jackals that preyed upon society. This time the enemy had crossed the line and nearly lured him into a death trap, killing innocents along the way as if they were of no consequence. The Executioner was through with them. It was time to fight them on his terms. Yeah, it was time to enact a blitz play and unmask all of the players in the game.

The look on Arisa's face as she burst through the door told the soldier he was about to get that chance. Her deep, intuitive eyes probed his face for a moment with a mixed expression of shock and perplexity. He knew immediately there was trouble, and he was off the bed with his Beretta in hand before she could open her mouth to speak.

"We have company," she said tightly.

"Do we know how many?" he asked, stepping away from the window and pointing his weapon at it expectantly.

"I'm not certain, but they aren't here for rice cakes and sake."

Her abrupt and crude humor seemed almost American in origin, definitely a twist from her normally reserved composure. It took him a little off guard, and Bolan couldn't repress a grin.

The tough mask immediately fell again. "You find this humorous?"

"Forget it," he retorted. "Where are they?"

"Sajn saw them pass twice before they stopped at the end of the street. Perhaps five or six, but at least four."

"Could they be Cho's men?"

"No," she said, shaking her head emphatically. "This isn't possible."

"Why?"

"These men are Japanese."

"Hakajima?"

She nodded.

The window suddenly imploded, showering the room with shards of glass. Bolan tracked the shadowy form with the Beretta, sighting in on the target as he squeezed the trigger. The shot never came because the gun was suddenly gone from the Executioner's grasp. The only evidence his attacker had even taken the weapon was the breezy gust of air Bolan felt sweep the air just above his hand.

The new arrival was clad entirely in black. A *hakama,* a traditional garment that looked like a skirt but was actually a pair of billowy pants, covered his legs, and his upper body was swathed in a thick *gi* top. A mask concealed the enemy's face except for dark, almond-shaped eyes. A red sash encircled the man's waist, and Bolan knew from previous experience that he was dealing with a master in martial arts. The man spoke softly in Japanese, then attacked, slashing toward Bolan's throat with a rigid-hand strike.

The Executioner stepped aside, narrowly avoiding the deadly maneuver, and grabbed the man's arm. He twisted his opponent's wrist toward him as he spun inward and attempted to snap the elbow over his shoulder. The *ha-*

kama brushed the back of Bolan's neck as the Japanese left his feet and twisted his body in a 180-degree turn. He came down in front of the soldier and drove a knee toward his opponent's groin.

Bolan twisted his hips and took the blunt of the impact on his thigh. It wasn't nearly as debilitating as it would have been had the man reached his target, but it seemed no less painful. The soldier maintained his grip and drove an elbow between them, landing it under his assailant's chin. The man seemed barely dazed by the blow, and he twisted from Bolan's grip.

The Japanese dropped to one knee and drove both hands into Bolan's unprotected solar plexus. Only hardened muscles developed from regular abdominal exercises prevented the blow from putting the Executioner down for the count. He doubled over with a forceful grunt. A fiery sensation burned in his diaphragm and ran up into his chest as the air left his lungs.

A black shape blurred in Bolan's peripheral vision, and it took a moment to realize it was the flowing, dark hair of Kawashita Arisa. The Japanese special agent seemed to materialize between Bolan and his attacker. He turned in time to see Arisa snap a hard kick against the side of the Japanese man's head. Both the speed and ferocity of her attack seemed to surprise her opposition, and it appeared Arisa wasn't about to lose that advantage. She immediately followed the kick with a knife-hand strike to the man's face, then an uppercut to his chin.

Bolan's original blow to the chin had to have softened the attacker some, because blood suddenly sprayed from his mouth and the mask ripped as it caught on a tooth. The blow staggered the Japanese man and sent him reeling blindly backward. He lost his balance as he tripped over the small stool in front of Arisa's bureau. The lithe, agile woman stepped in to finish the job by stomping on the man's throat.

Her enemy caught her foot when it was mere inches from his throat and twisted, wrenching with enough force to break the ankle. Only because Arisa turned with the technique did she spare herself such a nasty injury. She yelped with pain, and Bolan could immediately detect the tides shifting.

The Executioner sprang into action.

He drew his combat knife and rushed toward the man still trying to deal with the feisty Japanese woman who had shown him up. Bolan leaped over Arisa's falling body and landed next to the man's head. He dropped to his knees and drove the honed, razor-sharp steel blade into his opponent's eye. The blade pierced the orbit, crashed through the skull and continued into the brain. The man died with a shocked gasp, and his body went as still as quickly as it had appeared.

Bolan didn't try to retrieve the knife but instead rose and assisted Arisa to her feet. They stared at each other for a moment, both of them breathing hard with their exertion, and it seemed time stood still. Something replaced Arisa's strained expression. Something like respect and admiration—perhaps even attraction.

The moment passed and Bolan remembered where he was. "You all right?"

She nodded. "I am."

"What about your ankle?"

"It is not bad," she said, her eyes never leaving his.

Sajn burst through the doorway and said something short and terse to Arisa. She nodded, and Sajn barely shot a sparing glance at the dead intruder before leaving the room.

Bolan had turned his attention to the Japanese assailant. He quickly frisked the guy for ID, locating his Beretta in the process, then unmasked him. He tugged on the knife, but brute strength powered by sheer adrenaline had caused him to wedge the knife to the hilt. It wasn't coming out.

"Recognize him?" he asked Arisa.

"He is one of Hakajima-*san*'s men. As I suspected."

Bolan jerked his thumb. "Are they all like this one?"

"We should expect this."

"It figures."

The lights suddenly winked out, and the house was shrouded in darkness. Only a dim glow from the street-lights shimmered through the broken window, enhanced by a full moon that hung in the cold, clear sky.

Bolan grabbed Arisa's hand and urged her to follow. They left the bedroom and walked down the hall, but met no resistance along the way. Near the foyer, the soldier crouched and paused to listen. There were no movements inside the house and no sign of Eichi or the others. Where were they?

"Eichi and Yutaka already left," Arisa whispered in his ear as if she'd read his mind. "Sajn will attempt a diversion so that we may escape."

"Suits me," the soldier replied.

Bolan waited another moment, then signaled for her to stay with him. He rushed for the front door, pulled it open and stepped aside. Gunfire resounded from the street, and rounds burned the air where the couple had stood. Chunks of plaster and bits of wood erupted from the walls, filling the darkened interior with smoke. The Executioner risked a glance around the corner and quickly spotted the familiar shapes of the Gallopers that had chased him and Arkwright from Ingchok.

Muzzles winked again from the windows of the sleek gray autos and pounded the house with an incessant storm of lead. Windows shattered and pictures fell from walls. The vases and glass tables exploded as a rainstorm of autofire raked the house interior. Bolan pressed himself to the wall and shielded Arisa with his arms as the gunfire continued. After what seemed like an eternity, the night fell silent again.

"It's Cho," he growled. "Working with Hakajima's men."

"No," Arisa objected softly. "Hakajima does not use outsiders for such business. This is simply an act of fate."

"Lady, I make my own fate," Bolan snapped. He traded the Beretta for the Desert Eagle .50 AE and thumbed the weapon's safety. "On my signal, I want you to head for the car and don't look back. Drive straight to Pyongyang airport and I'll meet you there."

"What about you, Belasko?" she asked. "I need you to help me."

"I'll be there," he said quickly. "Now do what I say."

She studied him a moment in the semidarkness of the room, but Bolan tossed her a look meant to subdue her desire to argue with him. If there was anything he didn't need right now, it was a debate. This was his area of expertise and she knew it. Their relationship had somehow reached a new level, and Bolan didn't want this to end as abruptly as it had with Arkwright. His job was to keep the innocents out of the way, and Arisa hadn't signed on for the same war as the Executioner. Her personal feelings had nothing to do with it on that count.

"Do it!" the soldier grated.

Arisa burst around the corner and leaped over the porch railing. Bolan was impressed by the way she thought on her feet. She was an enigma of brains, beauty and sass.

Bolan hit the doorway a moment later as Cho's men turned their weapons in Arisa's direction. He knelt, sighted down the huge barrel of the .50 AE and squeezed the trigger. His ears rang with the first shot as a 300-grain bullet crossed the expanse and smashed through the driver's window of the lead Galloper. The autofire directed at Arisa abruptly quieted. Doors on the opposite of the vehicle flew open, and men's voices echoed back to the Executioner like the shouts of a crowd in an open arena.

Bolan immediately followed up with another shot, ripping back a large chunk of metal from the roof of the rear vehicle. He narrowly missed a man still seated in the driver's seat. An overhead streetlight illuminated his face as he sighted a machine pistol on Arisa. Bolan adjusted his aim and fired again. This heavy-caliber round cleared the door window, and the man's head exploded with the impact. His corpse flopped backward and disappeared from view.

The soldier watched as Arisa stared at him for a moment before jumping into the silver sedan. She fired the engine to life and accelerated down the driveway. Tires squealed on the asphalt drive of the cul-de-sac as Arisa powered the vehicle onto the street and roared away from the house, scraping the side of the enemy's SUV upon her exit.

Something made a scraping noise, and Bolan turned in time to see another hooded, shadowy figure rush him. The soldier was twisted sideways and knew he'd never be in time. Left with no other options, he dropped flat to the ground and rolled toward the man. Despite all its simplicity, the unexpected move worked. His would-be attacker tripped over Bolan and landed prone on the concrete porch.

The Executioner got to one knee and swung the muzzle of the Desert Eagle in the man's direction as the enemy jumped to his feet and whirled for another try. White-hot powder seared the man's *gi* top and the skin underneath as the .50-caliber slug followed. The round expanded as it tore through his midsection, blowing out pieces of his spine through a grapefruit-size exit hole. The impact lifted him from his feet and tossed him through the air. His body landed on the walkway below and rolled twice before coming to a halt.

Another ninjalike shadow suddenly appeared at the door and lunged toward Bolan. He never made contact. The monstrous form of Sajn emerged from the adjoining living area and yanked the Japanese assailant short. The surprised man recovered quickly and launched a series of rock-hard blows to Sajn's shins, knees and stomach. Sajn grunted with pain but hung in there, refusing to release the small Japanese man who now dangled almost a foot off the floor.

Bolan noticed Sajn's opponent smoothly but deftly reach into the folds of his *hakama*. He tried to shout a warning, but he was a moment too late. Some unseen light flickered momentarily off the cold, polished, stainless steel of the *sai*. The Japanese enemy swung the point of the three-pronged weapon gracefully, puncturing the soft indentation just above Sajn's sternum. The weapon sunk to the hilt, and Sajn's eyes widened with shock and terror. He stepped backward, wheezing and gasping for air because his windpipe had been completely severed from his lungs.

Bolan rushed forward, switching the Desert Eagle to his left hand as Sajn collapsed and the Japanese landed on the floor with catlike grace. The Executioner swung the barrel out and away from his body, aiming the butt for the enemy's skull. The man whirled just in time to miss the full impact of the blow, and the butt caught his shoulder. The receiver continued in motion and the sharp edge of the forward sight tore the mask and ripped a deep gash in the man's cheek.

The Japanese thug reacted as the true martial artist he was, grabbing Bolan's wrist with the intent of using the soldier's own motion against him. He also reacted just as Bolan had hoped. The soldier had already reached for the Beretta holstered in his shoulder rig, and now it was

pointed directly at the Japanese's stomach and set to
3-shot mode. The man's dark eyes swept downward in a
moment of realization as his hands clamped on to Bolan's
wrist. His position had left him wide open.

Bolan stroked the trigger, and the weapon chugged out
three rounds in succession. The 9 mm cartridges ripped
through tender flesh, nearly disemboweling the man. It was
a fitting end, since failure in some parts of Japanese society
meant the practice of seppuku, a horrendous form of self-
evisceration invented during the country's feudal period.
The impact sent the killer spinning, and he toppled against
a wall before slumping to the ground.

Bolan holstered his weapons and stood panting in the
darkness. For the longest time, he didn't move. Every muscle in his body ached, particularly his gut, and he would
have given anything in that moment for a place to lie down
and close his eyes. Once again, the enemy had almost
caught him off guard. He began to wonder why they were
so desperate to kill him.

They had followed him wherever he went—he'd
planned on this. What he hadn't planned on was that they
would strike so quickly. And if Arisa was correct in her
assessment of the simultaneous attack by Cho's and Hakajima's goons, then that meant there was some kind of
division between this alliance of Japanese and North Koreans. Somebody was acting without the knowledge of the
other party.

And the Executioner fully intended to use that to his
advantage.

CHAPTER NINE

Washington, D.C.

Hal Brognola was anxiously waiting in the Oval Office when the President arrived.

The two men didn't often meet under such circumstances, and Brognola knew it upset the country's leader to take time from his busy schedule when the need did arise. Nonetheless, the recent incidents in the Democratic People's Republic of Korea demanded priority. Otherwise Brognola would have never called an emergency meeting of this nature. The President knew this about the big Fed and he also knew Brognola wouldn't have made such a request unless it was extremely important.

The President smiled cordially at him as he shook his hand. He instructed the Secret Service agents and White House chief of staff he wasn't to be disturbed, and the two men were left alone.

"I assume you called this meeting because of something having to do with North Korea?"

Brognola nodded. "Correct. The situation there has become, well, unstable."

"Uh-oh. That doesn't sound good, Hal." The President faced Brognola with an expectant gaze. "Please continue."

"Striker ran into serious trouble shortly after he arrived. He was almost intercepted by regular North Korean soldiers, and his contact was murdered the evening prior to his penetration of the country. Shortly after that, he encountered more resistance from a special detachment of mercenaries, apparently hired or at least financed by someone in the higher ranks of the DPRK ruling party."

The President nodded slowly and sat back his chair. "What about Yang Tae-jung?" the President asked.

"He wasn't at Ingchok," Brognola replied grimly. "We were deceived from the start. To make matters worse, the Japanese are now involved in this thing."

"How so?"

"The same person pulling the strings with the Korean mercenaries, or whatever they are, is also in bed with a Japanese tycoon. His name will probably ring familiar with you. Sumio Hakajima?"

"Hakajima...Hakajima," the President said thoughtfully. "You don't mean the founder of COR-DEF Industries, do you?"

"One and the same."

"The Air Force is currently testing a prototype missile-defense system he invented. This can't be possible."

"Striker confirmed he's one of the culprits, sir," Brognola argued. "I have no reason to doubt what he's telling us. He's not infallible, but he's rarely incorrect about these things."

The President shook his head quickly. "I'm not suggesting that I doubt the man's integrity, Hal."

"Point taken," Brognola said.

"What are you doing about this?"

"Well," Brognola began slowly, looking at his hands, "I've sent someone into North Korea to make an extraction."

"You're pulling him out?"

"Not exactly. We're relocating him to Hungnam. He thinks there might be a connection between the recent goings-on in the DPRK and this conference."

The President turned an uncomfortable shade of white and Brognola felt a lump form in his throat. For some unexplained reason, this bit of news hadn't sat well with the Man, and the big Fed wasn't sure why. It wasn't as if Bolan would compromise the security of the delegates or disrupt the negotiations. His take on the whole matter was that Bolan wanted to do some looking around and see if he could pinpoint the other aggressor.

Brognola quickly voiced his observations.

"If you can guarantee there won't be trouble," the President finally replied, "I'll support the operation."

"I appreciate your concerns, Mr. President, and I'm always aware that Striker's methods are hard. But they're effective and generally permanent."

"And violent," the President interrupted, "which might create a debacle we couldn't afford."

"I understand," Brognola replied sympathetically. He waved his hand for emphasis, adding, "Striker believes that's exactly what these subversives inside North Korea want, and I agree with his assessment. To rush in without forethought would only further those aims. The whole purpose behind their plan was to manufacture a scandal that would support their claims regarding the training exercise in Seoul."

"It would also justify launching their new ballistic missile." The President nodded. "I'm well aware of what they're trying to do. And you are correct about our foolishness in this situation."

"All Striker wants to do is see if he can identify the North Korean party member responsible for this."

"And when he does?"

"I imagine he'll take appropriate action."

"And at the appropriate time," the President added. "I mean it, Hal. I don't want any problems."

"I'll make sure your directives are passed along, sir. We'll handle this with all possible discretion."

"Excellent. I'm counting on you for this. And tell your man I'm counting on him, as well. I know he'll get it done right."

"Yes, sir."

Brognola had received his signal that the meeting was finished. He bid a hasty farewell to the Man and then hurriedly left the Oval Office and headed for the rooftop helipad. A helicopter would whisk him back to Stony Man Farm. That's where he really belonged.

Brognola had never been a proponent of politics. The lofty, complacent mentalities of the representatives that congregated in Wonderland had replaced the wholesomeness and honor of their predecessors. America had definitely seen simpler, more honorable times—times of peace and prosperity. Times where people could walk down any dark street in any city without fear of violence and danger.

Corruption and personal gain had permeated the halls of power on every level of government, leaking down to the citizenry, and Brognola sometimes wondered why the members of Stony Man continued to strike wherever the enemy reared up. Without a doubt, much of their vigilance could be traced to the relentless war of one man.

Brognola thought of Mack Bolan now, and he realized that his views had changed after his first involvement with the Executioner. It seemed as if someone other than him had first taken up the fight to bring down the one-man army striking at the heart of the Mafia. The big Fed smiled when he remembered what a conscientious, anal-retentive, narrow-minded young upstart he'd once been. Brognola had sworn to bring Bolan in dead or alive. Now he had sworn a lifelong friendship with that same man. It amazed him when he considered the fact it was he who had changed and not the Executioner.

Bolan was still the same idealistic weapon of war that he'd always been. Sure, he'd seen quite a few additional miles since beginning his war. Nonetheless, the warrior was a consummate soldier and professional—he'd never lost that. And he'd never lost his burning desire to rid the world of the predators that sought to exploit a weaker and unwary society. It was this axiom that kept Brognola active in the cause of Stony Man and its personnel.

And strengthened his bond with the man called Mack Bolan.

Pyongyang

IT WAS WELL PAST MIDNIGHT when the Executioner arrived at Pyongyang International Airport, and he knew the enemy was close on his heels.

He'd walked to a subway terminal that was only a couple of miles from Arisa's former base of operations, eluding numerous police vehicles along the way. He kept to the shadows as they whizzed past. Some concerned citizens had probably reported the gunfire coming from that quaint little home in an otherwise unobtrusive neighborhood.

That was fine with Bolan. If North Korean law enforcement kept busy trying to sort out the mess he'd left behind, it lessened his chances of an unwanted encounter with them elsewhere. Given the recent violence throughout the city, the police would most certainly wish to detain and question any American dressed like Bolan. The soldier still wore his combat suit, and he solemnly wished he'd told Brognola to have Grimaldi bring a change of clothes.

Well, he could worry about that later. His priority was to find Arisa and then grab a safe place to wait until Grimaldi showed up. Bolan had to admit he'd be happy to see a familiar face, especially that of Stony Man's ace pilot. He'd known Grimaldi longer than any of the Stony Man crew, with the exception of the members of Able Team, and he relied heavily upon his old friend's skills.

At the moment, however, he was relying on his intuition to warn him of the danger that lurked in the shadows. When the men following him made their move, he wanted to be ready. He would deal with them swiftly because that left the smallest margin for error. Their patience was admirable, and Bolan wondered which side his tails represented.

Bolan knew he hadn't brought down all of Cho's crew. There were at least six guns that attacked them on the road near Ingchok, and he'd eliminated two in front of the house. That left at least four, and the soldier was betting they would stick together. Yeah, they would find comfort in numbers. Not that it had done them much good to this point.

Arisa had said Cho was dangerous. The evidence that his men were professionals wasn't incontrovertible so far, but Bolan could hardly bring himself to awe. They had made several sloppy mistakes and rushed into each situation without any apparent preparations. Nonetheless, he knew that overconfidence was the mother of all killers. Bolan had survived this long by granting due respect to his enemies. He wouldn't stop now.

Hakajima's men were something else entirely. They were skilled professionals all the way and extremely dangerous. Bolan knew he would have to exercise extreme caution in the future until he could find the Japanese crime lord and put a decisive end to his schemes. Much of Bolan's healthy fear had come from his firsthand encounters with the Japanese karate experts. The Executioner had walked on every continent and dealt with many kinds of combatants, but this force wasn't one easily reckoned with. He didn't relish another encounter with them.

Bolan began to push himself up the ramp that led to the street level. He'd purposely exited one stop from the airport's main entrance since he was loaded down with weaponry. He'd stripped away the hip holster and webbing, tucking the Desert Eagle into a large pocket of the overcoat he now wore. He'd found the coat in a closet at the house, and based on the size of the thing it had probably belonged to Sajn. It nearly dragged on the ground.

When he reached the street, Bolan saw the main gates ahead. They were unmanned at this hour, and that would make his job easier. There was no sign of Arisa's sedan, and the Executioner knew he'd have to walk the parking areas until he found her. She knew he was armed and with any luck she'd wait for him where they couldn't be compromised. However, he didn't want to bring the enemy to her. He would have to deal with them first.

Bolan stepped to his left and broke into a jog as soon as he was clear of the ramp. He drew his Beretta as he crossed the deserted two-lane road that led from the airport. In moments he'd entered an alleyway between two utilitarian buildings that stood isolated along the far side of the road. Once he'd ventured deep enough into the shadows, he crouched and waited for his prey.

CHO SHINMUN WATCHED the American step from the subway train and walk toward the airport. He couldn't imagine why his quarry would select this destination. The thought that he might try to slip quietly out of the country occurred to him, but he dismissed it out of hand. That seemed too easy. This man didn't strike Cho as the kind who would allow others within his capitalist government to pull his strings. The American was definitely a loner—he acted like it and he fought like it.

Cho and the remaining trio of his squad maintained a discreet distance, keeping in the shadows of the darkened subway station. The American moved quickly and with some obvious purpose. Cho thought it was possible that his target might have a meeting scheduled here. It was a public place with a lot of running room, although safety in numbers was hardly a viable option at this time of morning. Pyongyang International was a busy place, but it wasn't that busy.

No, the American professional had something else in mind.

Perhaps he was going to rendezvous with the Japanese woman. His association with her or the American agent Cho's men had eliminated surprised Cho. He was convinced the man tended to operate alone. Well, in a short time it wouldn't matter. He stopped and waited patiently as the American walked up the ramp and disappeared from view.

Cho knew it would soon be time to make his move.

BOLAN COUNTED the seconds as he awaited his tail.

He was certain that there were at least two who had followed and possibly more than that. The Executioner was still amazed that the enemy continued such a dogged pursuit. Even if Cho and his men weren't the best the North Koreans had, they were still relentless. Relentless men could be dangerous men; this was something Bolan had come to accept in his experience.

Two men suddenly exited from the same ramp Bolan had used, popping their heads over the ledge of the walkway where it met the ramp and looking around cautiously. The soldier froze in place, the Beretta clutched in his grasp. He knew he could probably take them from that distance, but he had to be sure he was dealing with enemy troops and not just lost bystanders. He never struck out at the enemy before he'd made a positive identification.

Bolan cursed the fact he'd been unable to get a closer look at Cho and his men. At this stage, any attack on unknown persons without confirmation they were aggressive was futile. That wasn't the way the Executioner did things, and he wasn't about to change now. His protection of the innocent and respect of law officers were two traits that many of the Stony Man team found redeeming. Yet Bolan wasn't afraid to step into the heat of battle when and if the need arose.

The pair finally progressed the remainder of the distance up the ramp and again checked their surroundings. Moments later, another two men joined them and the four began to study the immediate area for any sign of the Executioner. If Bolan's ruse worked, they would head in the direction of the airport and he would become the stalker. It seemed obvious these men had followed him, but it was entirely possible they were members of the North Korean secret police. Maybe they were plainclothes officers who were assigned to look for suspicious or criminal elements riding the subways.

While Koreans tried to maintain a more pacifistic appearance, they had the same problems as any other ethnic group. Poverty and starvation led to crime. The Executioner wasn't an expert in sociology, but he understood the basic nature of man. Some were generally good and others turned to their more vile and baser instincts. The subway at night would be easy pickings for muggers and rapists. Nevertheless, the North Korean authorities didn't condone such behavior. Justice and punishment were usually severe and immediate, and this was a deterrent. But like any society, it wasn't exempt from crime.

The men looked straight in Bolan's direction for a moment, and the soldier wondered if they had seen him. Suddenly, they turned and began to rush toward the parking lot. Bolan waited a few seconds and then stepped from the shadows. He started to tail them but then reconsidered. If he followed them and they *were* after him...? No, he couldn't risk a firefight under such circumstances. There was a better place and time for that. He had a higher priority and that was to find Arisa.

He waited near the corner of one of the utilitarian buildings until the men were distant specks against the backdrop of the airport terminal and then set off to find his female cohort. If the time came to handle the quartet, then he would act without hesitation. He hoped it wouldn't come to that.

Bolan began to search the parking lot carefully. It took him almost fifteen minutes to locate Arisa's sedan, which was sandwiched near the airport terminal between a minivan and an imported sports car. He crept up to the passenger-side door and peered inside. The sedan was empty, and a quick try of the door handle revealed it was locked.

Arisa was supposed to have come here and waited for him. He couldn't fathom any reason for her to leave her car and just disappear. It was possible that she was waiting inside the airport, but Bolan couldn't risk going to look for her. He would attract the undue attention of security, and that presented another set of problems he didn't need. The soldier decided he would just have to wait for her and hope she returned soon.

The sound of movement behind him sent warning signals, and he turned in the direction of the footsteps. He leaned against the minivan and brought his Beretta into play. He thumbed the safety down as gently as he could and held his breath.

The shapely form of Arisa Kawashita appeared with a steaming cup in her hand. Bolan rose from his cover gracefully, but Arisa didn't seem the least bit surprised to see him. She smiled at the soldier, her dark eyes twinkling in the lights of the parking lot, and her face went slightly flush.

"You are okay?" she asked. Her actions made it seem as if she'd only left Bolan for a few minutes.

"Tired," he replied easily, not even trying to hide the fatigue in his voice. "But it's nothing I won't get over."

She smiled and punched a button attached to a box on her key chain. The doors of the sedan clicked mechanically. She tossed the keys to him and immediately walked to the passenger-side door. Arisa climbed into the vehicle and shut the door behind her without another word.

Bolan circled the sedan and took his place behind the wheel. Arisa sipped at something that smelled hot and spicy. The odor began to fill the car, and Bolan studied the cup in her hand with a questioning gaze.

"It is tea," she said, offering the cup to him. "I was cold and I did not wish to run the engine."

Bolan took the cup gingerly from her. He took a sip and nearly spit it out. It was strong and bitter—way stronger than any tea had a right to be. He handed it back to her and shook his head. Arisa began to laugh as he smacked his lips and shook his head again. A warm glow began to run through his body, and he felt a wave of nausea coming on. Normally, the Executioner didn't have such a sensitive palate, but it had been many hours since he'd eaten anything and he had begun to feel the pangs of hunger.

"What is that stuff?" he asked with disdain.

"It is a special blend of teas, designed to enhance the *ki* and restore energy," she explained patiently. "Such drinks are one of the strong points of the DPRK. They have set a standard comparable to that of my country, and even surpassed it in some ways. I find this particular mixture to be quite pleasurable."

"What's in it?" Bolan asked with interest.

"I do not think you want to know."

"Yeah, I do. Tell me."

Arisa studied him with resolute skepticism, and Bolan tried to keep his face impassive. In that moment of silence and peace, he couldn't deny how beautiful this woman was. There was something very special about her hair, but he couldn't really discern it. The silky way that it seemed to pour from her head, feathered in many places. It wasn't thin and straight like most hair he'd seen on Japanese women. There was a different quality to it.

"They usually begin by fermenting raspberries and chamomile, and they dry this into powder. Then they crush the loins of the sacred yak—"

"Hold it," Bolan interjected, "I think you're right. I don't think I want to know."

"I told you this," Arisa protested.

"So you did," Bolan replied.

"What happened at the house?" she asked quietly.

"I was able to put down three of Hakajima's men and a couple of Cho's." He cleared his throat and added, "Sajn didn't make it."

Arisa remained silent for a long time.

"I'm sorry," Bolan offered.

"He was a good man. I shall miss him." Her voice was slightly shaky.

"How can you be so sure that Hakajima and Cho aren't in on this thing together?"

"That is not the nature of Sumio Hakajima. He is a proud man."

Her eyes narrowed and she stared at Bolan. There was something there that went beyond mere distaste, and the Executioner was immediately aware of its presence. It seemed like a deeper, more personal grudge—almost like hate. Something had triggered a strong emotion in her, and Bolan was convinced he hadn't heard the entire story. There was an unexplained animosity for Hakajima on Arisa's part, and Bolan knew he would have to get to the heart of it.

The soldier knew it wasn't his imagination. He'd learned to read people well over the years. Not that Arisa had done much to hide her displeasure at the very mention of the Japanese crime lord's name. He'd seen the same reaction before, on the drive from Sungho-Dong, but it hadn't seemed all that odd since he didn't know Arisa as well then. But now? Well, now was a different story.

"He is also an evil man," she continued. "Full of arrogance and presumption. It will be his undoing."

"I've met many men like that," Bolan replied. "And you're right—he'll trip on his own lunacy and break his neck."

Arisa now turned to study Bolan for a moment. "You are a wise man, Belasko," she finally announced. "I am happy to know you."

"Yeah."

Bolan used the silence to take in her elegance while he sorted out a few details in his mind. If fortune was smiling on him, Grimaldi would arrive before dawn with information on Hakajima, Cho and anyone else Price or Kurtz-man might think was involved.

"My people told me you know one of them person-ally," he said. "How did you meet?"

She tossed him a wan smile, and Bolan knew she rec-ognized the ploy. He was testing her, probing for answers and waiting for her to betray herself as another one of the enemy. It had only occurred to him at that moment that she might have lured him into the trap in Pyongyang and then had to cover her tracks when the attack on the house failed.

"We were once assigned together on a case," Arisa explained, "when she served as a mission controller for your National Security Agency. I was the liaison for a long-range mission involving members of Delta Force. She offered intelligence and even came to Tokyo for the dis-mantling of a corrupt mercenary force sponsored by a gov-ernment official."

"The two of you became friends?"

"Close associates," she added. "I do not know for whom she now works, but she contacted me and wondered if I could warn you of the trap at Ingchok. Somehow she knew that I was assigned to my own mission here inside this country."

"That doesn't surprise me in the least," the soldier said. "She keeps tabs on just about everything."

"It is amazing, her mind is. I respect her for her honor and courage."

"She's a good lady," Bolan replied with a nod.

Arisa put her hand on his. "And you are a good man. I can sense this."

"Thanks."

"You have not explained your purpose for sending me here. What do you hope to accomplish?"

"Well, that's the next step," Bolan replied honestly. "I've arranged to hook us up with a pilot. He's as good as they come and he'll get us to Hungnam."

"You think Hakajima-*san* will go there?" Arisa asked.

"I don't know about Hakajima, but I'm sure that whoever's behind this business on North Korea's end of it will be there. I plan to find out who that is and stop this once and for all."

"I am not sure this is the wisest course of action," she countered. "My government believes that Hakajima-*san* has something very considerable planned. Perhaps a major operation for the near future. He has invested a substantial amount of money and support for the project in Kumho."

"I know what you're thinking," the Executioner interjected. "Why is he in bed with the North Koreans and what's he really after?"

Arisa nodded. "This is troubling for my people. Hakajima-*san* is a very powerful man in Japan. Few would dare to accuse him of any illegal acts. However, I find his behavior treasonous. He has bartered the security of his own people for some cause he believes is greater."

"And you think it's got nothing to do with what the North Koreans want?"

"The DPRK wants only one thing. Nuclear superiority."

"Or at least equality with any countries it considers a threat."

"That does not explain what Hakajima-*san* wishes to accomplish."

"I think we'll find that out soon enough."

Bolan reached beneath his coat and withdrew the small box he'd kept with him since his raid on Ingchok. He opened the watertight case and removed a small black device with a miniature switch and red LED. He flipped the switch and the light began to flash rapidly. He set in on the seat between them and then returned the box to its place.

"What is this object?" Arisa asked.

"It's a homing device with a special scrambled signal. When the light stops flashing, it means our ride's here."

"This is impressive."

"Uh-oh," Bolan whispered.

"What is wrong?" she asked, turning to look through the front windshield.

"We've got company."

CHAPTER TEN

The four men seemed to materialize from the darkness as they advanced on the sedan.

"Cho's men," Arisa whispered.

Well, that clinched it. They were the same four Bolan had allowed to slip past him, and he now regretted that decision with the knowledge he'd allowed the enemy to pass unmolested. They strolled toward the sedan at first, but when they neared it they burst from their positions and fanned out. Weapons appeared in their hands, ranging from semiauto to fully automatic machine pistols.

Bolan fisted the Beretta and turned to warn Arisa, but the Japanese agent already had her weapon in hand. She clutched a stainless-steel, Colt Government Model .380 pistol fitted with an extended 10-round magazine. It was American made and a perfect fit for Arisa's tiny hands.

The Executioner nodded his approval before going EVA.

Arisa pushed open the door of the sedan and knelt behind it. She propped her elbows between the door and frame and fixed her sight post on the nearest gunman charging her. She held her breath as she squeezed the trigger. The .380 slug hit at center mass and cored through the liver and kidney before exiting through the man's back. The impact spun the gunner to his right just in time for his body to receive a second round from Arisa's pistol.

This bullet shattered his jawbone and ripped open his face before he collapsed to the pavement.

Bolan watched one gunner with a Chinese Type 79 SMG clutched in his grip sprint on a direct approach while another circled to flank the soldier on the left. The sedan provided enough cover, but it also hindered a clear line of sight. The Executioner would have preferred open territory, but the sedan was sandwiched between the two large vehicles. This provided protection while simultaneously covering the enemy's approach.

He took the guy ahead of him first, sighting down the slide of the Beretta and shooting a double tap. The twin 9 mm subsonic rounds took their target high. The first slug punched a hole in his sternum and the second cored his throat, lifting the aggressor off his feet and slamming him to the hard, unyielding concrete. He rolled over several times before his body came to a halt.

Bolan stepped away from the door and rushed in the dead man's direction. He scooped up the Type 79 and pulled the charging handle to insure a round was chambered, then continued forward and around the front of the minivan. He crouched and waited for the second enemy soldier to appear. He didn't have long to wait.

Arisa left her position and ran toward Bolan to join him behind the minivan. He signaled her with an emphatic shake of his head and gestured for her to find cover on her side. The fourth aggressor had seemingly disappeared into thin air, and the Executioner needed Arisa to watch his back. There had been nothing but moments of such explosive violence since he set foot in North Korea. It was definitely time to take the fight to the opposition and beat them at their own game.

The man came around the rear of the minivan just as Bolan had predicted, but he stopped short when he noticed the Executioner was no longer there. He swept the muzzle of his pistol back and forth as he stepped in closer for a look inside the sedan. Bolan counted four seconds, then burst from cover. He brought the muzzle of the Type 79 onto the target and depressed the trigger. The thunderstorm of 7.62 mm lead ripped the would-be assailant to shreds and shattered the driver's side window. Bolan emptied the Type 79, and then tossed it aside.

The sound of a scream erupted to his left, and Bolan turned in time to see a young Korean man withdraw the blade of a knife from Arisa's side. Her body collapsed to the ground, and her breath begin to come in short, labored gasps.

Bolan watched her lips form a silent word: Cho.

The Executioner reached for his Beretta, but Cho charged and slashed toward his chest with the knife. Bolan cleared the pistol from his shoulder holster but only had enough time to block the knife thrust with it. The blade contacted slick metal and bounced off. Bolan lost his grip on the Beretta as the sharp tip of Cho's knife ripped through the fabric of the heavy overcoat. The blade missed the tender skin beneath by mere inches.

Bolan realized his mistake a moment too late. Cho took complete advantage of his opening. He twisted sideways, drove an elbow into Bolan's stomach, then dropped to the ground and swept the Executioner's legs. The soldier landed hard on the pavement, and waves of pain traveled up his back. Despite the grueling blow, he managed to keep his head off the ground and avoid being knocked unconscious.

Cho immediately got to his knees and swung his knife in an arc. Bolan rolled away and regained his feet as the blade sang off the pavement. His eyes flickered momentarily toward Arisa's body, and he searched for any sign of life. Anger began to cloud his emotions, and Bolan repressed the urge to charge his enemy. Such an action was foolish under the circumstances. Cho was a highly trained specialist and experienced combatant. He would use whatever means were at his disposal to finish Bolan. He had probably stabbed Arisa simply to distract his opponent. The soldier wouldn't allow that distraction to kill him.

Cho stepped in and feinted several slashes toward different parts of the Executioner's body. The men circled each other in a game of dodge and parry as Cho taunted Bolan. The soldier ignored his enemy and concentrated on each attack. Cho was unwittingly giving Bolan the chance to size up his opponent—to identify the openings and the flaws in his movements.

The North Korean appeared much younger than Bolan. He had that, as well as speed and agility on his side. But there was one thing he didn't have, and that was the common sense that came from experience. As the Executioner studied his enemy, he realized that Cho was overconfident. There was a wild gleam in the man's dark eyes. He thought that he was simply taunting Bolan and that when it came time to kill, victory would be his for the taking. He was wrong.

Bolan stepped in and launched a jumping front kick toward his adversary's head. The man blocked it easily but didn't notice the haymaker that followed. Iron-hard knuckles connected on Cho's jaw and dislocated it. The blow sent the North Korean soldier reeling, and he landed hard on his knees.

Bolan rushed in as Cho shook his head to clear it. He attempted to snap his attacker's neck with a knife-hand strike to the spine, but Cho had enough command of his faculties to duck away from the blow and slash at Bolan with the knife. The blade ripped another furrow through the overcoat and a part of it nicked flesh this time.

The Executioner refused to relent and drove the heel of his boot into Cho's shoulder, aiming for the brachial pressure point. The blow connected and the knife fell from Cho's fingers, which were now temporarily useless because of deadened nerves in his biceps. The North Korean got to his feet and stepped backward, keeping one arm up to defend himself. Bolan drove his knee toward Cho's groin, and as the man blocked the knee he launched an uppercut. The maneuver caught Bolan off guard, but he managed to avoid most of the shock.

Cho had weakened and the soldier seized the moment. He snapped his elbow upward. Bones crunched as Cho's jaw went to mush under the abuse. The man's head snapped backward, and the soldier stomped his heel against the side of his opponent's knee. More bones and cartilage collapsed under the onslaught. He grabbed the back of Cho's neck and drove an elbow into the North Korean's sternum. Cho gasped for air and flew off his feet. He landed on his butt and sank backward.

Bolan took a step forward and noticed Cho's knife lying near his feet. He picked it up and looked at Cho in time to see the North Korean reaching inside his jacket. The man withdrew a Daewoo DP 51 pistol and aimed it at Bolan. The Executioner hefted the knife blade first and hurled it at him. The sleek, angular blade penetrated the target's chest just below the fourth rib and slid into the edge of the heart. Cho made one final attempt to pull the trigger, but the life began to leave his eyes even as he struggled to kill his enemy. He whispered something and then blood began to bubble from his mouth.

Bolan never heard Cho's dying words because he was already moving in the direction of Arisa's still form. He knelt beside her and put his cheek close to her nose, checking for breath while he felt for a pulse at her neck. Both signs were faint but present. The soldier expertly felt for another pulse at her wrist and found it was absent. Arisa's blood pressure was falling, and Bolan knew he needed to find the wound and plug the hole. Then he'd get her away from the area, because the gunfire was likely to bring police and airport security running very soon.

The lower parts of Arisa's shirt and jacket were slick with blood. Bolan tore open the shirt and quickly felt for the wound. He found the stab hole in the left flank area just outside the kidney. Fortunately, Cho had missed the mark, probably in his haste to confront the Executioner. Another inch and the wound would have been fatal, as was certainly the original intent.

Bolan shrugged from his overcoat and quickly tore a portion of material from the sleeve of his combat suit. He folded it several times to use as a compress for the wound and then tore some material from the other sleeve to tie a bandage. He then wrapped the woman in the overcoat, carried her to the sedan and slid her into the back seat.

He considered his next move as he stepped over the bullet-riddled body of one of Cho's thugs and got behind the wheel. As he started the engine, he looked down at the GPS transmitter and noted it was still flashing. It would probably be several hours before Grimaldi arrived, and Arisa didn't have that kind of time.

He knew he would have to find a hospital. He put the car in gear and quickly drove from the parking lot. The driver's-side window was shattered, and the chill winds bit at his skin as a breeze whipped into the sedan's interior. Bolan flipped on the heater and drove toward the highway, his thoughts completely focused on finding help for Arisa. He'd trained his mind to tune out physical discomforts like pain and cold and chose to concentrate on the mission.

He was behind schedule now and he didn't like it. Moreover, the enemy was still out there and gunning for him. Hakajima would certainly send someone to finish the job his other men hadn't, and there was still a potential threat from whomever Cho had worked for. Neither thought settled well with the Executioner, but he couldn't bother with them now. He needed to find medical help before Arisa bled to death.

Bolan drove down the main road that led from the airport until he saw a cross street that rang familiar. It only took the Executioner a moment to recall that Maruptang So was the road that Arkwright had lived on. He fell back on his keen sense of direction and within a few minutes he'd found the Pyong Ni South Highway. Bolan proceeded northbound and headed for the one place he knew might help Arisa without asking a plethora of questions he didn't want to answer.

It took almost forty minutes before Bolan finally located the NSA safehouse. He parked the car in the deserted lot behind a run-down two-story brick building with bars on the windows.

The soldier climbed from the sedan and lifted the woman from the back seat. As he walked toward the single glass door leading to the building's interior, she began to moan and thrash about. Bolan had to struggle to keep her under control. He could see beads of sweat had formed on her forehead, and she was becoming delirious. She had lost a tremendous amount of blood, and it appeared he'd arrived just in time.

Bolan stormed through the door and was immediately intercepted by a big, beefy man wearing military camouflage fatigues and a side arm. The guy had a muscular build but stood nearly half a head shorter than the Executioner. The silence weighed heavily in the room, and the soldier realized it wasn't time for niceties or introductions.

"She's hurt," Bolan said calmly, nodding at Arisa's limp form. "She needs help."

"Who are you?" the uniformed guard asked.

"I'll get to that later. Right now, get a doctor over here."

A tall, unkempt man in a blue suit appeared from another room and walked over to where the men stood. He eyed Bolan with a practiced gaze, then peered over the blanket to see the strained features of Arisa's face.

"All we have is a medic here," the man said.

"That'll work for now," the Executioner shot back. "He can get her stabilized."

The man nodded with uncertainty but instructed the guard to go find the medic. Once he'd departed, the man gestured for Bolan to follow him and led the way to a back room with several single bunks. The lighting inside the bedroom was poor, and scratchy olive-drab blankets covered the bunks. Nonetheless, it was clean and warm. Bolan deposited Arisa on the nearest bed and nodded to the man.

A young blond kid of about twenty-seven entered the room moments later and immediately took charge of his new patient. He did a quick assessment, shining a light in her eyes and inspecting the wound that Bolan pointed out.

"Nice patch job," the medic said, "if not a bit crude."

"I didn't have much to work with."

"It's okay," he said. "We'll have her up and dancing in no time."

"She'll live?"

He nodded.

The Executioner let out a sigh of relief.

With Arisa in good hands now, Bolan felt he could relax. He turned to leave the room and noticed the man with the suit watching him. The uniformed guard had returned, as well, and his hand rested on the butt of the .45-caliber pistol. Bolan realized that he would probably have to explain a few things even if he wished to avoid it. The looks on their faces said they weren't about to let him just walk out of there. Bolan waved them outside and closed the door to the bunk room before speaking.

"I guess you're wondering what's going on," he began.

"It had crossed our minds," the man in the suit replied.

Bolan offered his hand. "My name's Mike Belasko."

"Pleasure. I'm Dennis Cliff, NSA. Who do you work for?"

"I can't say and it's not really important," Bolan said easily. He jabbed his thumb in the direction of the bedroom. "But the woman in there is an agent for the Japanese government, which means she's on our side. I trust she'll get the care she deserves."

"We'll see to that." Cliff looked Bolan up and down. "Shit, man, it looks like you've been through a war."

"You're not too far off. I can't be specific here, but I can tell you that I'm scheduled to catch a private flight in the next few hours. Do you have any way to get me past airport security?"

Cliff smiled. "Dressed like that?"

Bolan returned the smile with a cagey grin of his own. "Yeah, I could use a change of clothes, too."

Cliff studied Bolan for a moment, and the Executioner remained silent. How he acted in the next few moments would decide the outcome. If Cliff chose to accept what Bolan had told him, then he would solicit whatever cooperation he needed and be on his way to Hungnam before dawn. Otherwise, Cliff could have him taken into custody and questioned, and Bolan had to admit he wouldn't blame the guy.

"Okay," Cliff finally replied. "We'll play it your way for now. But I trust you'll get someone to explain something to me before morning arrives. Deal?"

Bolan nodded. "You got it."

JACK GRIMALDI CHECKED his watch as he circled Pyongyang International Airport for the seventh time. The air traffic controllers below were starting to irk the ace pilot, and he was damn tempted to just put his plane down right in the middle of their field. It was almost 0430 hours, and he still hadn't obtained a landing clearance.

Grimaldi surmised that they might have detected the strain in his voice and were thoroughly checking his clearances. He smiled as he thought of the strings Brognola had pulled to even get him into North Korean airspace in the RC-35 Learjet. The cover story was that Grimaldi was actually returning an important member of the ruling party from overseas business. It was unlikely that they would call someone important to verify the information at that hour, so they were probably discussing it among themselves.

The sound of a heavily accented voice in his headset signaled they'd reached some decision. Grimaldi got his landing clearance and he immediately began his descent.

According to the information Brognola had forwarded for the Executioner, the situation was getting worse by the minute. He recalled his telephone conversation with the big Fed while Grimaldi cooled his heels in Guam and waited for the tsunami-like conditions to pass between the islands and Korean peninsula. The mission had been hot since Bolan's arrival, and it was about to get hotter. Brognola instructed the pilot to fly the warrior straight to Hungnam and render whatever assistance he could.

It wouldn't be much. Grimaldi probably knew the Executioner better than anyone, and it was an unspoken rule that Bolan worked alone. At least most of the time. Grimaldi couldn't count the number of support missions he'd flown or hot spots he'd pulled the guy out of since the beginning of their alliance. Not that it mattered all that much. Mack Bolan was welcome to call on Grimaldi anytime for any reason and he'd be there for the guy, no questions asked.

Once he was on the ground, Grimaldi taxied the reconnaissance plane to a distant corner of the airfield, shut down the engines and began his vigil. They had barely finished winding down when three shadowy forms made their way from the terminal toward his position. Grimaldi reached inside his jacket, withdrew the Glock 21 he carried, checked the load, then chambered a round.

In a way, Brognola had spooked him a little with all his talk about how they were misled in attempting to rescue Yang. It had apparently been one disaster piled on another. Well, Grimaldi wasn't about to get his ass shot off in some foreign land because of bad information. His job was to wait for Bolan and take him to Hungnam, and he'd do his duty come hell or high water.

As the figures neared the plane, the pilot noticed the outline of one of them seemed awfully familiar. He waited another moment to confirm his hopes, then leaped from the seat and immediately went to the entry hatch. Grimaldi dropped the door and looked into the graveyard eyes of none other than the Executioner.

"How's it shaking, Sarge?"

"Just fine, buddy," Bolan replied.

Grimaldi studied Bolan's two escorts. "I don't mind saying this is one of those times where I'm really glad to see you."

"Likewise." Bolan noticed Grimaldi's nervousness and waved it away. "They're on our side, Jack."

"Gotcha." Grimaldi felt better, and some of the tension began to ease from where it had lodged behind his eyes. "Are you ready to split?"

"Yeah." The Executioner turned to his escorts and shook hands with each of them, then hopped aboard the Learjet.

Grimaldi sealed them into the plane and grasped his old friend's shoulder. It was damn good to see Bolan alive, even if he did appear exhausted. The guy obviously hadn't had any sleep for a while, and he looked dead on his feet.

Not that the outward appearances mattered—especially when it came to Bolan. He had an uncanny ability to endure hardships that would have defeated lesser men.

"You look like you could use a few winks," Grimaldi said.

Bolan nodded tiredly. "Once we're airborne. But let's get out of here before the North Koreans change their mind."

"Consider us history," Grimaldi replied, and he headed for the cockpit.

Before the plane had leveled off, the Stony Man pilot looked back and saw the Executioner was out like a light. He smiled as he pointed the plane in the direction of Hungnam. Perhaps he would take a slight detour and let the guy get a few extra winks.

"WHAT DO YOU MEAN 'escaped'?" Sumio Hakajima demanded quietly.

Pak In-sung clutched the receiver and tried to ignore the scolding tone in the Japanese man's voice. His eyes burned and itched, and he felt dizzy despite the fact he was seated in a comfortable chair at his private office. A reliable informant had awakened the party leader with an urgent call. He related his eyewitness account of a firefight at the airport, the death of Cho Shinmun and the subsequent illegal departure of an unidentified aircraft with forged clearances. Pak immediately contacted Hakajima, who listened impatiently to the information.

"My intelligence sources have concluded," Pak replied, "that the man who killed my people, and has now fled like a coward, was probably the same one who attempted the rescue of Yang."

"I can assure you this man is anything but a coward," Hakajima said. "He is obviously both skilled and dangerous. You assured me the situation was under control."

"That may be, but this doesn't change our plans."

"I would not agree. This changes everything where I am concerned. I have invested a considerable amount of money in your schemes. Where has it brought us? Your men are dead and your government could trace this back to you."

"Highly unlikely."

"Is it?" Hakajima asked. "If someone should link these events to you, then that means they will eventually discover my involvement."

"The Americans are fools, as are their allies."

"Do not be so naive. This man is a scourge to you and your plans. Despite your elaborate schemes to entrap him, he has managed to escape. You said it yourself."

"He has fled the country," Pak said, trying to control the anger in his voice. "It is not up to you to reprimand my methods. I have held up my end of the bargain, and I expect you to do the same."

"My friend," Hakajima replied, his voice taking on a congenial tone, "let us not quarrel among ourselves. Our common enemy would like nothing more. I think I have a solution to the problem, but we must work together if we are to accomplish our goals."

Pak couldn't believe the sudden change in Hakajima. The man had treated him like a subordinate from the onset of their alliance, and now he had the gall to preach cooperation and partnership. Pak was beginning to realize how manipulative the Japanese tycoon could really be. This troubled him, but he was willing to listen. Hakajima had spoken the truth. With Cho Shinmun and his men gone forever, Pak had no recourse. He would have to facilitate good relations with Hakajima even though the man was a fool and a liar.

"You wish to profit financially," Hakajima continued, "and I wish to profit for more idealistic reasons. Agreed?"

"Continue."

"Therefore, we should each concentrate on our respective issues. You will be attending the conference in Hungnam?"

"I leave in a few hours."

"Excellent. In your absence, I will oversee the project on this end. I will await your signal that things are secure. At that time, I shall continue with the operation as planned and then rejoin you here in Pyongyang. We will toast to our victory and watch as these capitalist dogs grovel on their knees and beg the world's forgiveness."

"It is an excellent suggestion," Pak concluded, "but I am concerned that you might become overwhelmed. It was not in the plan for you to supervise this end of the operation."

"Your concerns are duly noted and appreciated, but I insist you allow me to do this. It would be an honor."

Pak sighed in resignation. There was nothing he could do. He knew that what Hakajima suggested made perfect sense. His attendance at the conference was requested at the highest levels. The premier was counting on his presence, and he had to make appearances if he wanted to salvage the operation. The idea of leaving DPRK special forces in the hands of this Japanese leech didn't sit well with the party leader—not in the least. However, it did leave him the option of absolving himself from guilt should things not work out.

"Very well, I will concede this point and leave it to your discretion."

"Excellent."

"I have only one question."

"And that would be?"

"What about this American operative? How do you propose to deal with him if he does interfere?"

"Swiftly."

CHAPTER ELEVEN

The echo of Jack Grimaldi's voice roused the Executioner from his slumber. "Rise and shine, Sarge."

Bolan opened his eyes and looked around the interior of the plane. He checked his watch and realized he had been asleep for nearly two hours. He stretched his sore muscles, passed a hand across his eyes, then got to his feet. He stood for a moment, then squeezed his large frame into the cockpit next to the Stony Man pilot.

"We're outside of Hungnam," Grimaldi stated. "There's no airport down there, at least not one that's going to allow me to land."

"What's the plan?"

"I located a dry field that's only a couple of klicks outside the city. See it?"

Bolan nodded in agreement. "You should be able to find some cover down there. We don't want to alarm any of the locals if possible."

"Roger that. If I don't miss my guess, the harvest is finished. I can see a farmhouse with some adjoining structures, but I already did a flyby. It looks quiet." He pointed to one open field, then gestured in the direction of a shallow hill that separated it from a second field. "I can approach from the east, and that should lessen the chance of someone seeing us. I just hope the ground's hard enough to support the landing. Otherwise, things might get a little rough."

Bolan shrugged with skepticism but fastened his seat belt anyway. "Take us down, ace."

Grimaldi tipped the Learjet's nose and put the plane in a steep bank. He leveled off and then began his descent. Bolan watched with interest as Grimaldi calmly handled the controls. Pockets of warm air buffeted the plane as it descended, but the pilot seemed unaffected by the wind shear. The ground rushed toward them, and the Executioner could feel his stomach churn.

"I could use something to eat," Bolan said.

"There are some MREs stored in back. Got them from the military guys in Guam."

"That wasn't exactly what I had in mind."

"Hey, beggars can't be choosers."

"Says you."

They dropped the playful banter, and Grimaldi focused on the task of setting down the plane intact. The landing was rough but not much more than if he'd had a paved runway. Bolan wasn't the least bit afraid of air travel anyway. As far as he was concerned, any landing where he got down in one piece was picture-perfect. He was hardly about to complain and counted himself fortunate that it was Grimaldi behind the controls and not some reckless hotshot.

The Learjet rolled to a stop under a canopy of trees, and Bolan disengaged himself from the copilot's seat as Grimaldi shut off the engines. It didn't take long for the soldier to locate the meal packages—turkey bits in gravy was the entrée with a side of crackers and cheese. A dehydrated fruit wafer served as dessert, and there were also packets of salt, pepper, instant coffee, creamer and sugar. Bolan ripped open the entrée and used a combination spoon and fork to dish out the contents. He bit hungrily into the food, sampling a morsel before he was satisfied with the military field rations. He had half of it gone when Grimaldi appeared next to him wearing a grin that ran ear to ear.

"What's so funny?"

"You look like you haven't eaten for a week."

Bolan shook his head and grinned. "I guess I was pretty hungry. Want something?"

Grimaldi looked past him at the wooden crate that held the other MRE packages. "Naw. That might be *your* last meal, but I certainly don't want it to be mine."

"Suit yourself."

Grimaldi dropped into a low chair and studied Bolan. "So, what's the plan?"

"I'm not sure. Did you get the information from Hal?"

"Yeah, it's right here."

Grimaldi reached into a compartment built into the cabin of the plane and withdrew a gray metal case. He flipped open the lid and reached inside to retrieve its contents. He handed a stack of papers, photographs and dossier sheets to the Executioner.

Bolan set his food aside and took the information. He riffled through the pages and shook his head. From his cursory inspection, he realized that Stony Man had been as thorough as always. He would have to take some time to separate the chaff from the wheat in order to secure the intelligence he needed.

The Executioner knew the job ahead wasn't going to be easy. Thus far, the events occurring inside the DPRK were a mystery to him. He'd half expected the "plight" of Yang Tae-jung was a ruse to lure the President to take action. But to what end? The ruling party stood little to gain by exposing American subterfuge inside North Korea. While it might have solicited sympathy from other countries, it was hardly the kind of event to spark an international incident. The CIA conducted similar operations in almost every nation on Earth, as did other intelligence organizations. Everyone within the powers that be knew this, and it seemed they simply chose to ignore it.

Everything that Arisa had told him made perfect sense. What Bolan couldn't figure were the reasons behind such an elaborate plot because the ruling party wasn't the only one with a stake in the outcome. Sumio Hakajima was in bed with them, and he'd seek returns on the investment tenfold. That meant fueling good relations between North Korea and Japan, something that had not existed to date.

Conversely, Japan usually threw itself in support of U.S. initiatives and rightfully so—America was Japan's meal ticket. It wouldn't have been savvy business for Hakajima to alienate himself from the good graces of the President, since he was hoping to sell his missile-defense system to the country. The only reasonable explanation was that the Japanese businessman thought he could play two ends against the middle and somehow keep himself out of the picture.

"Did you have a chance to look this over?" Bolan asked.

Grimaldi shrugged. "A little bit, yeah. I got a briefing from Hal, but I don't pretend that it makes sense to me."

"Don't feel bad, Jack. It doesn't make a lot of sense to me, either."

Bolan set the papers down and finished his meal as he perused the top sheet. It was a list of dignitaries who would attend the negotiations. He looked at his watch and realized that he only had a few hours to put himself in position at the conference. His presence there posed a danger to him, since one or more of the representatives from the ruling party knew what he looked like. They had tried to kill him several times already, and it was more than likely they would try again.

"Let me run this by you and get your take on it," Bolan

said. "The North Koreans have protested this training exercise every year, but they've never taken serious action to stop it. Why?"

"They probably don't want to start another war."

"Or maybe it's because they don't want the U.S. and its allies to pull financial support for the Kumho reactors."

"I could buy that."

"Arisa told me that this Hakajima is working with someone high up inside the ruling party. So let's say this party member stages the attack on the Haeju navy yard, knowing that we're going to send someone to investigate. And just to sweeten the pot, they manufacture this deal with Yang and the new ballistic missile."

"So we send someone in and they try to pin it all on us as hostile intent," Grimaldi concluded.

"Exactly. Only it doesn't go quite the way they wanted it to. Now they have to come up with something more spectacular. I figured this conference as the most probable place to do that."

"Seems logical enough."

"But does it?" the soldier countered. "These negotiations only serve to benefit North Korea. Two of the main issues here are financial and political support for their poverty and reunification programs. Never mind the Kumho project."

"I see what you're getting at. Why would they blow it?"

"It's possible they want another chance to make the President look bad. If they can show hostility on the part of America and South Korea, they can justify continued improvement of their nuclear capabilities. If Hakajima *is* footing the bill, then the money wouldn't matter to them anymore."

"Okay. But who would throw in support if we pull out of the negotiations?"

"Russia and China, to name a couple." Bolan furrowed his eyebrows. "Plus the Japanese, if Hakajima can convince them to turn support, as well."

"So you think he's lending all this money to sway his government?"

Bolan shook his head. "He wouldn't put himself in the public spotlight. I think he might be hoping North Korea, or at least someone in power here, will buy into his game and take rash action."

"And you think the peace conference is the target?"

"It's the only thing that makes sense. Look, they create an incident while the world watches, then point the finger of blame at America and South Korea. Now support for their cause would just fall into place."

"I don't know," Grimaldi replied skeptically. "It sounds like a gamble."

"But if it works, the payoff will be worth it for them."

"How do you think they'll do it?"

"That's the part I haven't figured out yet," Bolan admitted. "Maybe they'll use an outside force to take hostages. Hal was going to try to get an agenda, but I don't see it here."

"They're keeping that part under tight wraps," Grimaldi said with a nod. "He didn't have time to get the clearance he needed."

"Guess I'll figure it out once I get inside."

"That's not going to be easy."

"Tell me about it," the soldier agreed. "Once I get into Hungnam, I'll need a change of clothes and a way inside the conference."

"Oh, that reminds me," Grimaldi interjected. "Hal said to tell you that someone senior in the U.S. State Department would be attending."

Bolan nodded. "Yeah, I saw Ken Durham listed here."

"Well, he's apparently been told you're going to be

there under the cover of special security. Barbara made arrangements for you to hook up with Durham at his hotel.'' Grimaldi nodded at the papers he'd given the Executioner. "Details and directions are somewhere inside with that stuff. Durham's staff will provide you with all the necessary credentials. You'll have a bird's-eye view, Sarge.''

"Good. Did you bring weapons?''

"Everything I could carry. There's a suitcase in the back with plenty of hardware. Now all you have to do is find this North Korean party member.''

The Executioner's expression was grim. "I'm sure he'll come to me.''

SECURITY WAS TIGHT at the Mudo Kwan Hotel. According to Bolan's information, representatives from several countries were staying in rooms on different levels at the luxurious high-rise. Stony Man's intelligence indicated Durham and his entourage were situated in the penthouse suites. It would be nearly impossible for the Executioner to reach the State Department man without attracting attention.

The soldier sat in a small café across the street from the hotel and spent the better part of the morning watching the front entrance. The entire area was alive with the bustle of dignitaries and their support staff arriving in limousines marked with the flags of their respective countries. The street was a virtual logjam of taxis, buses and sedans. Officials dressed in everything from tuxedos and travel clothes to native dress entered the hotel under heavy escort. Bolan noted the uniformed security forces that guarded the front doors, their side arms in plain view. Through the several sets of glass doors, he could see a checkpoint established in the lobby. The DPRK wasn't taking any chances with their honored guests.

Bolan tried not to look out of place in the café. Only a few patrons spared him more than a cursory glance. The ill-fitting suit donated to him by the NSA crew in Pyongyang and the imitation-leather suitcase at his feet served well to maintain his appearance as just another American tourist. Thus far, nobody had approached him or asked questions.

The Executioner's Beretta 93-R was holstered beneath his jacket. The suitcase contained the remainder of his arsenal, including an M-1911 Government Model pistol and Heckler & Koch MP-5, both of which Grimaldi managed to procure from the military base on Guam. There were also two changes of urban camouflage fatigues and a new pair of boots to serve as replacements for his tattered blacksuit.

None of it would do him any good unless he found a way to bypass the North Korean security measures. A direct approach was out of the question—he'd never get past the scrutiny of the lobby guards. He'd considered waiting until nightfall and then making access via the roof but he couldn't risk waiting. With every moment that passed, he increased his chances of discovery.

Reaching a decision, Bolan rose from his table and left the café. He walked down the street to another hotel that was cheap and run-down and rented a room under his alias. The place was filthy with substandard accommodations, but he ignored his dismal surroundings. There was a phone, and that was the important element. Bolan pulled the intelligence brief from his suitcase and dialed the number to the Mudo Kwan Hotel.

"Hello?" a woman's voice answered in Korean.

"Ken Durham's suite, please," Bolan requested in English.

"One moment."

The line clicked a couple of times, then a fast ringing

buzzed in Bolan's ear. A man with a deep voice cut in
halfway through the second ring. "Hello?"

"Who am I speaking with?"

"This is Frank Schifflit, senior aide to Undersecretary
Durham."

"I need to speak with him immediately. Tell him it's
Mike Belasko."

Schifflit asked Bolan to hold, and the Executioner heard
him cup the phone with his hand. There was a brief conversation before another man's voice came on the line.

"Yes, Mr. Belasko, this is Ken Durham."

"Mr. Durham," Bolan greeted him respectfully, "I
don't have a lot of time, so listen carefully."

"Go ahead."

"There's no way I can make it past the security at your
hotel. I'm staying in a place down the street. I need the
material you promised to provide. Can you make it happen
quickly?"

"Absolutely," Durham replied cordially. "Give me the
address, and I'll send over my head of security right
away."

Bolan relayed the information, told Durham he'd meet
the security chief in the lobby of the hotel, then broke the
connection. The Executioner quickly stored his suitcase
under the bed and took a shower. He donned a nice suit
obtained from a men's shop earlier that morning and proceeded to the lobby. As he passed the front desk, he noticed the clerk nervously scrutinize him. It was a clear
signal for Bolan that something was amiss. The hairs stood
up on his neck, and a sudden sense of impending danger
washed over him.

The soldier turned in time to see four Korean men push
through the front door and enter the open vestibule. Their
eyes probed the dark interior of the lobby and all settled
on the Executioner. The leader of the group started to reach

inside his coat, and Bolan knew they weren't the escort promised by Durham. They had *enemy* written all over them.

The flash of motion almost distracted Bolan as he dropped to one knee, yanked the Beretta from shoulder leather and thumbed the safety. The movement belonged to an American the soldier didn't recognize as he swung the 93-R's muzzle in the direction of the new arrivals. The man tackled the Korean team leader before he could clear his pistol and began to hammer him in the face with his fists.

Bolan adjusted his aim and took the next target in line. He squeezed the trigger, and three rounds smashed through the Korean's midsection. The impact punched the Korean backward, forcing him through the decorative glass enclosure of the vestibule.

The two who remained on their feet dived away from each other, but they couldn't get far in the enclosed space. One turned his attention to help his comrade, and the other focused on Bolan. The Executioner saw the man try to retrieve a machine pistol from under his coat, but the soldier was already in position to repel the clumsy attempt. The Beretta barked again in Bolan's fist. The trio of Parabellum rounds drilled through the target's neck and head. Blood showered the Korean's shirt as he flopped onto his back and twitched.

The other two Koreans now had their hands full trying to contain the mysterious man assisting the Executioner. They were cloistered together in a ball of flailing kicks and punches.

Bolan surged forward and grabbed the Korean who straddled the other American. He curled his forearm around the man's neck, yanked backward and pulled his opponent clear of the fray. The Korean dropped to his knees and attempted to throw Bolan over him. The soldier brought his foot off the ground and drove a knee into his enemy's spine as he wrapped his fingers around the guy's neck. A quick jerk snapped the spinal column at the small of the Korean's back as the Executioner's viselike grip crushed his voice box. His body stiffened and blood gurgled from his mouth before he collapsed facefirst to the dirty floor.

The mysterious benefactor got unsteadily to his feet. His chest heaved with his exertion as he turned to Bolan and smiled. The smile quickly faded when his eyes flicked past the soldier's shoulder. The Executioner whirled to see the desk clerk standing behind the counter with a snub-nosed revolver in his grip. A momentary lapse in the action occurred before a resounding click echoed in the lobby. Everyone turned to see a dark-haired man in a three-piece suit pointing a stainless-steel S&W .645 at the clerk's head.

"Put it down," the man growled, "or I'll blow your brains out."

The clerk's head remained motionless as his eyes roved between the new arrival and Bolan. The lobby was bathed in a terse silence, and the soldier could see the clerk weighing his options. After several moments, the clerk placed his revolver on the counter and raised his hands as he backed away from it.

Bolan nodded to the man in the suit. "You're with Durham?"

"Yes, sir," the man replied as he stepped forward and secured the clerk's weapon. "Ted Strack. You're Belasko, I presume?"

"Yeah."

Strack nodded toward the man who stood quietly behind the Executioner. "And who's this guy?"

Bolan turned to look at the man. "That's a good question."

He was young, maybe midtwenties, with closely cropped hair and green eyes. Chest muscles bulged visibly under the crisp white polo shirt he wore beneath a black leather jacket. He was nearly as tall as Bolan was, and his sharp features contrasted with his dark complexion. He could have passed as Italian or Greek, but there was no mistaking the pinched East Coast accent when he spoke.

He held out his hand. "The name's Steve Rueben."

Bolan shook his hand and quietly replied, "Mike Belasko."

"Pleasure. I noticed you were by yourself. I kind of figured you for an American. Thought maybe you were on vacation."

"Business," Bolan said with a shake of his head.

Rueben looked at the corpses behind him and flashed a cocksure grin. "Tough business."

Bolan flashed a ghost of a smile before directing his attention to Strack and the desk clerk. The security chief had escorted the frail Korean around the counter and now set him in front of Bolan with the muzzle of his weapon trained a few inches from the man's neck.

"If you want to mop the floor with this guy," Strack offered, "I can wait outside."

"That won't be necessary." Bolan fixed the clerk with a cold stare and added, "Will it?"

"N-no," the clerk replied. His voice was heavily accented, and it was difficult to understand him. "I no want trouble with you."

"You should have thought of that before," Bolan growled. He grabbed the Korean by his shirt lapels and pulled him to within inches of his face. The man had to stand on his toes to keep his balance. "The phones. Were they tapped?"

"I—no...they—" the clerk stammered.

"You're stuttering," Strack interjected as he holstered his weapon.

"You've got three seconds to answer me," Bolan continued, gesturing toward Strack, "or I turn him loose on you."

"They are workers for party member."

"Which one?"

"I not know, I not know."

"How did they know I was here? Did you call them?"

"Y-yes. They came here early and described you. They say to call if I see you."

Bolan gripped his shirt tighter. "Where's the number?"

The clerk kept his left hand up and reached into his pocket with his right. He withdrew a slip of paper, and Bolan snatched it from him.

"Beat it!" Strack yelled, stepping toward the clerk as Bolan released him.

The Korean seemed to disappear from the lobby, almost tripping over his own feet in his haste to leave.

Bolan unfolded the piece of paper and checked the number, then handed it to Strack. "Can you trace this?"

"We can try," Strack said with a shrug.

"Do your best." The Executioner turned to Rueben. "So what's your story? I can't buy you're here as mere coincidence."

"It's not," Rueben replied, "but I don't think you'd believe me if I told you."

"Try me."

"I'm looking for my father. He's a political correspondent, and he came to Hungnam three days ago to cover the conference."

It was Strack who looked puzzled. "The conference was supposed to be a secret then. How did *he* know about it?"

"I told you. He's a reporter," Rueben replied in a sarcastic tone. "Do you really think the press wouldn't find out about this?"

"So where's your father?" Bolan asked.

"I don't know." Something distant and sad flashed in the young man's eyes. "He disappeared the day after he got here. I called all over this damn place. Nobody has seen or heard from him. He was supposed to get in touch with me. He never did."

Bolan's eyes narrowed and focused on the unmistakable chain around Rueben's neck. It was barely visible under his collar. A further inspection revealed two long, oblong rectangles beneath the polo shirt. The warrior redirected his gaze to Rueben, and he studied the man with grim curiosity.

"You're in the military, aren't you?"

"Yes, sir," Rueben said.

"AWOL?"

Rueben remained silent for several moments before nodding.

"This isn't good," Strack groaned. "You could get in some serious shit for this."

"I know," Rueben countered, "but this takes precedence here. My dad's the only family I got left. I won't abandon him when I think he's in trouble."

The Executioner's heart immediately went out to Rueben. The young man standing before him was like a reflection. He could recall that time when another young soldier came home to bury *his* family and realized there was a war on the home front that needed fighting. Ever since that first night in a little town in Massachusetts, Bolan had changed the course of his destiny forever. Johnny was his only remaining family, and he knew how Rueben felt.

"Hey, Belasko," Strack cut in, "we'd better take this

up somewhere else. The Korean cops will be here soon, and we don't want to be here when they show.''

Bolan nodded, then focused his attention on Rueben. "You come with us. Maybe we can help you find your dad.''

With that, the three Americans made a hasty exit from the hotel.

CHAPTER TWELVE

Pyongyang

Kawashita Arisa woke to discover IV tubes running into her arms and an oxygen cannula in her nose.

The dingy white walls of the hospital room slowly came into focus. Her memory of the recent past was little more than a blur of events. As she willed herself to calm the turmoil of her inner spirit, the room stopped spinning and she slowed her breathing. Arisa meditated to the beeping sound of the electronic heart monitor positioned near the bed and tried to recall the traumatic fragments of memory lodged in her mind.

The last thing she remembered clearly was Belasko gunning down one of Cho Shinmun's men. Then she'd heard the sound of someone creeping behind her and felt the agonizing pain in her back. Someone stabbed her and roughly shoved her to the ground. There were other moments after that, but she couldn't seem to define them clearly. The sounds of cold, rushing winds and Belasko's voice, pain and fever, someone carrying her in strong arms—protecting her. Then nothing until she awakened in the hospital bed.

Arisa strained her neck to inspect her surroundings. A shoddy wooden door was set in a wall across the room. It seemed like miles from where she lay. She felt stiff and immobile—they had probably drugged her with pain medication. Her stomach churned as she licked her parched lips. She tried to lift her head but to no avail. Every time she exerted herself, the room would start to spin again. She let her head rest against the pillow.

It could have been minutes or maybe hours before Arisa awoke to the sound of someone padding into the room. She opened her eyes slowly and saw a short, petite woman wearing a gray uniform and hair net. The woman stood next to Arisa's bed and smiled. Arisa reciprocated the gesture with a halfhearted smile of her own. The edges of her vision seemed hazy, and Arisa wondered if she was dreaming.

The nurse looked Oriental and her melodic voice spoke in flawless Japanese. "You are awake. This is good."

"How long have I been unconscious?" Arisa asked tiredly.

"About fourteen hours."

"That is not good!"

"Calm yourself, dear. You needed the rest."

"Where am I?"

"You are safe. That is the important thing."

"What happened?"

"You were brought to us by American agents. They said that you were attacked and your purse was stolen."

Americans? Arisa tried to make sense of what the nurse was telling her. Perhaps Belasko had taken her to some of his own people. She'd obviously been admitted as the victim of a crime. The Korean police would want to question her presence in North Korea. She might have already given away her true purpose and identity to them under duress or the influence of the pain drugs.

Arisa knew she must remain clear and concise if she

was to ensure the success of the cover story. In a way, she was angry with Belasko for putting her in such a position. He would need her help if he'd made it safely out of Pyongyang and gone to Hungnam. There was no way he could handle the situation without her assistance. Hakajima's men would still be looking for him, as well as the North Koreans. She had to find a way out of her predicament.

"You must rest," the nurse said. "The doctor will be here in a little bit to assess your healing. Until then, someone has patiently been waiting to see you."

She had a visitor? It had to be Belasko! So he hadn't abandoned her after all. She nodded enthusiastically and told the nurse to admit him. Arisa hoped she looked half-presentable. Not that it mattered—Belasko was the kind to look on the inside. In fact, when he looked at Arisa she couldn't help but wonder what he saw. There was something soft and gentle beneath the man's hardened shell. It was as if he possessed something in his spirit that only Arisa could touch.

The nurse left the room, and the visitor entered less than a minute later. Arisa couldn't contain her horror at the sight of Sumio Hakajima. The King of Tokyo walked to her bed boldly. He probed her with his dark eyes, and his hand nervously smoothed back her hair. Arisa cringed and looked desperately around her for something to stop him. She needed her weapon, but she could hardly focus through the mental fog that gripped her mind. It was overshadowed only by her sudden terror.

"You are not happy to see me," Hakajima purred. "I am disappointed. I have waited here for some time."

Arisa looked for a call button but she didn't see one. She turned her attention to Hakajima and narrowed her eyes in an attempt to intimidate him. He appeared unaffected by her cold, deadly stare.

"How did you get in here?" she demanded, her own words echoing in her ears.

"Now, why would you ask that?" Hakajima replied in a taunting tone. "Do you honestly think they would stop me?"

"They will stop you, Hakajima-*san*. And if they don't, then I will."

Hakajima looked her up and down and chuckled mockingly. "You are in a position unsuitable for threats, young flower."

"Get out," Arisa said hoarsely, feeling the blood rush to her face. "Get out or I will kill you."

"Hardly," he snorted, waving her rants away with a flick of his hand. "Oh, do not worry. You are correct about one thing in that you are in no danger here. There are a score of foreign diplomats just outside the room." He gestured toward the door. "Perhaps you should call for them. Tell them who I am and all of the terrible things I have done. I'm sure they will listen to you in your half-crazed state."

Arisa wanted to scream, but she couldn't bring herself to do it. She could barely hear Hakajima's voice when he spoke and she had little sense of time or distance. Hakajima was well respected by officials within the American government. While Belasko's friends like Barbara Price might have believed her, she knew that the locals didn't know Hakajima. His connections were influential, his money a powerful tool and he had one of the most feared team of enforcers at his disposal. Arisa didn't want to accept the fact that everything he was telling her was true.

The locals would simply label her a lunatic. They would say she was in shock after such a humiliating and traumatic experience. They would lull her into a false sense of security and then tie her down. And then the monster who now stood before her would just arrange for her disappearance and subsequent elimination.

"Yes, dear child," he continued, leaning so close that Arisa could smell the stale scent of opium clinging to his skin and tailored suit, "scream and cry. They will rush to your aid and take me away from here."

Arisa kept silent.

Hakajima stood erect and smiled. "You see? You are now powerless over me, just as you have always been. I will no longer bother with you. What the Americans have done, especially your loathsome friend who has interfered with us from the beginning, is far worse than anything I could invent."

"He is a greater man than you will ever be, Hakajima-*san*," she replied with a frigid whisper. "He will topple your beloved empire."

"Where has he gone to?" Hakajima asked loftily, turning to inspect a vase of fresh-cut flowers. He looked at her. "To Hungnam perhaps? Is he looking for Pak Insung?"

Arisa nearly displayed her surprise at the terrible blunder Hakajima had made. In his own arrogance, he revealed the name of his Korean cohort without realizing it. He'd obviously assumed they knew and that Belasko was headed to Hungnam to stop the man. Arisa knew that she had to get the information to the American. She would have to deliver it personally—she couldn't trust the local agents to do it and she had no idea how to contact Barbara Price.

"It will do him no good," Hakajima said. "Even if he finds Pak, he will not be able to prevent us from finishing what we have started."

"You are a fool," Arisa replied.

"This is your opinion and you are entitled to it. However, before the sun sets tomorrow, we will have taken the final step to restore the glory of our country and restore honor to our name. The greatest event in history is about to unfold, and there is nothing that you or your American conspirators can do to stop it."

Arisa watched helplessly as Hakajima bowed gracefully to her, then turned on his heel and left the room. Tears welled up in her eyes, but she choked back her sobs. It was time to be strong and she had to take command of her senses and think clearly.

She had to find Mike Belasko before it was too late.

GAIESH KOTO PATIENTLY waited for his master to return.

Hakajima's luxury sedan sat running with a driver and one of Koto's men in the front seat but the chief enforcer preferred to stand his vigil in the cool noontime air. The breeze felt good against his skin, and the sun warmed his head and shoulders as it blazed away in the clear skies. Nevertheless, Koto missed his own country. Korean architecture was so plain and lifeless—as lifeless as its people.

Koto had never agreed with Hakajima-*san*'s alliance with the filthy North Koreans, but he understood it. His destiny lay along the path of a follower and obedient servant. It was the code he'd lived by since his youth, and he adhered to it as staunchly as his exercise and training regimens. His priorities focused on combined matters of honor and discipline, elements long forgotten from the feudal periods of his ancestry. No one seemed more detestable to him than those without these traits. He didn't tolerate substandard performance from himself or his subordinates.

To become remiss in duty was to become a sloth unworthy of the master's affections or loyalty.

This was probably the greatest source of Koto's fresh hatred for the American who had defeated his men. To die amid success was honorable and acceptable; to die amid failure was to bring shame on oneself. It wasn't the way or the code. Koto could find little reason to respect those who died under the hand of the insignificant capitalists. War was the only exception; some loss was to be expected in those circumstances.

Koto had prepared himself to accept the blame and responsibility for their failure, but Hakajima-*san* wouldn't have it. Instead, the master blamed himself for not sending Koto to do the job personally. Now four of his men were dead and shame had cloaked the name of the master's empire. As chief enforcer, he wouldn't allow the mistake to be repeated.

Koto turned his eyes toward the three-story infirmary that catered to the foreign diplomatic community. A pair of guards stood silently at the wrought-iron gates of the rear entrance. Their eyes flitted occasionally toward the sedan, studying Koto with suspicion. The Japanese martial artist ignored their insulting attitudes and kept a vigilant watch for Hakajima-*san*.

Thirty minutes passed before the Japanese tycoon reappeared and walked to the car. Koto opened the rear door of the sedan to allow his master to pass, then slid into the seat. He ordered the driver to take them back to the house and waited respectfully for Hakajima to address him.

"Those putrid idiots working for Pak In-sung did considerable harm to her," Hakajima announced finally.

The master's eyes looked sunken and bloodshot, and there was a dangerous, almost purple hue to his face. His body trembled, and Koto immediately became aware of the turmoil welling inside of his charge.

"My original beliefs about Cho Shinmun and his men were incorrect. Clumsy savages, my master," Koto said softly. "They have paid for that."

"Yes, but not by our hand."

"It is of little consequence."

Hakajima threw Koto a furious look. "I do not consider it 'of little consequence.'"

"Forgive me. I did not mean to—"

"I am concerned that Pak will not follow through with his end of the plan, Koto," Hakajima interrupted offhandedly. "Perhaps you should go to Kumho and supervise the operation yourself."

"I will happily go where you think me most useful," Koto replied with a reverent bow.

Hakajima smiled and put his hand on the enforcer's shoulder. "You forget that I know you well. It is against your ideals to leave my side, but I am perfectly safe here. The Americans have left Pyongyang, and there is no direct threat to my safety now. I want you to make sure there are no errors."

"And what is it you wish me to do if Pak fails us?"

"Kill him."

"As you wish, my master."

THE AFTERNOON DREW to a close and evening settled on Pyongyang. When the nurse came in, Arisa pretended to sleep. Her mind would drift from one escape plan to the next, but nothing seemed appealing to her.

Her conversation with Hakajima led her to believe the room wasn't guarded by the DPRK. She'd managed to view the chart that hung on the edge of the bed at one point when she was alone. It indicated she was hospitalized in the infirmary for the diplomatic community. The place was very secure in all probability, and it would be as difficult to leave as it would to make entry—maybe even more difficult.

When the sky outside had dimmed sufficiently, Arisa gently extracted the IV tubes from her arm, using a torn piece of her gown at the crook of her elbow to stop the bleeding. She climbed from bed and went to the window.

The pain in her back throbbed. She let her hand drift unconsciously to the spot where Cho stabbed her. A large bandage covered the wound. She let her fingers slide beneath it and felt the stitches there.

The latch on the window frame suddenly caught her eye. It was a projected-type window that swung inward on guide rails. It provided minimal security, but it opened wide enough that Arisa could get out. The Japanese agent turned and went to the door. She pressed her ear against it and carefully listened. The area beyond her room sounded quiet.

Arisa began to search her room for her clothing. She could hardly venture out into the elements without adequate protection against the unforgiving environment. She opened each drawer in her nightstand without success, then searched under the bed and in a closet. She finally walked into the bathroom, although she was certain it would produce the same results. To her amazement she found the overcoat Belasko had worn and her pants hanging in a small closet behind the bathroom door. Her shoes were also there, but her shirt was missing. The infirmary staff had probably discarded it when she was brought in.

Arisa quickly stepped into her pants, donned her socks and shoes and shrugged into the huge overcoat. She checked the pockets of the coat but didn't find anything that would help her. They probably would have emptied their contents before having it cleaned anyway. Arisa didn't have the first idea as to the location of her identification or her side arm. Nonetheless, escape was the main thing on her mind. If she managed to leave the grounds undetected, she could find a way back to the house where she had clothes, weapons and a spare vehicle.

The woman returned to the window and quietly opened it. She peered under the edge of the frame and spotted a ledge with decorative spires. Her room was on the second story, which would make the descent much easier. She didn't have a rope, and that left the bedsheets. Arisa stripped the bed, forming two loops in one end, then put one leg through each loop and wrapped the working end around her arm. She used a nearby chair to climb over the window and slid down until her legs contacted the ledge.

Arisa forced herself not to look down. She wasn't afraid of heights but with the amount of medication in her bloodstream she couldn't trust herself not to develop vertigo and fall. The Japanese agent tied a slip loop around one of the spires. The thick metal was set firmly in the concrete ledge, and Arisa prayed that it would hold her small frame. Using the slip knot she gently lowered herself from the ledge. She had to disengage herself from the loops and drop the last couple of feet. The impact jarred her spine, and she gritted her teeth against the fresh waves of pain that ran through her back. She could only hope she hadn't torn out the stitches.

The woman pressed herself against the wall and clung to the shadows. Tall bars of wrought iron ran along the entire perimeter of the grounds. There was no way she could climb the fencing unit. Even if she could achieve the climb, she risked discovery by a possible roving patrol of guards.

Arisa skirted the edge of the building until she reached

a corner. She slowly peered around the corner and immediately noticed several cars parked in a lot adjacent to the U-shaped complex. It wouldn't be difficult to find one that was unsecured and hot-wire it. She crossed the lawn to the parking lot and found her salvation in a two-door sports sedan. Within a few minutes, she was leaving the parking lot and heading for the front gate.

As the Japanese agent approached the exit, her heart began to pound in her chest. Four guards stood at their post, and it appeared they were going to stop her vehicle. She slowed and tried to look as innocent as possible. At the last minute, one of the sentries waved her through and the twin gates swung out obediently upon a signal from another man inside the control shack. Arisa smiled sweetly and waved at the handsome young men as she passed through.

They returned her wave cordially, and she pulled onto the street. Her plan had worked! No one within the infirmary would have the first idea of her whereabouts. Now it was time to get a fresh change of clothes and her weapons. She would also abandon her stolen transportation and submit a brief report to her superiors in Tokyo before heading for Hungnam. With any luck, the North Korean police wouldn't have someone stationed at the house.

Arisa couldn't help but wonder where Mike Belasko would be or what he was up to. Well, she would find out soon enough. No matter what it cost, she had to find the warrior and warn him that something big was brewing. It was quite possible that he didn't have any idea that the enemy was actually waiting for him.

She was the only one who could save him from certain doom.

CHAPTER THIRTEEN

Hungnam

"I must admit, Mr. Belasko," Ken Durham said, "you definitely have influential connections in Washington."

Bolan nodded in agreement. "Yes, sir."

The U.S. State Department man was a pleasant-looking gentleman with salt-and-pepper hair and a mustache. His voice was deep with just a hint of Southern twang, and he had a tan complexion. Durham reminded Bolan of a famous actor he'd seen in a lot of spaghetti Westerns, but he couldn't recall the name. There was something tough and rugged about Durham while simultaneously he was a congenial and eloquent diplomat. The Executioner could understand the President's reasons for choosing to send the State Department man to Hungnam.

The two men sat in Durham's personal suite. The room was decorated with hand-carved wooden furniture upholstered with red velour. The floors were carpeted in a cream-colored shag, and one wall sported a complete bar and waist-high refrigerator. Heavy drapes covered windows and fancy glass doors that looked out onto the darkened city.

Strack had circumvented security by taking Bolan and Rueben through a rear door used for deliveries to the hotel kitchen. The men proceeded to the top floor in a service elevator. Strack now waited with Rueben in an adjoining room as Bolan met with Durham.

"Mr. Durham," Bolan continued, "I'm concerned for the safety of the delegates. That's why my people sent me here. The timetable prevented them from giving me an agenda."

"Well, I can understand your dilemma," Durham interjected. "It's difficult to plan when you don't have all of the information."

"Then I'm sure you also realize how unstable the situation could become."

Durham looked puzzled. "These negotiations serve to benefit the entire Southeast Asian theater, Mr. Belasko. What could anyone possibly have to gain from committing an act of terrorism?"

"You'd understand if you knew what I did, sir," Bolan replied.

"I'll bet."

The Executioner tried to keep his temper in check. He didn't have time to explain the situation to Durham. Moreover, there was just too much the politician didn't need to know. Bolan had to make him aware of the potential risks without paralyzing the man with fear. Durham didn't realize that his few bodyguards and the security in the hotel lobby weren't enough. If the North Koreans wanted to get to him or anyone else at the conference, Bolan needed to know when and where they were most likely to strike.

"Someone in the ruling party wants to start a war," the soldier offered.

"Could you be more specific?" Durham asked.

"I wish I could, but there's no time for that. What I can tell you is that this individual has allied himself with a Japanese businessman by the name of Sumio Hakajima."

"You're not talking about the man from COR-DEF Industries are you?"

"The same."

"So," Durham said absently, "Hakajima's working for the North Koreans."

"The Japanese government is certain that he's providing financial support for the power plants in Kumho. I ran into one of their agents, and that's when I learned of Hakajima's involvement."

"Perhaps you're correct in your assessment, then."

"What do you mean?"

"Well, this afternoon's activities were canceled due to the fact several delegates were delayed. They should arrive late tonight, and so the North Koreans have agreed to suspend the talks until tomorrow morning. But that's not the odd thing. After lunch, the entire conference is scheduled for a trip to Kumho to look over the power plants."

"That's it," Bolan replied. "That's when they'll make their move."

"I don't know, Mr. Belasko," Durham said, shaking his head with a doubtful expression. "I don't believe the North Koreans would take such a risk. It could have very nasty results."

"It's not the North Korean government I'm worried about, Mr. Durham," Bolan replied. "It's just a small faction. Perhaps one man. The intelligence is pretty sound on this issue."

Durham didn't reply at first but crossed his legs and pulled absently at his mustache. The Executioner could see the skepticism in Durham's expression—the guy just couldn't believe what Bolan had told him. For whatever reason, Durham didn't want to accept the fact that his life and the lives of the other delegates were in jeopardy.

"I'm willing to provide you with the credentials needed

to move freely," he declared finally. "I'm also willing to provide you with an agenda and any support you might need. But that's where I have to draw the line. Beyond that, you'll be on your own."

"Fair enough. I've taken enough of your time. Thank you."

As Bolan rose from his chair, Durham called to him. "Uh, Mr. Belasko?"

"Yes, sir?"

"The President has advised me that he doesn't want any trouble during the conference," Durham announced sternly, "so let me offer you a bit of sage advice. Don't stir a simmering pot. It could result in more trouble than we have already."

"Duly noted, sir."

Bolan left the suite and entered the room where Rueben and Strack waited impatiently. The two men rose as the soldier shut the door, and he knew from their expressions that the strain showed in his face.

"He didn't go for it, huh?" Strack ventured.

Bolan looked back at the door before replying quietly, "It's hard to protect someone who doesn't see the need for it."

"Amen to that. What are you going to do?"

"For the moment, he'll allow me mobility. That's definitely a plus in my favor."

Strack nodded. "It'll be a hell of a lot easier to find your guy if you can look in from the outside."

"Yeah."

Bolan realized Ted Strack was a sharp individual. The guy knew how to think on his feet, a trait he'd probably picked up as a former agent for the Secret Service. Strack had told Bolan a little of his past on the trip to the Mudo Kwan. The guy had guarded the last vice president and conducted various other protection jobs for ambassadors and members of Congress. His official title for the purposes of this conference was that of an aide, but the fact he carried himself like a bodyguard gave away his true status.

"Look, Belasko," Strack said, "I have to stay on top of things tomorrow, so I don't know how much I can help. But if you have any suggestions for what I can do on the inside, I'm all ears."

"Thanks. I'll keep that in mind."

"Excuse me," Steve Rueben cut in, "but what about me? Did you ask him about my dad?"

"No," Bolan replied. "I think we should handle the issue of your father ourselves."

"Fair enough."

The soldier cast another glance at Strack. "You know about this little trip to Kumho tomorrow?"

"Yeah. Scheduled to leave right after some luncheon. About 1500 hours if I remember correctly."

"I told Durham the people I'm after would probably make their move then. He doesn't trust my information, but that won't matter. I need to procure some wheels. I can take care of the rest."

"I think I can help in that department," Rueben said. "I've got a rental parked near your hotel. It shouldn't stick out like a sore thumb."

"That'll do the trick."

"Are you planning to follow us in?" Strack asked.

Bolan shook his head. "No, I'm going to scout the forward area."

"What if they make their move on the road?"

"Doesn't sound likely. Too many open spaces. They'll play their hand where the conference members are away from the security of the hotel. Maximum effect with minimum effort."

"That's what I'd do," Strack conceded. "Good thinking, Belasko."

"I'll take Rueben here back to the hotel with me. Can we get a lift?"

"Sure. Just let me tell Durham I'm leaving."

PAK IN-SUNG SAT with his head security adviser and the commander of the Black Army detachment that would conduct the next day's operation in Kumho. The party leader was nervous, and he didn't mind showing it. They were about to imprison a group of delegates from some of the most powerful nations in the world. It wasn't an act that the countries in question would take lightly. Timing would be crucial with Hakajima's efforts across the country. At least all of the pieces were in place. Now they simply had to let the game play itself out.

It was the waiting that bothered Pak the most. He'd never been an impetuous man, but he didn't like to wait. The longer he waited, the more he anticipated their victory. He could practically taste the impending success of the operation. By the following night, there would be a dozen countries lining up and gladly receiving the demands of the DPRK. His country would spearhead its aggression against the South Koreans and the capitalist nations that supported them.

China and Russia would certainly come to their aid and probably the Europeans, as well. The British would likely side with America, as would Israel and France. Who knew where the Middle Easterners stood in the whole thing, but Hakajima seemed convinced they would jump at any chance to strike back at the Americans.

The United Nations would probably collapse under the

threat of thermonuclear war. The DPRK's first targets would be South Korea and Japan, as well as the other Southeast Asian islands. Then they would induct the citizens into military service and march them across the rest of Asia. With support from Russian technology, and manpower and weapons from China, North Korea would once again rule a vast and powerful empire.

Even if the United States and her allies weren't annihilated, they wouldn't risk global warfare just to repress the DPRK war machine. Such ideals had disappeared with the defeat of Adolph Hitler's Third Reich. Every conflict in American history since World War II had involved minor wars with countries only marginally capable of defending themselves against a numerically and technologically superior force.

The North Korean people wouldn't topple so easily. They would rise up like a sleeping lion and deal a horrific blow to the warmongers that had subjugated the DPRK for so long. Their threats would bounce as harmlessly off his country's chest as their food and economic sanctions. When the North Koreans needed food or supplies in the future, they would simply strip them from those they defeated as spoils of war.

Pak was feeling better now as he considered the momentous events ahead of him. He turned his attention to the two men who sat respectfully waiting for him to address them. They were on the second floor of a hotel booked exclusively for members of the ruling party. There were a score of officials from his country there with him, but most of them would not be involved with the tour at the Kumho nuclear sites tomorrow afternoon.

"I cannot stress the importance of this operation," Pak told General Hap Mung-Li. "Your men must be ready. Failure is not an option."

"We shall await your signal with eagerness," Hap replied with a bow. "It will be a memorable occasion. It was foolish of these people to think they could divert us with this pathetic conference."

Pak smiled and inclined his head. The propaganda he'd spread throughout the country had apparently convinced his people of the implicit threat in the training exercise in Seoul. Even the members of the elite military corps were believing the rumors. Pak had purposely let it slip that the DPRK believed an invasion was imminent and would probably take place in the middle of the negotiations. He planned to set events in motion that would only strengthen those beliefs.

Pak didn't particularly like Hap, but he chose to tolerate the man because he was a brilliant military strategist. Pak could recall how he had relied on Cho's brilliance, and it resulted in complete disaster. Well, this was quite a different situation indeed. Just because the American had followed him to Hungnam didn't mean he knew whom to look for. Pak would never show his face. He would wait in the wings and run the operation from a safe distance.

Pak turned a haughty glance to the other man there. Nang Ki-wan was the head of the North Korean secret police. His men had failed to stop the American agent, and Pak was so angry about it he'd seriously considered having the man executed for his ineptitude. But Nang knew how to fix problems quickly, and he had sworn to Pak that he would bring the party leader the American's head.

"What do you plan to do about this...what is his name? Belasko?"

"We have the situation well in hand, sir," Nang replied.

Pak snorted with disbelief. "You call the incident at this hotel 'well in hand,' Captain Nang?"

"One of my men observed him leave his hotel with two

other Americans. Apparently, he did not defeat my agents alone. He might have help from those attending the conference.''

"My informants believe that this Belasko prefers to operate alone, and that he fights like a demon straight from hell.''

"He is hardly a threat, sir,'' Nang protested. "I have the suites of the American delegates tapped. We already know he will travel to Kumho tonight and try to uncover your plans. We shall be waiting for him. I promise you that he will not live to see the dawn.''

"I've heard these same empty promises before!'' Pak slammed his fist on the table next to his chair, and the men jumped in their chairs with horrified expressions.

Pak lowered his voice and continued, "I don't want promises anymore, Captain Nang. I want results. And if I do not get them this time, I will personally ensure that *you* do not live to see the dawn.''

"I will bring you his head.''

"I don't want his head.'' Pak sneered. "Do not be dramatic or foolish. This man is dangerous. I want him eliminated. See to it, Captain Nang. This is your final chance.''

Nang rose and snapped to attention. "It shall be done.''

Once he'd left the room, Pak turned to Hap and narrowed his eyes.

"Now, General,'' he began, "brief me again of your plans tomorrow.''

STRACK DROPPED off the two men at Belasko's hotel. As they got out of his car, the former Secret Service agent leaned toward the passenger seat and called to them through an open window. "We'll see you tomorrow.''

"Bet on it,'' Belasko said with a nod.

Steve Rueben accompanied Belasko to his room, where

the big guy retrieved a suitcase. He couldn't help but admire Belasko. There was something about the way the man carried himself. He was confident and alert, always watching and sizing up the situation. It seemed obvious that the kind of thing that had occurred in the hotel lobby earlier that day was nothing new to this guy.

Belasko reminded Rueben of his older brother in a lot of ways. Jerrod Rueben had lost his life during Desert Storm when the Iraqis blew up an airport hangar near the Kuwaiti shores. Jerrod had just disembarked from his plane and was in-processing before shipping off to a tank unit. He never made it, and Rueben could remember watching the flag-draped coffin at the airport as it was unloaded from a plane in Seattle.

Rueben had just turned twelve when his brother was killed. He could remember how the news of Jerrod's death nearly killed their father, Shem Rueben. The man had lost his wife a few years earlier to breast cancer, and now all they had left was each other. The tragedies in their lives only served to strengthen the bond between Rueben and his father. When his dad would go on trips during the summer, he would take his wide-eyed boy along. Before he graduated high school, Rueben had seen more of the world than most of his friends and experienced way more than most kids probably had to.

Nonetheless, Rueben didn't consider those experiences all bad. They held nothing but good memories for him because those were the times he could remember being happiest. Those were the times he felt closest to his father, and he knew in his heart that there was nothing that could hurt him as long as he could hide in Shem Rueben's loving embrace.

But they slowly drifted apart.

In his senior year of high school, Rueben attempted to

enlist in the Marine Corps under the delayed-entry program; his father wouldn't have it. Shem didn't want to see his only remaining son go off to some foreign country and get killed. In a way, Rueben's father was responsible for spawning his son into someone who loved to travel and experience the thrill of other cultures. He'd unwittingly set Steve Rueben on a path as a career soldier. But he refused to sign his approval for Steve's enlistment.

Their contradictory views created a rift between them, and Rueben enlisted as soon as he turned eighteen. He tried to compromise with his father in a way by enlisting in the Army rather than the Marines, but all Shem could seem to see was a repeat of Jerrod's rebellion and subsequent death in the line of duty.

Rueben had to admit to himself many years later that he'd stayed in the Army for reasons less lofty than those of duty, God and country. Part of it might have been an attempt to punish himself for not being the same kind of man his brother had been. Another reason he definitely knew now was escape, although this idea hadn't occurred to him when he was young and immature. Through his years in the military, he'd renewed the ties with his dad, and now something unforeseen had taken that away from him. Or was it someone?

"What do you do for the military?" Bolan asked.

"Field artillery."

"Good job."

"I enjoy it," Rueben said, adding hesitantly, "at least I used to. You don't really approve of my going AWOL. Do you?"

"It's not up to me, soldier," Belasko replied easily. "You helped me, and now I'm going to help you. That's all there is to it."

"Then you understand my reasons?"

"Yeah. I understand."

Bolan retrieved a large leather suitcase from under the bed and laid it on the mattress. He opened the case, and Rueben had to lean forward to inspect the contents in the poorly lit room. There were several different firearms in the suitcase along with fatigues and boots. One of the weapons was a machine pistol Rueben didn't recognize, but there was no mistaking the M-1911 pistols and the Mark XIX .50 AE.

"Damn, Belasko," Rueben whispered. "You must be tight with some heavy hitters."

Belasko turned and stared at him with a serious expression. "You packing?"

"No, not really. Unless you count a Gerber pocket-knife."

"I want you to understand something before we go forward here."

"Okay…"

"Just listen," Bolan said, shaking his head in a gesture that he expected silence. "I've got a mission to complete. It takes precedence over your father. The people I'm going up against don't like me, and you know yourself that they're trying to kill me. They won't be selective of anyone with me."

"Hell, they're welcome to try," Rueben cut in with more bravado than he actually felt.

"That attitude will get you killed quick, my friend," Belasko countered. "If I allow you to tag along, you do things my way. Understood? Otherwise, you're on your own, and I'll try to come back and help you."

"Okay," Rueben acquiesced, "I can deal with that. I'm actually pretty good with a firearm, and you need my wheels anyway. Remember?"

"I don't need them bad enough to cost you your life,"

Bolan replied as he turned and reached into the suitcase. "Just as long as you understand the risks and you're willing to accept them, I won't mind the help."

Bolan took one of the .45-caliber pistols from the suitcase. He rammed in a full magazine and handed the M-1911 to Rueben along with a spare magazine. Rueben took the weapon, expertly chambered a round, then thumbed the safety. He tucked the pistol into his waistband beneath his leather jacket and concealed the additional clip in a coat pocket.

The Executioner shrugged off his suit coat and pulled a lightweight, fleece-lined jacket from the suitcase. He pulled a Beretta 93-R from shoulder leather and popped the clip. In seconds he stripped down the pistol and quickly pulled a cleaning kit from the suitcase. He sprayed the parts with a liquid compound that had chemical properties similar to those in Freon. Within a few minutes, the Beretta was cleaned, oiled and reassembled.

"You've done this kind of thing a lot, huh?" Rueben said in a conversational tone.

"Yeah, a few times."

"Done time yourself?"

"Vietnam, two tours."

"I spent a short time as an armorer with my last unit. I got hurt and they pulled me from field duty for three months. I mostly took care of small arms like Berettas and M-16s."

"How long you been in?"

"Since I was eighteen. I would have had eleven years next month, but I guess I blew that."

Rueben went to the window and peered through it. The hustle and bustle of the day had tapered to a crawl along the windswept streets below. The sun had finally set, and there were few pedestrians on the sidewalks. It had become much colder and it appeared that dark, dismal clouds were rolling into the area. The residents of Hungnam were apparently smart enough to stay indoors and keep out of the weather.

"Looks like it might snow." Rueben turned from the window and looked at his newfound friend. "Heavily."

Bolan nodded. "We'll be on the road soon. Why don't you tell me about your dad while I prep the rest of this stuff."

"Oh, my dad," Rueben said, repeatedly banging the side of his forehead to show his frustration. "The guy doesn't listen to anybody, Mike. No, he knows best, regardless of what anyone else might think."

"How so?"

"I tried to tell him that it could be dangerous right now for him to be in North Korea. We were briefed about the attack at the Haeju naval base, and command said the DPRK brass was pissed. Our entire battalion went on alert. Hell, we couldn't leave the post or anything."

"You said he's a political correspondent?"

"Yes. He called me when he landed in Seoul. I guess he couldn't fly directly into North Korea. Some kind of political reasons or security issues or something. Anyway, he called me at my unit and told me he couldn't come see me right then, but he'd definitely stop on his way out of the country."

"So what makes you think he's missing?"

"He never called me when he got here. I mean, I was out in the field with the training exercise and all, but—"

Bolan's eyes snapped up from his task, and he looked at Rueben with what the young soldier interpreted to be just a glimmer of hope. "You were part of the training exercise down there?"

"Yeah," Rueben replied with a shrug, not sure what the big guy was trying to get at. "Why?"

"I'm convinced that this training exercise has something to do with the reasons I'm here."

"Really? That's kind of weird. The exercise has always been an annual thing."

"How many troops are involved with this thing?"

"I think I remember something in the avenue of forty thousand. It's mostly just the high-ranking officers sitting around in some big room using computer simulations to play 'what-if' scenarios. We just go where they tell us. The medical corps and some of the infantry guys get South Koreans to help them by acting as patients and victims of chemical attack. It's really a big deal here actually."

"Chemical weapons, huh?"

"Well, yeah. Sure."

"Have they ever tested response to a nuclear-weapons attack?"

"Nukes?" Rueben laughed. "You're kidding, right? The North Koreans aren't allowed to maintain nuclear arms. Not any that are worth a damn anyway. They agreed to halt their nuclear programs in exchange for aid."

"Well, they've apparently broken that agreement," Belasko replied thinly.

Rueben's eyes widened. "What do you mean they've broken it? They can't do that."

"Let me ask you a question. What if someone inside the ruling party used a nuclear missile against all of those troops massed in Seoul right now?"

"They wouldn't dare do something stupid like that. It'd start a freaking world war!"

"I think that's exactly what they want."

"My God," Rueben whispered.

The impact of the words stabbed him in the heart like

a razor-sharp saber. If the North Koreans decided to mistake the training exercise as a mobilization for invasion, it was possible they would repel the attack with significant force. If Belasko was correct in his assessment of their nuclear capabilities, a single missile could eradicate all of Seoul and a good portion of the surrounding areas. Millions of lives would be lost in an instant, and more than forty thousand American soldiers would be dead.

The retaliation would be swift and decisive. The United States would appeal to NATO, and then the President would request immediate action. Congress would more than likely declare war on North Korea, and in the midst of peace negotiations in Hungnam, the U.S. armed forces would respond with everything they had. They would bomb North Korea until it was no longer a peninsula. Other countries would jump in to protect their own interests in Southeast Asia, and the situation would be out of control before anybody really knew what happened.

"What you're saying makes sense to me," Rueben finally admitted, "but why would anybody want to start a war? For what reason?"

"I think we'll find the answer to that in Kumho," Belasko replied.

CHAPTER FOURTEEN

True to Steve Rueben's prediction, the ominous clouds and bitter winds brought sleet along with them. Visibility was horrendous, and the Executioner would occasionally have to stop the rental car so he and Rueben could clear the snow and ice collecting on the windshield wiper blades. At their present rate of progress, Bolan predicted it would take them more than two hours to reach Kumho.

They wound through the treacherous mountainous regions. Only an occasional vehicle passed them traveling in the other direction. Rueben said little to Bolan, opting for silence that allowed the soldier to concentrate on the snow-packed roads. Despite the slow, tortuous drive, the pair arrived in Kumho no worse for the wear a little before 2200 hours.

The city itself seemed quiet and unimpressive, but Bolan knew its looks were deceiving, particularly beneath the blanket of inclement weather. According to Stony Man, Kumho had become a thriving metropolis in comparison to many cities in the DPRK. Since the 1997 establishment of the liaison office in Sinpo, South Korean workers, technical staff and a score of hopeful merchants had flocked to Kumho and begun the long, agonizing ritual of urban growth and renewal.

All personnel with any interest in the completion of the twin thousand-megawatt reactors worked directly with the liaison office. The office was located at the construction site and provided counselor service by members of the Korean Peninsula Energy Development Organization to outside agencies. KEDO staff members included representatives from the U.S. State Department, Japanese Office of Foreign Relations and South Korean Foreign Ministry. Nine thousand tons of equipment and goods for the workers were primarily provided by JAPEX Industries and shipped monthly from warehouses in the South Korean port of Masan. Interestingly enough, JAPEX was a subsidiary distribution service for COR-DEF Industries in Japan—the company owned and operated by Sumio Hakajima.

It was all falling into place for the Executioner. There was no question that Hakajima had sunk millions, perhaps even billions of dollars into the construction. The original project had been estimated at around five hundred million dollars, a good portion of which was provided by South Korea. Now parties within the DPRK were determined to use monies dedicated to helping their own people for more sinister purposes. Bolan intended to put an end to the scheme once and for all.

"What's the plan?" Rueben asked, finally breaking nearly an hour of silence.

"I think the best place to start," Bolan replied, "is the KEDO liaison office."

"Why?"

"The information I have indicates that nothing goes into or comes out of this city without them knowing about it. I figure they might have information that could provide proof positive the North Koreans are using the installations at Kumho to build a new ballistic missile."

"Well, I won't argue with you since you obviously know a hell of a lot more about it than I do. But I can't understand why the North Koreans would announce that kind of thing to this KEDO place."

"They wouldn't," Bolan explained, "but that doesn't mean there wouldn't be clues that point to some sort of subversion."

"Such as?"

"Such as manifests with weapons-grade plutonium, triggers or fuses. Maybe certain alloys. I won't know exactly what I'm looking for until I see it."

The young artillery specialist fell silent for a time before saying, "You think the North Koreans would actually build a nuke and risk violating the treaty?"

"It's possible."

"It just doesn't make any sense," Rueben said, shaking his head. "The North Korean government turning on their own people. And for what?" He looked at Bolan. "What makes men do these things?"

"Let me tell you something," the soldier replied as he peered through the ice-encrusted windshield. "I've been in almost every country in the world at one time or another. Men commit atrocities in the name of almost every contemptible cause you can imagine. They murder, pillage, rape and manipulate the system to suit their own perverse needs. And it's almost always at the cost of innocent lives. But no matter what the cause is, the basis for it is always the same."

"And what's that?"

"Power. Whether it's over people, finances, governments or life and death itself, every one of them are driven by the same motive. That's what makes them lesser men."

"And what about a good man, Belasko?" Rueben asked seriously. "What do you think makes a good man?"

"His actions work toward the betterment of all mankind," Bolan said. He looked at Rueben and added, "That's what defines a good man."

Rueben nodded. "Do you consider yourself a good man?"

"I let my actions speak for me," Bolan replied with a shake of his head.

The Executioner noticed a small eatery that appeared to be open. He pulled his car to the curb, and the two men entered the establishment. It seemed like a cozy place, but the exterior did little justice to what was inside. The eatery was clean and modern with whitewashed walls and a gleaming tile floor. Emerald-colored carpets ran down a center aisle that accessed roomy booths on either side. Traditional Korean music resounded softly from hidden speakers, and candles cast flickering light at each table. Red flannel banners bearing Korean symbols and words hung from the ceiling.

The modern, romantic environment seemed out of place under the circumstances, but the aromas and scents of exotic Korean food churned the stomachs of the pair. They quickly selected a booth close to the exit, and Bolan insisted on sitting where he could observe the front door.

"I guess this reactor construction has been good to Kumho, huh?" Rueben observed.

"Yeah," Bolan said, taking another look at the eatery's decor.

A Korean woman attired in traditional garb seemingly appeared from nowhere and wordlessly poured the men tea, although neither of them had requested it. Her black hair was flecked with only a strand or two of white, and she looked fairly young to Bolan.

"May I help you?" the woman said in flawless English.

"What's the special?" Bolan asked.

"Kem-shi with rice and mandarin-seasoned fish."

Bolan looked at Rueben. "What do you think?"

"Well, she speaks good English," Rueben remarked.

He looked at the woman and smiled, then began to address her in Korean. The two spoke back and forth for about a minute before she hurried away with a slightly miffed expression.

"You speak Korean?"

Rueben chuckled. "I've learned to turn a phrase or two since I was assigned here. I speak some Spanish and German, too. And a little French. Guess you could say I'm a bit of a dabbler in linguistics."

"That's one way of putting it. What did you order?"

"That's the funny thing," Rueben said with a wide grin. "I asked if she could make us cheeseburgers and fries. She was happy to oblige but she said, 'You Americans always order the same thing.'"

The two men got a good laugh out of that, and the tensions of the day seemed to ebb from their conscious thoughts. Still, Bolan couldn't help considering the turn of events in the past twenty-four hours. He would be glad when the mission was over—whichever way it went.

"I'M SURE THERE ARE a few Americans here with the nuclear reactors going up," Bolan said. "I know for a fact the U.S. has members of the State Department and CIA here. Probably American engineers, as well."

"Yeah, I suppose you're right. I hadn't thought of that."

A long strap of bells suspended from the front door rang softly for attention as a small Korean man dressed in a black trench coat entered the eatery. Bolan was immediately alert for trouble, and Rueben noticed the intense look in the soldier's eyes.

The military man whispered tensely as the Executioner watched the newcomer with interest. "What's wrong?"

"I don't know," Bolan replied quietly. "Maybe nothing."

The waitress greeted the customer and escorted him to another table.

Bolan let out a breath and returned his attention to Rueben. "False alarm."

"All of this stuff's really got you jumpy," the young man said casually, "hasn't it?"

"I prefer to think of it as caution."

The men received their meal and hungrily dug into their American cuisine. The late supper passed without incident, and Bolan left a generous tip. The men exited the eatery and returned to the car. The snow had stopped and the clouds were replaced by a blue-black sky filled with brilliant stars that glittered like diamonds. The breaths of the two men crystallized in the frigid night air. They cleared the snow that had settled on the sedan's windows and then got into the car.

When they were inside and Bolan let the interior warm sufficiently, Rueben turned to him and said, "Did you see it?"

Bolan nodded. "Large van parked on that side street, no lights and engine running."

"Who the hell are these guys, Mike?"

"Probably more of the same like those from the hotel today."

Bolan flicked on his lights, put the rental car in gear and began to drive toward the liaison office. They were nearly out of sight before he saw the headlights in the far distance wink on and swing into the rearview mirror. The cessation of the storm would make it much easier for the soldier to keep his tail in sight. These newcomers would probably look for the right time and opportunity to make their move, if they were as predictable as their predecessors.

As he continued toward the power plants, Bolan wondered who might be working for the North Korean ruling party. Cho Shinmun's crew had been hard-core, professional soldiers, but the last group he'd encountered at the hotel didn't move with one-quarter of the efficiency.

Hakajima's partner was probably using conventional resources—perhaps members of the security agency or even mercenaries. They were definitely not professionals of the caliber of Cho, and the Executioner was grateful he wouldn't have to deal with that crew again.

Bolan made a left onto a narrow road that branched off the main drag. He drove about a mile before stopping in front of a darkened one-story building just off the side of the road. A large metal sign hung above the door and sported letters in at least a half-dozen languages. It only took a moment for Bolan to positively identify it as the liaison office. Directly ahead he could discern the dome shapes of the light-water reactor plants that were nearing completion. One of the plants was actually finished in the area of construction, and currently engaged in final testing before it went into service.

The Executioner reached into the back seat and opened the suitcase. He withdrew the MP-5, pocketed two spare magazines and put the weapon in battery.

"Listen up," he commanded. "I'm going EVA. Go around back, kill the lights and wait for me. Got it?"

Rueben indicated he understood, and Bolan left the car. The soldier sprinted to the front door, crouched and quickly studied the entrance. The headlights of the van appeared almost a minute after Rueben had left the roadway. With any luck, the occupants in the car would continue past the darkened building and drive to the reactors. The guards at the gates to the site would probably stop them, and they would realize Bolan and Rueben hadn't gone that far. Maybe this would stall the enemy long enough for Bolan to get a handle on what the North Koreans really had planned.

He already realized that a confrontation of some kind was inevitable.

The front door of the office was wire-mesh glass in an

aluminum frame. He inspected the lock and realized it was only a dead bolt from the inside. The van was now within a mile. Bolan ran the butt of the MP-5 into the glass near the lock. The glass caved on the second blow. He continued to plug away at the door until the wire snapped from his repeated hammering. He reached through the hole, unlocked the bolt and pushed into the darkness about ten seconds before the van rolled past.

Bolan pressed himself to the shadows and remained motionless, the MP-5 held at the ready. The Executioner hoped his ruse worked. The sound of the van's engine continued to fade in his ears, but he kept still until it was gone. When he was satisfied, Bolan flicked on a flashlight provided by Grimaldi and began to riffle through the file drawers of the inner offices.

There was nothing of value in the office of the South Korean or Japanese foreign-ministry offices—he couldn't read the documents there anyway. The State Department files were another matter. Bolan began to read inventory lists and shipping documents with interest. Among each shipment there were crates listed under ambiguous numbers and labeled machine parts. Moreover, there were shipments listed that seemed out of sync with the official reports that Washington was receiving. The Executioner skimmed the information and began to find a pattern. It primarily dealt with the types of materials coming in and vague references to the completion of the reactors. What bothered Bolan the most were that the messages were occasionally followed by a row of numbers, a date, then another series of numbers.

Bolan decided to hold on to the information—he couldn't know if it would come in handy down the line. He continued to search through the offices but found little else that would help him. Whoever was working with Hakajima was covering his tracks well. The soldier left the building and quickly rejoined Rueben, who was waiting anxiously in the back as instructed.

The Executioner climbed into the passenger seat and waved the sheaf of papers at his ally. "Found something that might be of use."

"Great," Rueben replied nervously. "Now can we get out of here?"

"Yeah, let's go."

Rueben pulled out of the lot, and as he turned in the direction they had come Bolan stopped him.

"Drive toward the reactors."

"But isn't that the way—" Rueben began, but he cut himself off with a sharp look from Bolan. "I know, I know. I agreed to do things your way."

Rueben redirected the nose of the car toward the reactors as Bolan studied the messages again. He just couldn't put his finger on the printouts. The messages seemed legitimate, but there was something that bothered him about them. Someone within the DPRK government had communicated with American KEDO members on a regular basis. Such communications would have been forwarded to Ken Durham, yet the State Department man had never mentioned them when Bolan brought up the issue of someone manipulating things with Hakajima's assistance. It was entirely possible the thought had slipped his mind, but Bolan couldn't convince himself of this.

As the rental car neared the front gates, Bolan could see the van ahead. The driver was standing outside of his vehicle, and it appeared he was discussing something with a uniformed guard. As they drew closer, Bolan could see that the guard was a Black Army trooper and the other man was a Korean in plainclothes.

The soldier flipped the selector switch on his MP-5 from safe to full-auto and ordered Rueben to rear-end the sedan. The younger soldier didn't hesitate, popping the clutch as he slammed the gearshift into overdrive. The rental car lurched forward and skidded on the snow but managed to find some ground. The front end rammed into the back of the van before either the driver or the guard could react.

"Quick! Get out and stumble toward them like you're drunk."

Rueben nodded and quickly indicated he understood the Executioner's plan. He obediently pushed open the door and clumsily climbed from the car. Bolan watched Rueben's award-winning performance as the young man nearly staggered into the snowdrifts along the side of the road. He managed to keep his balance, then trotted in unhesitant steps toward the pair of unwary men.

As soon as their attention was completely focused on Rueben, Bolan left the sedan and rushed to the passenger side of the van. He yanked the door open with his right hand and used his left to level the MP-5 at the chest of another Korean man seated there. The passenger was dressed in civilian clothes like the driver, and his eyes widened in terror when he saw the barrel of the subgun resting on his chest.

"Stay still!" Bolan ordered him. "Keep your hands clear of the rest of you."

The driver turned suddenly toward the van and began to reach inside his jacket, but Bolan was ready for him. He cleared his Beretta from shoulder leather, snap-aimed and squeezed the trigger. The 93-R chugged twice as twin 125-grain hollowpoint rounds slammed through the man's hand before he'd completed his own draw. The Korean danced away, his eyes filling with pain, then a hole suddenly appeared in his forehead as the echo of another gun resounded through the night air. Rueben had shot the man from his side.

The Black Army trooper tried to bring his Type 89 to bear, but he never made it as Rueben tracked on the soldier and blew off a double tap. The rounds took the special-forces soldier high in the face, ripping away flesh and bone and exposing brain matter to the frosty elements. Steam rolled from what remained of the soldier's head as he spun away and collapsed to the frozen ground.

In the distracting moments during Rueben's offensive, the passenger tried an offense of his own, grabbing the receiver of Bolan's weapon and forcing it away from himself. The man was little but he was quicker and stronger than Bolan predicted. The Korean launched himself from his seat and began to pummel the Executioner with his fists. Bolan rolled away from the vicious attack and came to his feet. The Korean charged the soldier as he leveled the MP-5 and squeezed the trigger. Nine millimeter Parabellum slugs sizzled across the short distance and tore ragged holes through the man's body. Chunks of wet, bloody flesh erupted from his back, and the force of the rounds punched him against his open door. The man collapsed hard as a scarlet tendril began to pour from his body and run through the snow.

An entire squad of Black Army guards approached the group with their weapons held at the ready. The side door of the van suddenly slid aside, and several more Koreans in civilian dress poured from it. They pointed their automatic rifles at Bolan, and the Executioner suddenly realized they held the upper hand.

Rueben appeared at the back and was prepared to fight to the death, but the Executioner stopped any foolish moves by shaking his head. He signaled for Rueben to follow suit as he dropped his weapons and raised his hands. The Koreans and Black Army soldiers quickly spread out and gathered their two prisoners. One of the men stripped Bolan's overcoat from him and exposed the camouflage fatigues he'd worn underneath.

They bound their prisoners' hands behind them, then

pushed them into the van and drove them through the compound. The back windows were completely blackened so that Bolan couldn't make an educated guess on where they were being taken. The eyes that stared at him and Rueben all gleamed with the same unadulterated hatred. Bolan wondered if he'd walked into another elaborate trap, but he didn't voice the thought to Rueben. The two only exchanged knowing looks before the Executioner considered their new situation. His attack on the van hadn't been an impulsive decision. He'd wanted to take the offensive—shake the tree and see who fell out. Bolan didn't have a clue who their captors were, but he was positive they worked for whoever inside the ruling party was manipulating the situation.

The van bounced along some rough terrain for nearly ten minutes before it stopped. The Korean guards quickly exited the vehicle, then gestured with their weapons for their two prisoners to do the same. Bolan and Rueben jumped from the van and the older soldier quickly looked around. He didn't see the power plants anymore, and he could only assume they were hidden from view behind the van.

The vehicle was parked a few feet from a cinder-block structure that looked about the same size as the liaison office. As they entered, Bolan noticed security cameras mounted along the walls and recessed bulbs that cast dim lighting through iron grates bolted across them. The interior was very cold, and Bolan didn't observe any heat vents. As they moved deeper into the building, a horrid smell began to assault Bolan's senses. It was the smell of human feces, and as they rounded a corner, he knew they were in some sort of structure that had once served as an outbuilding.

Now it appeared their captors had turned the place into a makeshift prison. They reached the end of the corridor, and the guards opened a heavy metal door. They shoved the two men through, then slammed it behind them with a sonorous clang. The echo of the key turning in the lock resonated through the cavernous room.

As Bolan's eyes adjusted to the gloom, he could make out a raised platform running along two of the walls. Further scrutiny revealed oval holes carved into the tops of the platforms and evenly spaced from each other. He quickly realized his original guess had been correct. They had imprisoned the two men in an unused and forgotten outhouse. The Executioner could feel a chill as he studied the area around him. The smell of human waste was nearly overpowering.

"I think I'm going to barf, Belasko," the field artillery specialist mumbled.

"Can't think of a better place to do it," the Executioner replied lightly.

The sound of a human grunt suddenly tackled their attentions. Both men turned simultaneously toward the source of the noise. In one corner, they could barely make out the rocking movement of someone crouched in the shadows. Bolan walked toward the man with caution, but as they drew near he could hear Rueben draw in a sharp breath. Before he could stop the young soldier, Rueben was rushing toward the shadowy form.

"Dad?" Bolan heard Rueben say.

Rueben knelt over the form and pulled the man away from the wall. It was extremely difficult to make out the man's features, but Bolan could see the raised, swollen areas with little effort. The guy continued to rock for a moment, throwing up his hands and screaming as Rueben grabbed his arms. The man screamed again and again and Rueben attempted to calm him.

"Dad...shh, easy. It's okay, Dad." As his patience began to wear thin, Rueben started to shake his father. "Dad!

Calm down and talk to me. It's all right. Nobody else is going to hit you!''

The older Rueben suddenly stopped screaming and a look of recognition flashed in his eyes. His voice cracked as he said, "Stevie?"

"Yes, Dad, it's me. You're all right."

Rueben hugged his father and held him close as the older man began to sob. Despite the pathetic circumstances, their reunion warmed the Executioner's heart. It also burdened him. Now that he'd somehow miraculously kept his promise to help Rueben find his father, he felt the pressing responsibility to get them out of the situation alive.

Bolan turned from the two men and looked around, but he was unable to dredge up the slightest hope. There were no windows and no exits other than the door. He didn't have the slightest clue where to go if they did manage to escape, and it didn't appear that Rueben's father was in the best shape to travel. Moreover, he had less than twenty-four hours before the delegates would arrive, and he still hadn't identified the North Korean in bed with Hakajima.

The worst part was that he'd allowed it to come to this, but yet he couldn't beat himself up over it. It wouldn't have made sense to resist the forces back at the front gate. He and Rueben would have died senselessly, then there would have been no chance for him to accomplish his mission. This way he at least had time to think of a plan. At least his theory about the operation taking place at Kumho seemed correct. There were Black Army troops everywhere, and that seemed like overkill for a couple of nuclear power plants that weren't even operational yet. No, the North Koreans had something else planned, and the Executioner had only a short time left to stop it.

CHAPTER FIFTEEN

Hungnam

Arisa could barely keep her eyes open as she approached the city limits. She rolled down her window and fought the urge to sleep—or maybe just pass out. The effects of the drugs had completely worn off, leaving only excruciating back pain and the desire to vomit. Her mouth was dry and her eyes burned with sleeplessness. Nevertheless, she had to find Belasko. It was entirely possible she was already too late, but she couldn't quit now.

Not when she was this close!

She scolded herself as she remembered her failure to call her Tokyo case officer before leaving Pyongyang. Well, it didn't matter. She knew where the conference was being held and how to contact the American delegates in attendance. Belasko had mentioned his belief that the enemy would target the negotiations. His assumptions made sense. Perhaps he'd already stopped Pak In-sung from selling out his country's security.

She couldn't help her feelings of animosity toward the American warrior. He'd left her in capable hands, certainly, but excluded her from his mission. It didn't matter all that much that her condition warranted his actions. She befriended him, trusted him to help her accomplish her mission in North Korea. He then had the audacity to betray that trust. While his intentions were clearly honorable, his actions weren't. Arisa's government had a stake in what happened, as well, and *she* definitely had a stake in it.

It wasn't completely his fault. Belasko didn't fully understand the situation or her relationship with Hakajima-*san*. The better part of her career as a special agent for the ministry of foreign affairs concerned bringing down Sumio Hakajima's self-proclaimed empire. The American didn't realize the atrocities the tycoon had committed in the name of good business. Hakajima was an egomaniac with an insane zeal for his own private causes. He didn't want money or power—he had plenty of both. What Hakajima-*san* wanted transcended the plane of reality. The man lived in another world created by his own delusions, and when coupled with his influence it made him one of the most dangerous men in the world. Now she was on a personal crusade to neutralize that danger.

Since her departure for the coastal city, Arisa had listened intently for any news related to the conference. There was a delay but no clear explanations as to why. She knew much of the information surrounding the agenda was classified until the negotiations were under way. In any case, it bought her some extra time.

She considered it fortunate that the North Korean police left the house in Pyongyang unattended. She now wore a change of clothes and an old Miroku .38. The pistol was bequeathed by her father, a decorated policeman in Japan who died in the line of duty, and she carried it as a backup for times like these. The weighty, snub-nosed revolver felt comforting holstered against her side.

Arisa slowly depressed the accelerator of her sedan— her stolen vehicle now abandoned and parked in an alleyway near the house—but not so much that she would lose control on the snow-packed streets. It took her almost an hour to locate the hotel where members of the Japanese Office of Foreign Relations were staying.

Arisa parked down the street from the Mudo Kwan Hotel and exited the sedan. She walked purposefully toward the front entrance and bit back the throbbing ache that coursed through her with each step. Four armed soldiers stood on the sidewalk, drinking something from steaming cups and stamping their feet against the early-morning chill. The KPA troops snapped to alertness at the Japanese woman's approach.

"Halt!" one of the soldiers called in Korean. "State your purpose."

Arisa started to reach inside the pocket of her long wool coat but stopped short when the KPA troops leveled their weapons. She raised her free hand slowly and agonizingly as she withdrew a wallet containing her foreign-ministry credentials. She passed it to the closest soldier while the remaining trio trained the unwavering muzzles of their automatic rifles on her.

The soldier gestured for her to remain in place and disappeared inside the hotel. Arisa complied with the request, confident the KPA troops would open fire with the slightest provocation. The man returned less than a minute later accompanied by an older gentleman dressed in an overcoat similar to hers. The newcomer had Oriental features and a warm smile as he began to speak to her in Japanese.

"What may I do for you, miss?" he asked with a formal bow.

Arisa inclined her head but didn't dare bend at the waist. "I must speak with Makasawa-*san*. It is a matter of national security."

"Who sent you?" the man persisted.

"You have seen my credentials," Arisa countered.

"You have no right to detain me. This is a direct matter for the foreign-relations ambassador."

"I beg your pardon, Agent Kawashita," he replied formally, "but I am Hojo Ieyasu, head of security for Ambassador Makasawa, and I have every right to detain you. Or to deny you admittance if I deem it appropriate."

"I do not wish to be insulting," Arisa managed to reply, bowing ever so slightly this time, "but the ambassador is in danger. I have no wish to discuss this in front of these men. Please..."

The Japanese eyed her for a moment, then studied her credentials. Arisa could see he was weighing his options. He was absolutely correct; she couldn't supercede his authority as a bodyguard for the ambassador. Ishumu Makasawa was a very important man and quite influential within the Japanese society. Many people respected him and just as many posed a danger to him. Arisa's procedure was highly irregular—it was customary to call and leave a message requesting an appointment. She could understand the bodyguard's reticence, especially given the time of morning and her appearance.

"Very well, you must come with me," Ieyasu finally said. He tapped the wallet and added, "However, I will hold on to this for the time being. Are you armed?"

Arisa nodded and pulled her coat aside to reveal the pistol. The man stepped forward and perfunctorily snatched the Miroku revolver from her holster. He gestured for her to follow him after nodding calmly to the soldiers that they should allow her to pass. The KPA guards lowered the weapons, but their eyes tracked Arisa's every movement as she followed the man into the hotel.

The two passed through the interior checkpoint, and an elevator off the lobby whisked them to the top floor. Within a minute, Arisa found herself in a posh, upper-class room with elaborate furnishings. The decor was thoroughly Korean, but Arisa forced herself to dismiss such mundane matters. She was on a mission of importance, and the lives of millions probably hung in the balance with every passing moment.

Ieyasu instructed for her to sit and then disappeared into an adjoining room. Five minutes passed, then ten. Arisa bit back the urge to collapse as another surge of pain washed over her. Leaving the infirmary wasn't the smartest move she'd ever made, but it was a closed matter now. The more daunting task ahead would be to convince the Japanese ambassador that her information was valid, and then he would have to convince the rest of the diplomats.

Arisa immediately recognized Ambassador Ishumu Makasawa when he entered the room, dressed in a black terry-cloth bathrobe with a red dragon embroidered on the left breast. She tried to stand, but the effort was nearly too much and she had to remain seated. She bowed and Makasawa returned the gesture with perfunctory grace.

"Agent Kawashita, it is an honor. Your name is considerably respected in certain circles of influence."

"Thank you, Ambassador. You also are a man of honor."

"What has brought you here on such errant business?" Makasawa asked immediately now that the pleasantries were dispensed.

"Ambassador, you are in danger," Arisa said. Her tongue felt thick in her mouth and she squinted, trying to focus the man's blurry outline. "This entire conference is in danger."

"What?" Makasawa said with a laugh. "What makes you think so?"

"The North Koreans are planning to stage a coup

against the training exercise in Seoul. They plan to strike at this assembly with terrible fury."

"Do you have proof of this?" Makasawa demanded, appearing slightly irritated now. "You have leveled a serious accusation against our hosts."

"You...must...believe me, sir." The words sounded slurred in her ears.

"Agent Kawashita?" His voice echoed inside her head. It rolled across her consciousness several times as if he'd shouted to her from across a deep chasm.

Arisa nodded but the pain was now unbearable. "I...there is a man named Pak In-sung. He is a member of the r-ruling party. He will betray all of you."

Before she could say anything more, her world went black.

GAIESH KOTO CONSIDERED his options.

The arrival of Kawashita Arisa at the Mudo Kwan Hotel hadn't surprised him in the least. He'd watched the entire affair outside the high-rise complex. Arisa had undoubtedly come to warn the dignitaries of Pak's plans. She was extremely resourceful; her escape from the infirmary proved that. It only served to reinforce Koto's assessment of the enemy. Pak's personal minions had underestimated them, and now they were all dead. Some of his men were dead, as well. Oh, yes, his new enemy was extremely dangerous—especially the American agent.

The fact Arisa was in Hungnam did pose an unforeseen problem. Pak probably wasn't aware of this yet. Koto considered going to the North Korean and informing him of these developments, but he dismissed it just as quickly. He didn't work for the man. His loyalties were to Hakajima, and he was here only to make sure that Pak held up his end of the bargain. If things got out of control, then Koto would take action. Until then, the North Koreans were on their own.

The master had called and wanted him to go directly to Kumho. Black Army troops guarding the reactor apparently caught the American trying to break into the site. Koto's orders were to extract whatever information he thought he could from him. Such measures seemed pointless, but Koto would obey. He took no pleasure from torture. He believed in the warrior spirit of the samurai—to do battle on equal terms was the honorable way of his code. He would prefer to meet the American in combat rather than under such putrid conditions. The very idea disgusted him.

The thing that bothered Koto was that Arisa would probably implicate the master in the upcoming coup. He couldn't allow that. He would have to protect Hakajima's interests and silence her before going to Kumho. It suddenly occurred to him that if he could get Arisa out of the hotel alive, he stood a much better chance of extracting information from the troublesome American. What would loosen the man's tongue quicker than if Koto threatened to do away with his attractive cohort?

Coming to a decision, Koto started his car and drove past the hotel. The sun broke above the horizon, and he considered the irony of it. The rising sun—an omen to his skill and dedication. Yes, it was a good plan, a good decision on his part. The master would be pleased with the results.

Koto rounded the corner and left his car at the curb. He got out and quickly studied his surroundings. After ensuring nobody was observing him, he sized up the wall of the hotel, then extracted a very thin cord attached to a steel claw-shaped grappling hook. Koto swung the hook and let it fly up to the third floor. It wrapped around one of the stone balcony railings, and the hooks bit in securely against. Koto tested his weight on the cord, then scaled it with the ease that came from years of conditioning. He landed silently on the balcony and pressed his ear to the window. No sounds emerged from the interior, and within a minute he had the flimsy double door open. He stepped into the warmth of the darkened room and took a cleansing breath.

Only silence greeted him. Koto crept past an open door that led to the master bedroom suite. Through the open doorway he noticed the bed was neatly made and unoccupied. He continued to the front door and disengaged the chain. He opened it enough to slip past the gap and closed it firmly behind him. The hall branched in either direction. Koto spied a door at one end that marked the stairwell and proceeded to it.

He began to ascend the stairs, bound for the top floor.

THE ROOM SLOWLY CAME into focus.

Arisa was lying nude in a bed beneath clean sheets and several blankets. She shuddered with chills, but the pains in her back were considerably diminished. A woman sat in a chair next to the bed and smiled at her reassuringly. She wore a white lab coat, and her hair was pulled back from her head in a traditional Japanese style. A stethoscope encircled her neck, and a name badge hung from the lapel of her coat. Arisa couldn't read the words imprinted on the badge but that was okay. She knew the woman meant her no harm.

"Welcome back, Agent Kawashita," the woman said softly. "Try to relax. You have a high fever."

"Who are you?"

"I am personal physician to Makasawa-*san*. I was summoned after you collapsed in his suite."

"Where is he?" Arisa asked with concern. "I must speak with him."

"No, you must rest," the doctor replied. "You have not been unconscious for very long, but you are severely injured."

"Where is the ambassador?" she repeated.

"He is outside speaking with some of the other foreign dignitaries. He instructed that you not be disturbed."

Arisa wanted to argue with the woman, but that was improper. Physicians were highly respected in Japan, and to contend with them was considered very disrespectful. If the ambassador was speaking to the representatives of other countries, it probably meant he had taken her words to heart. How they proceeded on the information was another matter, but she knew there was little she could do about that. At least she'd managed to get their attention.

Arisa wondered about Mike Belasko. It was possible he was with the men outside her room, but she didn't dare ask. She could endanger his cover by inquiring about him. If word leaked out to Pak In-sung or his people about Belasko's presence, they would probably try to kill him. He had risked his life to save Arisa, and she couldn't take such blatant liberties by interfering. He knew what he was doing, and she would have to trust her conscience with the knowledge that he would only reveal himself if he thought it was necessary.

A soft knock drew her attention. The doctor rose and went to the door, opening it only slightly. There was a brief, hushed conversation, then she stepped aside and allowed Ishumu Makasawa to enter. He was accompanied by a short, handsome man with thick sideburns and mustache. He was dressed in a nice suit that revealed impeccable Western tastes.

"Agent Kawashita," the ambassador greeted her, "it

pleases me to introduce you to Undersecretary Kendall Durham of the American State Department.''

Durham nodded, and Arisa tried to mask her pain with a smile. Beads of sweat broke out on her forehead. She fought back the fresh nausea and concentrated efforts on blocking out her discomfort. Arisa remembered her training and breathed deeply several times to calm herself. The mind controlled the body and Arisa had spent many hours perfecting the self-control that brought balance and harmony between the two.

"It is a pleasure," Durham said quietly. "Your ambassador speaks very highly of you. I understand you risked your life to come here."

"Thank you," Arisa replied.

She turned her attention to Makasawa and spoke to him in Japanese. "Ambassador, I must talk to you. You have to believe me when I say that you're in extreme danger."

Makasawa nodded grimly. "I've already spoken with Undersecretary Durham on this matter. He has offered some valuable insight. It is being handled as we speak. A full inquiry will be made immediately following the negotiations, but we cannot risk insulting the North Koreans prematurely."

Arisa's eyes widened. "But, Ambassador, you must believe me. This conference was called for the sole purpose of luring all of you into a trap!"

"Agent Kawashita," Makasawa interjected, "I have contacted the foreign ministry. They were not aware you had come here. Now, I understand your concern for my safety and it is greatly appreciated. Nonetheless, these are sensitive affairs of diplomacy and international relations. They must be handled with complete discretion and tact. The safety of every member is the individual responsibility of our security teams. Every precaution has been taken.

Now, you are ordered to rest by my physician. You will return to Tokyo as soon as you are well enough to travel.''

"Sir, I do not think—"

"This matter is finished, Agent Kawashita. Do not ruin your good standing by being disrespectful. I am quite grateful for your concern, but I will not tolerate insubordination. Do you understand?"

Arisa sighed with defeat, then fell silent with a nod.

"Take your rest, my dear," he added in a more personal tone. "You have earned it."

With that, the two men departed from the room and left Arisa alone with the doctor. The woman propped her up in bed with pillows behind her and offered Arisa some tea. She sipped gingerly from the cup and fought back the urge to cry.

What she couldn't understand was why her own people were so willing to dismiss her without even verifying the information themselves. The ambassador's assurances were of little comfort. Neither he nor Durham appeared the least bit concerned with the notion that Pak In-sung had some insidious plan for the negotiations. Moreover, their security measures wouldn't hold up against Pak's operation. The party leader had every advantage including surprise and authority. The rest of the delegates were on foreign soil, and their respective governments had little recourse when Pak made his move.

Arisa knew she was too weak to stop Pak herself. All she could do was hope that Belasko was already prepared to counter Pak's plans with one of his own. In the meantime, she would try to regain some strength, then maybe she could help her country and its allies even if they wouldn't help themselves. It meant she would probably have to disobey the orders of her superiors, and that wasn't considered an honorable or respectable action in her culture. As she drank her tea, Arisa wondered what Belasko would do.

The sounds of shouting and people running outside in the hall startled Arisa. The doctor rose and went to the door. She was just about to open it when one of the Japanese security men pushed inside and ordered her to lock all doors and windows. He noticed Arisa in the bed, whispered something else to the doctor and in the next moment he was gone.

"What is it?" Arisa asked as the doctor immediately closed the door and locked it behind her.

The physician began to dart about the room and secure all the windows and the adjoining door where Makasawa and Durham had made their entry. Arisa repeated her question as the doctor returned to her bedside and tried to act as if nothing were wrong.

"Please, you must tell me. I cannot sit here if—"

"Do not concern yourself with this," the doctor said firmly. "The ambassador's men are simply investigating a problem."

"What problem?" Arisa demanded.

"Be silent and rest. This is best for you."

Somehow, Arisa wasn't convinced.

"WHAT'S GOING ON, Ted?" Ken Durham asked.

"I'm not sure yet, sir," Strack replied as he hung up the phone. "Wait here with the men."

The security chief issued instructions for the other bodyguards to remain with Durham, then left the suites. He trotted down the hallway and encountered the head of the Japanese ambassador's security team stepping off the elevator. Strack had met Hojo Ieyasu upon the arrival of his team the previous morning. The man was quiet and proper, but there was no mistaking the competence in his moves.

He seemed trustworthy and carried a reliable aura of strength beneath his unassuming personality.

"What's up?" Strack greeted him.

"Someone has entered the hotel," Ieyasu replied with a pinched, Japanese accent. "A maid saw him leaving a room on the third floor and enter a stairwell."

Strack shrugged. "So what?"

"The room is not occupied."

"Shit. That's not good."

"I thought you would agree."

"We'd better check it out."

Ieyasu nodded, and Strack reached into his pocket. He stepped into the elevator before the doors closed and inserted a key supplied by the hotel management. A quick turn of the lock stalled the elevator on the top floor. Strack motioned for Ieyasu to follow him as he rushed to the stairwell. He pushed through the doors and began to descend the stairs two at a time. As the two men alighted on the next landing, Strack could hear shouts a couple of floors below.

"Those are my men," Ieyasu said.

They continued down the stairs and rounded a corner of the landing in time to see one of the Japanese bodyguards drawing a pistol from beneath his jacket and pointing it at someone concealed just out of view. A foot lashed out and knocked the pistol from the security man's grip. A small, wiry Oriental dressed in black appeared from nowhere and launched a series of vicious punches and kicks. The Japanese bodyguard collapsed under the blinding assault.

Ieyasu pushed past Strack and vaulted off the landing. He hit the bottom in a crouch as the newcomer fired a punch that whistled over his head. The Japanese security specialist swept the attacker's legs and knocked him off balance. The enemy twisted away from the force and quickly regained his feet. Ieyasu executed a side kick, but his opponent easily countered the attack. He pulled the leg toward him and drove an elbow into Ieyasu's sternum. Strack could hear the air forced from the man's lungs as his opponent followed up with a throw that tossed Ieyasu over the railing.

Strack descended the stairs as he drew his pistol and tracked on the shadowy target. He ordered the man to stop and hesitated a moment as the dark eyes stared into his own. Strack squeezed the trigger of his S&W .645, but his first two rounds missed. Before the former Secret Service agent realized it, his enemy was gone, leaving only the slow movement of the door that led into the hallway. Strack continued to the landing and called for Ieyasu.

"I am okay," he shouted, the weakness apparent in his voice. "Be cautious. You must stop him."

Strack shouted a brief word of assurance and then proceeded through the door. He tracked the hallway with his pistol, but only an eerie silence greeted him. He could feel the enemy's presence—their mysterious infiltrator was close. Strack walked down the side of the hallway with his pistol in front of him and his back to the wall. A young woman poked her head out of the door, and Strack immediately ordered her to close and lock it. She nodded fearfully and quickly disappeared from view.

Strack continued until he reached a center hallway that intersected that corridor. He stepped across the hall and pressed himself to the hall, taking a deep breath before he swung his pistol around the corner. That hallway was empty, as well. Strack began to wonder where his quarry might have gone when there was a whisper of movement above him. He looked up as the black-clad wraith dropped from the high ceiling to land to his rear. Strack started to bring his pistol around but he was too late.

He caught the blur of a fist traveling toward his head a moment before a sharp pain hit him behind the ear.

ARISA THREW THE COVERS off her body and slowly climbed from the bed. The relative chill of the room against her bare skin struck her hard, and she sucked in a surprised breath. She padded across the room to a dresser.

"Where do you think are you going, Agent Kawashita?" the doctor demanded.

"Away," Arisa snapped. "It is not safe here."

"This is the safest place you can be!" her caregiver insisted as Arisa began to search the room for her clothes.

"I do appreciate your concern," Arisa said as she located her clothes hanging neatly in a closet, "but this is a matter of security for our government."

"You must not go. Your fever might continue to rise and you could die."

Arisa turned to face the doctor and smiled. As she dressed, she replied, "I would prefer to die on my own terms, Doctor. I think you can respect that."

"I respect it," the woman replied, her pale complexion flushing with her obvious anger. "However, I do not agree with your decision."

"I understand."

Arisa finished dressing and realized that once again she was unarmed. She quickly searched the rest of the room but didn't find any weapons. This didn't surprise her. The only guns allowed on the premises were probably safely in the custody of the security force. They weren't about to relinquish that advantage. Arisa knew she would have to take her chances.

"I must get the ambassador to safety," she announced.

"The ambassador is already in the best of hands. Please

listen to me," the doctor begged Arisa. "Please do not leave."

"You are correct," Arisa replied, ignoring the woman's pleadings. "He will be safer here."

A fresh group of shouts resounded outside the room, followed by gunfire. Sirens wailed in the distance—probably the local police force responding. Arisa went to the window and looked down to the street. The soldiers were still outside and standing their post. It was unlikely anyone could get inside or leave the building, and even less so that the Koreans weren't aware of what was happening within the hotel. That meant Pak was already making his move.

Arisa went to the door, opened it and peered into the hallway. Two of the Japanese security force members lay either dead or unconscious on the carpeted floor. There was no movement and Arisa looked to the right. The door to the ambassador's suite was closed and secured. She stepped into the hallway and quickly rushed to the bodyguards. Both men had a pulse. She reached inside the coat of one of them and felt for his pistol.

Gone! Arisa immediately checked the second man but came up with nothing. She was about to venture down the hallway when there was the slightest hint of sound behind her. In the silence of the hall, she could hear the regulated breathing of a human. Arisa tried to focus on his position—he was definitely male, well-balanced and stood probably an inch or two taller than she did.

Arisa stepped back two small steps and fired a back kick. Against most individuals the blow would have connected. It was easily deflected and a rigid hand grasped her by the shoulder. The Japanese agent tried to swing a back fist at her attacker, but it proved useless. The man drove a rigid spear hand into her solar plexus and knocked

the wind out of her. Arisa crumpled to the carpet and began to wretch. Her spasms subsided after a minute or two,
and she looked up to see her opponent standing over her.

Gaiesh Koto flashed her a cold smile. "I've been looking for you."

CHAPTER SIXTEEN

Kumho

Mack Bolan's toes felt numb in his boots. He stamped them regularly to try to restore some blood flow, all the time considering different plans of escape and then dismissing them just as readily. He had to admit to himself that the situation was beginning to look extremely bleak.

Steve Rueben had spent most of the night with his arms wrapped around his father to keep the older man warm. Shem Rueben probably hadn't said a half-dozen words. As the morning light began to swallow the darkness, the Executioner could see that the man was returning to coherency. He'd stopped muttering some time during the night, much to Bolan's and the younger Rueben's relief.

The interior of their makeshift prison became brighter with each passing minute. Rueben finally rose from where he'd spent most of the night and joined Bolan. His voice was a harsh whisper as he spoke to the soldier, broken only by an occasional glance at his father.

"Hey, Mike. How you doing?"

"Not bad, considering the circumstances." Bolan nodded toward Rueben's father. "How about your dad?"

"He'll be okay," Rueben said. "I think. Looks like

these bastards rolled him pretty good, though. I'd like to kick their collective asses given half the chance.''

"Easy there, soldier," Bolan cautioned. "Don't let revenge get the best of you. It clouds good judgment.''

"Yeah, maybe." Rueben sighed before asking, "Any ideas on how to get out of here?"

Bolan shook his head and began to walk around and move his arms to keep warm. "Nothing that wouldn't get us killed within a minute.''

"A stinking outhouse. I feel like a POW or something.''

Bolan frowned. "This is *nothing* like being a POW, guy.''

Rueben nodded apologetically. "I guess you're right.''

Bolan dismissed the thought and studied Rueben's father. The guy was awake now, and returning the warrior's appraisal with one of his own. Some brightness seemed to have returned to Shem Rueben's eyes, and a sudden thought struck the Executioner.

"Hey, Rueben," Bolan called to the younger man.

"What?''

"Do you think your father could talk to me now?''

Rueben looked in his father's direction. "Dad, you feel like talking to my friend here?" He paused and when there was no response he added, "He's a good guy. Why don't you come to talk to him? His name is Mike Belasko.''

The older Rueben nodded before slowly getting to his feet. He walked out of the corner and into the light where Bolan could get a better look. He was tall and lithe with many of the same features as his son, although the hair was gray and the skin less healthy. Bolan could only imagine what horrors the poor guy had suffered at the hands of his captors, but that was what had interested him.

"Have a seat, Mr. Rueben," Bolan suggested, pointing toward one of the benches.

"Such as it is, eh?" Shem replied in a gravelly voice.

The guy smiled but accepted Bolan's offer and sat. He grimaced in pain with the effort but gritted his teeth against griping or complaining about his discomfort. The Executioner had to admire the man for taking such a beating and not whining about it. Sure, his condition hadn't been exactly great the previous night, but that was only because he thought that Bolan and his son were actually his captors come to deal out more violence.

"Mr. Rueben," Bolan began, "tell me what happened. How did you get into this mess?"

"That's easy," he replied with a snort. "I got too close to the North Koreans and their little scheme here."

Steve Rueben stepped forward, interested now in what his father had to say. "What scheme?"

Shem looked at his son for a moment, then refocused his attention on Bolan. "How did he get involved in this, Belasko? Did you tell him he had to help you?"

"He didn't do anything of the sort, Dad," Rueben cut in. "Jeez, what the hell's the matter with you? This guy saved my ass."

"Why don't we relax?" Bolan growled. "There's no time for that."

The younger man fell silent with a hard look from the Executioner. He put his hands in his pockets and shuddered against the early-morning chill but remained quiet.

Bolan nodded a silent thanks, then studied Shem. "Your son was in Kumho looking for you and I offered to help. I know about the North Koreans, and that someone with the ruling party has something planned for the negotiations in Hungnam. I just don't know what."

Shem studied Bolan for a second, apparently probing him, watchful for some falsehood. Whether he convinced himself that Bolan was okay by what he saw in the soldier's eyes or because what he'd heard had a ring of truth, the Executioner couldn't tell. Either way, the two seemed to reach some silent but mutual understanding and Shem Rueben visibly relaxed.

"Then you only know half of it, pal," Shem declared. "The North Koreans caught me snooping around, and when I got too close they jumped me, knocked the shit out of me and here I am."

"You took a pretty good beating," Bolan agreed.

Shem touched his swollen eyes self-consciously and nodded. "You're telling me."

"Why?"

"What do mean, 'why'?"

"Why did they beat you?"

"Don't ask me, ask them."

"Did they interrogate you?"

"Now that you mention it, I think they did ask me some questions but in Korean. I speak a little bit of the language, mind you, but not that much."

Bolan nodded. "Maybe they wanted to know what you knew."

"I'm sure they did," Shem replied, "but I wasn't about to give those bastards the satisfaction of thinking they got the better of me."

"So you took your lumps."

The older Rueben smiled. "I played stupid."

"You're lucky you're not playing dead now, Dad," Rueben scolded his father. "These people aren't kidding."

Shem pointed a finger at his son. "Don't sass me, young man." He looked at Bolan and continued, "The guy you're talking about inside the party? His name is Pak Insung, and he's a mean SOB. I think the men who rolled me might have been from the security agency."

"Secret police?" Bolan nodded and looked at Rueben.

"The guys in the van. They must have followed us from Hungnam."

"But how?" Rueben replied. "How did they know where we'd go?"

"Did you tell anybody else?" Shem asked.

His son shook his head and shrugged. "Just a guy named Ted Strack. He's head of security for the American delegates."

"Makes sense," the older Rueben announced. "They've got all the hotels wired for sound."

"They tried to send a few for me shortly after I got there," Bolan said, now understanding who was behind the attack at his motel. "What do you know about this Pak?"

"Not much. I tried to dig up what I could on every one of the North Koreans attending this peace gig. Pak is one mysterious character. He's probably the most powerful man in the country next to the premier, but there's very little known about him."

"I'm sure that's by design," Bolan commented.

"He's also got somebody on our side working with him."

Bolan's curiosity was piqued. "Who?"

"Now, I can't be a hundred percent sure here," he cautioned, "but I'm figuring it's somebody working for the Japanese."

"Maybe somebody from the KEDO office?"

He splayed his palms and shrugged. "Could be, I suppose."

Bolan reached into the cargo pocket of his fatigues and withdrew the information he'd procured from his recon of the KEDO liaison building. He handed the communiqués to the older Rueben and pointed to the names of its recipients. He also gestured to the numbers and made an inquiry regarding the information.

"Well, neither of these guys sounds familiar," Shem said, indicating the two American KEDO members. "But I'll bet these numbers at the bottom mean something."

"I already figured that much."

"Well, let's see. If I were a betting man, I'd say these KEDO guys were on the take."

"Those numbers could be monetary amounts," Bolan said matter-of-factly. "Maybe the money financed by Sumio Hakajima."

"Who?" Shem interrupted.

"Hakajima's a Japanese businessman who's been using Pak to keep an eye on the reactors for the sake of the missile project."

"What project?" Shem asked.

"The Taepodong III," the Executioner explained. "They're bringing the delegates from the conference here, but it's not the conference they're interested in. This isn't a tour they're going to conduct. It's a demonstration."

"Holy shit," Steve Rueben said slowly. "If they *have* built a missile here, do you think what you said last night is true? About them dropping that thing on the troops in Seoul?"

"I don't know," Bolan replied. "That was only a theory."

"But is it possible?"

"Anything's possible. But I don't see what that would accomplish. Sure, it would kill a bunch of South Korean and American troops, but that's hardly a devastating blow."

"Killing forty-thousand-plus soldiers isn't devastating?" Shem asked incredulously.

"Not in the long-term sense," the soldier said. "No lasting benefits."

"So what are they up to?" the younger Rueben interjected.

"That's what I plan to find out."

The Executioner was just about out of ideas when he looked at the dark openings ranged around their makeshift prison. It suddenly occurred to him that there had to be some kind of sewage runoff—a piping system that sent the excrement somewhere. He considered that perhaps it was a self-contained system but quickly dismissed the thought. The North Koreans would never have allowed something like that. It would have violated their religious laws regarding cleanliness and affected their hygienic sensibilities.

Bolan broached the idea with the other two men.

"You're kidding, right?" Rueben argued. "You mean you really want to go down there?"

"Unless you have a better idea," the Executioner shot back.

He looked at Shem after the younger man shook his head to indicate he didn't. "You?"

"That's not going to be too pleasant, Belasko, but you're right. I don't see any other alternatives," Shem conceded.

Bolan nodded, then stripped the canvas military load-bearing belt from his fatigue blouse. He gestured for the two men to follow him and then led them to the nearest hole. He handed the web belt to Rueben, who took it with a skeptical expression, and then leaped onto the toilet area. He sat down and put his legs down through one of the openings, then grabbed one end of the belt.

"You two lower me down," he instructed father and son.

"You got a light?" Shem asked.

Bolan shook his head. "I'll have to wing it."

Shem reached into his pocket and withdrew a small, cardboard box of matches. "Here, these might help."

"Bad idea," the soldier said. "There's probably methane gas and lots of it. I don't feel like incinerating myself so soon."

"Oh, yeah," the man replied, putting them away with a shrug. "Well, it was the thought that counted."

"Yeah, all that methane, Mike," Rueben interjected. "And you're going to breathe it. I'm not so sure this is a good idea."

Bolan tossed him a reassuring smile. "Don't sweat it. I'll be all right. And I'll come back."

"See that you do," Shem Rueben snapped.

"Count on it," the Executioner replied, and with that they lowered the soldier into the cold and putrid darkness.

EXITING THE Mudo Kwan Hotel with his prize didn't prove difficult for Gaiesh Koto, considering the commotion. The remaining security forces were more worried about protecting their assignments than preventing anyone from leaving, and Koto used that fact to his advantage. It was joined with the simple fact that Kawashita Arisa was in no condition to resist him.

The sun peaked in the bright blue, cloudless sky as Koto entered Kumho. The markets and downtown commercial areas were unpopulated in the aftermath of the heavy snow, cutting down on the number of visible pedestrians and vehicles. His luxury car bounced along the uneven hills and ruts of compressed snow that formed a slick, treacherous sheet of heavy ice. Koto wasn't used to driving in such weather, and he fought the wheel with every maneuver. He willed himself to remain passive, to simply feel the road ahead of him. The antagonistic nature of the drive slowly ebbed from his conscious thought as his control continued to improve. It was an illustration he wished his pupils and underlings could have seen. Perhaps it would have taught them the power and strength that could be drawn when one used the mind to overcome the body— or to control destiny, for that matter.

Koto spared an occasional amused glance at his prisoner as she struggled against her bonds. Arisa was as obstinate and self-sufficient as he'd come to realize over the years, and she would return his looks with cold defiance. The Japanese enforcer couldn't bring himself to feel threatened. He knew this prize he held was infinitely more valuable. His prisoner knew it, as well, which made the thought only that much more pleasing to him.

"You will not succeed with me," Arisa snarled. "Given the chance, I will kill you with my bare hands."

Koto said nothing and refused to look at her again. This was the most degrading and insulting thing he could have done to her. The master wouldn't allow it to go beyond that. He began to consider his plan to use her against the Americans. He couldn't actually kill the woman—he didn't really know how far he *could* go. It had always been clear that anyone who dared eliminate the meddlesome foreign agent would incur the master's ultimate wrath. Yet, Sumio Hakajima trusted Koto implicitly and would never strike his faithful servant down without due cause. The Japanese martial artist would have to use his soundest judgment in this case.

When Koto arrived at the Kumho site, the guards admitted him quickly and one jumped into the back seat to direct him. Koto followed the KPA soldier's instructions and soon pulled parallel to a plain square building constructed from dilapidated cinder blocks. He estimated it was about forty feet square and looked like an old outhouse. A strong odor after he exited his North Korean luxury car told Koto his original assessment was accurate. He walked around the front of the sedan as the Black Army soldier brutally tried to pull a kicking, squirming Arisa from the front seat.

Koto interceded and easily shoved the special-forces soldier backward. The Korean staggered from the seemingly light, effortless push. He got to his feet and dusted himself off as he reached for the rifle.

"Do not do this," Koto warned him quietly in an even tone. "I will kill you before you have time to pull the trigger."

The Black Army trooper hesitated as Koto pointed to Arisa.

"This is my prisoner and I will deal with her. No one else. I work with the authority of Pak In-sung. Is that clear?"

The guard nodded, his dark eyes boring into Koto. He relaxed and Koto could tell the guy planned to bide his time. He would probably try to jump his new enemy when Koto least expected it. Not that there would ever be such a time. Koto would welcome the challenge to toy with the Black Army soldier for a while before maiming or perhaps killing him.

Koto reached into the car and effortlessly plucked Arisa from the seat. He escorted her into the building after obtaining some information from the guards just outside the door. It seemed they had three prisoners, all American, and one of them was definitely the big one who had single-handedly eliminated Pak's entire mercenary group. It was news he accepted eagerly.

Koto anticipated the meeting. He needed to see this man for himself and to discover his weaknesses. Although he wasn't consciously aware of it until that moment, Koto had let his curiosity fester into almost an obsession. He didn't understand why he felt that way but the fact remained. The chief enforcer found it difficult to believe this American warrior could elicit emotions from him. It took the reins of control from him, and this was something that normally Koto never allowed to happen. *Never.*

The Japanese met two more men inside, including the leader of the Black Army detachment sent there under personal orders from Pak. Koto couldn't remember his name, but he knew the man was a personal aide to General Hap Mung-Li, who would command the rest of the Black Army forces in coordination with the master back in Pyongyang.

One of the most frustrating things for Koto was the secrecy with which this entire operation was conducted. There were things about the master's alliance with the North Koreans that even he wasn't privy to, which caused him some distrust and uneasiness. The master had never withheld information from him before, but it seemed he was holding back in this case, and Koto couldn't understand why. Not that it mattered. His sole purpose in life was to serve Sumio Hakajima, and he would honor that bond to the death.

They arrived before a heavy metal door and the guards unlocked it with a large skeleton-type key made of thick brass. Koto pushed Arisa inside the room before entering himself and saw two figures standing in the shadows on the far side. Neither of them seemed to present a threat, and Koto suddenly realized there was something missing.

Koto turned to General Hap's aide. "One of the men outside said you had three prisoners. Where is the third?"

The man looked dumbfounded for a second, then ordered his men to sweep the vast interior. One of them covered the two in the corner while the remaining pair scoured the open, smelly outhouse turned holding cell.

They reported back negatively, and the aide's face filled with fury. He marched to the two remaining men and stopped just behind and to the left of his machine-gun-toting guard.

"Where is the other American?" he demanded in heavily accented English. "Speak!"

"Up yours," Steve Rueben replied.

The officer whirled toward his men, his face red with anger. "Send out an alert! One of the prisoners has escaped and I want him found! *Hurry!*"

The Black Army soldier whipped a radio from his belt and began to speak rapidly into it.

Koto left instructions to guard the rest of the captives, including Arisa, then whirled and exited the cell. The one prisoner he was most anxious to confront had escaped. However, it was good because Koto could now feed off his blood lust. And his hunger would increase as he drew nearer to the enemy.

IT TOOK THE Executioner quite some time to gain his bearings in the slippery sludge of the knee-high wastewater. The walls were slimy and cold to the touch, but the soldier knew it was no time for nit-picking. He had a job to do and he could worry later about amoebic dysentery or any one of the other hundred diseases he might contract from such an environment. The temperature belowground was comparatively chilly to say the least, and it did little to suppress the pungent odors that assailed his nostrils.

Bolan forced himself to ignore his conditions and concentrate on escape. He traversed the walls and continued to feel for some kind of opening. He'd covered a considerable part of the area and was about to give up hope when the wall suddenly disappeared and the soldier nearly toppled into the muck facefirst. He regained his bearings and

waved his hand around the opening until he found the edge
where the wall had vanished. He let his hand run along
the opening and realized it was a large, circular egress
from the septic tank.

The Executioner emerged from the mucky wastewater
and stepped onto the dry floor of the tunnel. He put his
body in a crouch and duckwalked along the tunnel. The
soldier maintained contact with his surroundings by running one hand along the wall and the other just in front of
him. He couldn't afford to meet any sudden drop-offs.

The minutes ticked by slowly and eventually turned into
a couple of hours. Bolan wondered if he would find his
figurative pot of gold at the end of this crude rainbow. He
imagined the surprise of his captors when they discovered
he was gone. He knew the Rueben men wouldn't tell them
a thing, even at the risk of a beating. Both of them were
good guys, and the Executioner had to admire men of their
caliber. They deserved the warrior's respect and they had
it.

Bolan had to admit that he didn't have the first clue on
his next move. Things were moving at a breakneck pace.
The luncheon was undoubtedly wrapping up in Hungnam—if not already concluded—and the delegates were
probably on their way to the reactor site. On the off chance
they hadn't departed yet, Bolan realized it was unlikely he
could get out and find a way to contact Grimaldi before
they did leave. That left him with only one alternative: let
the situation play out and see what happened.

The Executioner hardly found that acceptable. It seemed
obvious that only a short time remained before zero hour,
and the clock was ticking relentlessly. Moreover, the soldier wasn't even sure if his assessment of Pak and Hakajima's plan was correct. He didn't have the first idea on
where the Taepodong III missile was located *if* it even

existed, and he didn't know how Pak planned to handle the diplomatic entourage scheduled to tour the reactor sites. To add insult to injury, Bolan couldn't determine Hakajima's part in the plan, either. There were still too many variables and unanswered questions.

Bolan suddenly realized that the tunnel was getting brighter. He continued traversing the tunnel for about two more minutes, then the floor began to slope downward in front of him. The soldier followed the tunnel as it descended, then rounded a corner after maybe twenty yards. There was a bright light ahead of him now, and he picked up the pace. Within five minutes, he emerged through an opening that led into a concrete pool of brackish-looking water.

The pool was surrounded by a walkway that led along a trail bordering large cylinders. The hum of machinery was evident, and there was a definite warmth that felt good against Bolan's tired, aching muscles. His legs were cramping, and he dropped gingerly to the walkway with relief. A further inspection revealed a set of metal stairs that ascended to a grate-type walkway above the central part of the vast room. It didn't take long for Bolan to conclude he was in a water-treatment plant, probably an unmanned facility.

He vaulted up the steps, soon found an exit door and pushed through to descend some more steps to the rocky, half-frozen ground. The fresh air of outdoors hit him like a gust of wind, and Bolan counted himself fortunate. Fate had smiled on him this time. In another sense, his elation at escape was short-lived when he considered his newest predicament. He was somewhere deep in the heart of North Korea with no transportation and no means of communication. His clothes weren't dry and the temperature would drop quickly with the sun. He was also without supplies or weaponry. But other than that, the Executioner felt fine.

Until a KPA truck suddenly swung around a large stand of trees and roared toward him.

CHAPTER SEVENTEEN

If the Executioner had learned anything in his long career as a soldier it was that the best strategy against an enemy was sometimes the one that made the least sense. Bolan decided to apply that theory and took off at a hard sprint in the direction of the truck.

The surprised expressions of the driver and officer in the cab were obvious through the windshield. The driver reflexively stomped on the brake. Bolan terminated his suicide course at the last second and grabbed the mirror mount on the passenger side as the vehicle slid past him. Yells and curses of surprised men in the back of the truck reached the soldier's ears as he opened the door and yanked the stunned officer from his seat. The man sailed past and slammed into the frozen, packed earth.

Bolan jumped from the truck's running board and knocked the officer unconscious with a rock-hard punch to the point of his chin. He reached inside the officer's hip holster and withdrew a pistol just as the driver leaped from the cab and ran around the front of the truck. He clutched a Chinese Type 56-1 assault rifle. Bolan spun to one knee, snap-aimed and fired three times as the driver raised his own weapon. The 7.65 mm Browning rounds slammed home, two ripping through the stomach and the third puncturing a lung. The heavy rounds lifted the driver a few inches off his feet and slammed him against a tire. The

Executioner leaped up and sprinted toward the driver's side, scooping up the assault rifle on his way. He climbed into the truck as the now recovered KPA troops began to pour from the rear.

Bolan waited until the last possible instant, then put the truck in gear and nailed the accelerator. The tires spun against the hard ground as the vehicle lurched into motion and tossed the remaining occupants onto their disembarked comrades. He swung the truck into a one-eighty and accelerated toward the confused KPA troops. The disheveled group dived in every direction to avoid the five-ton missile bearing down on them. Bolan swung the assault rifle out his side window and shot two soldiers attempting to draw a bead on him. A couple more died under the impact and bone-crunching weight of the Executioner's newly acquired transport. The soldier could hear a few stray rounds strike the bed of the truck, but he was well out of range before the opposition could recover.

The element of surprise had worked well for him in this case. Actually, he was lucky his rash move hadn't cost him his life and he knew it. Nonetheless, Bolan chose to look at his actions from a tactical standpoint. Yeah, he'd bargained with fate but it wasn't the first time. Sometimes a soldier just had to work from the gut. And this time, like every time before, it paid off. Now he had transportation and a little bit of firepower.

He needed to find a phone and touch base with Grimaldi. Then he would deal with Pak.

Stony Man Farm, Virginia

"WE'VE RECEIVED some new information, Hal," Barbara Price announced as she entered the War Room.

Brognola stood behind Kurtzman; the two of them were focused on a terminal screen linked directly to Stony

Man's vast mainframe system. They had spent the past few hours trying to sort through the complicated itinerary of the conference in Hungnam, and develop a foolproof theory that might explain a conspiracy between the DPRK ruling party and COR-DEF Industries. It would have been a lie for Brognola to tell the mission controller they were making tremendous progress.

Price carried a thick red folder in her hands with Confidential marked all over it. She dropped it on the table and slumped into her chair. The fatigue was evident in her eyes and rumpled clothing—she'd hardly slept a wink since Bolan's departure. The coffeepot was working around the clock, and Brognola had to admit he was beginning to feel the effects of their vigil with no end in sight. He could only imagine what the Executioner had to be going through and contemplated where Bolan might be right at that moment.

"What's the story?" Brognola asked tiredly, leaving Kurtzman to his task and taking a seat across from Price.

"We've managed to obtain some concrete evidence that would tie Hakajima with the North Koreans *and* the Kumho reactors," Price said.

"Explain."

"Hakajima's been involved in the project from the get-go," she began, "although never directly. The guy has his fingers into every phase of this thing but he's managed to bury it under one corporate front or another. JAPEX is a shipping company that sends monthly supplies and equipment to Kumho. SUMO-CORP provided the electronic equipment that they'll use to control and monitor the reactors. Back in 1999, TOK-REAC won the bid to manufacture nuclear rods for plants in the U.S. Now they're doing the same for the Kumho reactors."

Kurtzman whirled in his chair and cleared his throat. "Hey, I remember that."

His statement didn't come as a surprise to Brognola. Kurtzman's mind compared to a steel trap, and there didn't seem to be any limits to his mental file. He constantly processed information into his computer to maintain Stony Man's monstrous database. His practice of cramming computer memory with bit pieces of seemingly worthless information might have seemed futile to outsiders. Brognola understood the man quite differently, however, and occasions repeatedly arose where those practices paid off.

"Go on, Aaron," the Stony Man leader prompted.

"Well, the NRC did this huge study on more cost-effective means of energy production for the country," he explained. "The results showed that TOK-REAC could produce the rods at a fraction of what it cost domestic manufacturers without compromising quality. Congress then signed this huge deal with them and they set up house right here in the States. Before long they were working for other countries, as well."

Brognola nodded with interest. "So it stood to reason that when KEDO was formed, the United States would sponsor TOK-REAC to manufacture the rods."

"Right," Price said. "And guess who owns all of these companies?"

"COR-DEF Industries?"

"Right again."

"The Man didn't seem convinced when I told him of Striker's theory about Hakajima working covertly with subversives inside the DPRK."

"That doesn't surprise me," Price replied. "Hakajima has a good reputation in the corporate world. In most cases, his companies well exceed ethical standards. He's considered a respectable businessman and entrepreneur. He donates sizable sums of money and support to worthy organizations everywhere, and he has the ear of some of the heaviest political hitters in the world."

"Maybe so," Brognola interjected, "but there's one question no one seems to be able to answer, including Striker."

"Which is?"

"What does Hakajima stand to gain by the completion of the nuclear reactors in Kumho?"

"That doesn't make a whole lot of sense to me, either," Price said. "There's no love lost between the North Koreans and Japanese. They've always considered Japan nothing more than a U.S. puppet."

"I have to concur. There's something else here we're not seeing." Brognola looked at Price. "What about your friend Arisa? Did she give you any sense of her government's position on Hakajima?"

Price nodded. "Arisa works as an intelligence officer for the Japanese foreign ministry. Her superiors have members in KEDO, as well. She thought it was possible Hakajima might stage a disaster. Perhaps an accident similar to the kind in Chernobyl. But those accusations are totally unfounded."

"And that still doesn't give us a motive," Kurtzman said.

"I know."

"One step forward and two back," Brognola said gruffly.

"I'm very concerned about Arisa, anyway," Price added. "She was left injured at an NSA safehouse in Pyongyang. They had her in the infirmary for the diplomatic community, but she disappeared and nobody has the first clue where she is."

"What about Striker?"

"Also MIA," Price replied. "I spoke with Jack a short time ago. He's lying low at some place in Hungnam and hasn't heard anything from him in the past eighteen hours."

"Do you think there's a relationship between their disappearances?" Kurtzman asked.

"I don't see how," Price stated. "Hungnam and Pyongyang are practically on the other side of the country from each other."

"Well, I knew it would be difficult to keep tabs on Striker," Brognola offered. "We know he made contact with Durham of the State Department."

"How did Durham become involved in this, Hal?" Kurtzman asked.

"He's the undersecretary for global affairs at the U.S. State Department. The members in the KEDO liaison office work directly under him."

"Moreover," Price added, "he's one hell of a smooth operator. The guy could charm the habit off a nun."

Brognola chuckled. "I guess that's one way of putting it. Nonetheless, the President takes great stock in his powers of persuasion. I've met Durham personally on several occasions, and he's definitely a suave diplomat. Smooth and urbane as they come."

"By the way," Kurtzman said, turning to his computer and punching in a coded number on the keyboard, "I did manage to find something that I thought might help us."

Brognola and Price fell silent and waited with interest. There was little they stood to gain by brainstorming the situation further, but Brognola wasn't prepared to rule anything out just yet. Somewhere they missed a vital piece to the puzzle—some link in the chain of events that continued to elude them. And if anyone could find it, Kurtzman could.

"Ah, here it is," Kurtzman said absently, studying the screen as he spoke. "I dug through every record I could find when we pulled up the information on Hakajima and that Cho Shinmun. It took a while for me to get everything, but I ran into an interesting little tidbit."

"On Hakajima?" Brognola asked.

"Yeah," Kurtzman said with a nod. "Remember how Striker had mentioned Daewoo Precision Industries manufactured those K-2s? It seems one of Hakajima's other ghost companies machined parts for them. North Korea became very interested in the efficiency of the company for the same reasons the U.S. did. At the time, the individual interested in them was a minor official by the name of Pak In-sung." Kurtzman turned in his chair and frowned. "Today, Pak is a senior member in the ruling party."

Brognola's eyes became wide as he realized the implication. "You think that's Hakajima's partner?"

"Well, it seems more than a coincidence that Pak is also on the list of DPRK delegates scheduled to attend the conference," Kurtzman replied. "He's also a major influence on DPRK officials that spoke out against this training exercise in Seoul."

Price inhaled sharply. "The training exercise. You don't think—"

"Yes, I do," Kurtzman said grimly. "It's possible this Pak has something very nasty planned for the conference. Maybe he's going to send a more forceful message about the training exercise. Maybe one in the form of a certain missile."

"Well, I'll be damned," Brognola said hoarsely.

"We'd better call Jack," Price suggested.

"Do it. ASAP," Brognola ordered. He turned to Kurtzman and added, "Aaron, get the Pentagon on the phone and pronto."

Kumho

MACK BOLAN STOPPED just outside the city and found a phone where he could reach Grimaldi. The ace pilot promised to meet him within the hour, even if he "had to set the plane down on the site itself." The Executioner had no doubts that Grimaldi meant what he said, and something in his gut told him he was going to need the Stony Man pilot before all was said and done anyway. It was time for action.

Bolan abandoned his truck about half a mile from the reactor site and now watched from a small rise as the first score of vehicles arrived with the delegates from Hungnam. The cars and utility vehicles passed through the gates with increasing regularity. The soldier suddenly remembered that Durham and Strack would be riding in one of those cars.

Chances were good that the North Koreans probably had something set up inside the site, maybe a tour through the completed reactor that was undergoing tests. They would want to impress the visiting dignitaries with technological gadgetry and awe them with the power that even one of the huge facilities could produce. Then when they were most vulnerable, Pak would make his move. But so would the Executioner.

Nonetheless, his next problem involved weapons. Bolan knew he couldn't go far on five rounds in the Type 64 pistol and about two dozen 7.62 mm in the assault rifle's 30-round banana clip. That meant he would need to acquire additional firepower before he could rescue Steve and Shem Rueben or stop Pak from whatever plan the party official had in store for the peace conference. The guard shack near the front gate seemed like a logical place to start.

The sun was falling quickly as Bolan crawled toward the gate. He counted a half-dozen guards along with a couple of plainclothes men—probably members of the security agency. Shem Rueben had indicated Pak used them regularly, and that meant there was a good chance the party leader was already here. Good. At least Bolan wouldn't have to go far for his enemy.

The Executioner reached the fence line and lay still as he sized up the group. Most of the men stood at the gate and relaxed, smoking and talking while the two plain-clothes officers made frequent trips into the guard shack to escape the biting chill, which increased as night drew nearer. Bolan kept himself prone and waited patiently for the right time to move. He crawled toward them one small movement at a time.

The shadows seemed to swallow him up, and the guards didn't see him even when it appeared one or two were looking right at him. The eyes could play tricks on sentries after a while, especially as they grew more restless and uncomfortable. They would probably cut the security by half once the remaining delegates arrived, but Bolan didn't have that long.

When he was practically within spitting distance of the nearest guard, the soldier rose to a crouch and aimed the muzzle of the assault rifle at the center of the group. He unleashed a hail of fire, and the 7.62 mm ammo shredded flesh as it tore through the six guards.

The two security officers burst from the shack, reaching for their weapons as the bolt locked back on the Executioner's rifle. The soldier dropped and rolled several times as the North Korean pair aimed and fired at him a moment too late. Bolan came to a crouch, the Type 64 pistol clutched in a two-handed Weaver's grip. He sighted on his targets and fired two shots. The first round dropped one of the plainclothes agents, but the other missed its intended target.

The survivor was joined by the senior guard, and the two men rushed to converge on Bolan's position, trying to pin him down with erratic fire. The soldier stood his ground and returned their shots, ignoring the buzzing rounds that zipped past his head. Bolan's marksmanship paid off, one of the cartridges taking the security agency man high in the chest while the other drilled through the Black Army officer's head. Both men were dead before they hit the ground.

Bolan rose and quickly collected weapons and all the ammunition he could carry from the dead guards, including a pair of AK-74s. He intermittently looked through the fence and waited for a storm of KPA or Black Army troops to come, but they never did. Obviously, the front gate to the site was too far from the actual buildings to warrant attention. Bolan went into the guard shack and located a small panel with a monitor that displayed a picture of the gate and two switches. He flipped both of them and watched the black-and-white video monitor as the gates began to part obediently at the center. The Executioner retraced his steps outside and rushed through the opening. He would have to find Strack and Durham first—he needed to get them alone and warn them about Pak.

Quickly but cautiously, Bolan pressed onward toward the completed reactor. He didn't follow the road that wound through the site from the gate to the reactors themselves, electing to make the trip cross-country. He would make much better time that way. The reactors seemed to be an eternity away even though Bolan could see their outlines loom nearer on the horizon with each step. The sun was finally gone and the twin, domelike structures seemed to glow in the large lights that reflected off their gleaming surfaces.

Bolan thought of the Ruebens as he got closer to the reactors. He had no idea where exactly to find the outhouse where they were prisoners. Moreover, he didn't have any assurances the men were even still alive. Pak might not have risked the delegates discovering that there were American prisoners on the grounds. Assuming, of course, that Pak didn't have the same plans for the rest of the men and women of the conference.

The negotiations had definitely put a twist on Bolan's mission. His original task was to rescue Yang Tae-jung from imagined peril and investigate claims of the Taepo-dong III's alleged existence. Now he was attempting to rescue delegates from an unknown fate crafted by men he'd never seen, much less heard of. Bolan shook his head with the irony of the whole thing, and with the complexity of it. Even if he managed to thwart Pak's plans, it didn't put him any closer to stopping Hakajima. There was no way he could bring himself to just let the Japanese crime lord walk. He was too close to this thing with the North Koreans. If Bolan let him slip away, Hakajima would just return at another opportune moment and create some other havoc. No, he had to stop them both.

It took almost forty minutes for Bolan to reach the re-actors, but it was worth the effort. The slew of cars and utility vehicles he'd seen pass through the gates were now parked neatly next to one another outside a nondescript entrance to one of the nuclear power facilities. Bolan crouched in the brush that lined the uncompleted parking area and watched for sentries. There was no movement inside the vehicles, and he didn't see any sign of drivers or guards.

Bolan stepped from the bushes and trotted past the ve-hicles until he reached the plain door set into the side of the building. He opened the heavy, metal door painted drab gray, which moved soundlessly and easily on its new hinges. The door led into a narrow corridor that terminated at another door.

The Executioner quickly crossed the expanse and opened that door a crack. The room beyond appeared to be a large, circular space with amphitheater-type seating that faced a central stage. Many of those seats were now filled with representatives from the conference, as well as their security teams and the drivers. On a small dais on the stage stood a small Korean man dressed impeccably in a fine suit with a green-and-yellow armband. There was some sort of Korean symbol on the armband, but Bolan couldn't make it out clearly from his position.

Things looked quiet enough, and the Executioner began to rethink his plan. It was possible he'd made an error in judgment. It didn't appear there was any trouble, and Bolan couldn't help but consider other options. He'd spotted Durham, Strack and the rest of the American group but signaling to them would have drawn the kind of attention he didn't need. After all, he was attired in urban camouflage fatigues, smelling of human waste and toting enough firepower to start a war.

A moment later it didn't matter.

A DOZEN Black Army commandos suddenly appeared from doors scattered throughout the top tiers of the room.

"What is the meaning of this?" Ambassador Ishumu Makasawa demanded, leaping from his seat.

"Sit down!" Pak In-sung spat.

The party leader directed several of the Black Army troops to keep the delegates under cover while the remainder descended the stairs and quickly disarmed the security agents.

Ted Strack looked at Durham, who just nodded quietly and indicated he and his team should surrender their weapons. Strack had to think long and hard before he finally obeyed. It wouldn't do him or his people good if he resisted. They would probably gun them all down.

Once the task was accomplished, Pak called for the outraged group to calm down so that he could address them. It took some time to get the situation under control, but the delegates finally quieted and the room was once again in order. Pak gestured for them to take their seats and don the headsets that would provide translations to the respective representatives in their own languages.

"Honorable members of the Hungnam Peace Conference, I do apologize for this intrusion," Pak began. The individual interpreters probably wouldn't convey his words with the same affability, but the tone in his voice would hopefully fill the language barriers. "These men are North Korean special forces, and they are here only for security purposes."

"Bullshit," Strack muttered. He looked up and tried to count the seemingly endless row of automatic weapons dangling above their heads.

"Please do not misunderstand our intentions," Pak continued. "We will happily return all side arms to your security teams as soon as we can suppress the emergency. In the meantime, you may enjoy the complete freedom of our beneficent protection."

Strack leaned over and said to Durham, "I'd give real money if someone would just shoot this prick, sir."

"Since you have all taken time from your busy schedules to come to our beautiful country," Pak droned, "we have prepared a pleasant surprise for you. One that is sure to attract your interest. If you would direct your attention to the large monitor on my right, I will be happy to show you the fruit of efforts by those countries represented here today."

All eyes turned in the direction of the monitor. The area was strategically placed so that everyone in the room, regardless of where they were seated, would have a clear view. A series of fuzzy lines and static appeared but were then replaced by the huge, cylindrical-shaped picture of a missile. The room became deathly quiet, leaving only the cackle of Pak's laugh.

"I see that perhaps I understated your reaction," the party leader said in a victorious tone. "You are quite surprised by what you're seeing. It probably will also come as some surprise that you are now prisoners of the Democratic People's Republic of Korea.''

"Prisoners?" Durham said, rising now and pointing his finger at Pak. "What right do you have to hold us prisoners? We're not at war!"

The delegates began to murmur among themselves and some even stood with Durham and shouted protests, as well. The quick clack of bolts from the rifles above silenced any further outbursts.

"I am truly sorry that I must implement these emergency procedures," Pak replied, "but I have just received word that we are, in fact, at war. At this very moment, a unit of South Korean troops from the Seoul training exercise has advanced over the demilitarized zone and into North Korea. They are now attacking North Korean citizens. Until we can confirm this information with the South Korean authorities, we must protect ourselves."

Durham slowly lowered himself to his seat and looked at Makasawa, who sat nearby. Strack noticed the exchanged looks of worry between the two men, and he could see they'd been misled by Pak. So Belasko had been right. Now, there was nothing he could do to help the guy stop Pak. He would just have to wait with the rest of the group until an opportunity presented itself.

BOLAN JACKED the slides on the two AK-74 rifles. He pressed his back to the wall and began to wonder if a forward assault was the best. If he came through the door with guns blazing, he stood the chance of starting a firefight and putting the delegates at considerable risk. On the other hand, he had the element of surprise in his favor and he knew Strack would rally the others to turn on their Black Army guards in the few moments of confusion.

Bolan formulated a plan and then counted to three before yanking open the door. He pointed the muzzles in opposite directions, aimed for the two closest targets and squeezed the triggers simultaneously. A volley of 5.45 mm rounds crashed into the Black Army troops and slammed them into the doors from which they had emerged. Bolan didn't wait for the other soldiers to respond before he shouted for Strack to seize the advantage. The security forces present acted with admirable competence, pushing the delegates to the ground, then going after the nearest Black Army troops.

The Executioner initiated covering fire as the troops above prepared to shoot the unarmed group below. Smoke belched from the muzzles of the AK-74s as the soldier poured on the firepower. Several more Black Army commandos fell under the random shots as Strack's men and several of Makasawa's protectors overpowered the troops on the ground level. They were in control and had neutralized the special forces by the time Bolan dropped the last trooper on the upper level.

The delegates slowly began to get to their feet as the Executioner crossed the room and shook hands with Strack. The big ex-Secret Service agent smiled from ear to ear.

"Nice job, Belasko!" he boomed.

"Likewise," Bolan replied with a quick nod. He turned to the undersecretary. "Mr. Durham, all of you have to get out of here. Now."

"We'll be happy to," Durham said, "just as soon as you explain what's going on."

"No dice," the soldier snapped. "I've got work to do, and you don't want to be here for it."

"For what?" Durham pressed.

Bolan nodded toward the screen. "I'm going to destroy that missile."

"And you will fail!" Pak In-sung's voice echoed in the soldier's ears.

CHAPTER EIGHTEEN

"That's what you think." The Executioner crossed the room to the dais and snatched Pak by the collar, yanking him away from where one of Strack's men had him covered. Pak tried to hide the fear behind a chuckle as Bolan nearly lifted him off the ground.

"I should think not," he said. "You are too late."

"That thing hasn't launched yet," Bolan replied angrily, snapping his head in the direction of the monitor. "Shut it down."

"I cannot," Pak insisted. "I've already told you that you are too late."

"Shut it down," Bolan repeated, pressing the muzzle of the AK-74 under Pak's chin, "or I'm going to strap you to the side and send you on to whatever final destination you have planned for it."

Pak began to stammer now, obviously fighting to hide the tremor in his voice, but he seemed unable to suppress the shaking in his small frame. "You fool! It's not here. Besides, I do not have the authority to launch the Taepodong III. That is not the true aim of the party. South Korean troops have invaded the north, and this is enough to make my government act."

"This is ridiculous!" a South Korean dignitary interjected. "We would never do such a thing."

Bolan silenced the man with a hand of caution, then

revisited his attention on the quaking man before him. "So the real target was the training exercise in Seoul?"

"Yes," Pak mumbled.

"And Sumio Hakajima is your partner?" the soldier pressed.

Pak nodded.

"The whole thing was a ruse. The attack on Haeju, the imprisonment of Yang and the threat with the missile bought you time to manipulate the training exercise in Seoul. Right?"

"You are just as I suspected," Pak said in way of reply. "Clever, insightful and self-reliant. A formidable enemy. It does not surprise me that you were able to defeat Cho Shinmun and his men so easily."

"Do you have any idea how many people have died because of this?" Bolan snarled. "Or do you even care?"

Pak remained silent. The soldier dragged him down the steps of the dais, then up an aisle until he reached Strack. The look in his eyes spelled death as did the gnawing in his gut. He couldn't do something that would create an international incident until he had all the facts. His first inclination was to blow off the ruling party leader's head, but that wouldn't have served any purpose. The North Korean government would deal with him. He tossed the party leader into Strack's waiting arms, then surrendered one of his AK-74s.

"Keep this guy covered," Bolan ordered. "There are more troops somewhere near here who are holding Steve Rueben and his father prisoner."

"No shit?" Strack replied with disbelief. "So that's what happened to his dad."

Bolan nodded. "Yeah. He apparently stumbled onto their little plan and they locked him up. I'll find them and get them out. Keep things in hand here until I get back."

"Check, boss," Strack replied quickly, nodding his assent and tossing a look that showed he recognized Bolan was in charge. "Anything else?"

"Start evacuating the delegates back to Hungnam." The soldier turned to look at Durham and added, "All of them."

Durham decided not to argue with Bolan, and the soldier knew he could at least be grateful for that fact. He got the keys to one of the American-rented utility vans from Strack's driver and proceeded toward the assemblage of vehicles parked outside. As he left the room Strack called after him.

"Hey, Belasko, watch your ass! These people mean business!"

"Count on it," Bolan shot back before exiting the reactor building.

He quickly found the sport utility and climbed behind the wheel. The engine roared to life with the first turn of the key, and the vehicle was angling down the main road within seconds. It took him about fifteen minutes to wind his way back to the front gate. He tried to get his bearings and remember which way the van had turned when he and Rueben were captured. In the hazy light of a half moon, Bolan spotted a makeshift trail cut along the fence line. He swung to the left and followed it toward what he was certain had been his prison just a few hours before.

It seemed obvious to the Executioner that Hakajima was running the show outside of Seoul, whatever it might be. There was no telling what the Japanese crime lord was up to, and he didn't have time to get it out of Pak. He still needed to rescue the Ruebens. Once they were safe, he would have Grimaldi fly him to Seoul and try to figure out what was happening there.

Ten minutes passed before Bolan met a rise in the trail. The engine hummed with increased power as he topped the small hill and immediately spotted the familiar cinder-block building in the near distance. The Executioner quickly killed the lights on the utility vehicle. He checked the load in the Type 64 and AK-74 before going EVA. Bolan approached the building on the run, keeping low and wasting no time in his approach. The seconds ticked in his head as he mentally readied himself for resistance.

The first appeared in the form of a KPA regular trooper stepping outside the building to light a cigarette. He never saw Bolan. The warrior was within ten yards before the KPA soldier heard him. The man whirled and reached for his rifle, but Bolan was more than ready for such a play. He leveled the muzzle of the Type 64 pistol and squeezed the trigger on the run. The 75 mm slug bored through the man's chest and ripped at heart muscle. Blood sprayed from the fatal wound as the soldier dropped to the ground.

Two more troopers suddenly appeared, but Bolan had the AK-74 locked and loaded in his fist. He aimed the barrel in the direction of the startled duo and opened up. The echo of the reports was thunderous in the cold, still air as a mass of 5.45 mm rounds blew holes in them. Steel-cored projectiles punched gruesome spiral patterns and ripped away flesh, spilling the intestines of one of the soldiers onto the ground. Both men collapsed to hard earth.

Bolan stopped and frisked the bodies until he found the key to the cell door. He rounded the corner of the entryway and stopped short. A small but well-built Asian man stood blocking the path to the Ruebens' cell. He was dressed in black, loose-fitting pants with matching top, and a red sash encircled his waist. The sash was just like those worn by the men who'd attacked Arisa's headquarters in Pyongyang. The only difference he noted was that this man's belt was embroidered with black-and-gold lettering that looked like either Chinese or Japanese.

The Executioner raised the pistol and squeezed the trigger, but as the gun bucked in his hands, he noticed his target was no longer there. The bullet slammed against the back wall and tore a large furrow in one of the cinder blocks. The crack left in the crumbling wall wouldn't have nearly compared to the one left in Bolan's head had his senses not alerted him to trouble. He ducked in time to avoid a rigid hand slashing toward his temple. The man seemed to materialize next to Bolan where he'd stood at least five or ten yards from him just a moment prior.

The soldier dropped to one knee and tried to fire a shot toward the man's midsection, but his attacker leaped over him and flipped through the air. He came to rest almost soundlessly behind Bolan as the Executioner turned to face his opponent. This guy was definitely as good as those men he'd faced in Pyongyang, possibly better. Bolan was guessing this was another one of Hakajima's goons.

The soldier leaped to his feet and struck up a defensive fighting posture. He didn't want to risk the time and effort with hand-to-hand combat, but it quickly became apparent small-arms combat wasn't ideal in such cramped quarters. The pistol was suddenly jarred from his hand as a foot contacted the ulnar nerve in his wrist. Bolan swung the stock of the AK-74, aiming for the enemy's head, but the little man simply stopped the maneuver by shattering the stock with his forearm, snatching the weapon from Bolan's hand and tossing it away.

The Executioner nodded curtly at his enemy. "Hakajima doesn't know when to quit, does he?"

"You have repeatedly interfered with the master's plans," the man hissed. "Now you will pay for your interference. And your insolence."

"And I suppose that's why he sent you?" Bolan inquired.

The Japanese martial artist smiled. "You are correct. Now you are dead."

"I feel okay. Who are you anyway?"

He appeared to seriously consider Bolan's question and finally replied, "It is unimportant, except that a man should have the right to know his executioner."

Bolan was almost humored by the reference.

"You may know me as Koto."

Koto leaped through the air and snapped a perfectly executed side kick. Bolan managed to twist away enough to avoid the blow intended for his sternum. The human missile instead landed on his ribs. The sheer force of the kick knocked the wind from the soldier and sent him reeling into the corridor wall. He slid to the ground and rolled away, gritting his teeth with the agony. He'd definitely fractured a rib or two. The Executioner again sidestepped fate, inadvertently rolling just before Koto reached down to hammer a fist into his solar plexus. The martial-arts expert slammed his hand against a cinder block and broke a good portion of it from the wall.

Bolan got to his feet and tried to balance on wobbly legs. He was increasingly winded from the fight. The man before him was extremely fast and decidedly powerful. He had a warrior's cunning and strength, and he didn't give up. There was something uniquely adversarial in his attitude toward Bolan, and the Executioner pondered the oddity of that thought. If Koto had somehow become obsessed with him, Bolan knew he might be able to taunt the man into making a mistake.

"They build you guys slow," the soldier stated.

Koto's eyes flashed with anger, and the mask of discipline was now gone. The Japanese killer leaped forward and tried to gouge out Bolan's eyes. The soldier ducked to the right and stepped back several feet, always allowing himself a way out.

"I think that other guy of yours back in Pyongyang," Bolan continued, "was faster than you."

"You are a fool," Koto spit.

"Yeah. And you hit like a schoolgirl."

Koto became angry and screamed a mouthful of obscenities. He leaped from the floor and tried to do a spinning double kick, but the soldier simply dropped to the ground and let his furious enemy pass harmlessly overhead.

Bolan whirled as Koto landed on the opposite side of the corridor. He looked down and noticed the AK-74 lying nearby. The Executioner jumped for the weapon a moment before Koto realized what he was thinking. The Japanese killer rushed to stop Bolan, but the soldier already had one fist around the handle as Koto reached him. He swung the jagged edges of the shattered stock against Koto, tearing fabric from his shirt and ripping ugly gashes in the skin of his belly. The martial artist let out a cry of surprise and stepped backward, staring incredulously at his stomach as blood began to pour freely from the deep wounds.

Bolan immediately knew they weren't serious enough to kill his enemy. The soldier spun the muzzle of the AK-74 in Koto's direction and winced with the pain in his side as he did. Koto ducked under the barrel just microseconds before Bolan squeezed the trigger. The weapon chattered thunderously within the confines of the hallway as Koto threw his shoulder into the Executioner's gut. The blow staggered Bolan and knocked him down. His enemy was on him. The Japanese enforcer straddled him and wrapped a viselike hand around his throat. Koto began to squeeze, and the light around the edges of the soldier's vision quickly became dim and blurry. If he didn't do something quickly, he knew his chances of survival were slim to none.

Bolan realized he still had the AK-74 in his grip, but both of his arms seemed pinned by the deadweight of Koto's knees. However, he could turn his wrist and it was enough to swing the barrel of the Russian assault rifle into action. He pressed the barrel against Koto's back and depressed the trigger. A half-dozen rounds cored through Koto's back and tore vital tissue from his lungs, liver and right kidney. Koto arched his back for a moment, then began to convulse with the sudden shock of his injuries. Blood began to run from his mouth as he leaned to the side and slowly slid off Bolan.

The Executioner lay there a moment and caught his breath. He carefully disentangled himself from Koto, then painfully got to his feet. He stopped a moment to stare at the body of Hakajima's late enforcer and wiped a mixture of sweat and blood from his forehead. He reached up and discovered a new, tender cut above his eyebrow. He couldn't remember actually obtaining the injury, but it wasn't that important.

Bolan turned and rushed to the cell. He quickly inserted the key into the door and stepped into the interior. It was much darker and smelled better than he remembered it, but that wasn't surprising. After his little romp through the belowground sewers, this was a paradise in comparison. Bolan was merely relieved to see the fresh and excited faces of Steve and Shem Rueben. It was the third face that surprised him—a lovely feminine face but a surprise all the same.

"Arisa?"

Kawashita Arisa smiled at Bolan. "I was beginning to wonder if you would come back for us."

"Yeah, Belasko," the younger Rueben chimed in. "Where the hell you been?"

"It's a long story."

"We must hear it later," Arisa announced. "Right now I have very important information for you. The other man working with Hakajima-*san* is the head of the ruling party. His name is—"

"Pak In-sung," Bolan cut in with a nod. "I already know."

"What?" Arisa replied. "But how could you know this?"

"Another long story. I have a lot of long stories. What I don't have a lot of right now is time to tell them. There's some transportation outside."

"Then we shall talk on the way," Arisa said, marching past Bolan and heading for the front door.

As Steve Rueben walked past Bolan, he grinned. "Guess she told you, Belasko, huh?"

Shem Rueben said nothing as he walked by, but Bolan couldn't mistake the slight smirk that played on his features. The Executioner followed the trio outside and around the back of the building to the van that brought them there. They also found the younger Rueben's smashed sedan and Bolan's bag of weapons and gear was still in the back seat. The enemy had obviously figured there was nothing of value inside their car. Either that or they hadn't even bothered to look. In any case, it would give Bolan the opportunity to clean up and change before Grimaldi arrived.

They all climbed into the van, Arisa in the front seat with Bolan behind the wheel. Father and son rode in the back. Bolan started the engine and let it warm up before turning and pointing them in the direction of the reactors. He stopped a moment so that and he and Arisa could bail from the van and jump into his borrowed sport utility vehicle. The Ruebens followed them in the van, and Bolan led them across the bumpy trail.

Arisa hadn't said a word up to this point, but Bolan could tell there was something on her mind.

"What?" he prompted her.

"I beg your pardon?" she replied.

"What do you want to say to me?"

"What makes you think I have anything to say to you?"

"Cut it out and get to the point, Arisa," Bolan growled. "I'm not stupid."

"Why did you leave me in Pyongyang?" she blurted angrily.

The loss of sudden composure and childlike tone in her voice seemed very uncharacteristic to the Executioner. He was a little surprised at her question, but he didn't need to consider his answer before replying.

"Well, the fact you were unconscious and bleeding probably had something to do with it."

Arisa glanced in his direction, and the look on her face showed hurt. "There is nothing humorous in what you say."

"Wasn't intended to be," Bolan replied with a shake of his head. "You couldn't do anything else for me at that point, and I needed to get to Hungnam. I knew they would take care of you."

"They took excellent care," Arisa replied coldly, "except the point at which they let Hakajima-*san* into my room."

Bolan shot her a look of incredulity. "What are you talking about?"

"This is not important," Arisa replied quickly, shaking her head. "He came merely to taunt me and that was a foolish error. It is when I discovered he was working with Pak In-sung. But this is not the point."

"What is the point?"

"That you left me after I helped you. I have a mission here, as well, and it is to stop Sumio Hakajima at any cost. You deserted me, left me for dead with men I did not know. What kind of man would do this?"

Bolan stomped the brake pedal and brought the utility vehicle to a skidding halt. He could hear a squeal of protest coming from the van behind them as Steve Rueben had to jam on his own brakes to avoid rear-ending them. The Executioner turned in his seat and tapped his beautiful but spunky, outspoken accomplice on the shoulder.

"Listen up, lady, because I won't repeat myself. A lot of people are dead on both sides, and for no other reason than Pak and Hakajima. I want both of them to pay just as much as you. The difference is that I have everybody to think of in this thing."

"But this does not excuse—"

"Shut up a second, I'm not finished," Bolan cut her off. "What do you think is really going on here? Do you believe that Hakajima is pulling the strings on this thing alone? Think about it, Arisa. There are North Korean military officials involved in this operation, not to mention members from your foreign-ministry office. Maybe even some people from the U.S. State Department."

"You mean members of our own government?" Arisa asked in disbelief.

"Possibly. I don't have any solid proof yet. The point is that I couldn't take the time to worry about you. I got you medical attention and figured you were out of danger. If that's abandonment, then I guess I'm guilty. But remember that's only your opinion. The safety of bystanders is paramount. Needs of the many, remember?"

Arisa nodded slowly and the look in her eyes was filled with resignation. "I owe you an apology. You are correct, of course. The safety of civilians is our highest consideration. I will not forget this again."

Bolan nodded before returning his attention to the trail and continuing toward the twin reactors illuminated on the horizon. He hadn't enjoyed lecturing her, but Arisa was going to have to remember that he had a job to do. It wasn't a time for personal feelings and he certainly hadn't come to North Korea to play slap-and-tickle with the other intelligence organizations involved.

Right at that moment, the two Koreas were on the brink of war. Somebody from the South was probably on the phone with the North Korean premier trying to explain why troops had crossed the border. The Thirty-eighth Parallel was the DMZ between the two countries. It wasn't only a blatant act of war but also a violation of the armistice for either country to enter any portion of that area with weapons of any kind. The situation there was quite similar to that in Guantánamo Bay, where a mere twenty yards of DMZ zone between two fence lines was the only thing to separate long-time bitter enemies.

There was nothing that could stop a full invasion force now if the South Koreans *had* in fact violated the armistice. The Executioner was having a tremendously difficult time believing that. The whole thing was a setup by Pak— the ruling party leader had already admitted that much. What Bolan didn't know were the specific details. One thing was certain. He needed to get to Seoul and neutralize the enemy before their actions sparked a war.

When Bolan arrived at the reactors with Arisa and the Ruebens, he was greeted by the beaming face of Jack Grimaldi. The men shared a brief moment of handshakes and back-clapping outside the reactor building before Ted Strack appeared with the AK-74 hanging from his shoulder.

"What's the word?" Bolan asked the former Secret Service agent.

Strack shook his head. "That Pak is an asshole. He's still refusing to talk, although I consider that a blessing in disguise. I got all of the delegates out of here in a hurry, just like you said. They're under armed escort back to Hungnam."

"What about Ken Durham? What's he planning?"

"Durham's hot, man," Strack replied, shaking his head again. "He's going to file a dog pile of complaints about this whole situation. I don't think he's very happy with you, either."

"Tough. I can't please everybody, and he's at the bottom of the list right now."

"I understand."

The Executioner turned to Grimaldi. "You are definitely a sight for sore eyes, Jack."

"Likewise." Grimaldi excused them from the rest of the group and pulled his friend away for a private aside. "We've got big trouble, Sarge. The Farm called right after you did. They say this Hakajima guy has his fingers deep into both the reactor project and the missile. They figure the real target is the training exercise in Seoul, but I guess you already know that now."

Bolan nodded. "Pak In-sung was the other half of the puzzle. With him in custody, Hakajima's the only one we have to worry about. We need to—"

The sound of gunfire inside the reactor cut Bolan short. He unslung the AK-74 and gestured for Strack to accompany him. He quickly ordered Grimaldi to stay with Arisa and the Ruebens. Once Strack had joined him, the Executioner moved inside the building. The two proceeded to leapfrog down the hallway and entered the building in time to see the two guards fall under a hail of gunfire. About twelve KPA soldiers fanned out and rushed toward Pak.

Bolan swung the muzzle of his assault rifle at three of the men closest to Pak before the bodies of their victims hit the ground. He squeezed the trigger and rode the rise of the muzzle, keeping the weapon low to maintain accuracy. The steel-cored rounds slammed home. One KPA trooper was sent spinning into a second man just before his comrade's head disappeared in a hail of slugs. The third danced around with each hit before crashing into a row of chairs. Bolan was already tracking on more troops before the first three had died.

Strack pressed the butt of the AK-74 tightly against his shoulder and lined the sights on a group trying to spread out in the crowded confines of the amphitheater-type room. His first shots were high, but he quickly corrected his aim and knocked out a pair of soldiers standing too close to each other. The force of the impacts flipped them over the seats and into the row behind them. Strack was sighting on a new target when something burned in his gut and drove the air from his lungs. He staggered backward, dropping his rifle when he looked down to see parts of his intestines hanging out of his body.

Bolan saw the hit, but there was little he could do about it. Four soldiers on the upper rows had him pinned down. He fired on them as the remaining KPA soldiers swept Pak through an exit door on the opposite side. The Executioner watched helplessly as his one link disappeared from view. He cursed himself for not having Strack send Pak with the rest of the delegates. Well, it could have put the entire group at risk then. It was better to have it out here where there would be fewer casualties. One by one, the enemy covered their escape with a load of automatic-weapons fire.

Bolan managed to drop the last KPA soldier just as he had reached a door on the overhead tier. The warrior left his cover and rushed to help Strack. Blood and damaged tissue covered his stomach. One look told Bolan he wouldn't be able to stop the clutches of death for Strack now. Even as he looked at the bodyguard, he knew the man was fading. A moment later, his feelings were confirmed—Ted Strack was dead. His memory would certainly live with the friendly ghosts within the deep recesses of the Executioner's mind.

Bolan got to his feet and stared at Strack another moment before turning toward the door that led from the reactor building. He wouldn't bother pursuing Pak. The greater concern now was to stop whatever was transpiring in Seoul. It was time to dish out some of what he'd been taking and give back to the enemy. Yeah, it was time to end this war and do it quickly.

The Executioner gripped the AK-74 tighter as he left the reactor building.

CHAPTER NINETEEN

"I'm running out of time," Mack Bolan announced to the weary group.

"Agreed," Grimaldi replied.

The two men stood near the Learjet Grimaldi had parked close by the perimeter of the Kumho reactor site upon his arrival. Arisa sat on the ground and tried to ease the pain in her back. Steve and Shem Rueben stood near the Executioner, listening intently as he looked over a map of Seoul and the immediate areas surrounding it.

"According to Pak," Bolan continued, "a large unit of troops crossed the border into North Korea."

"Okay," Steve Rueben interjected, "but what we don't know is where."

The Executioner nodded and turned his attention to Jack. "I need you to get me to Seoul. Pronto."

Grimaldi gestured his assent and then climbed into the plane to prepare for their departure. Bolan studied the layout of the Korean border and shook his head. The possibilities were endless. How effective Bolan would be against the enemy would depend largely upon two factors. First, he would have to find the group. This probably wouldn't present too much of a problem if he could get Stony Man to utilize satellite technology. Troop movement was fairly easy to detect if the unit was large enough. The second problem was a bit more practical in its scope. Who was the real enemy and how many of them was he up against? It was a given he wouldn't face actual South Korean army soldiers, so that left either a military faction from the North or some kind of specialized squad—maybe a larger version of Cho's group.

There were so many questions that remained unanswered, and Bolan knew it would continue to be a mystery until he could actually locate and identify the enemy.

"I'm going with you," the younger Rueben announced.

Bolan shook his head. "No dice. You need to stay here and take care of Arisa and your father."

"They can take care of themselves," Rueben argued. He pointed to Arisa and added, "Especially her. And my dad can use that SUV to get back to Hungnam."

"Doesn't matter. I've got enough blood on my hands. I don't need to add yours."

"Look, Mike, you're not the only one with a stake in this," Rueben protested.

"I must agree with him, Mr. Belasko," Arisa added. "You are being rather obtuse in your assessment of the stakes."

Bolan looked at all three of them. "Was I obtuse when Arkwright got killed?" He gestured absently in the direction of the reactors. "Or Ted Strack?"

He looked coolly at Steve now. "Your dad's been beaten nearly to death, and Arisa here's still not up to par. Sorry, but I can't let anyone else get involved."

"I already am involved," Rueben snapped. "Besides the fact I'm AWOL and it's time for me to get back to my unit. If they're in trouble, then they're going to need me."

"I don't have time to stand here and argue."

Rueben turned and marched toward the plane. He stopped at the hatch and turned on his heel. "Then we'll argue on the way to Seoul. You can't stop me from going, Belasko.''

Bolan studied the young man. Rueben was definitely a tough customer and he had a point. He'd risked his neck to help the Executioner. Sure, Bolan had returned his favor and helped him find his dad, not to mention pulling him out of their filthy prison. Nonetheless, Steve Rueben had contributed to the soldier's success in his own way and carried his weight through a tough time. And aside from the physical sense, there really wasn't anything Bolan could do to stop Rueben if he wanted to go. He looked at Rueben's father, who shrugged helplessly, then returned his gaze to the younger man.

"All right,'' Bolan conceded, "you can tag along. But the rules still apply.''

"I know, it's your show,'' Rueben said as he turned and vaulted into the jet.

Bolan nodded and then turned to Arisa as the engines began to whine. She got to her feet and looked into his eyes. There was still something unquestionably desirable beneath the exquisite visage; it was the same look she always gave him. She had a gentle beauty wrapped around a soul that the Executioner knew was tough as nails. Something bothered him about her expression and he mentioned it, practically shouting to be heard above the steadily growing roar of the plane.

"What is it?''

"I must follow Pak,'' she replied. "He will surely go to wherever Hakajima-*san* is.''

"No.'' Bolan shook his head. "Go back with Shem Rueben to Hungnam. Don't go after Pak or Hakajima or anybody else, Arisa. I mean it. I'll deal with them.''

Arisa nodded but Bolan wasn't convinced. She wouldn't listen to him—it wasn't in her nature. She was independent and scrupulously correct in her observations. Perhaps Bolan had allowed himself to become blunted to the involvement of others in the present situation. Arisa was only trying to protect her people, just as Bolan was trying to protect his. But the Executioner knew the most effective way to do that. Alone, as always, because that was the method that allowed for the fewest errors and least loss of life.

He turned and shook hands with Shem Rueben before boarding the plane himself. He spared one last glance at them before closing the door. Bolan signaled for Grimaldi to proceed, and they were airborne in a short time.

Grimaldi set the plane on autopilot as Bolan joined him in the cockpit. Steve Rueben was already asleep, and his snoring reached the two men up front. The Executioner tried to relax and catch up on his own sleep, but rest wouldn't come. He was too restless, anxious for the upcoming action. He let his mind drift and tried to concentrate on his plan but it was difficult. The lack of sleep combined with little food and the smell that clung to his filthy body served as distractions. He still hadn't changed his clothes or cleaned up—he would definitely have to attend to that before meeting with the commanding officer in Seoul.

"Where exactly do you want to go, Sarge?" Grimaldi asked, obviously aware that Bolan was having trouble sleeping.

"Rueben said the headquarters for the exercise are located at the Eighth Army base in the central section of Seoul. The joint-forces commander is a four-star by the name of Dearbourne."

"How cooperative do you think he'll be when he hears what you have to tell him?" Grimaldi ventured.

The soldier shrugged but kept his eyes closed and his head propped against the back of the seat. "Doesn't matter. We'll already have Hal pulling strings by that time.

Speaking of which, I need to touch base and bring him up to snuff.''

The Executioner reached between them on the console to find the special satellite communications hookup. Bolan thought a moment of the numeric codes before punching the number he'd memorized for that day into the handheld receiver. There was a brief whir over the line, followed by clicking sounds before the voice of Barbara Price came through loud and crisp.

"Hey, soldier," Price greeted him. "Are you all right? Jack said—''

"I'm in one piece," Bolan cut in sharply. He quietly added, "Thanks. I need to talk to Hal right away."

"Hold on, he's right here."

The head Fed's voice echoed in the Executioner's ears like a cymbal. "Striker, what's going on? We've been trying to get in touch with you. Aaron's pulling his hair out with a gob of new intelligence."

Bolan chuckled lightly. "And just when I was beginning to think you cared."

"Fill me in."

He explained the situation in detail, and Brognola listened in contemplative silence. It took the soldier a bit of time to get through his narrative, but there were definitely grunts and groans on the other end of the line as he updated the Stony Man chief. When he finished, Bolan waited for some reply. He didn't have to wait long.

"Aaron can give you more on Hakajima and what we've uncovered. And you're right about Dearbourne. I'll see to it you get every cooperation. I happen to have friends in high places who want results."

"I'm afraid that might not help me in Ken Durham's case. I lost his respect."

"It's no loss, believe me."

"That doesn't sound good."

"I'm afraid it isn't," Brognola replied grimly. "Durham may be heavily involved in this little stunt Pak In-sung pulled."

"I kind of wondered," Bolan interjected. "He seemed pretty resistant to the idea of confronting Pak. I think he got the Japanese and South Korean delegates in his corner, as well, under the fear of straining negotiations."

"Well, we have evidence that suggests he was taking kickbacks from Hakajima's numerous corporations," Brognola explained. "The State Department's investigators are looking into it now. Looks like sizable amounts of cash were deposited periodically into personal and investment accounts, and it appears they are from rather dubious origins."

"Sounds like you have it under control."

"At least we've convinced ourselves we have," Brognola quipped. "Hang tight and I'll put Aaron on the line. And Striker?"

"Yeah?"

"Good luck."

"Thanks."

Bolan could hear the sincerity in his friend's voice. The soldier's lonely existence bore few close friends, but Harold Brognola was definitely one of them. From their earliest ties, Bolan could remember seeing something in the big Fed that seemed honest and decisive. Moreover, he couldn't say he knew a man more dedicated to the safety of the entire world. Brognola wasn't in it for just America—he was in it for all mankind.

"Hey, Striker," Kurtzman said over the digital, satellite linkup system that was his own brainchild. "I've got a lot here but I'll try to break it down in bite-size chunks."

"Do it," Bolan prompted him.

"First, there's the issue with Hakajima. This guy managed to get his companies in the bidding for the Kumho reactor projects because at that time nobody had any reason to tie him to Pak. While his business did manufacture rods and what have you, they also managed to use that as cover to assist Pak and his cronies in building the Taepodong III. There's only one problem.''

"What's that?"

"The Taepodong III doesn't exist. It's a pipe dream!''

"What are you talking about?" Bolan asked, unconvinced with what he was hearing. "I saw the thing, Bear.''

"Live and in person?"

"No, through a—" Bolan cut himself off. "That Pak is one slick operator.''

"Uh-huh, and that's not all," Kurtzman replied. "We're fairly certain that Hakajima doesn't know the money actually went to line the pockets of some pretty heavy hitters within the ruling party and KPA.''

"Payoffs for the training exercise?"

"Correct. Not to mention supplies, weapons and a whole bunch of stuff requisitioned through the KEDO liaison office and approved by the Japanese foreign ministry. They took one look at the stuff, saw Hakajima's name on the bill of goods and then stamped their approval all over the damn things.''

"Meanwhile," Bolan interjected, "Hakajima and Pak are getting ready to pull off the greatest deception in military history.''

"You guessed it," Kurtzman agreed. "They had everyone fooled. Even our intelligence organizations.''

"What can I expect out of them from this point?"

"Well, it hasn't been difficult to track the movements of these renegade South Koreans. Amid a considerable hubbub of international press, our staff in Hungnam managed to determine that the hostilities weren't initiated through any official channels of government. As this is really our baby, the South Koreans have agreed to let us handle it and the North is waiting to see just how we do that."

"I hear a 'but' coming here."

"Yeah," Kurtzman said more quietly. "They've given us twenty-four hours to implement some kind of control on the situation. Otherwise, they will."

"That shouldn't be a problem. It's identifying the enemy that will be tough. Will this Dearbourne be of any help to me?"

"Hold on a sec," he said suddenly. There was a brief pause before he returned to the line. "Hal said to tell you that the word's being passed over to Wonderland right now. You should have all the cooperation you can handle."

"Check that," the Executioner said. "Tell him I'm on it. Out here."

Bolan ended the call and returned the cellular phone to its position between him and Grimaldi. He craned his neck to check on Rueben in the RC-35's cabin before noticing his old friend's askance expression.

"We're going to get this Dearbourne's cooperation. Right?"

"Supposedly," Bolan replied. "Hal says so anyway. If anything I'll need fresh weapons and equipment."

"And transportation," Grimaldi reminded him. "Preferably something fast and maneuverable."

"Right. Nothing Pak or Hakajima have done to this point's been half-assed. If Pak was telling the truth, they'll go for broke on this deal."

"What kind of numbers do you think you're up against?"

"A lot," the Executioner replied.

ARISA HAD NEVER BEEN this close to catching Sumio Hakajima. She wasn't about to give that up, regardless of what Belasko thought. What bothered her most was the turn her relationship had taken with the tall, dark-haired American. It seemed he cared nothing for her or her mission now. He had his own enemy to fight. She wished him well, but it didn't mean she could turn her back on her own mission.

Arisa couldn't bring herself to tell Belasko the entire truth—he wouldn't understand. The whole thing went much deeper than he could have imagined. Arisa had many reasons for wanting to end Hakajima's criminal reign, not the least of which was the safety and welfare of all the Japanese people. Part of it stemmed from a sense of duty to her government. She could understand this part of Belasko's ideology—he did what he did out of duty. But the deeper reasons that drove them on divergent courses were not so blatantly obvious. Perhaps she'd been unfair then in calling him obtuse. He wasn't really a bad man; his focus was simply different from hers. She refused to blame him for that.

Arisa rode in silence as Shem Rueben drove them back to Hungnam. Once there, Rueben went to make contact with the American delegates. He wouldn't have too much trouble gaining access with his press card. During the trip, he'd told her of his many victories in the media. He was a well-known and respected journalist with worldwide connections. He would be fine.

After arriving in Hungnam and talking briefly at the hotel with Ken Durham, the two said their goodbyes and Arisa climbed behind the wheel of her sedan. She did a U-turn, waving at Rueben as he stood outside the hotel and watched her drive by, then headed down the road that would take her back to Pyongyang.

Barring military checkpoints or an unexpected encounter with North Korean police, she would make it to the city by early morning. The entire country would undoubtedly be on stepped-up alert as the news of the pseudoinvasion spread. Arisa even pondered the possibilities of never reaching Pyongyang if martial law was declared throughout the country. She could only hope that North Korean officials from the southern borders would convince the government that the entire thing was an elaborate hoax.

As to finding Pak and Hakajima, Arisa knew exactly where to look. Before leaving the Mudo Kwan Hotel, Ken Durham released information to her and she would be happy to pass it on to Mike Belasko, of course. Belasko had apparently given Strack a telephone number and asked him to trace it. The number finally came back listed to a residence in the country just north of Pyongyang. Arisa was guessing that's where Pak had gone, and wherever Pak was at, it was more than probable Hakajima-*san* would be with him. At least she wouldn't have to face Koto—Belasko had finally dealt with him once and for all.

Actually, it surprised Arisa that Belasko defeated the Japanese enforcer. Koto had always been a man that instilled fear in his opposition. Hakajima-*san* would not take the news of his death lightly. Arisa had never liked Koto. He'd leered at her in her younger days when she stayed at Hakajima's huge rural estate well outside the spherical influence of Tokyo. Koto watched her like a dog watched someone setting food before it. His eyes had hungered with desire.

That was just one of the many things that Arisa recalled about living with Sumio Hakajima. Nothing she could remember about her uncle was happy. Her thoughts were tainted by the horror of discovering what he did and who he really was. She couldn't remember exactly how she'd come to find out about Hakajima-*san*'s sordid past, but it was of little consequence now. Remembering it again now only made her shudder.

Seoul, South Korea

JACK GRIMALDI WAS GIVEN immediate clearance to land at the Eighth Army base in Seoul. Larger planes such as cargo transports and major MAC flights apparently had to land at the civilian airport, but there would be no such necessity for the small RC-35.

A quick plug into the Stony Man's computer banks via the invaluable satellite linkup and onboard laptop gave Bolan the rundown of both the base and its commanding officers. The place was actually called Yongsan Garrison, and it was located in the heart of Seoul. Yongsan maintained the lifestyle of a small suburb, boasting almost eight million square feet of building space and covering nearly sixteen hundred acres. It was home to the United Nations Command, U.S.-ROK Combined Forces Command, the U.S. Forces Korea and the Eighth U.S. Army. Much of the logistics and operations responsibilities for the training exercise rested on the shoulders of the Thirty-fourth Army Support Group, including base support to all units in the designated sites known as Area II, which spanned some twenty-two installations and subinstallations. According to the information Bolan glanced through, the Thirty-fourth ASG had its work cut out.

The Learjet touched down and taxied to a nearby oversize Quonset hut. It was a drab and dilapidated building, but it served its purpose along a row of identical structures. The unusually warm and balmy weather that evening, combined with the military surroundings, reminded Mack Bolan of his first jaunt into Vietnam. There was something all too familiar about Army airstrips in Asian countries—something the Executioner could readily identify with. Little had changed since the Vietnam War. The enemy was still at large and Bolan had a duty to do. He shook off his reverie and focused on the task ahead.

Six MPs in camouflage and full battle gear greeted the trio as they disembarked from the Learjet. Bolan took the lead with Rueben behind him and Grimaldi bringing up the rear. The soldier noted one of the military policemen was a lieutenant. The man stepped forward and saluted him. Bolan was a bit taken aback by the gesture. Brognola had definitely pulled some strings, and the Executioner realized he had no idea whom Dearbourne had been told to expect.

Bolan decided to play the game and see what evolved. He returned the man's salute smartly.

"Welcome to Seoul, sir," the officer said quickly. "I'm Lieutenant Mercer. I've been instructed to take you straight to General Dearbourne at the training exercise headquarters."

"That's fine, Mercer," Bolan replied. "But I'd appreciate a shower and change of clothes first."

"Of course, sir," Mercer replied. "This way."

The man led them to a waiting government van, a GMC repainted in OD green. Mercer and one of the MPs climbed aboard while the remaining four took station in an M-998 Hummer parked behind the van. Bolan took the rear seat with Grimaldi next to him and Rueben positioned behind them. The driver put the van in gear and soon they were cruising across the airfield and headed directly toward a set of squat brick buildings illuminated in the distance.

Yongsan Garrison was definitely vast. It had a huge lodge known as the Dragon Hill along with a commissary, AAFES facilities, the 121st General Hospital and more than eight thousand individual quarters. Yongsan was also home to more than one hundred tenant units and headquarters for all of the major subordinate units in South Korea. Bolan had to admit that he was impressed with the size of the base considering its foreign roots, and he could see for the first time why the North Koreans might be nervous at the thought of so many troops training that close to their border.

The driver stopped the van before the first brick building he came to, and the groups bailed from their respective vehicles. The lieutenant showed them to some sparse but adequate quarters that included a shower and small kitchenette. Bolan quickly showered while Rueben and Grimaldi hungrily tore into a stacked set of boxed lunches chilling in the refrigerator. The Executioner felt like a new man after exiting the hot, sterilizing waters—some shampoo and soap could do wonders for his demeanor at times. After a quick change into a fresh uniform provided courtesy of the Army, Bolan snatched a box lunch and ate in the van on the way to see Dearbourne.

"What's the current status of your situation, Mercer?" Bolan asked.

"I should probably let General Dearbourne give you that information, sir," he replied hesitantly. "Most of it is classified. I can tell you that all of Yongsan Garrison is at full alert. We're still in the investigation stages."

"What do you think of this?" Grimaldi asked offhandedly. "Do you really think a bunch of South Korean troops suddenly went ape and decided to invade without orders or provocation?"

Mercer looked at Grimaldi with a grievous expression. "Quite frankly, sir, I'm not sure what to think at this point. I've never been much for these people."

"What do you mean, 'these people'?" Rueben chimed in. "Don't tell me you're prejudiced against the South Koreans."

"Like I said, I'm probably not the best person to tell you what's going on."

Mercer looked at Bolan and added, "Understand that I'm not necessarily prejudiced against them, sir. It's just I'm not sure how much I trust them is all."

"A little mistrust isn't bad, Mercer," Bolan replied, "as long as it's not carried beyond personal opinion."

"Yes, sir."

The group rode the rest of the way in silence, and Bolan tossed Rueben a warning look. He couldn't afford strained tensions between them. He was going to need the Army's cooperation. Not that he wouldn't get it, but he wanted Dearbourne to offer it willingly. Slapping the man in the face after accepting his hospitality wasn't the way to start off on the right foot. Nonetheless, he could understand Rueben's reticence. The guy was AWOL and that probably wasn't setting well with him; his pride and sense of duty went much deeper than that. In a way, he probably felt guilty for "abandoning" his people in their time of need. But Rueben would have to deal with that in his own time and in his own way.

They arrived at the headquarters ten minutes later. Inside the place was definitely hopping with activity. All of the senior officers from the various commands appeared to be present, cloistered around a large map on a raised area in the middle of the room. Surrounding them were dozens of computer terminals where U.S. and South Korean military personnel typed furiously. There was a row of desks off to one side, each manned by support members from both military and civilian corners, filling in documents and marking smaller maps of different areas.

The MPs guided Grimaldi and Rueben into a separate lounge area while Mercer led Bolan to the center of the room. The military policeman saluted a harried-looking man with circles under his eyes and fair skin. The man's hair was thinning and gray, and he studied Bolan with mock complacency. Behind his eyes, the Executioner could see the tension and strain of the past few hours. He was feeling some of it himself but he couldn't let that get to him during such a critical juncture.

"So you're Colonel Belasko?" the uniformed man asked sharply.

"Yes, sir."

He extended his hand. "I'm General Dearbourne. Welcome to Yongsan Garrison."

"Thank you, sir." Bolan offered him a salute, then shook his hand.

Dearbourne looked at his officers with surprise, then quickly returned the gesture. Several others offered salutes, as well, and then two men stepped aside so that Bolan could get a better look at the map they'd been studying. It was a huge section of Seoul, with part of the peninsula laid out, as well as the immediate elements over the border. Red pins were marked on several areas, and others were dotted with miniature flags of blue, green and orange.

"This is the operations map," Dearbourne explained. "We have each of the respective forces marked off. The green designates U.S. troop placement, the orange is South Korean and the blue stipulates combined forces."

"Understood," Bolan replied. He looked at Dearbourne directly. "You've been told to expect me, so I assume you know why I'm here."

Dearbourne studied the Executioner a moment before turning to the other officers gathered around the room. "Would you gentlemen excuse us, please?"

They moved away and tried to busy themselves with other tasks. Dearbourne excused Mercer, as well, then returned his attention to Bolan. The soldier could see his presence didn't meet with the general's approval, but he didn't really care. Technically, the guy was his superior officer. Bolan had attempted to show him all military courtesy, but he figured Dearbourne for a sharp one and that meant the guy probably wasn't buying his cover. Only time would tell.

"I was told you were coming," Dearbourne said quietly. "I also couldn't give a rat's ass. You understand that? We've got a serious situation here, Belasko, and I don't need some SF wacko coming in here and fucking it up. Is that clear enough for you?"

"Sure," Bolan replied. It was time to take a harder tack. "But if someone told you I was coming, then I'm sure they also told you that I'm here to help. I'd rather get your cooperation by peaceable terms, General, but I have other options available." Bolan lowered his voice and added coldly, "Now, if you're attached to those stars you're wearing, let's work together and get the problem solved."

Dearbourne's jaw dropped. Bolan wished the man hadn't pushed him to that route, but he didn't have time to argue. He needed Dearbourne, and Dearbourne needed him. It was just that simple. The next few seconds would decide the careers of both of them. The easy part for Bolan could have been to simply walk away, but he was committed and he now required that same commitment from Dearbourne. One way or another, he planned to get it and he sensed the CO knew that.

"Fair enough, Belasko. You're my kind of guy. Short on bullshit and long on balls. Okay, here's the situation...."

CHAPTER TWENTY

The Executioner knew he'd signed up for more than he bargained as Dearbourne gave his briefing.

The training exercise was only into its fifth day, and they were already experiencing problems. The original purpose of the exercise was and always had been to improve the joint coordination of the staff leaders and enhance deterrence of an enemy attack.

"The trouble began during a simulation along a major road in northern Seoul," Dearbourne advised. "One of the South Korean units apparently broke off from the main group and didn't return with the others this evening. The officer in charge didn't realize not all his people were accounted for until they turned in weapons."

"Do you know how many troops are in this phantom force?" Bolan asked.

"About a hundred, give or take," Dearbourne replied quietly.

Bolan shook his head. "What's the explanation from the South Koreans?"

"They claim all personnel and weapons are present, but we have eyewitness accounts coming in now." He gestured to the map again. "Look, we know that South Korean army troops definitely crossed over border points here and here."

"Or at least troops wearing SKA uniforms," Bolan offered.

"Okay, whatever," Dearbourne shot back impatiently. "The point is that we have an unidentifiable threat from a hostile force. Now, the North Koreans have agreed to not take actions to repel these attacks until we have more information."

"That was my understanding. We have twenty-four hours."

Dearbourne looked at the clock and replied, "Actually, there are only nineteen left, but okay."

"You mentioned multiple points of entry," Bolan observed. "They split up?"

"Yes. Apparently, there are three targets currently under their control now. A local medical center here, a small village near that and then a KPA observation station on the DMZ border."

Bolan nodded as he studied the map. "Just south of Panmunjon."

"Correct."

"I can see the reason behind the observation station, and maybe even the village. But why the medical center?"

"We're not clear on that yet," Dearbourne said, "but we're working on it."

"Well, a hospital full of ill and injured will have to be the priority. If you're correct in your assessment of troop strength, I imagine most of the forces will be committed to the KPA camp and second highest to the village."

"Makes sense," Dearbourne replied matter-of-factly. "How do you want to handle this?"

"Quickly and permanently," Bolan said, "before the North Koreans change their mind. I'll need some equipment. High explosives, preferably C-4, along with an A-2 over-and-under and a mountable M-24. And plenty of ammo for all of them."

Dearbourne nodded once. "No problem. We have all of that on hand."

"Also some air transportation. I'll supply the pilot and the logistical support directly from my people. The only catch is I'll need something equipped with satellite linkup capability."

"That might be a problem," Dearbourne interjected. "Most of our stuff is tapped out, given the alert and all. I was going to let you use my own personal UH-60, but it's not equipped with a linkup."

"The linkup's a must," Bolan countered. "I have to be able to coordinate with you, as well as my own people."

"I might have an alternative. It's an OH-58D."

"A Kiowa Warrior? Might work but I'd have to run it by my pilot."

"It's on loan from the Thirty-fourth. Only outfitted with light observation stuff right now, but it's definitely high tech in the communications department, and my people could equip it with an XM-296 in no time. That's standard armament, and it's just a matter of mounting the damn thing."

"Do it," Bolan replied with a nod. "I'll wait here until you're ready."

"Fine." Dearbourne paused for a long time and looked helplessly at the map. Finally, he asked, "What do you think your chances are of stopping these fanatics?"

"I wish I knew," came the Executioner's deathlike whisper.

"I'M GOING," Steven Rueben insisted.

"You're not," the Executioner replied.

They were standing in the lounge area of the exercise headquarters. Grimaldi sat on a sofa that looked as if it was overused for catnaps by senior staff. The rest of the room was plain and unimpressive, with a table in one corner supporting a couple of coffee urns and foam cups. Beneath the table were cases of chocolate-chip and peanut-butter cookies, along with vanilla creams to which Grimaldi had helped himself. A refrigerator held more of the plain box lunches that seemed so popular with the Army, as well as baskets of fruit and a few cartons of fruit juice.

"It's the only way I'm going to get back into the good graces of the Army," Rueben insisted.

"The agreement was that I allow you to come back to Yongsan," Bolan announced. "We didn't say anything about this mission."

"But—"

"But nothing," Bolan interrupted him. He jabbed a finger into Rueben's chest and added, "Look, it's time for you to face the music. I'm sure the Army will cut you a break under the circumstances. I put a good word in for you with Dearbourne. But as far as you coming along on this mission, the answer's no. You got me, soldier?"

"Yes, sir," Rueben muttered, dropping his eyes.

A few seconds of silence elapsed, and Grimaldi finally looked at Bolan and raised his eyebrows. The Executioner shook his head to indicate the matter wasn't open for further discussion, and Grimaldi clammed up on another vanilla cream. Bolan whirled at the sound of footsteps coming through the door. It was Dearbourne, and his face seemed solemn. The features had paled even more than they were normally, and Bolan immediately knew it wasn't good news.

"What's up?" the Executioner asked.

"The, uh…" Dearbourne choked back something before continuing. "The CIA agent we had inside the medical center was discovered. They shot him on the spot. And five of the patients."

"You didn't say a damn thing about having CIA inside the medical center."

"We didn't want to compromise his position," Dearbourne replied.

"And now he's dead."

"I don't know you, Colonel," Dearbourne snapped. "I don't even know if your real name is Belasko. Whatever the case, I don't give a damn. But I've been told you're the only one who can stop what's happening here. Just stop these people, Belasko, before the situation gets any worse. Your chopper's ready."

Dearbourne turned on his heel and stormed from the lounge. Bolan nodded to Grimaldi, who immediately jumped from the couch and headed for the Kiowa. The Executioner turned and faced Steve Rueben for perhaps the last time.

"We've lost enough good people in this war, Steve," the soldier told him. "Be patient and let me do my job."

"Okay." The younger man held out his hand, and Bolan shook it. "Good luck."

Bolan gave him a thumbs-up. "Live large, Steve."

The Executioner turned on his heel and started to leave the room when Rueben called after him. "I forgot to tell you that my dad called a little while ago."

"Is he all right?"

"Oh, yeah, he's fine. But he wanted me to give you a message. Arisa apparently left. Said she was going back to Pyongyang to finish the job."

"Pyongyang?"

"Yeah, or something like that." He snapped his fingers, pulled a piece of paper from his pocket and handed it to Bolan, adding, "He said Durham gave her some address and asked her to pass it on to you. It's got something to do with that number you asked Strack to trace. My dad thought it was strange she didn't just tell Durham you had gone to Seoul, so he memorized the address."

Dammit! Bolan had warned Arisa not to go, and she'd

done it anyway in spite of his concerns. Well, he figured she probably wouldn't listen. She was competent and determined. Maybe her training would keep her alive long enough to change the course of this disaster. In any case, Bolan didn't have time to worry about her. She was on her own now. Just as he was.

It was time to start a small war in order to avert a larger one.

THE BELL OH-58D Kiowa's Allison power plant was already warming up by the time Bolan reached the chopper. Grimaldi sat behind the throttle in a new Army flight suit and a tinted helmet visor that was linked into the new heads-up armament system. He couldn't see the usual gleam in the pilot's eye, but there was no mistaking the grin below that visor.

Bolan jumped into the back of the two-man rear compartment, closed the sliding door behind him and immediately donned a headset that would voice-link him with the Stony Man pilot.

His weapons were laid out as requested, along with the ammo crates and forty pounds of C-4 plastique. There were also about a dozen M-26 fragmentation grenades secured against the back wall. All of the hardware Dearbourne equipped him with would provide more than sufficient armament to deal with the North Korean threat.

BOLAN FIGURED he would deal with Black Army troops. It seemed like a logical assumption, since Pak was behind all of this and was obviously impressed with the KPA's answer to special forces. Black Army troopers weren't nearly as adept as Navy SEALs or Army Green Berets, but they were known for their fighting skills and fierce devotion to the cause of the government. Given the views of the North Koreans toward honor and duty, it came as a surprise to the Executioner that they would have killed some of their own people.

He blew into the headset microphone to check it was in working order before speaking. "All set, Jack?"

"On your word, Sarge."

"Let's move."

The whine from the four-blade rotor increased, and a few seconds later the Kiowa left the ground. Bolan took a moment to look out the side of the Kiowa's window and watch as the lights of Yongsan Garrison began to shrink. The installation spread out far and wide, and as they climbed higher into the air, the lights of Seoul began to fill his view like stars in a black sky. Bolan checked his watch and noted it was almost 2300 hours.

"Are we in contact with Dearbourne?" he asked Grimaldi.

"Yeah. There's a channel selector up here and you're set. All you have to do is hit the red button on your headset and you can transmit directly."

"Good. What about the linkup with Stony Man?"

"Coordinates for the medical center are coming through now. Bear says the place is called Yung Hamshi. It's a fifty-five-bed facility with urgent-care and basic diagnostic capabilities. Most of the serious cases apparently get sent to Panmunjon or Kaesong, so there are no acutely ill there."

The Executioner scowled. "Killing hospital patients in their beds. Bastards."

"What could possess them to do something like that?"

"I don't know," Bolan replied, "but we're about to reverse fortune and see how they like it. How long until we get there?"

"About twenty minutes."

"Okay, I'll have you drop me on the roof."

"Roger that."

The Executioner turned to the task of preparing his weaponry. He slipped into the LBE harness provided by Dearbourne, then stocked the pouches with six spare clips for the M-16/M-203. The M-16 was actually an A-2 model, which would allow the warrior the 3-round burst capability to which he'd become so accustomed. He loaded the 40 mm high-velocity HE M-383 grenades into a backpack-type satchel along with ten pounds of C-4, then slung it over his shoulder.

Next he prepared the M-24. The sniping rifle was actually an upgrade of the original Army sniping rifle based on the Mauser-type bolt system of the Remington 700. In essence the M-24 came packaged as an entire system, and included a bipod, deployment kit, carrying case and various sights. It was also mounted with a 20-power scope and fitted with an M-40X custom trigger. The weapon chambered 7.62 mm cartridges of special sniper ball ammunition that the Army designated as M-118s. Bolan couldn't repress a small grin—it seemed Dearbourne wasn't completely ignorant of the methods of men like the Executioner. Mounted near the door, and in the hands of an expert like Bolan, the sniper rifle would prove a faithful ally.

By the time the soldier had finished checking his gear, they were on a direct approach for the medical center. There couldn't be the slightest margin for error. Bolan estimated the enemy to number at least fifteen or twenty, and they would be scattered throughout the facility. He could only hope they would respond to the threat rather than taking it out on the hostages. The plan would call for split-second timing.

Through the front portal, Bolan could see the medical center illuminated in the lights along its perimeter. It was a two-story building made of brick with casement windows and a small parking lot. One section of windows was completely dark, but the remainder of the place looked wide-awake. Bright lights spilled from the building in other areas, and several South Korean army trucks were positioned in one small parking area that looked as if it accessed the urgent-care section. It adjoined another lot reserved as a helipad.

"I'll drop you on the north topside of the building," Grimaldi called into the headset. "Looks like there's a scuttle hatch there for you to make entry."

"Check."

"Take care, Sarge."

Grimaldi set the Kiowa into a hover a few feet above the tar-and-gravel roof. Bolan was out the door and on it in seconds. He rushed for the hatch as Grimaldi lifted the chopper up and away from him. Sounds of autofire were immediately evident as several sentries on the ground began to open up on the Kiowa. Bolan abandoned his route and rushed to the edge of the building. He peered over the side of a knee-high parapet and saw four troops firing toward Grimaldi.

Bolan knelt and popped an HE round into the M-203. He leveled the barrel in their direction and immediately squeezed the trigger. The shotgun kick of the weapon barely phased the soldier as the high-explosive round landed on target between the Black Army troops. A bright explosion of orange flame washed over their position, and a moment later three of the men dropped.

Bolan was already loading a second HE shell as the remaining soldier turned toward the source of the shot. The Executioner slammed the shell home and flipped up the leaf sight. He put the post directly on target and fired. The heavy round traveled a straight and narrow path, striking the target in the shoulder as the soldier raised his assault rifle to sight on Bolan. The commando exploded with the impact and the HE charge blew him apart. Bits of flesh and bone rained upon his motionless comrades.

Bolan was up and running back to the scuttle hatch before the grisly debris finished falling. He pulled the hatch aside and noted the fold-up stairs secured above false ceiling tiles. They were connected to a door that looked as if it could only be lowered from the inside.

The soldier slung his rifle, then whipped a block of plastique from the satchel. He tore half of it away, primed it with a detonator, then stepped back from the hatch. He attached the wires from the detonator to the electronic signal box and flipped a switch. Less than a second elapsed before the detonator ignited and the C-4 blew. A heavy explosion erupted through the scuttle hatch and blew upward. Smoke belched from the hole.

The Executioner stepped forward and peered through the jagged opening. The door was gone, as was the staircase, but he could see to the floor about eight feet below. He pocketed his fuse box, unslung his M-16/M-203 and dropped through the opening. Bolan landed on the hallway floor in a crouch and swept the muzzle in every direction. No one appeared to challenge him, but several women in nursing uniforms stood in the hallway with surprised expressions. The soldier gestured for them to get down, and it took only a moment for them to grab some floor.

Resistance did arrive a moment later in the form of two commandos toting AK-74s. They burst through a doorway at the far end of the hallway and immediately aimed in the Executioner's direction. Bolan threw himself against one wall and brought the M-16 into acquisition by his cheek. He flipped the selector switch to 3-round bursts as steel-cored slugs from the AK-74s ripped away sections of the floor and wall around him.

The M-16 barked with repeated fury as Bolan laid down an unerring field of fire. The 5.56 mm ball ammo took the first commando high in the chest and spun him into the door frame. Bolan tracked down and to the left for his second target, and his autofire struck home, ripping open his enemy's guts and continuing through. Blood sprayed the man's shirt. He let out a scream of pain before collapsing to the floor dead.

Bolan regained his feet and immediately checked the two nurses. Both of them appeared unharmed. He gestured for them to rise and kept his voice as level and calm as he could manage.

"Do either of you speak English?"

The shorter of the two raised her hand. "I speak some. A little."

"Don't be afraid," he said, gesturing with the muzzle of his weapon to the two commandos. "How many more are there?"

"Many...not sure. There are much soldiers."

"All right. Stay here and keep quiet."

The Executioner moved away from the woman and did a closer check on the enemy. A quick inspection confirmed the warrior's suspicions. Black Army troops, which meant resistance ahead and plenty of it.

Bolan pushed through the doors and accessed another wing. This one was lit by only a few lights at either end of the corridor. A brief reconnaissance of several rooms in that wing revealed the area was deserted. The Executioner quickly found the stairwells and began his descent to the first floor. By his count, he'd dropped six of the enemy. That probably left at least a dozen he still had to contend with.

In the recesses of his subconscious, he tried to remember what he could about Black Army troops. Aside from their ferocity in combat, NKSF were instrumental in preinvasion plans for South Korea. They would spearhead a blitzkrieg attack on Seoul and coordinate the subsequent occupation, which many military experts declared would be the goal of any invasion from the North. Tunnels were dug all along the DMZ, fortified with every kind of modern military piece of equipment available to the KPA, including chemical weapons.

That kind of preparedness didn't come from poor training techniques. Black Army troops weren't necessarily the best, but that didn't make them any less dangerous. Particularly when the odds were stacked so high against the Executioner. He would have to be doubly cautious as he proceeded and grab every tactical advantage he could.

The Executioner reached the first-floor landing and propped open the door with the muzzle of his M-16/M-203. Three sentries were visible through the crack, their eyes roving up and down the hallway with their backs to the door. It was a grievous error, and Bolan made full use of it as he opened the door and sprayed the commandos before they had a chance to react to the noise of his presence.

Two of the troops never even completed their turn as the 5.56 mm rounds tore through their clothing and ripped flesh from their upper torsos. The remaining guard managed to avoid any fatal shots, but a trio of rounds burned through his shoulder. The man's weapon clattered uselessly to the linoleum floor as Bolan stepped into full view and swung the muzzle in the sentry's direction. The Black Army commando reached for a side arm as he sought cover behind a nearby desk. The Executioner triggered his weapon again and drilled his enemy through the head.

Bolan turned his attention to the rear and saw another pair of commandos charging through an entrance door at the end of the long corridor. There were no rooms at that foyer, and the soldier made a snap decision. He raised the M-203 to hip level and stroked the trigger. The 40 mm incendiary grenade traveled the thirty yards in under a second and exploded on the door frame above the commandos. Showers of hot phosphorous rained upon the men and washed over them. Their bodies combusted and they screamed and staggered around, finally bumping into one another before dropping lifelessly to the floor.

Bolan was on the move in seconds, sprinting away from the fiery remains of his enemy and rushing in the direction of the urgent-care section. He drew another grenade from the satchel, this one high explosive, and crammed it into the smoking breech of the M-203 on the run. He could hear shouts now—probably commanders ordering their troops to find him. The Executioner was on a roll now, and the Black Army soldiers wouldn't have to look hard. He was going to bring the war to them.

Bolan rounded a corner and saw a cluster of six soldiers attentively receiving their orders from a seventh man. The men turned, and some of them swung the barrels of their AK-74s in the warrior's direction. Two of the KPA crack troops realized they were up against more than just small-arms autofire as Bolan raised the over-and-under combo to his shoulder and sighted on the group at center mass. They dived into an adjoining hallway, one of the men yanking the officer with him as they escaped certain death.

The other four weren't as lucky. Bolan didn't flinch as 5.45 mm rounds burned the air around his head and shoulders. He didn't hear the familiar plunk of the M-203 over the enemy gunfire, but the kick followed by a terrible explosion signaled his success. The concussion of the M-383's RDX and TNT filling blew out a set of glass windows that looked upon a small courtyard at the center of the U-shaped medical center. Superheated gases and a heavy shock wave dismembered the bodies of the Black Army troops, sending limbs in every direction.

Dust and plaster rained from the crumbled walls and ceilings at the site as one of the escaped soldiers leaned around the corner and sent several short bursts in Bolan's direction. The Executioner dived to the floor and rolled into a nearby alcove. He pressed his back to the wall and ripped an M-26 from his LBE suspenders. Bolan yanked the pin and leaned out long enough to roll the explosive charge down the hallway. He heard shouts of surprise and scrambling a moment before the grenade blew.

Bolan burst from cover and rushed the enemy's position, keeping low and moving in a zigzag pattern. As he reached the intersection of the two corridors, he dived to the floor and slid along the linoleum on his shoulder. Two mangled bodies were strewed immediately in front of him, and the officer was retreating down the corridor with only his right arm attached. The man turned, and the Executioner could see the expression of shock and fear on his face. He got to one knee as the officer reached toward a hip holster. Bolan brought the stock of the M-16/M-203 to his cheek and fired before the officer could clear the pistol. Three rounds connected with the officer's chest and knocked him off his feet. He hit the ground hard and lay still.

The Executioner regained his feet and studied the aftermath of his attack. Thus far, his offensive was working. There were no more innocent casualties among patients or staff, and he'd taken the majority of the Black Army force out here. He moved down the hallway in search-and-destroy mode. He would take no prisoners in this blitz. The enemy would soon understand there was no escape from his wrath.

The soldier reached the urgent-care section and discovered the place was deathly quiet. All too quiet—the opposition lay in wait for him somewhere. He went through each of the rooms, but all were vacant. He continued along the main corridor until he spotted a door ajar. He couldn't read the writing above it, but a part of some huge machine was visible in the hall lights that spilled into the darkened room. Bolan perceived the slightest muffled sound in that room.

Making a slow and cautious entry was tantamount to suicide and he needed to survive to finish his enemy. Settling on a decision, the Executioner moved on and continued down the corridor until he reached another hallway. He stepped around the corner and crouched, waiting patiently for his quarry. Whoever was in that room wouldn't wait there forever, but rather just long enough to be comfortable with the fact the enemy had left.

The gamble paid off. A man emerged a few minutes later, this one dressed in the uniform of an SKA officer. A short, dark-haired nurse was with him, and he had one hand around her mouth. Bolan watched from the shadows as the officer looked around before turning away. Now he could see the man held a small, wicked-looking pistol at the small of the woman's back. The Executioner stepped into the hallway and moved silently up the corridor.

As the officer and his hostage reached the nurse's station, Bolan rushed his opponent. The man turned with a surprised glance, but he was too late to do anything about it. Bolan slammed the butt of his M-16 A-2 squarely against the bridge of the Black Army leader's nose. Blood sprayed his hostage and the officer released her, staggering backward, his hostage forgotten.

The Executioner didn't wait for his opponent to recover. He rammed the butt at the man again, this time driving the stock flat into the man's neck. The hard plastic and rubber shattered his windpipe, and he sucked down bone and blood with a grotesque noise. His eyes rolled up into his head as he sunk to his knees and reached for his fractured throat. Bolan slammed a boot into the man's chest and knocked him flat to the floor. The man gasped once, then died.

The soldier turned to see the nurse stare at him with a

frightened expression. There was only quiet in the medical center now. Bolan knew he'd have to do another walk-through, but he was certain his job there was finished. It was time to move on. He raised his hand to reassure the petrified nurse, then reached to the radio mike attached to his webbing.

"Eagle, this is Striker. All secure. Meet me on the helipad in five minutes."

"Copy, Eagle."

Yeah, there was still a lot of work to be done.

CHAPTER TWENTY-ONE

"One down, two to go," Bolan announced over the headset and roar of the Kiowa's rotors.

"Any casualties?" Brognola asked. His voice was clear and crisp over the intercom system. It was a digital wave technology radio installed into the helicopter's state-of-the-art communications system. Not only did the headset Bolan wore allow hands-free operation, but he could barely hear the normally deafening sounds of the Kiowa's engine. There wasn't even so much as a whine coming through, and the Executioner was impressed with the newest upgrades to the OH-58D chopper.

"Only on their side," he replied.

"What's your take on the opposition?" Brognola asked. "Any idea who we're really dealing with?"

"I've pretty convinced it's a Black Army unit," Bolan replied.

"What makes you think so?"

"An identifying mark I found on one of them. That, and Pak seems to use them for everything else. There's also the issue of those unaccounted funds that Hakajima supposedly paid for the Taepodong III. I'm sure Pak used the money to pay off this private little army of his."

"Okay. I'll talk this over with the Man and have him let the North Koreans know that we suspect these are their own people gone bad."

"They're not going to buy it, Hal."

"You're probably right. We'll just have to convince them. In the meantime, you watch yourself, Striker."

"Roger."

Bolan punched a button on the computer console in front of him in the copilot's seat. Once he'd ended the transmission, he switched the radio headset frequency to the dedicated channel and called for Dearbourne.

"Base One, Eagle One," Bolan said evenly.

"Eagle One, this is Base One," Dearbourne's voice came back. "The channel is secure. What's the story?"

"I've neutralized enemy placement at the medical center. Advise North Korean Command they can send in a mop-up crew. I'm now headed toward the village."

"Copy," Dearbourne replied. "We have some better intelligence now."

"Let's have it."

"Troop estimates at the village are between twenty and twenty-five. Vehicles include a deuce-and-a-half and a couple of mechanized combat vehicles."

Bolan raised his eyebrows. "Armored?"

"It's possible," Dearbourne said grimly. "Initial satellite photographs we're getting from NSA aren't that great. Pretty grainy because there's a high-altitude weather storm, but my tacticians here are pretty sure they're BMP-2s."

That wasn't good news. The BMP-2's predecessor was invented in the mid-1960s. Its biggest failures were the armament, and Bolan searched his memory for the most recent modifications made by the former USSR. The BMP-2 favored a 30 mm cannon over the old 73 mm smoothbore gun of the BMP-1. The rapid-fire cannon could elevate high enough to neutralize low-flying aircraft, particularly choppers, with its staggered 500-round com-

318   DECEPTION

plement of HE-T or AP-T ammo. Never mind it was also
equipped with an AT-4 Spigot antitank guided weapon that
fired a heat-seeking warhead.

"Those are Russian made," Bolan stated.

"Yeah," Dearbourne agreed. "They'll sell anything to
anybody for the right price."

"Yeah, but the North Koreans and Russians were
friendly to begin with."

"How do you want to work this?"

"I don't have anything on board here that can handle
something like that," Bolan replied. "And you can't very
well fly a tank killer into DPRK airspace."

"Agreed. Do you want to come back for something
heavier?"

"No dice. The clock's ticking, and I don't like the numbers."

"Okay, Belasko, it's your show. But how the hell are
you going to take out BMPs with an over-and-under and
an XM-296?"

"I'll have to take it as it comes. Out here."

Bolan switched off the intercom and looked at Grimaldi.
"You heard?"

"Yeah," Grimaldi said, nodding slowly while keeping
a careful eye on his instruments. "BMP-2s are some serious shit, huh?"

"Very serious. Most of them sport appliqué armor along
their sides."

"You have a plan—" he cast a sideways glance
"—don't you?"

"Yeah." He looked at Grimaldi and frowned. "But it's
going to take split-second reflexes on your part. It could
be damn dangerous."

"That's me," the Stony Man pilot said with a broad
grin. "Jack 'Damn Dangerous' Grimaldi. I'm with you all
the way on this one, Sarge. But whatever you're planning,

you'd better fill me in quick. We've got five minutes to that village.''

Bolan borrowed Grimaldi's cigarette lighter and then quickly climbed into the back of the Kiowa as he explained his plan. While he detailed his plan to the pilot, he pulled all of the remaining grenades from the satchel and stuffed it with another ten pounds of the C-4 plastique, adding to the ten already inside. Grimaldi listened to the Executioner and when the warrior had finished he agreed that the plan was good. Bolan then checked his watch and waited patiently as they drew closer to the enemy.

"Forty-five seconds," Grimaldi announced.

Bolan moved to the door and knelt. He opened the bag just enough to light the C-4. The stuff burned hot but slowly, and as the first one-pound block caught, it began to catch on the other ones like charcoal piled in a grill.

"Thirty..."

The Executioner watched as tracer rounds began to sail toward them. Grimaldi expertly maneuvered the chopper. Bolan felt his stomach seesaw with the smooth, rolling motions of the Kiowa.

"Fifteen..."

Bolan watched as the 30 mm AP-T rounds whizzed past the OH-58D, some coming uncomfortably close to the fuselage. He gritted his teeth against the tremendous forces of Grimaldi's evasive maneuvers. A couple of times, he could hear the pinging of rounds as they grazed the thin skin of the helicopter. His plan would have been utter suicide had someone other than the Stony Man pilot been behind the controls, but the Executioner knew when to tempt fate and when it was a futile effort. This was definitely not one of those latter times. He had an ace card to play, and its name was Jack Grimaldi.

Bolan slid open the door as Grimaldi counted off. "Four...three...two..."

The chopper swung into a one-eighty, and Grimaldi positioned it fifteen yards above the turret of one BMP-2 nestled between a couple of one-story houses. The mechanized combat vehicle was dug in about two or three yards belowground to provide some cover, but it wasn't going to do them any good with the Executioner on the job. The face of a commander positioned in the center of the enlarged turret looked straight up at Bolan seconds after the soldier leaned out and dropped the flaming bag of almost twenty pounds of C-4.

"Go!" he ordered, but Grimaldi already had the Kiowa in motion.

The fiery explosion swept over the turret on impact, scorching everything in its path including the gunner, vehicle commander and driver. Bolan's plan had been ingenious in its simplicity. The turret could rotate 360 degrees, but its maximum angle of elevation was seventy-four degrees. Therefore, it couldn't shoot a target directly above it. Moreover, it wasn't important to take out the vehicle itself if he could take out the personnel operating it.

Grimaldi glanced back at his friend in amazement. "Good job, Sarge!"

"No sweat," Bolan said, although he could feel droplets on his forehead. As he pocketed a few of the high-velocity M-383 grenades and used the rifle scope's soft case for the last of the C-4, he added, "Put us down somewhere safe and I'll take care of the other one while I'm out."

Grimaldi landed in a small clearing on the outskirts of the village and Bolan hit the ground running, the over-and-under clutched in his fists. He made a beeline through a yard and arrived on the main street where the BMP-2 sat neutralized. The top of the fighting vehicle was still awash in flames. From where he stood, it looked as though some of the heat had melted the back portion of the 30 mm cannon's barrel. The Executioner could barely make out the twisted, hulking remains of the AT-4 Spigot device. Smoke rolled from the open turret where fire had begun to consume some of the interior.

The Executioner advanced down the street and let his senses guide him in the general direction of the second BMP-2. It didn't take long for him to find the thing, as he nearly walked right up to it while rounding a corner. The soldier ducked back into the shadows and watched the vehicle from the edge of the commercial building adjacent to its position. The armored fighting machine was facing away from him, its powerful weaponry aimed down the street. The tank commander sat in the turret and studied the darkened area with a pair of NVD binoculars, accompanied by his driver and a gunner manning the special AT-4 system.

Bolan crept up to the dual rear doors of the BMP-2 and pulled on the heavy steel latch. It rose smoothly and quietly. Bolan opened the door and swept the dismal interior with the M-16/M-203. There were no troops in back. The Executioner smiled as he pulled a pair of M-26 fragmentation grenades from his harness, thumbed away the pins and tossed them into the vehicle interior. He closed the door quickly but quietly, then turned and sprinted from the BMP-2. He rounded the corner just as the grenades exploded in succession. Bolan didn't bother to inspect the damage; the resultant explosions spoke for themselves.

The soldier knelt in the shadows of the flaming wreckage to face the structures across the street and studied the dark, deserted surroundings. The houses looked nicer than those in Onchon, and he could see signs of prosperity here. It wasn't all that surprising, since the chances were quite good that the majority of the village workers were crossing into South Korea and taking underpaying jobs in Seoul. The North Koreans, just like their southern neighbors, were heavily steeped in pride and heritage. But that didn't make them stupid. It was better to work for less money under decent conditions than slave away in some DPRK sweatshop and starve along with the rats and the livestock.

Only a few seconds elapsed before trouble manifested itself in the form of a squad of heavily armed Black Army troops. The special-forces men poured from a nearby house and fanned out. They drew beads on the Executioner's position, and Bolan raised the M-16/M-203 to his shoulder, triggering several 3-round bursts. His fire took down a couple of the enemy commandos before they could even fire at him.

Bolan regained his feet and launched himself toward one of the two-story houses. Hot trails of 5.45 mm rounds nicked dirt and gravel behind the soldier's heels as he sprinted toward the poorly lit structure. He reached the front door and tried the handle. The damn thing was locked, and the Executioner didn't have time to knock. He put his foot to the door, and it gave in under his adrenaline-enhanced strength.

The sight of a family huddled in the corner was the first thing to greet him. A small man stood in front of his wife and two small children and his eyes studied the ghostly wraith decked in camouflage fatigues and black cosmetics. Bolan realized he had to have been a frightening sight, and he raised his hand to show he meant no harm. He pointed to the man without saying a word, then indicated to his family before pointing his finger toward the ceiling. Then he gestured for the guy to step it up. The North Korean immediately understood and quickly shooed his wife and kids past the Executioner and toward the stairs.

The echo of the footfalls above Bolan reached his ears as a fresh hail of autofire began to riddle the downstairs windows and door. The Executioner hit the floor and rolled away as more of the heavy-caliber slugs ripped through glass, furniture and antique ceramics. Vases that were probably priceless family heirlooms shattered under the intense gunfire, and a crystal chandelier exploded with the sheer force and magnitude of the assault.

Bolan got to his feet and found a cleared window as the fire died down. He flipped the leaf-sight into acquisition on a fire team of about four troops rushing toward the house. Another team of four men covered them. The Executioner wasn't visible in the darkness of the house, and he waited until the approaching group was practically on top of him before he triggered the M-203.

The high velocity M-383 exploded on impact between the group, and the concussion lifted them from their feet. Two of the men were close enough that they slammed against the front of the house. The other two were set on fire by the explosion, and Bolan fired mercy rounds into one of the men who ran around and screamed until put out of his misery.

Another fusillade of rounds poured from the muzzles of the other fire team behind cover. Bolan went prone and crawled on his belly toward the back of the house. There had to be a back door. He'd tempted fate by entering the house and putting innocent villagers at risk, but there was a greater purpose in his overall plan. He wanted to get as many as possible of them in a small, contained area. Then he could take out the whole force with a minimal effort. But it didn't look as if they were going to cooperate with that plan.

Bolan didn't find a door, but there was a small casement window in the kitchen that looked onto a backyard. He pushed out the window. It took some effort to squeeze his muscular frame through the narrow rectangular opening. Once outside, Bolan took a moment to crouch against the wall of the house and get his bearings. The sounds of gunfire had ceased and the only remaining noise was the incessant call of crickets.

The Executioner waited a minute before getting to his feet and sprinting across the yard. He reached a tall, thick tree with lots of branches and looked up, realizing the tree would provide perfect cover for him.

Bolan slung his over-and-under and returned to the edge of the house. He carefully opened the scope case and removed the twenty, one-pound blocks of C-4. He rapidly piled them up beneath the casement window and burrowed a blasting cap into one block deep beneath the pile. He strung wire from the cap to the tree and put it between his teeth. After rubbing his hands together, he jumped up and grabbed the lowest branch. Muscles strained beneath the fatigues as he pulled himself up. Slowly and carefully, he picked his way higher and deeper into the foliage. Pretty soon the leaves of the tree seemed to swallow him.

Bolan unslung his weapon and cleared a few small branches until he had a perfect view of the house. He was above the roofline, and he could see the second fire team approaching with two more support teams. They still thought he was in the house; it was time for Bolan to implement his plan. He linked the wires to his electronic detonator, then reached up to his LBE harness and keyed the microphone.

"Eagle, this is Striker," the soldier whispered.

"Go, Striker."

"I need you up in the air right now. Watch for my signal and then put down on top of me."

"Copy, Striker. Eagle out."

Bolan switched off, then continued to wait patiently. In the near distance, he could hear the whir of the rotors as Grimaldi started the powerful Allison power plant on the Kiowa. The Executioner loaded a fresh clip into the M-16 and slammed another 40 mm home, this one a red smoker. Grimaldi would just circle far enough above to avoid any danger from enemy fire, then swoop down on Bolan's position when the signal was given.

The last of the troops advanced on the house, and Bolan could hear the squawk of blaring radios as they approached. By his count, the enemy was falling right into the trap. At least six had bought the farm between the pair of BMP-2s, and six more went down in the last skirmish. Three fire teams of four men each were advancing on the house, which brought the count to twenty-four. Even if there were still one or two stragglers, they wouldn't be effective enough against a whole village.

Bolan's waiting became tense as he heard the sounds of the woman and children screaming. His heart agonized for them, but he couldn't give up his advantage. He now had the majority of the troops inside the house. They were contained, and that's what he needed. The screaming abruptly stopped and the minutes ticked by. The Executioner could hear the Kiowa somewhere above him, flitting back and forth nervously under the deft control of its nervous but expert pilot.

Relief swept over the Executioner when he saw the shadowy forms of the family leave the house and run down the street. A few more minutes elapsed, then he could make out the mass of troops inside the house. Their dark forms came near the window. Bolan waited a moment longer as one man actually put his head through the window and followed a moment later with his whole body. The pile of C-4 was hardly noticed in the darkness. One by one, the troops followed. Bolan waited until the first four were outside before activating the C-4.

A massive explosion blew away the better portion of the wall, and the concussion and flame literally tore the four men outside to shreds. Bolan twisted in the tree and sent the smoke grenade sailing into the clearing on his right.

DECEPTION

He then loaded the M-203's breech with a fresh HE round and sighted on the hole in the house created by the C-4. Bolan triggered the weapon and it bucked in his fists as the M-383 arced gracefully through the air and sailed right through the center of the hole. Another brilliant explosion rocked the night.

The Executioner quickly descended from the tree and pumped two more HE rounds into the house, followed by an incendiary, before he rushed toward the clearing. The chopper came down in a picture-perfect landing and Bolan jumped aboard. Grimaldi lifted off as the soldier donned the headset and ordered him to circle the house. Red-orange light poured from every window as the house began to ignite into flames. The construction standards in North Korea were nothing like in the U.S., and Bolan surmised the place would burn to the ground. He felt sorry for the family, but at least they had escaped alive and he'd restored their freedom.

"What are we doing?" Grimaldi asked.

"Checking for stragglers."

Grimaldi nodded and continued to circle for several minutes before Bolan gave him the thumbs-up signal.

The Stony Man pilot pulled away from the decimation and blew a sigh of relief. He finally looked at his friend and longtime ally. Mack "the Bastard" Bolan was still a soldier by any other name; he was like the reflection of death incarnate. Grimaldi could remember hearing about a verse in the Bible when he was a good Catholic kid where Death rode on a horse and Hell followed behind, or something like that. For some strange reason, Grimaldi felt as if he were piloting that horse now and that the Executioner, his trusted friend and ally, were Death riding upon his aircraft-aluminum steed.

Yeah, Grimaldi thought. And hell followed with him.

THE HINT OF DAWN stretched out behind Kawashita Arisa, the first tentacles of light playing over the skyline in her rearview mirror.

As she entered Pyongyang and began to drive north on the Pyong Ni Highway, she considered the fate of herself and the handsome, dark-haired mystery man who called himself Mike Belasko. She wouldn't have openly admitted to anyone, but she missed him with almost agonizing emotion. He had a way of attracting all of those around him.

Belasko's skills were beyond measure. He was a soldier in every sense of the word, and nothing stood in his way when he saw duty calling him. The responsibilities and burdens he carried on his shoulders were measurable only by the depth and character in those cold blue eyes and determined visage. She couldn't help but admire him, and she wished she'd had the courage to tell him so before he left.

Arisa shook away her vain thoughts and scolded herself for not paying attention to the task at hand. There was a time for daydreaming and this wasn't it. Just a few miles ahead, she knew death lurked, moving stealthily through the grand estate of Pak In-sung. Arisa had located a phone and contacted Eichi and Yutaka. They agreed to meet her at Pak's house and assist with the capture of Hakajima. She appreciated their devotion to her. They could have returned to Tokyo but they waited for her—they wouldn't leave one of their own. It was both an honor and a pleasure to work with such faithful people.

Arisa took the appropriate exit, and soon the road had turned from pavement to gravel. She parked her car behind some thick brush and waited patiently. Eichi and Yutaka emerged from the shadows of a grove of trees and sprinted toward her sedan. They climbed into the car, Eichi in front and Yutaka taking the back seat. Arisa inclined her head respectfully to both of them.

"Domo arigato," she said pleasantly. "You are no

longer my subordinates but rather my friends. I will not forget your faithfulness.''

"It is an honor to serve with you," Eichi replied. He withdrew a brand-new Colt Government Model .380 from beneath his jacket and handed it to her. "Your spare pistol.''

Arisa nodded absently and said, "I lost my father's.''

"I am sorry.''

"This is the way of things," Arisa said. "Perhaps now that we are close to capturing Hakajima-*san*, that destiny is beginning to separate me from those things in my past.''

"Do not dwell on this, Kawashita. Let us move forward.''

Arisa nodded and the three of them got out of the sedan. Arisa led her two Japanese subordinates on a random course through the trees until they reached the fenced border of Pak In-sung's sprawling rural home. They vaulted the fence, completely bypassing the single row of barbed wire atop it, and spread out. The approach to the estate was slow and agonizing. It was becoming lighter by the moment, and Arisa had hoped to make their entry under the cover of darkness.

They were about forty yards from the house when Arisa detected the sounds of running feet behind them. She turned and shouted a warning, raising her pistol to defend herself, but it was too late. Something blurred toward her arm and knocked the .380 pistol from her fingers. Her hands went numb but she tried to ignore the pain. The years of discipline in martial arts paid off as she barely avoided the meaty fist of her assailant.

She stepped into the attacker's domain and drove an elbow into his groin. The security forces member grunted with pain and dropped the Daewoo DP-51 in his own hand. He stepped back and stood sideways, a misty look visible in his eyes as he choked back the painful and unexpected blow.

Another man, Korean and slightly taller than his partner, took up an aggressive flanking position.

Arisa attempted to watch both of her opponents for sudden moves, but she wasn't quite ready for the sudden staccato of machine-pistol fire. The two allies and faithful associates whom she had known for years suddenly died under the merciless hail of bullets delivered from Russian-made PPS-43 SMGs. A line of security team members advanced as their 7.62 mm slugs drilled through Eichi and Yutaka at a rate of 700 rounds per minute.

The blood of Arisa's friends spilled onto the grounds of Pak's estate.

The Japanese woman screamed and launched herself at the closest man. She leaped into the air and snapped a vicious side kick that broke the man's jaw. Less than a second elapsed as she turned from the falling body and attacked the second security man, but she already knew it was hopeless. With any luck, they would kill her in the next few seconds, and she would join her friends on the great plain of Buddha's joy.

Something hard and unyielding slammed into the back of her head just as she managed to fracture the second target's collarbone with a knife-hand strike. The pain seemed to cause a lump in her throat and a groin spasm before they collided with the shock at the level of her stomach. She could feel the darkness nearly overtake her as the trauma of the impact set her teeth on edge. Whether from the blow or sheer exhaustion, Arisa collapsed to the ground facefirst.

She bounced back and forth between consciousness and unconsciousness, and she could barely feel herself being lifted roughly onto someone's shoulder. A few minutes went by, and she woke up to find herself inside. But where? The huge mansion was the most likely place, but she couldn't get her eyes to focus on her surroundings.

The pain in her back had returned with all its fiery resolve, and Arisa just wanted to give up. To end it all in the sweet sleep of death would have been the most merciful way for her enemy to end the suffering. But she knew, even as she heard a familiar voice taunting her at moments, that it would be a long time before death came.

had, and Brad sent the information to Stony Man in the
hope they could get radiomen in Pyongyang to act.

I've got about a dozen troopers in the heads-up here,
Bear," Grimaldi informed him.

"Take over, Jack."

"Righteous."

The Kiowa banked sharply left. Grimaldi made
another low-level acquisition run, circled the helmet
that dangled from a rack behind him, so he could see what
complaint was against. Small patch dots emerged as troops
of the army, and the soldiers.

A chopper's minuscule pulse, the whine of the Kiowa
...

CHAPTER TWENTY-TWO

Northern Border of the DMZ

Death had come to the small KPA observation station
south of Panmunjon in the form of Mack Bolan.

The Executioner watched as Grimaldi brought the
Kiowa on a straight course for the station. Schematics and
diagrams of the observation post were now displayed on
the computer in front of him. Bolan carefully considered
the layout. The North Korean troop strength at the station
averaged only ten strong. It was a small signal squad attached to a larger unit actually housed at a military station
in Panmunjon.

Attempts by the NKPA command to establish communication with the forward observation post had failed. Un-
like the village, Comsat intelligence showed no evidence
of armor or heavy equipment by the invading Black Army
forces.

The entire escapade engineered by Pak and Hakajima
had failed miserably, and the Executioner found it unfath-
omable they could kill their own people. Even if he de-
stroyed the site and defeated the remaining Black Army
commandos here, there was no guarantee he could find
Arisa or locate Hakajima and Pak. The address was all he

had, and he'd sent the information to Stony Man in the hope they could get authorities in Pyongyang to act.

"I've got about a dozen troops on the heads-up display," Grimaldi informed him.

"Take them, Jack."

"Roger that."

The Kiowa nearly swept the ground as Grimaldi maneuvered into target acquisition. Bolan donned the helmet that dangled from a rack behind him so he could see what Grimaldi was seeing. Small black dots appeared in front of his eyes, and the soldier mused that it was like playing a computer simulation game. The sights of the XM-296 changed from red to green when a target was in range. Heavy .50-caliber shells clanked from the casing at a rate of 600 rounds per minute as Grimaldi triggered the weapon system. The weapon functioned the same as an M-2 except it was remotely fired using an electrical solenoid.

Between the Stony Man pilot's skill behind the controls and the advanced weapon system, the troops below stood little chance of survival. In the early-morning sun, steam rose from the blood as the 12.7 mm ammo ripped large holes through the enemy. The XM-296 performed impressively under the circumstances, manipulated in 2-axis movement by a gimbal ring assembly between the gun's cradle and trunnion. Bolan watched the commandos below scatter in every direction as Grimaldi brought the Kiowa around for another pass.

"Sweep them again, and then get me down just above that tower," Bolan instructed.

"You got it, Sarge."

Grimaldi fired the weapon once more and delivered another hail of .50-caliber mass destruction on the commandos running across the compound. At least six more of the Black Army escapees fell under the heavy machine-gun fire. The pilot completed the pass, then rotated into a hover to the rear of the tower.

The rotors whipped the air as the Executioner jumped into the back and opened the sliding door. A Black Army commando inside the tower leaned out through the wide opening and sighted on the OH-58D with a VAL Silent Sniper rifle. Bolan took up a position behind the mounted M-24 and squeezed the trigger. The 7.62 mm slug crashed into the soldier's face and continued through, blowing off the back of his skull. The enemy soldier spun from the impact and toppled over the opposite side of the tower.

"Hold her steady!" Bolan shouted.

He slung the M-16/M-203, then disconnected the M-24 from the mount. He brought the sniper rifle sling onto his shoulder, securing it barrel-down, then gauged the distance to the tower before leaping out into the chill morning air. The Executioner landed on the roof with a grunt, then quickly dropped over the edge and swung his legs through the rectangular opening. He landed gracefully on the wooden floor, breathing heavily with exertion.

Grimaldi pulled out as Bolan looked through the front opening in the tower and spotted an officer trying to re-group his men for a counterassault. Nobody had apparently noticed the Executioner's maneuver, and he figured to use that as an advantage.

He keyed up his mike. "Striker to Eagle, pull back a mile or two. Make them think you split."

"Copy, Striker."

The *whup-whup* of the rotors faded, and soon the Kiowa was gone from sight, leaving only death and chaos in its wake.

The Black Army commandos cautiously broke cover and ran to the officer who was barking orders. Bolan took up a comfortable firing position and set up the M-24. He lined the sights on the officer who was shouting and policing up his men. The crosshairs settled on a point just above the man's breastbone. The Executioner took a quick estimate of distance and range, then adjusted for the steady wind blowing across the open area of the compound. When he was comfortable with his estimate, he pulled the stock tightly against his shoulder, let out half of a deep breath and stroked the trigger.

The 7.62 mm round flattened on impact with the officer's chest and continued to tumble through his heart before ripping out the back. The man dropped, landing on his knees first before falling prone to the cold, hard ground. The panicked troops froze long enough for Bolan to extract the bolt, return the sights to the next commando in line and squeeze the trigger. He also fell under the Executioner's flawless marksmanship.

Several of the men threw themselves to the ground while others rushed for cover. Bolan dropped a third man before leaving his position in the tower and descending a rope ladder he located at the back. Once on the ground, the soldier didn't hesitate to confront his enemy head-on. He took the offensive and stepped into the open area, leveling the M-16/M-203 at his waist and taking out some of the confused troops with 3-round bursts.

Several of the Black Army commandos tried to organize themselves into fire teams, but it didn't do any good. One group did manage to reach the cover of a small wooden building with an overhang but the Executioner was way ahead of them. He fired the M-203 with the incendiary grenade he'd loaded earlier, and the area covered by the overhang burst into flames.

Bolan turned in the direction of several more soldiers who tried to flank him with a fire-and-maneuver technique. The Executioner dived to the ground and rolled, coming up in a new spot before the opposition could realign their fire. A burst of 5.56 mm slugs tore through the bodies of the cover troops huddled only partially behind posts or cantilever walls. Without covering fire, the man in the open realized his vulnerability and tried to retreat. He'd nearly reached some adequate cover when the Executioner blew him apart with a maelstrom of autofire from the M-16 A-2.

Bolan keyed up his microphone again. "I'm wrapping it up here, Eagle. I need you back with some heavy-duty fire."

"Roger that."

The Executioner got to his feet and rushed toward the largest building in the compound. According to the blueprints he'd memorized, that would have been the headquarters area for the compound. He was guessing that the KPA soldiers were probably housed inside that structure, since no other building was realistically habitable for more than six men at any given time.

He went boldly through the front door of the observation post's HQ and found the men. It wasn't a sight he would soon forget. They were all there, their bodies piled up in one corner. Congealed blood lined the floors and walls where the Black Army troops had obviously lined them up and slaughtered them. It was as Bolan had suspected—no regard for human life. The money from Pak had to have been good for Black Army soldiers to slaughter their own.

The warrior left the gruesome view and stepped into the fresh air. More Black Army commandos were advancing on his position, obviously coming out from hiding since they no longer saw a great threat. The Executioner swung the muzzle of his rifle into action and began to fire on them. A few of them fell immediately, but the others decided that it was better to die with valor and honor than to run in cowardly shame. The troops stepped into the open and pressed onward, triggering their AK-74s and blanketing the area around Bolan with heavy autofire.

The Executioner dropped to the ground behind the brick stem wall just outside the building and keyed his radio. "Striker to Eagle, I need that support."

"I'm on it, Sarge," Grimaldi replied.

Over the thunderous echo of AK-74 fire, Bolan could hear the unmistakable sound of the .50-caliber machine gun. Grimaldi brought the Kiowa into view and began to hammer the area with the XM-296. The Black Army commandos had foolishly clustered themselves together, probably in the hope of taking out the Executioner by sheer numbers. It proved to be a fatal mistake as Grimaldi gunned down one after another before they knew what was happening.

The soldiers turned their weapons toward the Kiowa, but the Stony Man pilot buzzed away before they could gain target acquisition. Now Bolan leaped from his hiding spot and burned them with 3-round bursts from a fresh clip. The last man fell as Grimaldi reappeared from the other direction and saturated the area with another series of .50-caliber slugs.

The grounds fell deathly quiet except for the sounds of Grimaldi landing the helicopter. The Executioner had finally put an end to the deadly deceptions of Pak and Hakajima. He looked at his watch and realized he still had time to get to Pyongyang. Stony Man was really going to have to pull some strings with the North Koreans for permission to fly the Learjet into their airspace. The way he saw it, the DPRK owed them at least one favor for cleaning up this mess—but they'd broken the rules before and they could do it again if necessary.

Bolan jogged to the chopper and climbed aboard. He

squeezed into the copilot's seat and donned the helmet so that he could talk with Grimaldi. The chopper rose smoothly, and the Executioner waited until they were airborne before describing the bad scene in the headquarters.

"Looks like we were a day late and a dollar short, Sarge," Grimaldi said. "I'm sorry."

"Nothing we can do about it," the soldier replied. "It's up to the North Koreans now. I just hope they get a decent burial. The DPRK has never been overly friendly with us, but I didn't consider those men enemies, either. They died senselessly at the hand of animals."

"It's too bad the people of the world can't get along."

"Yeah, I hear you."

THE AFTERNOON SUN DIPPED lazily toward the horizon as Grimaldi put down the RC-35 at Pyongyang's Airport. This time he was landing with official clearance. The Executioner was dressed in tan slacks, black military-style sweater and a brown leather jacket. Stony Man had made arrangements with the North Korean ruling party to seize Pak In-sung at his rural home, but the premier halted the affair. He wasn't completely convinced that Pak was guilty of any wrongdoing, and leaned toward the side of discretion.

Bolan could actually understand the party's position in the whole thing. It would serve as a public embarrassment if the voting castes found out their government was involved in a plot to kill its people. It made no difference that Pak had acted on his own. Even with the party leader as their sacrificial goat, Pak wouldn't be the only one to dangle from a rope when the citizens discovered the party had even allowed it to happen. There would be a loss of control and a complete breakdown of their society.

The Executioner didn't necessarily agree with the way

the DPRK did things, but that didn't mean he had any desire to see the country thrown into anarchy. Besides, this allowed him to deal with Pak and Hakajima in his own way. They would succumb to his terms, and the only rules of engagement would be those established by the Executioner.

"You want me to go along?" Grimaldi asked after bringing the plane to a stop and shutting down the engines.

"Not this time, Jack. I've got to do this alone."

"Okay, but watch yourself, Sarge."

"I always do."

Bolan left the plane and entered the terminal building through a solitary door. He was late for the rendezvous with his allies at the prearranged spot. He walked down a long, deserted corridor until he reached another door and soon found himself in front of the terminal building. Just as planned, there was a car waiting and the familiar face of NSA Agent Dennis Cliff grinned at him. Cliff leaned against the hood with his arms crossed. He dropped his sunglasses on his nose and peered at Bolan over them.

"Welcome back, Belasko."

"How goes it?" Bolan asked congenially, shaking the agent's hand.

"As slow as the day is long. You're the most excitement I think we've had in at least a year."

The Executioner nodded, then frowned. "I guess you heard about Arkwright?"

"Yeah. Those bastards need a lesson taught to them."

"Well, the professor is in the house," Bolan countered quickly. "My people said they would see to the arrangements for Arkwright. He was a good man."

"Yeah, and he's got a service record, too, so I heard they'll bury him at Arlington."

"Couldn't agree more with that decision."

Cliff nodded and patted the roof of the government sedan. "She's all gassed up and ready for action, big guy."

"Thanks."

As Bolan got behind the wheel and started the vehicle, Cliff leaned down and peered through the open passenger window. The look on his face told the soldier that he wasn't happy, and Bolan could see he was itching for some payback. He could understand how Cliff felt, but he had to do this job on his own.

"Listen, Belasko, you get these guys. You hear me? You do justice by Arkwright and you plant these sons of bitches once and for all. Will you do that for me?"

"You bet."

Cliff shook Bolan's hand. "Good luck."

The Executioner drove away and within a few minutes he'd entered traffic. According to the directions supplied by his NSA contact, the drive to Pak's would take him about thirty minutes. He took the time to contemplate a plan of attack.

Ever since his earliest wars against the Mafia, Bolan had always based his success on the "hit-and-git" philosophy. Only in those times of a soft probe or role camouflage would he linger among the enemy. His tactics had changed little over the years, primarily because they still worked. This was one of those times where he needed to make a silent entry, eliminate Pak and escape. If Hakajima was there, that would simply be a bonus. He could only hope that Arisa hadn't been captured or killed attempting to locate the Japanese crime lord.

The other problem was intelligence. He had no idea of the number or training of the enemy force. Pak would surely have some sort of security team on the grounds, but that was hardly enough to go on. Quiet penetration was the best choice in that case, and he was rigged for silent running. His only weapons were the Beretta 93-R in shoulder leather and an Army-issue combat knife. Toting a noisy assault rifle or lugging the bulky Desert Eagle .50 AE wasn't practical for this particular mission. Both weapons required a lot of ammunition, and it made little sense if he planned to escape detection.

The Executioner left the highway and drove about a mile when he suddenly spotted a familiar-looking vehicle. He left the roadway, killing his headlights and pulling up behind the sleek, silvery car. A full moon played shadows from the trees, and Bolan couldn't shake the sense of foreboding that washed over him. He got out of the government sedan and stepped closer to the other vehicle. There was no question in his mind—it was Arisa's car.

That left an indelible impression on the warrior's psyche. So Arisa had found the place and tried to stop Pak on her own, failing to heed his warning. Without a doubt, she'd probably been captured and was almost certainly dead by now. He tried to remain optimistic, but something in his gut told him that Pak would snuff out her life without a moment's thought if he caught her.

Bolan pressed on through the woods and found a chain-link fence on the other side. He kept to the wood line and walked a parallel course with the perimeter until he reached one corner. The trees blocked the moonlight there and Bolan stepped from the woods and withdrew the fighting knife. One end of the razor-sharp blade had teeth designed to cut through wire. He efficiently sawed through enough links to allow entry and crept silently across the grounds.

As he drew nearer to the mansion, its outlines became more visible. Bolan reached a hedge and knelt to study the layout of the monstrous house. Light spilled from a few of the windows. Crickets chirped in the otherwise eerie silence, and the distant call of geese permeated his consciousness. The Executioner felt impatience burning his gut, but he waited it out. Hastiness could lead to trouble, and if he had learned anything it was patience.

His vigilance paid off as the shadowy form of a man suddenly rounded one corner of the house and walked along the perimeter. The sentry wore a bulky jacket and toted a machine pistol in his hands. He continued along his assigned post, passing Bolan on the other side of the hedge. The Executioner quietly drew his knife and waited until the man's back was to him before making his move. He vaulted over the hedge and took the guy at a run. Bolan threw his weight into a flying tackle and brought the man down hard. He drove the point of the blade through the back of the sentry's neck and cut the spinal cord. The man let out a sickly gasp and lay still.

Bolan withdrew the blade before dragging the guy into an area thick with bushes and moss. He continued to the house and walked along the edge until he found a pair of glass patio doors. The Executioner tried them, but they were locked tight. He felt along the crevice separating the doors until he identified the lock. The wood was thin and flimsy, not surprising as the doors were designed more for appearance than security. He jammed the tip of the knife blade between the thin gap and eventually managed to pry the clasp back.

The soldier opened the door just enough to squeeze inside, then closed it behind him. He was in some sort of den, maybe an office. A desk occupied one wall, and there were several different chairs scattered about. He let his eyes adjust to the semidarkness before continuing across the room to another door. He opened this one and peered through the crack.

The lights were on, revealing a large, expansive room

with flagstone steps leading down into a circular foyer. A small indoor pond with fish and a central fountain trickled softly. The pond was lined with expensive stones and ornate carvings. Life in the ruling party had apparently been good to Pak In-sung. The rest of the large, open-air room sported priceless furnishings and artwork.

Bolan proceeded through the doorway and walked along the foyer until he reached the front door. A hallway led from the main entryway to the other side of the house. A grand circular stairway rose to a second floor where a banister walkway overlooked the foyer. The Executioner chose the hallway and walked past several doors. He stopped to inspect each room but found they were dark and empty of human life. The hall branched off to the left and Bolan crept along one wall. He heard voices at the end of the hall, and he fisted the Beretta as he drew near.

A quick inspection revealed Pak sitting in a wingback chair with a glass in his hand. Another man sat directly across from him in an identical chair. The guy had a thin, wispy face with brooding, almond-shaped eyes and pale lips. The lofty and smug expression on his face left an aura of power and self-assurance. Bolan knew he was probably looking at Sumio Hakajima. It was almost too easy—the both of them together like this. He would have to proceed with caution.

Bolan stepped from the shadows of the hall and leveled the Beretta in the direction of the two men. They turned at the sound of his movements and both studied him impassively. The Executioner said nothing but held the Beretta 93-R where they could easily see it. The look in his hard visage probably said it all. He could see that they knew he meant business.

"Good evening," Pak greeted him. "We were wondering if you would dare to show yourself here."

"Really," the Executioner growled.

"Yes." Pak looked at his guest, then returned his attention to Bolan. "We just received word that you managed to take out our entire force single-handedly. Once again, your reputation precedes you, Mr. Belasko."

The other man shifted nervously in his chair, and Bolan jerked the muzzle of the Beretta in his direction. "Keep your hands visible."

"Mr. Belasko, please," the man replied in a deep, distinguished voice. His English was flawless. "It would be very unfortunate for you to shoot me. Do you have any idea who I am?"

"A pretty good guess," Bolan replied, "and I don't really give a damn."

The man studied his nails with feigned disinterest in Bolan. "Your capitalist government relies heavily upon my corporation." He looked at the soldier with obvious disdain and added, "If I am lost, so is all of my work."

"It's no loss, Hakajima."

"So, you do know who I am."

"Yes. And as I said, I don't really give a damn. Your work, and that of your partner here, has cost the lives of a lot of innocent people. I'm here to rectify that. Permanently."

"Do not be so dramatic, Mr. Belasko," Pak interjected. "Even if you kill us, you will not escape my home alive. Right now my security forces have surrounded this place. They will gun you down before you can escape. So put your weapon down and surrender. I promise that you will die quickly."

"You first," Bolan stated calmly and squeezed the trigger.

The silenced Beretta was barely audible in the room as the 125-grain Parabellum round crossed the expanse and punched through Pak's forehead. The force of the round knocked the party leader out of his chair and deposited him on the floor in a crumpled heap.

Bolan swept the barrel of the 93-R at Hakajima and narrowed his eyes. "Where is Arisa?"

"M-Mike?" a soft, strained voice said from behind him.

Bolan whirled to see Arisa standing there. Her face was badly bruised and dried blood matted her normally long, silky hair. Her lips were swollen and cracked. One of the security men had a pistol to her head and his other arm encircled her throat.

The Executioner left the muzzle of his weapon trained on Hakajima and stepped back so that he could keep an eye on the Japanese crime lord in his peripheral vision.

"It is futile, Mr. Belasko," Hakajima taunted him. "You have lost your precious country to the whims of your own government. You might kill me, but another will rise in my place. This is what happens when you entrust your will, and your very life to a country that's slowly rotting from within. Your politicians are corrupt, your leadership inept and your people in constant turmoil."

"You're an expert on turmoil, Hakajima," Bolan snapped, never taking his eyes from Arisa and her captor. "You attempt to manipulate the system with money and power, and wield a sword of hatred against anyone who opposes you. I've seen many men fall and break their necks under such delusions."

Hakajima laughed menacingly. "Perhaps. You are a very astute and dangerous man. In other circumstances, you would have been a tremendous ally."

"I will never be your ally."

The sounds of sirens in the distance suddenly became audible, and Hakajima's expression became panicked. A moment later, an explosion rocked the mansion and shattered a window.

Bolan seized the moment of confusion and launched a side kick into Hakajima's chest. The man sailed backward with the force, and the chair tipped over with him in it.

Arisa twisted from the security man's grasp and dropped suddenly to the floor. Her captor hesitated for a moment, trying to decide if she or Bolan was the greater threat. The hesitation cost him his life as the Executioner swung the Beretta into target acquisition, thumbed the selector switch to 3-round bursts and pulled the trigger. The 9 mm Parabellum rounds cored through the security man's chest and slammed him against the wall. He slid to the ground, leaving a messy streak of blood and tissue behind him.

Bolan turned to see Hakajima trying to scramble for something inside his coat. He pinned the man's hand to his chest with one boot and leveled the Beretta at his forehead.

"No!" Arisa screamed. "Don't kill him!"

Bolan eased off the trigger and turned a surprised expression in the woman's direction. "What are you talking about? He—"

"He is my uncle."

"What?"

"My father's brother. I did not know how to tell you before." She got to her feet and took a couple of hesitant steps forward. Her voice became quiet. "Please, do not shoot him. I must return him to Tokyo alive where he can answer for his crimes. This is why it was so important for me to come here."

Bolan shook his head and tried to fathom what the beautiful woman was telling him. He looked back into Hakajima's eyes, and the crime lord's expression told him it was the truth. The man cowered beneath his boot in fear.

The thought of the innocents who had died by his hand welled up in the form of a lump in the Executioner's throat. Nonetheless, the pleading look on Arisa's face burned itself into his brain, and he couldn't bring himself to kill Hakajima.

Bolan turned to see Arisa had the security man's gun now and she was pointing it at him. "I—I don't want to shoot you, Belasko. But if you kill him, you leave me no choice."

The Executioner stared at Arisa with cold resolve, but the woman didn't waver. He finally lowered his Beretta, reached into Hakajima's coat to withdraw a single-shot .22-caliber pistol, then turned to leave. The North Korean authorities were arriving, and he couldn't afford to be detained by them. His job was finished, and it was time to move on.

As Bolan made a hasty exit for a rear door, Arisa called to him. "Thank you, Belasko. For everything."

"Sure."

"Belasko?"

Bolan stopped at the door and turned to face her. "What?"

"I will never forget you."

EPILOGUE

Arlington Cemetery, Virginia

The funeral was a fitting one for Caleb.

Danielle Arkwright sat in the stiff, metal chair and stared longingly at the flag-draped casket of her beloved brother. She tried to remember all of the great times the two had as kids. As the older child, Danielle had always tried to protect her rambunctious sibling. Caleb was always in some kind of trouble—he didn't know how to keep still and just spend time idly. Too much imagination. Yes, that was it…just too much…

Danielle choked back her tears and tried not to let the sound of the rifle fire scare her. The twenty-one-gun salute was followed by a lone bugler playing taps while a group of six Marines in dress blues raised the flag off the casket and neatly folded it with military precision. The officer at the head of the group took the flag and turned sharply to his right. He stepped forward and handed the flag to Danielle.

She took the flag meekly as the officer spoke some brief repose. Tears stained her cheeks as she realized the ceremony was concluded. One by one, the small group of mourners filed away. Frank Sheerer, an old service buddy and childhood friend of Caleb's, stood and waited until

Danielle had regained her composure. She rose and allowed her escort to guide her back to the gleaming black limousine that awaited them.

As Sheerer opened the door for her, Danielle noticed someone in a long black trench coat walk toward the memorial site. She stopped and watched as the tall, dark-haired man stopped at the casket and laid one hand on it. He stood there for a moment, raised his face to look in Danielle's direction, then turned and walked back in the direction from which he'd come.

Danielle clutched the flag against her bosom as she watched the man continue to walk away. She marched purposefully back to the casket and looked down at it. There were flowers laid across it, the ones she'd arranged to have delivered and placed there herself. But now there was a small, shiny object that glinted in the noontime sun there as well. She picked up the oddly shaped ornament and studied it.

Sheerer walked up next to her. The man she was watching was now only a distant black speck on the horizon. He finally put a hand on her shoulder.

"Are you okay, Dani?" he asked.

"Yes, I'm fine."

"Who was that guy?"

Danielle looked down at the ornament once more before handing it to her escort. "I'm not sure, but he left this."

"Huh," Sheerer grunted, holding it up in the light. "I'll be damned."

"What is it?"

"It's a medal. An Army marksman's medal."

Take
2 explosive books
plus a
mystery bonus
FREE